# JUSTINE, OR THE MISFORTUNES OF VIRTUE

Qui ved, lorsque le Ciel nous
frappe de ses coups,
Si le plus grand malheur n'est
pas un bien pour nous?
*Phil. de Adversité*

VIRTUE between Lust and Irreligion. To the left is Lust, under the figure of a young man, whose leg is entwined by a serpent, symbol of the author of our evils; with one hand she lifts the veil of chastity; which concealed Virtue from the gaze of the profane; and with the other, as well as with her right foot, guides the fall in which she wishes to make her succumb. To the right is Irreligion, who forcibly holds back one of Virtue's arms, whilst with a perfidious hand, she tears from her bosom a serpent, in order to poison her. The abyss of Crime is yawning beneath their steps. Virtue, still strong in her conscience, raises her eyes towards the Eternal, and seems to say:

Qui sait, lorsque le Ciel nous frappe de ses coups,
Si le plus grand malheur n'est pas un bien pour nous?

*Œdipe chez Admete.*


Who knoweth, when Heaven doth strike us with its darts, But the greatest evil to us some good imparts?

# JUSTINE, OR THE MISFORTUNES OF VIRTUE

*A Philosophical Romance*

By
Marquis de Sade

Introduction by
Fabienne-Sophie Chauderlot

BARNES & NOBLE BOOKS

NEW YORK

# CONTENTS

# INTRODUCTION

*Justine, Or the Misfortunes of Virtue* by the *Marquis de Sade* was published in 1791 at the height of the French Revolution, in times as tumultuous as the story of its heroine. At the tender age of twelve, *Justine* and her elder sister *Juliette* are unexpectedly thrust into life on the streets of Paris. In order to survive, *Juliette* chooses to use her body to obtain the favors of powerful men, but *Justine* is determined to remain virtuous at all costs. *Justine* struggles to champion honor, decency, and honesty in a world ruled by corruption, betrayal, and crime. *Sade*'s narration of her plight ruthlessly describes the archetypal confrontation between vice and virtue, and the novel's striking motifs are sadly still relevant today.

*Sade*'s name alone brings to mind the darkest creations of the human imagination, although the man remains a mysterious figure for most readers. Both perpetrator and victim of crimes, *Sade* had a destiny as unpredictable as that of his heroine's. *Comte Donatien Alphonse Francois de Sade* was born in Paris in 1740, the son of a minor diplomat. As a young boy, he lived at the royal court, where his mother was *dame d'honneur* (lady in waiting) for the *Princess de Condé. Sade* was raised with the princess' son, the famously brutal little prince *Louis-Joseph de Bourbon. Mme de Sade* was well known for her coldness toward both her husband and son; this is echoed in the cruelty women demonstrate toward children in *Sade*'s novels. When she abandoned her young son to retire to a convent prophetically located in *Rue d'Enfer*—Hell Street—*Sade* returned to his father's estate in southern France, where his uncle, the *Abbot de Sade*, became his principal tutor. Now deliberately unattended ruins, the castle of La Coste still overlooks the soft and colorful curves of the Provençal countryside, east of Avignon. The *Abbot de Sade* was an erudite follower of the *libertines*; young *Sade* was exposed to his uncle's unfettered lifestyle until his return to Paris at the age of ten. After studying at the famous Jesuit high school Louis-le-Grand, *Sade* served in the military until the end of the Seven Years' War in 1763. By this time, *Sade* was already leading a dissolute life. In an attempt to curb his behavior, *Sade*'s father forced him to marry, but his wife, *Renée-Pélagie Cordier de Launay de Montreuil*, did not replace his gambling or partying. At the age of twenty-three, *Sade* was incarcerated for the first time, probably for acting out a pathological sexual practice. By the time he died in 1814, at seventy-four, *Sade* had spent thirty years in various institutions and jails, including the legendary Bastille and the infamous Charenton asylum, where he was sent for having written *Justine*. Beyond the actual reasons for his various incarcerations—debauchery, seduction, kidnapping, molestation, sodomy, poisoning, and eventually a false claim that he was insane—it was *Sade*'s persona and the social impact of his texts that were too subversive to be tolerated by either the monarchy, for which orgies were common entertainment, or later, the Republic, which destroyed thousands of its own people in a civil war.

*Sade* lived in a particularly tormented era. While eighteenth-century French thinkers were elaborating on ideas of justice, freedom, knowledge, and social progress, the necessity of overthrowing the political system that prevented their implementation was generating tragic consequences. *Sade*'s destiny was woven in the turmoil that destabilized his resisting but condemned class. By 1791, the French Revolution was under threat. The 1789 uprising of starving and overtaxed peasants guided by the Parisian bourgeoisie had successfully toppled *Louis XVI*, a lazy and cowardly king whose incompetence and greedy advisors were ruining the country. Inspired by thinkers who advocated equality and human rights, the movement turned into a force for political reform and social justice. The two major symbols of the *Ancien Regime*'s power, the palace of Versailles and the Bastille prison, had been repossessed by the people. However, neighboring monarchies saw both the progressive philosophy and the rebellious attitude of the French people as a threat to their own absolute power and they gathered to invade France. Material conditions rapidly deteriorated in the isolated capital. Fear and dissension split the revolutionaries into such ferociously opposed factions that *Robespierre*, the most radical leader, seized control of the government and decided to systematically suppress anyone who represented a potential threat to the newly created republican regime. Thanks to the recently invented and extremely efficient guillotine, the Revolution became the Terror: More than 25,000 people, most of them aristocrats, were beheaded between 1793 and 1794.

Though it took horrific forms, popular anger against the French nobility was understandable. The aristocrats benefited from numerous privileges that allowed the elite few to live in extreme luxury, while the people barely survived—and died—in dire misery. Through a perverted discourse and religious propaganda, the nobility justified their self-proclaimed right to exploit others without restraint for pure self-interest. Although an intermediate class, the *bourgeoisie*, was forming and its members denounced these injustices, the Revolution was rapidly turning into a bloodbath.

The lacerated flesh of *Sade*'s characters embodies the general rending of his century, the particular demise of a movement, and his own suffering in prison. It also illustrates the corruption of a singular concept: *libertinage*, or libertinism. Contrary to contemporary definitions that reduce it to moral and sexual dissolution, *libertinage* was a productive trend. In the famous *Encyclopedia* published by *Sade*'s contemporary Diderot (1713-1784), *libertinage* is inseparable from its etymology: *libertinus*, the slave made a free man in the early days of the Roman Republic. It is also associated with a Dutch group of religious fanatics who believed, in the middle of a repressively evangelical sixteenth century, that one's soul dies with one's body, and that it was the spirit of God who created everything, both good and evil. For these original libertines, as well as for *Sade*, paradise is an illusion, hell a phantom conceived by theologians, and religion an invention of those with political power to better "contain people and make them obey their laws." The *Ency-clopedia* article condemned such beliefs, but still concluded that it was an error to equate these free-thinking *libertins* with blasphemy and moral depravation. In fact, *libertinage* paralleled progressive political, social, and religious changes initiated by Enlightenment philosophers—among others the recognition of women's equality to men that prevails in Diderot's work and is also granted to *Sade's* female libertines. The seventeenth-century *libertins* were scholars like *Cyrano de Bergerac* who desired freedom from overly strict moral and religious principles inherited from the dark ages. They inspired much of eighteenth-century French philosophy, and a moral version of them that was dedicated to combating oppressive prejudices can be traced in eighteenth-century French art, litera-ture, and social practices.

But *Sade* brought *libertinage* to its apogee, advocating absolute license. In his novel *Aline and Valcour*, he summarizes his outlook on life:

> Allied, thanks to my mother, to the most powerful in our kingdom; in control, thanks to my father, of what was most distinguished in our Languedoc province; born in Paris amidst luxury and abundance, I believed, as soon as I was able to reason, that nature and fortune had gathered to shower me with their gifts; I believed it because those around me were stupid enough to tell me so, and this ridiculous pre-conceived idea made me scornful, despotic, and choleric; it seems nothing could resist me, that the entire universe was there to fulfill my whims, and that it was simply up to me to conceive of and better satisfy them.

Many of *Sade's* characters embody this perverted philosophy. For *Saint-Florent*, the tormentor whose life *Justine* saves, it consists of "the history of the passions, and my principles incline me to think that no curb ought to stop their impetuosity; when they speak, they must be waiting upon: it is my law." *Sade's* law would have been similar if the authorities and his mother-in-law had not put an end to all but one of his passions: literature. Indeed, *Sade* wrote most of his numerous novels, tales, plays, letters, and philosophical essays while in prison. Many of his works were destroyed by the police or his family; others were lost, including the savage *The 120 Days of Sodom*, which he wrote on a thirty-five-foot-long roll of paper that he had to abandon in a prison cell. Rediscovered and published in 1931, this sequence of atrocious acts would retroactively illustrate the pathological sexual behaviors catalogued and classified by *Dr. Richard von Krafft-Ebing*, who had already coined the term *sadism* in parallel to *masochism* in his *Psychopathologia Sexualis* (1886).

*Justine*'s fate is as complex an illustration of sadistic behaviors as her story is simple. The daughters of a rich banker, *Justine* and her older sister, *Juliette*, had a sheltered childhood and were educated in a famous Parisian convent. When their father, crushed by bankruptcy, died and was soon followed to the grave by their desperate mother, neither their relatives nor the abbesses were willing to help the suddenly destitute young girls. When they were expelled from the convent with a small dowry, fifteen-year-old *Juliette* realized that her only way to survive on the streets was to seduce and swindle powerful lovers. *Justine*, who was only twelve, opted for honesty and trust. Though it soon proved to be an obvious mistake, *Justine* responded with infinite virtue to the endless crimes that simple people, nobles, and clergymen alike perpetrated against her. Thus the tale of *Justine* is a subverted *Bildungsroman*, an edifying life story whose main subject is the moral and psychological development of a young heroine.

But current readers should not be deceived: Though a novel typical of its time, *Justine* pushes to their extreme core components found in comparable works of the same period like *Dangerous Liaisons* by *Choderlos de Laclos* or *Diderot*'s *Nun. Justine* also reshapes the archetypal elements of gothic novels found in Horace Walpole's *The Castle of Otranto* or Ann Radcliffe's *The Mysteries of Udolpho* into stunning images that are the forerunners of contemporary horror movies and reflect our modern aggressiveness. In order to demonstrate the grandeur of virtue that remains unflinching despite the omnipotent triumph of vice, *Sade* inflicts one sadistic pervert after another on his heroine. In ritualistic scenes of her violation, he maintains the suspense by making us wonder what it will take for *Justine* to finally denounce virtue. Does her resoluteness stem from absolute stupidity or defiant self-confidence? This question constitutes the book's obvious enigma but a more perplexing one concerns the extent of human fascination with power. While the melodramatic plot and epic adventures are narrated in a casual tone, in *Justine* power takes the least subtle and most horrific forms.

*Justine* is neither a text for sensitive souls, nor one for disturbed minds: If this book were *simply* the story of endless rapes, torture, and crimes, its appeal would have faded long ago. On the contrary, *Justine* remains as despised and targeted as it is admired and protected. In the nineteenth century, Sainte Beuve, Flaubert, and Baudelaire considered it a masterpiece. The surrealists rehabilitated *Sade* in the twentieth century, but his works were still attacked as late as 1957, when the French editor Jean-Jacques Pauvert was tried for having published a new edition of *Justine.*

*Justine*, the most unflinching of all literary figures of martyrdom, is the only female character *Sade* ever allowed to have a voice—a decision he apparently regretted since he took her first-person narrative away in a later version of the story. The attentive reader will soon perceive that *Justine* is much more than a victim of sexual or criminal perversion, she is also a symbol: She suffers because she refuses to abandon her principles. But contrary to appearances, what she stands against is not so much freakish individualized behaviors as a unified and universal power. As a group, libertines embody the indomitable force of a self-granted right to take control over others; they form a class that is beyond all laws because their corruption is always rewarded while the virtue they promote for average people only serves to better oppress them. Thus it is not *Justine*'s virtue that we should value; that she never gives up thanks to the strength she finds in a God who does nothing to protect her is neither a condemnation of nor a tribute to Christianity, but simply marks its irrelevance to a socially bound human condition. Instead, what *Sade* pays homage to in *Justine* is humanity itself.

Although *Justine* is irritating—she makes the same mistakes over and over again, telling her story to any stranger, trying to convince the worst sadists to look into their hearts, begging for mercy—it is impossible not to admire her willpower.

Beyond *Justine*, the enduring significance of *Sade*'s writings stems from the validity of his insight into the social nature of human violence. *Justine* challenges its readers to rethink a phenomenon with which they are doubtless well acquainted, regardless of their time: the unfairness of life. *Sade* points out this quandary in introducing *Justine*: Although we are "respectful of our social conventions and never erring from the duties they impose upon us, it happens, notwithstanding this, that we have met only with briars, while the wicked were gathering but roses." If you have ever wondered why the least intentional mistake you make creates a world of trouble but your hard work, dedication, and generosity lead you nowhere or even backfire; while at the same time you see that those who deliberately cheat and lie, willingly abuse their power, and carelessly dispose of others are successful, enriched, and often inhabit the highest ranks in society, then *Justine*'s story is but a radical version of your own. The villains are no longer called libertines, but sadistic exploitation of those who are weak for the benefit of an omnipotent elite persists on a larger scale. This is why *Justine* remains relevant today.

If the depths of its author's psyche are unfathomable, *Justine, Or the Misfortunes of Virtue* is anchored in the mundane reality of *Sade*'s prison cell. As *Simone de Beauvoir* has noted, in captivity "a man agonizes, but an author is born." After three years in the prison of Vincennes, *Sade* still had no idea how long his detention would last. Deprived of any outlet, he indulged in those few activities available to him: He ate voraciously, smoked rabidly, and wrote furiously about out-of-control characters who spiral down into abysmally destructive recreations. Through a long series of lewd episodes, the pace of *Justine*'s adventures is ruptured by abrupt changes in the rhythmic use of time that produce a sensation of vertigo. In the Surgeon *Rodin* episode, for example, an hour-long session of punishment can occupy three pages, months are covered in a single sentence, and many years are summarized in a short paragraph. While reading the novel, it can seem like a lengthy itemization of *Justine*'s misery; yet in the end, it lingers in our memory like a race. Thus the impact of *Justine* differs from other famously scandalous novels of the time like *Dangerous Liaisons* (1782), which is similarly replete with cynical plots, perverse seductions, self-indulgent delectations, as well as duels, madness, syphilis, and death. Compared to the misfortunes that befall virtuous *Justine*, *Cécile de Volanges'* ordeal in *Dangerous Liaisons* is like a quiet walk in the park. Then again, *Choderlos de Laclos* was only very briefly imprisoned for his political activity, while *Sade* spent a mere twelve years between the age of thirty-two and seventy-four as a free man. The rage that animates many of his characters and the increasing fury with which they treat their victims is in some way understandable.

*Sade*'s stance, however, remains subversive, disturbing, and fraught with a formidable danger. Only recently was *Sade* granted literary *lettres de noblesse* when he joined the ranks of the world's greatest writers in the legendary *Pléiade* catalogue. Calling itself the Rolls-Royce of editions, this famous French collection publishes authors' complete works with expert commentaries printed on fine paper and bound in leather. It took the prestige of such a luxurious edition to de-marginalize *Sade*. Yet *Justine* still resists containment. The novel has generated a multitude of literary analyses and interpretations, and inspired countless illustrations in art, film, and psychiatry. Thinkers like *de Beauvoir, Klossowski, Barthes,* and *Deleuze*; contemporary scholars like *Michel Delon, Lucienne Frappier-Mazure,* and *Philip Stewart*; and others such as the filmmaker *Pier Paolo Pasolini* and the intensely sharp post-feminist author *Kathy Acker* have all attempted to decode or re-embody *Sade*'s world. Yet in academia, media, or performance art, *Sade*'s work retains the secret of its manifold energy.

Even more than in Daniel Defoe's *Moll Flanders* or Abbé Prévost's *Manon Lescaut,* the story *Justine* tells her sympathetic listener explores social history, moral theory, ethics, and psychology. But the textual borders that normally separate these fields are carefully hidden: One passes smoothly from history (the debatable reasons the count of *Gernande* gives for the historical oppression of women) to philosophy (*Sade*'s conception of power vis-à-vis nature), via gory descriptions of body piercing. Whenever one tires of repetitive scenes that painstakingly detail *Justine*'s torment, such as in the Monk *Severino* episode, a lesson on virtue, equality, or taste re-anchors the discourse in a perverted but fascinating critique that keeps one from putting the book away. Although cruelly beaten by one of the depraved monks, *Justine* still finds the courage to accuse him of having depraved tastes. This prompts *Clement* to interrupt his chasing and hitting her and to start disserting about a topic very current at the time—the variety of tastes and how they depend upon such complex human faculties as perception and imagination:

> Two irregularities have, I perceive, already stricken thee among us; thou are astonished at the poignant sensation felt by some of our fellows for things usually known as fetid or polluted, and thou are likewise surprised because our voluptuous faculties may be shaken by actions which, according to thee, bear only the emblem of ferocity. Let us analyze each of these tastes, and try, if possible, to convince thee that there is nothing simpler in the world than the pleasures which result therefrom.

This seamlessness explains the magnitude of *Sade*'s influence on both 'erotic' literature and literature more broadly. Paradoxically, despite the masks, the whips, and widespread deviance, *Sade*'s anti-morality is universal. Precisely because virtue does not prevail over vice, *Justine*'s fate speaks to the most fundamental ethical issue: the casual and mundane vileness, violence, and violation of human decency that most of us witness and let happen every day, whether out of helplessness, passivity, or selfishness. As *Chantal Thomas* explains in unequivocal and accurate terms:

> The utopia of a form of freedom that would have no limits even in crime does not entail a departure of imagination from social reality. The force of the Sadian utopia comes

from the fact that it is nothing but the radicalization of a factual state of affairs. The discourse of the libertine, in its untiring will to say every single thing, equates the political omnipotence that has an absolute power of doing harm.

*Sade*'s characters dare to voice out loud the unspoken principles on which all elite-based governments are founded. *Justine* should be understood in the context of the limitless impunity that privileged members of the ruling class consider their original right. This license is self-granted although they may claim it is a divine inheritance, and it places these elites beyond the reach of human rules as well as godly laws. Moreover, they use their license to prevent ordinary people from challenging what thus becomes a self-fulfilling mastery. *La Dubois* sums it up nicely early in *Justine*:

> I like to hear them, those rich folks, those titled persons, those Magistrates, those Priests, I like to see them preaching virtue to us! It is exceedingly hard to free one's self from theft, when one has three times more than is needed for living; very difficult never to conceive murder when one is surrounded only by flatterers or slaves whose laws are our wills; very painful, indeed, to be temperate and steady, when one is at every hour before dainty dishes [. . .] But we, *Therese*, [. . .] we who are looked on disdainfully, because we are poor; whom they tyrannize over, because we are weak [. . .]; thou wilst have us abstain from crime, when its hand alone opens to us the gate of life, maintains us therein, keeps us together, and hinders us from losing it?

Such license should have been extended to *Sade* himself based on his aristocratic birth, but family and history took his privileges away and made him their victim. Thus with each woman beaten, child deflowered, body defiled, vein pierced, *Sade* displays, in a theater of grotesque cruelty, singular occurrences of the no less murderous and horrifying inequality people experience on the universal stage of life in the form of poverty, abuse, deprivation of civil and human rights, or elective wars. This injustice struck him all the more powerfully as it even worked against *Sade* himself.

*Justine*'s struggle against power, though literally embodied in sexual confrontations, characterizes the political dimensions of both *Sade*'s thinking and his times. An avid reader of his contemporaries, he did not adhere to any new system of thought produced during his intellectually active century, yet beneath the provocative surface of *Sade*'s work, one finds a patchwork of various theories. *Rousseau*'s already famous *Discourse on the Origin of the Inequality among Men* (1755) and *Social Contract* (1762) questioned the nature of and right to freedom; the *Social Contract* opens with the now famous quote: "man was born free and he is every where in chains." The libertine's way of life illustrates the contradiction: Its fundamental principle is the exact opposite of *Rousseau*'s idea. In the wake of *Montesquieu, Hobbes,* and *Locke, Rousseau* asserted that no one's moral and civil liberty should be infringed upon for the benefit of someone else. Rather, *Rousseau* posited that each citizen should agree to renounce part of his or her individual freedom and submit to laws that protect the general interest in return for security and the protection of his or her equal rights. In other words, law and human culture would compensate for the Darwinian natural tendencies of the strong to impose arbitrary force on the weak. But *Sade*'s libertines ferociously oppose *Rousseau*'s concept because it distributes power more evenly and thus goes against their interests:

> Men were all born isolated, envious, cruel and despotic; wishing to have everything and give up nothing, and incessantly fighting to maintain either their ambition or rights, the legislator came and said: Cease from fighting thus; in yielding a little on both sides, tranquility is about to spring up again. I do not blame the proposition of this pact, but I hold that two classes of individuals ought to never submit to it: those who, feeling themselves the strongest, and no need of parting with

anything in order to be happy, and those who, being the weakest, found themselves parting with infinitely more than was secured for them.

Similarly, many of *Sade*'s arguments radicalize, distort, denounce, or defy the thinking of other of his contemporaries, including *Diderot* and the Encyclopedists, the rationalist *Voltaire*, and the materialist *La Mettrie*. *Sade*'s work is thus an alternative but intrinsic part of his epoch. It also offers an infinite anomaly: The timeless allegory of vice and virtue one too hastily sees in *Justine* self-destructs. Defined by culture, virtue is subject to change, and that challenges the basis of its validity as soon as it is proclaimed:

> I am not therefore wrong when I assert that [virtue's] necessity is only of opinion, or of circumstance; virtue is not a fashion of an incontestable price, it is but a manner of conducting one's self, which varies according to each climate and which consequently has nothing real: that alone proves its uselessness. That only which is constant is really good; that which perpetually changes could not pretend to the character of goodness. That is why they have placed immutability in the rank of the perfections of the Eternal; but virtue is wholly deprived of this character: there are no two nations, on the face of the globe, which are virtuous in the same way, therefore virtue has nothing real, nothing intrinsically good, and nowise deserves our worship; it is necessary to use it as a stay, to politically adopt that of the country in which one lives, in order that those who practice it from taste, and who ought to revere it from taste, may leave you in peace. . . .

Contrary to appearances, *Justine*'s virtue does not stand for allegedly universal "moral" principles because such morality is decided by the local political and social forces that impose it. However, *Justine*'s suffering embodies the resistance that people can demonstrate to the particular vices of their own era. In today's troubled and dangerous times, when virtues are all too clearly defined by those in power and used to rally the masses in support of abusive acts and violations of human rights that only serve the elite, *Justine* serves as a deeply disturbing but vital reminder of the urgency of rethinking violence. Though we may be shocked and revolted by what the novel's sadistic characters do, nevertheless like them we treat lightly the daily forms of oppression that are common to our culture and the various wars of our own new century. Like *Justine* does for her masters, we enable our leaders to kill and torture, and we neglect the victims exploited by society's elites in pursuit of their own selfish interests. *Sade*'s corrupt darkness withstands time and accusations because it is itself an indictment of corruption; yet he does not accuse the perpetrators, instead he denounces the witnesses. Just as *Justine* creates a discourse of self-justification as she prepares the women or undresses the children, we participate, albeit indirectly, in the crimes that feed today's greed and hunger for power. *Justine* recounts tortures; we contemplate wars, class, gender and race struggles, ethnic cleansing, religious mutilation, institutionalized poverty, and preventable famines that sacrifice victims by the millions. *Justine* flees; we turn our eyes away. *Sade*, the ultimate libertine, was put in prison; yet the libertines of our own age remain at large. Until we can answer why this is so, *Justine*'s sublime sadness will remain not only part of our own story, but also our shame, and the world's sorrow.

**Dr. Fabienne-Sophie Chauderlot** teaches French studies and philosophy. A scholar of the French, English, and German Enlightenment as well as phenomenology, existentialism and post-structuralist theory, she is a specialist in the works of Diderot and Deleuze and she writes on the intersection of textual and visual aesthetics and on global ethics.

# PREFACE [1]

THE original edition of the famous *Justine, Or the Misfortunes of Virtue,* by the *Marquis de Sade,* is a book in some manner unknown to readers of the present generation. The author disowned it, pretending, according to custom, that an unfaithful friend had robbed him of his manuscript and had published therefrom only quite a shabby extract, unworthy of him whose energetic crayon had sketched the true *Justine.* He was strangely mistaken. This pretended extract is, on the contrary, the main work of the too celebrated monomaniac, and the alterations and additions to which he afterwards subjected it, completely spoiled it. Undaunted courage is necessary to face the reading of *Justine* in four volumes, followed by *Juliette* in six others, and, should one attempt it, *ennui* and disgust soon get the better of the most tenacious will. Here the case is quite a different one. In the two medium-sized tomes, of which the original edition is composed, we have the writer's first conception, such as he had expressed it, before, emboldened by success, he undertook to outdo his own eccentricities; we possess the book which caused so much sensation from 1791 to 1795, that Revolutionists did not disdain to peruse, and which, having become exceedingly rare, is to-day wholly forgotten.

The analysis of this work, having been given in the *Literary and Bibliographical Curiosity* [2], dispenses us from entering here into detailed criticism; we refer the reader to it.

It will suffice for us to state that this primitive *Justine,* contrary to the long rambling which was afterwards drawn out of it, is not only readable, but may be read with interest. It is a document. The system which the author presents therein as an intuition of a man of genius, a fundamental truth until then unobserved and which was his lot to reveal to the world, viz., that true voluptuosness, complete voluptuousness, ought to have for its seasoning the cries of suffering from the victims delivered up to frightful tortures, is a monstrous system; his demonstration is moreover illogical, for the paintings of *Justine* are more appropriate to give one the nightmare, than to provoke erotic passions: but there is in this strange amalgamation, in this chaos of tenebrous imaginations and criminal follies, a curious subject of study for the scholar, the philosopher. The moral, political, religious, social and other dissertations, which serve as interludes to the scenes of debauchery and torments, show that the *Marquis de Sade* was not simply a monomaniac enraged after lust: he had read very much, and, what is surprising, meditated a good deal. He is not alone the echo of *D'Holbach* and *La Mettrie*, with whom he is evidently inspired: he has ideas of his own, and sometimes new ideas. Who would expect, for instance, to find in germ within a book such as *Justine*, Darwin's doctrines on the evolution of species and the selection through struggle for life? Such was the ordinary fermentation of minds, at the dawn of the French Revolution, that we encounter proofs thereof even within documents where we should not certainly dream of looking for them.

# TO MY LADY FRIEND

YES, CONSTANCE, *to thee I dedicate this work; to thee at the same time the honor and example of thy sex, uniting to the most sensible soul the most upright and enlightened mind; it becomes only thee to recognise the sweetness of the tears which unhappy Virtue forces. Abhorring the sophisms of libertinism and Irreligion, incessantly combatting them by the actions and discourses, I fear not on thy account whom the class of set personages has necessitated in these Memoirs; the cynicism of certain sketches (softened down nevertheless as much as possible) will not frighten thee either; it is Vice who, bemoaning because of its being unveiled, cries out shame as soon as it is attacked. The suit against* Tartuffe *was carried out by bigots; that of* Justine *will be the work of libertines. I care very little about them: my motives, revealed by thee, shall be disowned by none; thy opinion suffices for my glory, and I ought, after having pleased thee, either to please universally, or to console myself for all censures.*

*The design of this Romance (not so Romantic as one would think) is undoubtedly novel; the ascendancy of Virtue over Vice, the reward of good, the punishment of evil, that is the ordinary plan of all the Works of this kind; should people be not sick of it?*

*But to present Vice everywhere triumphing and Virtue victim of her own sacrifices, to show an unfortunate woman erring from misfortune; the playtoy of wickedness; the merry-maker of all debaucheries; exposed to the most barbarous and monstrous tastes; giddy with the most impudent, the most specious sophims; a prey to the most crafty seductions, to the most irresistible subordinations; having, to oppose so many reverses, so many plagues, to* repel so much corruption, but a sensible soul, a natural mind and very much courage; in fine, to hazard the boldest paintings, the most extraordinary situations, the most dreadful maxims, the most energetic strokes of the brush, with the sole aim of obtaining from all this one of the sublimest lessons of ethics that man has as yet received: this was, you will agree, to arrive at the end by a track but slightly beaten up to the present.

Shall I have succeeded, Constance? Will one tear from thine eyes determine my triumph? After having read Justine, wilt thou finally say: "Oh! how much these pictures of Crime render me proud to love Virtue! How sublime she is in her tears! How misfortunes embellish her!"

O Constance! let these words drop from thy lips, and my toils are crowned.

# JUSTINE, OR THE MISFORTUNES OF VIRTUE

## PART I

THE master-piece of philosophy would be to develop the means which Providence employs to attain the ends it proposes over man, and to mark out accordingly a few lines of conduct which might make known to this unhappy biped individual the way in which he must walk within the thorny career of life, that he might guard against the whimsical caprices of this fatality to which they give twenty different names, without having as yet come to understand or define it.

If, respectful of our social conventions and never erring from the duties they impose upon us, it happens, notwithstanding this, that we have met only with briars, while the wicked were gathering but roses, persons deprived of a stock of virtues as sufficiently proved to place themselves above those remarks, will they not then conclude that it is better to abandon one's self to the torrent, than to resist it? Will they not say that Virtue, however fair she may be, becomes the worst party one may espouse, when she is too weak to struggle against Vice, and that, in an age wholly corrupted, the surest way is to do as the others? A little more instructed if you will, and abusing the lights they have acquired, will they not say with the angel Jesrad of *Zadig*, there is no evil from which some good does not spring, and that they may, according to this, give themselves up to evil, since it is only in fact one of the ways of producing the good? Will they not add that it is indifferent to the general plan whether such or such a one be good or wicked by preference, that, if misfortune persecutes Virtue and prosperity accompanies Crime, things being equal in the sight of Nature, it is infinitely better to espouse the party among the wicked who prosper, than among the virtuous who fail? It is therefore important to guard against the dangerous sophisms of a false philosophy; it is essential to show that the examples of unhappy virtue, presented to a corrupted soul, within which remain however a few good principles, may lead back this soul to the good as surely as if one had pointed out to it, in this path of virtue, the most brilliant palms and the most flattering rewards. It is undoubtedly hard to have, on the one hand, to paint a host of misfortunes overwhelming the gentle and sensible woman, who respects virtue the most, and, on the other, the affluences of prosperity over those who crush and mortify this same woman. But if there springs however some good from the painting of these fatalities, shall one feel remorse for having offered them? Can one be sorry for having established a fact from which it will result, for the wise man who fruitfully reads so useful a lesson of submission to the orders of Providence, and the fatal warning that it is often to bring us back to our duties, that Heaven strikes down at our side the being which appears to us to have best discharged its own?

Such are the feelings which are about to direct our toils, and it is in consideration of these motives that we beg the Reader's indulgence for the erroneous systems placed in the mouths of several of our personages, and for the sometimes rather painful situations, which, for truth's sake, we are obliged to bring under his eyes.

The Countess of *Lorsange* was one of those Priestesses of Venus, whose fortune is the work of a pretty face and much misconduct, and whose titles, however ostentatious they be, are only to be had in the archives of Cytheria, forged by the impertinence which assumes them, and sustained by the silly credulity which imparts them. Dark, of fine waist, eyes of singular expression; that incredulity of fashion, which, while lending another savour to the passions, causes the women in whom it is expected to exist to be sought after more carefully; somewhat wicked, no principles, believing no harm in anything, and still without corruption enough in her heart to have extinguished the sensibility thereof; proud, lewd: such was Madam of *Lorsange*.

This woman had nevertheless received the best education: being the daughter of a large Parisian Banker, she had been brought up with a sister called *Justine*, three years younger than herself, in one of the most famous Abbeys of this capital, where until the age of twelve and fifteen, no counsels, no masters, no books, no talents had been refused to either of these two sisters.

At this period fatal for the virtue of two young girls, everything failed them in one sole day: a frightful bankruptcy cast their father into so trying a situation, that he died of sorrow. His wife followed him a month later to the tomb. Two cold and distant relations thought over what they should do with the young orphans; their portion of an inheritance, absorbed by debts, amounted to a hundred crowns for each. While nobody caring to take charge of them, the Convent door was open to them, their dowry handed to them, they being left free to become whatever they pleased.

Madame of *Lorsange*, who was then called *Juliet*, and whose character and mind were nearly as formed as they were at thirty years old, the age she attained at the time of the history which we are going to relate, appeared sensible only to the pleasure of being free, without reflecting an instant on the painful reverses which were severing her chains. As to *Justine*, being as we have stated, twelve years old, she was of a gloomy and melancholy character, which caused her the better to feel all the horror of her circumstances. Endowed with a tenderness, a surprising sensibility, instead of her sister's craft and cunning, she had but one ingenuity, one integrity, which were to make her fall into many snares. This young girl united to so many qualities a sweet physiognomy, absolutely different from that with which nature had adorned Juliet; the more artifice, intrigue, coquetry you beheld in the countenance of the one, so much the more chastity, decorum and timidity did you admire in the other; a virgin's look, large blue eyes, full of soul and interest, a dazzling skin, a supple and flexible waist, a pathetic voice, teeth like ivory and the loveliest golden hair: such is the sketch of this charming younger sister, whose natural graces and delicate features are beyond our brushes.

The both got twenty-four hours notice to quit the Convent, being left the care of providing for themselves, with their hundred crowns, wherever they liked. Juliet, delighted at being her own mistress, wished for a moment to wipe away *Justine*'s tears; then, seeing she was not succeeding, she began to scold instead of consoling her; she reproached her with her sensibility; she told her, with a philosophy much beyond her age, that it was not necessary to afflict ourselves in this world except with what affected us only personally; that it was possible to find within ourselves physical sensations of a voluptuousness keen enough to extinguish all the moral affections of which the shock might be painful; that this procedure became the more essential to be put into practice, as doubling the sum of one's pleasures, than in multiplying that of one's pains; in fine, that there was nothing which ought not to be done in order to deaden in one's self this perfidious sensibility of which only others profited, whilst it brought us but chagrins. But a kind of heart is with difficulty hardened: it resists the reasonings of a bad head, and its enjoyments console it for false sparks of wit.

Juliet, making use of other resources, then told her sister, that with the age and form each of them had, it was impossible for them to die of starvation. She cited for her one of their neighbors' daughters, who, having fled from the paternal roof, was to-day richly kept up and undoubtedly far happier, than if she had remained in the bosom of her family; that we should take care not to believe that it was marriage which rendered a young girl happy; that, a captive under the laws of matrimony, she had to suffer with much whimsey, expect a very slight dose of pleasures; whereas, delivered up to libertinism, they could always assure themselves of lover's humour, or console themselves by their number.

*Justine* had a horror of these discourses; she stated that she preferred death to ignominy, and at a few fresh importunities which her sister made her, she resolutely refused to lodge with her, from the moment she saw her decided on a conduct which caused her to shudder.

The two young girls separated therefore, without any promise of seeing each other again, as soon as their intentions were so opposed. Juliet, who was going, as she pretended, to become a grand lady, should she consent to receive a little girl whose virtuous, though base, inclinations would be capable of dishonoring her? And, *Justine*, for her part, should she like to risk her behaviour in the society of a perverse creature, who was about becoming the victim of vile lewdness and public debauchery? The both then bade each other an eternal adieu, and the both left the Convent on the following day.

*Justine*, being since the time of her childhood caressed by her mother's Dressmaker, fancies that this woman will be sensible of her misfortune; so she goes to her, informs her of her disasters, asks her for work . . . she is hardly recognized; she is rudely repulsed. —"Oh Heaven!" cries the poor little creature; "is it necessary that the first steps I take in this world be already marked by such sorrows! This woman loved me formerly, why does she reject me to-day? Alas! it is because I am an orphan and poor; it is because I have no longer any resources in the world, and that people are esteemed only in ratio to the helps and pleasures that others imagine to receive from them." *Justine* goes bathed in tears to her Parish Priest; she paints her state to him with the energetic candor of her age. . . . She was dressed in a little white frock; her lovely hair carelessly bound up under a large bonnet; her throat, barely appearing, was concealed beneath two or three ells of gauze; her face rather wan, owing to the sorrows which were eating her up; a few tears stood in her eyes and lent them still more expression. "You behold me, Sir," says she to the holy *Ecclesiastic* . . . "Yes, you behold me in a very afflicting position for a young girl: I have lost my father and mother. . . . Heaven takes them from me at an age when I have most need of their help. . . . They died ruined, Sir; we have no longer anything. . . .

There is all they left me," continued she, in showing her twelve *louis* . . . and not a nook wherein to repose my poor head. . . . You will take pity on me, will you not, Sir. You are a Minister of Religion, and Religion was always the virtue of my heart; in the name of that God whom I adore and whose voice you are, tell me, like a second father, what I must do . . . what "I must become?" The charitable Priest answers, while eyeing *Justine*, that the Parish was very *burthened;* that it was impossible for it to *embrace* new alms, but that if *Justine* wished to serve him, that if she wished to do *the rough work*, there would be always a piece of bread for her in his kitchen. And, as while saying that, the interpreter of the Gods had slipped his hand under her chin, in giving her a kiss by far too worldly for a Churchman, *Justine*, who only too well understood him, repulsed him in saying: "Sir, I ask you for neither charity nor a servant's place; I left too short awhile ago a state above that which could cause me to desire these two favors, in order to be reduced to beg them: I solicit the counsels which my youth and misfortunes need, and you wish to make me purchase them a little too dear." The clergyman, ashamed of being discovered, drove quickly away this little creature, and the unhappy *Justine*, twice repulsed since the first day she is doomed to *isolism,* enters a house where she sees a bill, hires a small furnished closet on the fifth floor, pays for it in advance, and there abandons herself to her tears, the more bitter as she is sensible and her little pride has been just cruelly compromised.

Shall we be allowed to leave her here awhile, to return to Juliet, and state how, from the simple state out of which we saw her go forth, and without having more resources than her sister, she became however, in fifteen years, a titled woman, possessing an income of thirty-thousand livres, very fine jewels, two or three mansions both in town and country, and, for the moment, the heart, fortune and confidence of *Mr. de Corville,* Counsellor of State, a most influential man, and on the eve of entering into the Ministry? The career was a thorny one, surely nobody doubts of it. It is through the most shameful and hardest apprenticeship that those young ladies make their way; and such today in a Prince's bed is she, who still bears perhaps on her the mortifying marks of the brutality of libertines, into whose hands her youth and inexperience cast her.

Juliet, on leaving the Convent, went to a woman whom she had heard named by that young friend of her neighborhood; perverted as she had a mind to be and perverted by this woman, she accosts her with her little bundle under her arm, a blue gown much out of repair, her hair dishevelled, the prettiest form in the world, if it is true that indecency can have charms in certain eyes; she relates her story to this woman, entreating her to protect her as she did with her old friend.—

"How old are you?" *la Duvergier* inquires of her. — "Fifteen years old in a few days, Madam," replies *Juliet*. . . . — "And no mortal ever . . ." continued the matron.— "Oh! no, Madam, I swear to you," replied Juliet.— "But it is because sometimes in those convents . . ." says the old hag, "a Confessor, a Nun, a Comrade. . . . I want sure proofs. — It depends only on yourself to procure them, Madam," replies *Juliet* in blushing. . . . And the Duenna having clapped on a pair of spectacles, and having scrupulously scrutinized things everywhere:— "Come," she says to the little girl, "you have but to stay here; with much respect for my counsels, a great stock of complacency and submission to my customers, cleanliness, economy, candour towards me, policy towards your fellows, and knavery with men, shall, in ten years, put you into a position of retiring to a third floor, with a chest-of-drawers, a pier glass, a servant; and the skill you shall have acquired in my house, will afford you the means of procuring yourself the rest."

Having given these recommendations, *la Duvergier* seized on Juliet's little bundle; she asks her if she has not some money, and the latter having to candidly acknowledged that she had a hundred crown-pieces, the dear mamma confiscates them, while assuring her new boarder that she will place this small fund at a lottry for her, but that a young girl must not have money. "This is," she says to her, "a means of doing evil, and in so corrupted an age, a wise and well-bred girl ought to carefully avoid all that may drag her into some snares. It is for your own good I am speaking to you, my little darling," added the Duenna, "and you ought to take kindly of me what I am doing."

This sermon being over, the new comer is introduced to her fellows; they show her the room she is to occupy in the house, and from the next day her first fruits are for sale.

In four months the ware is successively sold to nearly a hundred persons; some content themselves with the rose, others more deli- cate or more depraved (for the question is not solved) want to blow out the bud which is blossoming aside. Every night *la Duvergier* straightens, sets in order, and during four months it is still the first flowers that the knavish woman offers to the public. At the end of this hard novitiate, Juliet obtains the patents of lay-sister; from this moment she is really recognised as maid of the establishment; since then she partakes of its pains and profits. Another apprenticeship: if in the first school, with a few slight exceptions, Juliet served Nature, she now forgets its laws in the second; she entirely corrupts her morals therein; the triumph she sees vice obtaining wholly degrades her soul; she feels that, born for crime, she ought at least to go at large and cease languishing in a subordinate state, which, while causing her to commit the same faults, while equally abasing her, falls far short of bringing her the same profit. She pleases an old and very debauched Lord, who gets her to come at first for the business of a moment; she possesses the skill of having herself mag- nificently kept up by him; she appears, in short, at the spectacles, on the promenades, along side the order of knights of Cytheria; she is admired, invited, desired, and the cunning creature knows so nicely how to get the right way, that in less than four years she ruins six men, the poorest of whom had an income of one hundred thousand crowns. Nothing further was wanting to make her repu- tation; the blindness of men of the world is such, and the more one of these creatures has proved her dishonesty, so much the more jealous are they to figure on her list; it seems that the degree of her abasement and corruption becomes the measure of the sentiment which they have the boldness to proclaim for her.

Juliet had attained her twentieth year, when a certain Count of *Lorsange*, an Angevin Gentleman, about forty years of age, fell so madly in love with her, that he resolved to bestow his name upon her; he allotted to her an income of twelve thousand livres, assuring her of the rest of his fortune should he chance to die before her; he gave her a mansion, servants, livery-men, and a kind of esteem in the world, which, in two or three years, succeeded in causing her *debuts* to be overlooked.

It was here that the unfortunate Juliet, unmindful of every sentiment of her birth and good education; perverted by evil counsels and dangerous books; eager to enjoy alone, to possess a name and on ties, dared let herself be carried away by the guilty project of shortening her husband's days. Having conceived this odious scheme, she fostered it: she considered it unfortunately in these perilous moments, when the natural is inflamed by the errors of the moral: instants when people least deny themseles, as then nothing is opposed to the irregularity of vows or to the impetuosity of desires, and as the received voluptuousness is alive only by reason of the multitude of laws violated, or of their sanctity. If one became wise, when the dream is vanished, the inconvenience would be a moderate one; it is the history of the wrongs of the mind: one knows that they offend nobody, but they go further unfortunately. What will be, dares anyone state, the realisation of this idea, since its mere aspect has just exalted, has just stung to the quick? One vivifies the cursed chimera, and its existence in crime.

Madame of *Lorsange* executed so secretly, fortunately for her, that she secured herself against every pursuit, and buried with her spouse the traces of the terrible crime which precipitated him into the tomb.

Having become free and a Countess, Madam of *Lorsange* resumed her former customs; but, fancying herself somebody in the world, she displayed rather less indecency in her conduct. She was no longer a kept up maid: she was a rich widow who gave fine supper parties, into whose house the Court and city were only too happy to be admitted. Briefly, she was a decent woman, who not withstanding used to *go to bed* for two hundred *louis,* and bestowed herself for five hundred a month. Up to twenty-six years of age, Madame of *Lorsange* still made some brilliant conquests; she ruined three foreign Ambassadors, four General Farmers, two Bishops, one Cardinal and three Knights of Orders of the King; but as it is rare to stop after a first crime, especially when it has succeeded, the unfortunate Juliet blackened herself with two fresh crimes like the first; the one, to rob a lover of hers who had entrusted her with a considerable sum, ignored by his family, and which Madam of *Lorsange* was able to secure by this frightful action; the other, in order to have the sooner a legacy of a hundred thousand francs which one of her adorers made her in the name of a third person, charged to render the amount after decease. To these horrors Madame of *Lorsange* added three or four infanticides. The fear of spoiling her pretty waist, the desire of concealing a double intrigue, all prompted her to stifle within her womb the proof of her debaucheries; and these crimes, ignored like the others, did not prevent this crafty and ambitious woman from daily procuring fresh dupes.

It is therefore true that prosperity may accompany the worst conduct, and that, even in the midst of disorder and corruption, all which men call happiness may spread over life. But let not this hard and fatal truth alarm; let not the example of misfortune pursuing virtue everywhere, as we are going to show, annoy honest persons either. This felicity of crime is deceitful, it is only apparent. Independent of the punishment which Providence most certainly reserves for those who have been seduced by its successes, do they not feed in the depth of their soul a worm, which incessantly gnawing them, prevents them from being rejoiced with those false gleams, and leaves in their soul, instead of delights, only the bitter remembrance of crimes which brought them to what they are? With respect to the unfortunate man whom destiny persecutes, he has his heart for consolation; and the inward rejoicings which his virtues procure him, soon recompense him for the injustice of men.

Such was the state of affairs with Madam of *Lorsange*, when *Mr. de Corville,* aged fifty, enjoying the trust and consideration which we have painted further back, resolved to entirely sacrifice himself for this woman, and to attach her forever to himself. Be it attention, proceedings, or policy on the part of Madam of *Lorsange*, he had succeeded therein, and lived with her for four years, quite as with a lawful spouse, when the acquisition of a very fine land property near Montargis, obliged them both to go and spend some time in the Province.

One evening when the beauty of the weather had caused them to prolong their walk, from the grounds they inhabited to Montargis, the both being too tired to undertake to return as they had come, they stopped at the inn where the Coach from Lyons draws up, on purpose to dispatch a man hence on horseback to fetch them a car. They were resting themselves in a low and fresh room of this house, looking over the yard, when the Coach we have just mentioned entered it.

It is an amusement natural enough to watch people alighting from a coach: one may bet on the kind of persons that are on it, and should you name a Fast-Girl, an Officer, a few Abbots and a Monk, you are almost sure of winning. Madam of *Lorsange* gets up, *Mr. de Corville* follows her, and the both enjoy themselves seeing the jolting society coming into the inn. It appeared there was no longer anyone inside the coach, when a marechaussee[1] Cavalier, alighting from the box, received into his arms, from one of his comrades likewise placed in the same spot, a girl of about twenty-six or twenty-seven years old, dressed in a short shabby Indian caraco, and muffled up to the eyebrows with a large dark taffeta mantle. She was bound as a criminal, and so weak, that she would have certainly fallen had not her guards held her up. At a cry of surprise and horror which escaped from Madam of *Lorsange*, the young girl turns round, and presents to view, with the loveliest waist in the world, the noblest, the most pleasing, the most interesting form; in fine, all the charms the most deserving of pleasing, rendered a thousand times still more enticing, because of this tender and touching affliction which innocence adds to the features of beauty.

Mr. *de Corville* and his mistress can not forbear from taking an interest in this wretched girl. They draw nigh, they inquire of one of the guards what this unfortunate girl has done.— "She is accused of three crimes," replies the Cavalier; "it is about murder, robbery and house-burning; but I confess to you that my comrade and I have never conducted a criminal with so much reluctancy; she is the mildest of creatures, and appears the honestest." — "Ah! ah!" exclaimed Mr. *de Corville,* "might there not be in this case a few of those blunders usual to subordinate Tribunals?. . . And whereabouts is the crime committed? — In an inn a few leagues from Lyons, where she was tried; she is going, according to custom, to Paris for the confirmation of the Sentence, and she shall come back to be executed at Lyons."

Madam of *Lorsange,* who had drawn nigh, who was listening to this tale, softly intimated to Mr. *de Corville* the eagerness she had to learn, from this girl's own lips, the story of her misfortunes; and Mr. *de Corville,* who also conceived the same idea, informed the two guards of it, while telling them who he was. They saw no reason for opposing it. It was decided they should spend the night at Montargis; they request a comfortable apartment; Mr. *de Corville* pledges himself in behalf of the prisoner; she is unbound. And when they had administered her a little food, Madam of *Lorsange,* who could not forbear taking the liveliest interest in her, and who doubtlessly said to herself: "This creature, perhaps innocent, is still treated as a criminal, whereas everything prospers about me . . . about me who have stained myself with crimes and horrors!" Madam of *Lorsange,* I say, as soon as she saw this poor girl somewhat refreshed, somewhat consoled by the caresses that they hastened to bestow upon her, persuaded her to relate by what adventure, with so sweet a physiognomy, she was in so unlucky a circumstance.

— "To relate to you the history of my life, Madam," says this lovely unfortunate one, while addressing herself to the Countess, "is to offer you the most striking example of the misfortunes of innocency, is to accuse the hand of Heaven, is to complain of the will of the Supreme Being; it is a species of revolt against his holy intentions . . . I dare not . . ." Tears then abundantly flowed from the eyes of this interesting girl, and after having given them vent, she began her recital in these terms:

You will permit me to conceal my name and birth, Madam; without being illustrious, it is honorable, and I was not destined to the humiliation to which you now see me reduced. I lost my parents while I was quite young; I thought that, with the little help they had left me, I could wait for a becoming employment, and refusing all those that were not so, I got through, without perceiving it, in Paris where I was born, the trifle I possessed; the poorer I became, the more I was despised; the more I was in need of assistance, the least I expected to obtain any; but of all the trials I experienced at the beginning of my unhappy situation, of all the horrible proposals which were made to me, I shall only mention the one which befell me at *Mr. Dubourg's,* one of the richest rate collectors of the capital. The woman at whose house I was lodging sent me to him, as to a person whose name and riches could the most surely alleviate the rigor of my destiny. After having waited a very long while in the antechamber of this man, I was introduced; *Mr. Dubourg,* of about forty-eight years old, had just got out of bed, wrapped in a loose morning-gown which scarcely hid his disorder; they were preparing to coif him; he dismissed them and asked me what I wanted. — "Alas! sir," I answered him quite confused, "I am a poor orphan who am not yet fourteen years old, and am already acquainted with all the shades of adversity; I implore your compassion, have pity on me; I do beseech you." And then I gave him an account of all my woes, the difficulty of finding an employment, perhaps too somewhat of the pain I felt about taking one, not being born for the state; the misfortune I had had, all the while, to get through the trifle I possessed . . . the lack of work, the hope I was in that he would facilitate me for the means of living; in fine, all that the eloquence of misfortune dictates, ever sweeping in a sensible soul, ever a burden to opulence. . . . After having listened to me with many distractions, *Mr. Dubourg* asked me if I had been always good? — "I

13

should be neither so poor nor so embarrassed, sir," replied I, "had I wished to cease being so". — "But," to this *Dubourg* said, "by what right do you pretend that the rich should relieve, if you are of no service to them?" — "And what service do you pretend to speak, sir?" replied I; "I desire nothing better than to render those which decency and my age permit me to do. — The services of a child like you are of but little use in a house," *Dubourg* answered me; "you are neither of the age nor make to be placed as you request. You had better to busy yourself in pleasing men, and try to find somebody that may consent to take care of you; this virtue of which you make so great a boast is worthless in the world; you may bow ever so much at the foot of its altars, its vain incense will not feed you. What flatters men the least, what they think the least about, what they despise the most thoroughly, is the wisdom of your sex; they value here below, my child, only what brings them profits or delights; and of what profit is woman's virtue to us? Their disorders serve and amuse us; but their chastity does not interest us in the slightest. In short, when men like us bestow, it is never except with the hope of receiving; now, how can a little girl like you repay what is done for her, if it be not the most complete giving up of all that is required of her person?" — "Oh! sir," I answered with a heart big with sighs, "there is then no longer either honesty or beneficence among men?" — "Very little," replied *Dubourg*; "there is so much said about it, why should you have it so? people have recovered from that mania of obliging others gratis; they have discovered that the pleasures of charity were but the enjoyment of pride, and as nothing is so soon dispelled, they have desired realer sensations; they saw that with a child like, for instance, it was infinitely better to reap, as fruit of their advance money, all the pleasures that lust can afford, than those very trivial ones of alleviating her for nothing; the reputation of a liberal, alms-giving, generous man, is not worth, even at the instant he enjoys it the most, the slightest pleasure of the senses." — "Oh! Sir, with the like principles, the unfortunate one must then perish!" — "What matter? there are more subjects than are wanted in France; provided the machine has always the same elasticity, what does it matter to the State the more or fewer individuals who press it down? — But do you believe children respect their parents, when they are thus treated by them? — What does it matter to a father, the love of children who trouble him? — It would have been then better had we been smotherd from the cradle! — Surely such was the custom in many countries, such was the custom of the Greeks; such is that of the Chinese: there, unfortunate children are exposed or put to death. What is the good of letting these creatures live, which, being no longer able to rely upon the assistance of their parents, either because they are bereft of them or because they are not owned by them, serve only from then to over-burden the State with a commodity of which it has already too much? Bastards, orphants, badly framed children ought to be condemned to death from their birth: the former two, because having no longer anybody to watch over or take care of them, they sully society with a dreg which can but become fatal to it one day; and the latter, because they can be of no use to it. Both of these classes is to society what excrescences are to the flesh, which, feeding on the sap of the sound members, degrade and weaken them; or, if you prefer, like those parasitic vegetables which, while binding themselves to the good plants, spoil them in adapting to themselves their nutritive seed. Telling abuses are those alms destined to feed such a scum those richly endowed houses which people have the extravagance of building for them; as if the human species was so exceedingly rare, so exceedingly precious, that it was necessary to conserve even the vilest portion thereof! But let us drop a policy of which thou understandest nothing, my child; why complain of one's lot, when it depends on one's self to remedy it? — At what price, good Heavens! — At that of chimera a thing which has no other value than the one thy pride sets on it. Moreover," continues this barbarian in rising and opening the door, "that is all I can do for you; agree to it, or get out of my sight; I do not like beggars. . . ." My tears flowed, could not retain them; will you believe it, Madam? they irritated this man instead of softening him. He shuts the door and, seizing me by the collar of my dress he says to me with brutality that he is going to make me do through force what I do not wish to grant him with good will. In this desperate instant, my misfortune lends me courage; I rid myself of his hands, and rushing to the door: — "Hateful man," I say to him while getting away, "may Heaven so grievously offended by thee, punish thee one day, as thou deservest, for thy execrable obduracy! Thou are neither worthy of these riches of which thou makest so vile a use, nor even of the air which thou breathest in a world stained by the barbarities."

I hastened to relate to my landlady the reception of the person to whose house she had sent me; but what was my surprise to see how this wretch loaded me with reproaches instead of sharing in my grief! — "Thou mean creature," she says to me in a rage, "dost thou imagine that men are dupes enough to bestow charity on little girls like thee, without exacting the interest of their money? *Mr. Dubourg* is too kind to have acted as he has done; in his place I should not have let thee go out of my house without having satisfied myself. But, since thou wilt not profit by the succours I offer thee, dispose of thyself as thou pleasest; thou owest me: to-morrow money, or the prison. — "Madam, have pity. . . ." — "Yes, yes, pity; people starve with pity!" — "But what will you have me do?" — "You must go back to *Dubourg*'s; you must satisfy him, you must bring me back some money; I shall see him; I shall make up, if I can, for your silliness; I shall offer him your apologies, but mind you behave better."

Ashamed, in despair, not knowing which side to take, seeing myself cruelly repulsed by everybody, almost without resource, I say to *Madam Desroches* (this was my landlady's name) that I was ready for everything, in order to satisfy her. She went off to the financier's, and told me on her return that she had found him very angry; that it was not without difficulty she had prevailed on him to yield in my favor; that by dint of entreaties she had however succeeded in persuading him to see me again the next morning: but that I had to look after my conduct, because if I thought of disobeying him again, he would himself undertake the care of having me locked up for life.

I arrive quite excited. *Dubourg* was alone, in a more indecent state than on the eve. Brutality, libertinism, all the marks of debauchery shone in his sullen looks.

— "Thank *la Desroches*," he says to me roughly, "because I condescend on her account to render you awhile my kindnesses; you ought to feel how unworthy you are of them, after your conduct of yesterday. Undress, and if you again offer the slightest resistance to my desires, two men are waiting for you in my antechamber in order to lead you to a spot out of which you shall never go during your life." — "Oh! Sir," I cried in tears and throwing myself at the knees of this barbarous man, "let yourself relent, I do beseech you; be generous enough to succour me without exacting from me what costs me sufficiently to offer you rather my life than to submit to it. . . . Yes, I had rather die a thousand times than transgress the principles I received in my childhood. . . . Sir, sir, do not constrain me, I do implore you; can you conceive happiness in the bosom of disgusts and tears? Do you dare suspect pleasure to be where you shall behold only repugnance? You shall have no sooner consummated your crime, than the spectacle of my despair will overwhelm you with remorse. . . ." But the infamies to which *Dubourg* was giving himself up hindered me from proceeding; could I have thought myself able of affecting a man who already found in my very grief a vehicle more to his horrible passions? Will you believe it, Madam? inflaming himself at the bitter accents of my bewailings, relishing them with inhumanity, the unworthy wretch was preparing himself for his criminal attempts! He gets up, and at last showing himself to me in a state in which reason seldom triumphs, and in which the resistance of the object which caused it to be lost is but another stimulus to the delirium, he seizes me with brutality, impetuously lifts the veils which still conceal what he is burning to enjoy; by turns he abuses me . . . flatters me . . . he uses me ill and caresses me. . . . Oh! what a picture, great God! What a strange medley of hardness . . . of lust! It seemed that the Supreme Being wished, in this first circumstance of my life, to imprint for ever in me all the horror that I ought to have for a kind of crime, from which the abundance of evils with which I was threatened was to spring! But was it the case to complain then? Undoubtedly, no; I owed my safety to his excesses; a little less debauchery, and I was a dishonoured girl; the fires of *Dubourg* were extinguished in the effervescence of his enterprises; Heaven avenged for me the offenses to which the monster was going to abandon himself, and the loss of his strength, preserved me from being the victim thereof.

*Dubourg* became only the more insolent at it; he accused me for the wrongs of his weakness, . . . wished to redress them by fresh outrages and abuses still more mortifying; there was nothing he did not say to me, nothing he did not try, nothing his base imagination, the hardness of his nature and the depravity of his morals did not cause him to undertake. My awkwardness tired his patience, I was far from wishing to act, it was a good deal even to lend myself, my remorse is not yet extinguished. . . . However nothing succeeded, my submission ceased to inflame him; in vain, he successively passed from tenderness to severity . . . from severity to tyranny . . . from the look of decency to the excesses of filth, we both found ourselves tired, fortunately without his being able to recover what was necessary to direct against me the most dangerous attacks. He gave it over, made me promise to come to him the next day, and the more surely to determine me to do so, he wished absolutely to give me only the amount I owed to *la Desroches*. I returned therefore to this woman's house, exceedingly humbled by such an adventure and firmly resolved, whatever might befall me, not to expose myself there a third time. I warned her about it when paying her, and while loading with maledictions the rascal capable of so cruelly taking advantage of my misery. But my imprecations, far from drawing on him the wrath of God, only brought him good-luck; I learned, eight days after, that this notorious libertine had just obtained from the Government a General Exciseship, which increased his revenues to more than four hundred thousand livres yearly; I was absorbed by the reflections which similiar inconsequences of destiny cause to rise, when a ray of hope seemed an instant to shine in my eyes.

*La Desroches* came to tell me one day that she had at last found a house where I would be willingly received, provided I conducted myself well in it. — "Oh! Heavens, Madam," I cried throwing myself with rapture into her arms, "this is the condition that I should myself lay down; fancy whether I accept it with pleasure!" The man whom I was to serve was a famous Parisian usurer, who had enriched himself, not only in lending on pledges, but also in robbing with impunity the public every time he thought he could safely do so. He lived in the *rue* Quincampoix, on a second floor, with an old creature of fifty, whom he styled his wife, and at least as wicked as himself. — "*Therese*," he says to me (such was the name I assumed in order to conceal my own. . . .), "*Therese*, the first virtue of my house is uprightness; if ever you convert to your own use from here the tenth part of a penny, I will have you hanged, do you understand, my child? The little sweetness we enjoy, my wife and myself, is the fruit of our immense toils and sobriety. . . . Do you eat much, my darling?" — "A few ounces of bread a day, Sir," I answered him, "some water and a little soup when I am fortunate enough to have any." — "Some soup! zooks, some soup! Look here, my dear," says the usurer to his wife, "lament the progress of luxury: that thing seeks a condition, that thing is starving since a year, and the thing wants to eat soup! Scarcely do we take any once on the Sundays, we who work like galley-slaves. You shall have three ounces of bread a day, my girl, have a bottle of river water, my wife's old gown, every eighteen months, and three crown-pieces of wages at the end of the year, if we are satisfied with your services, if your economy answers ours, and in fine if you make the house prosper by order and arrangement. Your service is light, it is the affair of one glance: you have to rub and clean this apartment of six rooms three times a week; make our beds, to answer the door, to powder my wig, to coif my wife, to care for the dog and parrot, to look after the kitchen, to polish the utensils thereof, to assist my wife when she is preparing a bit to eat and to spend four or five hours a day in making linen, stockings, caps and other little household trifles. You see it is nothing, *Therese*, you will have whips of time left, we shall allow you to utilize it for your own account, provided you are good, my child, discreet, especially economical, that's the essential." You easily imagine, Madam, that it was necessary to be in the frightful state I was to accept such a place; there was not only infinitely more work than my strength allowed me to undertake, but also could I live on what they offered me? I took good care however from acting the hard to please, and I was installed on the same evening.

If my wretched situation permitted me to amuse you awhile, Madam, when I ought to think only of moving you to pity, I should venture to relate to you a few acts of avarice of which I was witness in that house; but so terrible a catastrophy for me was awaiting me there since the second year, that it is very difficult on my part to detain you with these amusing details, before entertaining you with my misfortunes.

You shall know however, Madam, that there was never any other light in the apartment of *Mr. du Harpin,* except the one he used to rob from the street-lamp happily placed in front of his room; neither of them ever used linen; they stowed by that which I made up, they never touched it during their living; there was on the sleeves of the master's vest, as well as on those of Madam, an old pair of cuffs sewed to the stuff, and which I washed every Saturday evening; no sheets, no towels, and all to avoid the washing. Wine was never drunk in his house, pure water being, *Madam du Harpin* used to say, the natural drink of man, the wholesomest and the least dangerous. Every time bread was cut, he was wont to place a basket under the knife, in order to catch what was falling; they added to this with great exactitude all the crumbs which might be made at meals, and this mess, fried on Sunday, with a little butter, composed the banquet dish of the days of rest; the clothes were never to be beaten or the household stuffs either for fear of wearing them, but they were to be lightly swept with a feather duster. Master's soles, as those of Madam, were lined with iron, they were the same as those they had worn on their wedding day; but a far stranger practice was that they made me exercise once a week: there was in the apartment a pretty large cabinet the walls of which were not papered; I was obliged to go with a knife and grate a certain quantity of plaster from these walls, which I next sifted in a fine sieve; that which resulted from this operation became toilet powder with which I adorned every morning the Master's wig and Madam's chignon. Ah! would to God, that these turpitudes had been the only ones to which these niggardly folks had delivered themselves! Nothing is more natural than the desire of conserving one's wealth; but what is not so much so, is the envy of increasing it with that of others. And I was not long before perceiving that it was thus the *du Harpins* were enriching themselves.

There was lodging over our heads a private man very well off, possessing pretty fine jewels; and his effects, either on account of the vicinity, or because of their having passed through my master's hands, were well known to him; I often heard him regretting with his wife a certain gold box of from thirty to forty *louis,* which would have infallibly remained with him, he used to say, had he known how to hold on to it with more craft. In fine, to console himself for having restored this box, the honest *Mr. du Harpin* planned to steal it, and he entrusted me with the business.

After having preached me a long sermon on the indifference of theft, on the utility itself it was in the world, since it re-established therein a sort of equilibrium, completely disturbed by the inequality of riches; on the rarity of punishments, since out of twenty robbers it was proved that not two of them perished; after having demonstrated for me with an erudition of which I should not have thought *Mr. du Harpin* capable, that theft was held in honor throughout all Greece, that several nations still approved of it, favoured it, rewarded it as a bold action proving at the same time courage and skill (two virtues essential to every warlike Nation), in fine after having extolled his credit which would get me out of every scrape, if I were discovered, *Mr. du Harpin* handed me two false keys, one of which was to open the neighbor's apartment, the other the desk in which the said box was; he bade me fetch him forthwith that box, and for so signal a service, I should receive during two years a crown-piece over and above my wages. "Oh! Sir," screeched I in shuddering at the proposal, "is it possible that a master dares thus corrupt his servant! Who hinders me from turning against yourself the arms you put into my hands, and what will you have to oppose me, if one day I render you the victim of your own principles?" *Du Harpin*, being confounded, fell back upon an awkward subterfuge: he told me that what he was doing was only on purpose to test me; that I was very fortunate to have resisted his proposals . . . that I was lost had I given way. . . . I paid myself for this lie; but I soon felt the wrong I was in for answering so boldly: evil-doers do not like to meet with any resistance in those they seek to seduce; there is unluckily no medium from the moment one is pretty much to be pitied for having received their proposals: you must necessarily become from that time either complices, which is very dangerous, or their enemies, which is still more so. With a little more experience, I should have left the house on the instant, but it was already written in the Heavens, that every one of the honest movements which was to come to light from me, would be paid off by misfortunes.

*Mr. du Harpin* let nearly a month slip by, namely, almost until the end of my second year's stay in his house, without saying a word, and without expressing the slightest resentment at the refusal I had made him, when one evening, having gone into my room, to taste therein a few hour's rest, I heard all of a sudden my door flung inside, and saw, not without fright, *Mr. du Harpin* leading a Justice of the peace and four Soldiers of the Guet[2] near my bed. "Do your duty, Sir," he said to the man of justice; "this unfortunate girl has robbed me of a diamond worth a thousand crowns, you will find it in her room or about her, the fact is certain." — "I, to have robbed you, Sir!" said I in casting myself all troubled out of my bed; "I, good Heavens! Ah! who knows better than you do the contrary? Who ought to be better penetrated than you with the degree to which this action is repugnant to me, and with the impossibility there is of my having committed it?" But *du Harpin*, making a deal of noise that my words might not be heard, continued to order the perquisitions, and the unlucky ring was found in my mattress. With proofs of this forcibleness, there was no answer to be made; I was instantly seized, handcuffed, and led off to prison, without its being even possible for me to make a single word heard in my favor.

The trial of an unfortunate girl who was neither credit, or potection, is speedily got over in a country where virtue is deemed incompatible with misery . . . where misfortune is a thorough proof against the defendant; there, an unjust prevention causes it to be believed that the one who ought to commit the crime, has committed it; feelings are compared with the state in which the culprit is found; and so soon as neither gold nor titles establish his innocence, the impossibility of his being innocent becomes then proved[3].

I might defend myself ever so much, I might furnish with the best means ever there were my Counsellor of form sake whom they gave me for an instant: my master was indicting me, the diamond was found in my room: it was clear I had stolen it. When I wanted to cite the horrible act of *Mr. du Harpin*, and prove that the misfortune which befell me was but the fruit of his revenge, and the consequence of the mind he had to rid himself of a creature who, possessing his secret, became mistress over him, they treated these complaints as a recimination; they told me that *Mr. du Harpin* was known these twenty years for an upright man, incapable of such a horror. I was removed to the Jail, where I saw myself at the moment of going to pay with my days, the refusal of participating in a crime; I was coming to my end; a fresh offence could alone save me: Providence would have crime serve once at least as an ægis of virtue, that he might preserve her from the abyss in which the imbecility of judges was about to swallow her up.

I had near me a woman of about forty, as celebrated for her beauty as for the species and multiplicity of her transgressions; they called her *Dubois,* and she was, as the unhappy *Therese,* on the eve of undergoing a sentence of death. Alone the genus puzzled the judges; having made herself guilty of all imaginable crimes, they found themselves almost obliged to either invent for her a new punishment, or make her undergo one, from which our sex is exempt. I had inspired a sort of interest in this woman, a criminal interest no doubt, since the basis thereof, as I found out afterwards, was the ardent desire of making a proselyte of me.

One evening, two days perhaps at most before that on which both of us were to lose our lives, *la Dubois* bade me not to go to bed, and to stop with her without affectation as close as possible to the prison doors. "Between seven and eight o'clock," continued she, "the Jail will be set on fire, it is the work of my cares; many persons will be undoubtedly burnt, it matters but little, *Therese*," dared this wretch tell me; "the lot of others ought to be always nought from the moment there is question of our well-being; what is certain, is we shall be saved; four men, my accomplices and friends, will join with us, and I answer thee for thy liberty."

I told you, Madam, how the hand of Heaven, which had just punished innocence in my person, served crime in my protectress; the fire broke out, the conflagration was horrible, there were twenty-one persons burnt, but we escaped. On the same day we reached a poacher's hut of the forest of Bondy[4], an intimate friend of our band.

"There thou are free, *Therese*," *la Dubois* says to me then, "thou mayst now choose whatever kind of life thou pleasest; but if I have a counsel to give thee, it is to renounce the practices of virtue which, as thou seest, have never succeeded with thee; a misplaced delicacy has led thee to the foot of the scaffold, a dreadful crime saves me from it; see what is the use of good actions in the world, and whether it is worth the trouble of immolating one's self for them! Thou art young and pretty, *Therese* : in two years I undertake thy fortune; but do not fancy I lead thee to its temple by the paths of virtue: we must, when we wish to make our way, darling child, undertake more than one trade, and serve more than one intrigue; make up thy mind therefore; we have no safety in this hut; we must go hence within a few hours."

— "Oh! Madam," said I to my benefactress, "I am under great obligations to you, I am far from wishing to flee from them; you have saved my life; it is dreadful for me that it be through a crime! believe that were I obliged to commit it, I should have prefered a thousand deaths to the grief of participating therein; I feel all the dangers I have traversed in order to abandon myself to the upright sentiments which shall ever remain within my heart; but whatever be, Madam, the thorns of virtue, I shall unceasingly prefer them to the perilous favors that accompany crime. There are in me principles of religion, which, thanks to Heaven, shall never go from me; if Providence renders the career of life painful for me, it is to reward me for it in a better world. This hope consoles me, it sweetens my sorrows, it calms my complaints, it fortifies me in distress, and causes me to brave all the evils it will please God to send me. This joy would be immediately extinguished within my soul, should I sully it by crimes, and with the dread of chastisements in this world, I should have the woeful aspect of punishments in the other, which would not leave me an instant in the tranquility I desire." — "Those are absurd systems which will soon bring thee to the Poor-house, my girl," said *la Dubois* in frowning; "believe me, lay aside the justice of God, his chastisements or his future rewards; all that nonsense is good only to make us starve. O *Therese* ! the cruelty of the Rich legalizes the bad behaviour of the Poor; let their purse be open to our needs, let humanity reign within their hearts, and virtues may be established in ours; but so long as our misfortune, our patience in bearing it, our good faith, our servility serve only to double our fetters, our crimes will become their work, and we should be great dupes to deny ourselves them, when they may lessen the yoke with which their barbarity overloads us. Nature has caused us to be born equals, *Therese* ; if hasard takes pleasure in putting out of order this first plan of general laws, it involves upon us to correct its caprices and redress by our dexterity the usurpations of the strongest. I like to hear them, those rich folks, those titled persons, those Magistrates, those Priests, I like to see them preaching virtue to us! It is exceedingly hard to free one's self from theft, when one has three times more than is needed for living; very difficult never to conceive murder, when one is surrounded only by flatterers or slaves whose laws are our wills; very painful, indeed, to be temperate and steady, when one is at every hour before dainty dishes; it does them great harm to be sincere, when no interest for telling lies is offered them! . . . But we, *Therese,* we whom that barbarous Providence, of which thou hast the madness to make thy idol, has condemned to crawl in humiliation like the snake in the grass; we who are looked on disdainfully, because we are poor; whom they tyrannize over, because we are weak; we, whose thirst is quenched only with gall, and whose feet press but briars, thou wilt have us abstain from crime, when its hand alone opens to us the gate of life, maintains us therein, keeps us together, and hinders us from losing it? Thou wilt that everlastingly subjected and degraded, whilst this class which domineers over us has for it all the favors of fortune, we reserve for ourselves only trouble, dejection and sorrow, only want and tears, only disgraces and the scaffold? No, no, *Therese*, no; either that Providence that thou reverest is made only for our contempt, or those are not its wills. Know it better, my child, and be convinced that from the moment it places us in a situation in which evil becomes necessary, and leaves us at the same time the possibility of exercising it, it is because this evil serves its laws as the good, and that it gains as much from the one as from the other; the state in which it created us, is equality; he who puts it out of order is not guiltier than he who seeks to set it in order again; both act according to the received impulsions, both ought to follow and enjoy them."

I confess, if ever I was shaken, it was by the seductions of this cunning woman; but a voice stronger than hers refuted her sophisms within my heart, I surrendered to it; I declared to *la Dubois* that I was determined never to allow myself to be corrupted, — "Well!" she answered me, "become what thou wilt, I abandon thee to thy evil destiny; but if ever thou gettest thyself hanged, which can not escape thee, through the fatality which inevitably spares crime in immolating virtue, remember at last never to speak of us."

While we were reasoning thus, *la Dubois'* four complices were drinking, with the poacher, and as wine disposes the soul of the malefactor for new crimes, and causes him to forget former ones, our villians had no sooner heard of my resolutions, than they decided on making a victim of me, being unable to make a complice of me; their principles, morals, the dark by-place in which we were, the kind of security under which they fancied themselves to be, their drunkenness, my age, my innocence, all, all encouraged them. They rise from table, they hold a council, they consult *la Dubois*, proceedings the sad mystery of which makes me tremble with horror; and the final result is an order to lend myself at once to satisfy the desires of every one of the four, either willingly or forcibly: if I do so willingly, each will give me a crown-piece to bring me whatever I liked; if they are obliged to use violence, the thing will be done all the same; but that the secret be better kept, they will stab me after having satisfied themselves, and bury me at the foot of a tree.

I have no need to paint you the effect that this most appalling proposal caused me, Madam; you easily comprehend it; I flung myself at *la Dubois'* knees, I conjured her to be a second time my protectress: the dishonest creature only laughed at my tears. — "Oh! zookers," said she, "thou art very unfortunate! . . . What! thou shudderest at the obligation of successively serving four fine able fellows like those? but knowest thou that there are ten thousand women in Paris who would bestow half their gold or their jewelry to be in thy place? Listen," she added however after a little reflection, "I have sway enough over those queer fellows to obtain thy forgiveness on the terms that thou renderest thyself worthy of it." — "Alas! Madam, what must I do?" I cried in tears, command me, "I am quite ready!" — "To follow us, to enroll thyself with us, and commit the same acts without the slightest repugnance: at this price alone I spare thee the rest." I did not think I ought to waver; in accepting this hard condition, I ran fresh dangers I grant, but they were less urgent than the latter; perhaps I could free myself from them, whereas nothing was able to get me out of those which were threatening me. — "I shall go everywhere, I promise you; save me from the fury of these men, and I shall not leave you during my life." — "Children," said *la Dubois* to the four banditti, "this girl belongs to the troop, I receive her into it, I install her in it; I do entreat you to offer her no violence; let us not disgust her with the trade on the first days; you see how her age and form may be useful to us; let us make use of her for our interests, and not sacrifice her to our pleasures."

But passions have a degree of energy in man, when nothing can bring them under submission. The fellows with whom I had to do were no longer in a state of hearing anything, the whole four surrounding me, devouring me by their fiery looks, threatening me in a still more terrible manner; ready to seize upon me, ready to sacrifice me. . . . "She must pass by there," said one of them; there is no means of giving her quarter: "would they not say that it is necessary to show proofs of virtue to be in a band of robbers? and will she not be of use to us as well deflowered as maiden?" I soften down the expressions, you understand, Madam; I shall likewise weaken the pictures; alas! the obscenity of their coloring is such, that your chastity would suffer from their *naked part* at the very least as much as my timidity.

A meek and trembling victim, alas! I quaked; I had barely strength to breathe; kneeling before the whole four, sometimes my feeble arms were raised to implore them, and sometimes to bend *la Dubois*. . . . "One moment" cried one called *Cœur-de-Fer*, who appeared the head of the band, a man of thirty-six, endowed with the force of a bull and the form of a satyr; "one moment, my friends! it is possible to satisfy everybody; since this little girl's virtue is so precious to her, as *la Dubois* so well expresses it, this quality, diversely put in action, may become necessary for us, leave it with her; but we must be appeased; we have no longer our heads on us, Dubois, and in the state in which you see us, we should perhaps kill yourself if you were opposed to our pleasures; let *Therese* instantly strip herself as naked as the day on which she came into the world, and let her adapt herself thus by turns to the various positions we may choose to exact, while *la Dubois*, appeasing our passions, will make the incense burn upon the altars the entry of which this creature refuses us." — "To strip myself naked!" I cried, "oh Heavens! what do you want? When I am delivered up in this way to your looks, who can warrant me. . ." But *Cœur-de-Fer*, who did not appear in a mood to grant me any more or to stay his desires, railed at me while striking me in so brutal a manner, that I clearly saw obedience was my last lot. He placed himself in *la Dubois'* hands arranged by himself in the same disorder as mine, and when I was as he wished, having made me set my arms on the ground, which caused me to resemble a beast, *la Dubois* appeased his flames by positively approaching a kind of monster to the peristyles of both altars of Nature in such a manner that at every drive she should strike those parts most vigorously with her open hand, as the battering-ram of old did knock at the gates of besieged towns. The violence of the first attacks caused me to go backwards; *Cœur-de-Fer*, being in anger, threatened me with worse treatments, if I worked myself out of those; *la Dubois* has orders to redouble, while one of these libertines holds back my shoulders and keeps me from staggering under the bounces: these become so rude that they make me black and blue, and I am unable to avoid any of them. "Indeed," said *Cœur-de-Fer*, stammering out, "in her place I would rather deliver up the gates than to behold them shattered thus, but she will not have it so, we do not fail in the capitulation. . . . Vigorously. . . . vigorously, Dubois! . . ." And the bursts of passions from this lewd fellow, almost as violent as those of thunder, just spent themselves on the molested breaches without their being but a little opened.

The second fellow made me place one of my knees between his legs, and while *la Dubois* was appeasing him like the other, two proceedings entirely occupied him: one while he smote open-handed, but in a very nervous manner, either my cheeks or my breast; another while his unhallowed mouth just sullied mine. My chest and face became in an instant purple-red. . . . Being suffering, I begged for truce, and tears flowed in my eyes; they irritated him, he redoubled; in this moment my tongue was bitten, and the two strawberries of my bosom so bruised that I threw myself back, but I was held. I was pushed again upon him, I was squeezed tighter everywhere, and his extasy decided. . . .

The third made me get upon two separated chairs, and sitting underneath, excited by *la Dubois* placed between his legs, he got me to incline until his mouth was perpendicular to the temple of Nature; you do not imagine, Madam, what this obscene mortal durst desire; I had, willingly or not, to satisfy some slight needs. . . . Good Heavens! what man so depraved as to taste for an instant such things?. . . I did as he desired, I drenched him all over, and my entire submission obtained from this filthy man a fit of intoxication that nothing could have brought on without this infamy.

The fourth fastened strings to every part of me it was possible to adapt them; he held their ends in his hand, being seated seven or eight feet away from my person, and greatly excited by the fondlings and kisses of *la Dubois*; I was upright, and it was with hard chucking of each of these strings by turn, that the savage excited his pleasures; I staggered, at every moment I was losing my equilibrium: he became enthusiastic at all my stumblings; he then finally pulled all the strings together, with so much irregularity, that I fell upon the ground close to him: such was his sole aim, and my forehead, bosom and cheeks bore the proofs of a delirium which were duly to this mania.

That is what I suffered, Madam, but my honor was at least found respected, if my chastity was not. Being somewhat tranquillized, these banditti spoke of setting out, and on the same night they reached the Tremblai in the intention of getting near the woods of Chantilly, where they expected to make a few good hauls.

Nothing equalled the despair I was in at the obligation of following such persons, and I resolved only to do so being thoroughly determined to abandon them as soon as I could without risk. We slept next day on the outlets of Louvres, under haycocks; I wanted to harbour with *la Dubois*, and spend the night by her side; but it appeared to me that she intended to make use of it otherwise than in preserving my virtue from the attacks I might fear; these fellows encompassed her, and the abominable creature gave herself up to the three at the same time under our eyes. The fourth came up to me, he was the chief: "Lovely *Therese*," he said to me, "I hope you will not at least deny me the pleasure of passing the night close to you!" And as he perceived my utter repugnance: "Be not afraid," said he, "we shall gossip, and I shall undertake nothing against your good will."

"O *Therese*," continued he, while hugging me in his arms, "is it not a great piece of folly, this pretention you have of conserving yourself pure with us? Should we even agree to it, could this be settled with the interests of the gang? It is useless to conceal from you what we count only on the snares of your charms to make dupes." — "Ah me! Sir," replied I, "since it is certain that I would prefer death to those horrors, of what use can I be to you, and why are you opposed to my going away?" — "Surely we are opposed to it, my angel," answered *Cœur-de-Fer*; "you must serve either our interests or our pleasures; your misfortunes impose this yoke upon you, it is meet you should bear it; but you know, *Therese*, everything can be arranged in the world. Hearken to me then, and effect yourself your own destiny: consent to live with me, dear girl, consent and belong to me alone, and I shall spare you the sad role laid out for you." — "I, Sir," I cried, "become the mistress of one. . . !" — "Speak the word, *Therese*, speak the word, of a rascal, is it not? I grant it, but I can offer you no other titles, you are well aware that we do not wed; matrimony is a sacrament, *Therese*, and equally contemptuous of all sacraments, we never approach any of them. However reason a little; in the indispensable necessity you are of losing what is dear to you, is it not better to sacrifice it to one man alone who will become thence your prop and protector, than to prostitute yourself with all?" — "But why is it necessary," I asked, "that I have no other party to espouse?" — "Because we hold unto you, *Therese*, and because the reason of the strongest is always the best; *La Fontaine* said so long ago. Indeed," continued he rapidly, "is it not a ridiculous extravagance to set, as you do, so high a price on the most trifling things? How can a girl be so simple as to believe that virtue can depend on a little larger or a little smaller size of one of the parts of the body? Ah! what matter is it to men of God whether this part be whole or withered? Nay more: the intention of Nature being that every individual should discharge herebelow the duties for which he was formed, and the women existing only to serve the men for enjoyment, it is visibly to outrage her by resisting thus the intention she has over us. It is to wish to be a worthless creature in the world, and therefore contemptible. This chimerical wisdom, of which they had the absurdity of making you a virtue and which, from childhood, being far from serving Nature and society, visibly outrages both, is therefore nothing more than a reprehensible conceit of which a person so witty as you ought not to wish to be guilty. Never mind, continue listening to me, dear girl; I am going to prove to you the desire I have of pleasing you and of respecting your weakness. I shall not touch upon, *Therese*, this phantom the possession of which causes all your delights; a girl has more than one favor to bestow, and Venus is hallowed with her in more than one temple; I shall be contented with the meanest one. You know, my darling, near the altars of Cypris, there stands a dark cave where love goes to reside alone, in order to seduce us the more efficaciously; such shall be the altar upon which I shall burn the incense; there, not the slightest inconvenience, *Therese*; if childbearing frightens you it cannot take place in this manner, your pretty waist will never be deformed; those first flowers which are so dear to you will be conserved without blemish, and, to whatever use you may put them you can offer them undefiled. Nothing can betray a girl on this point, however rude and manifold be the attacks; as soon as the bee has pumped out the juice, the chalice of the ose closes up again; nobody would fancy it had ever blown. There are girls who enjoyed such a life ten years in this way, and even with several men, and are nevertheless married, as quite fresh after. How many fathers, brothers have thus abused their daughters or sisters, without the latter having become less worthy of sacrificing afterwards to hymen! How many confessors has not this same route served to satisfy, without the parents' knowledge! This is, in a word, the refuge of mystery: there it is linked to love by the chains of wisdom. . . . Need I say more to you, *Therese*? If this temple is the most secret, it is at the same time the most voluptuous; there we find only what is requisite for happiness, and the spacious ease of its neighbor is far from being worth the striking features of a local which is reached but by effort, where one is with difficulty lodged; women themselves win thereby, and those women who reason forces to recognize these kind of pleasures, never regret the others. Try, *Therese*, try, and we shall be both contented."

— "Oh! Sir," I answered, "I have no experience of what it is about; but that ill-conduct you cry up, I have heard it spoken of, Sir, it outrages women in a still more sensible manner. . . . It most grievously offends Nature. The hand of Heaven avenges it in this world, and Sodom presents an example thereof!" — "What innocence, my dear, what childishness!" replied the libertine; "who taught you thus? A little further attention, *Therese*, and I am going to set your ideas right.

The loss of the seed destined to propogate the human species, dear girl, is the sole crime that can exist. In this case, if the seed is put into us on the sole grounds of propogation, I grant it you, the misplacing of it is an offence. But if it is proved that in placing this seed in our loins, Nature is far from having had for object the employment of the whole thereof in propogation, what does it matter in this case, *Therese*, whether it be lost in one place or another? The man who misplaces it therefore does no more evil than Nature, which makes no use of it. Now these losses of Nature, which it depends only on us to imitate, do they not take place in a great many cases? First, the possibility of causing them is a primal proof that they do not offend her. It would be against all the laws of equilibrium and profound wisdom, which we know in everything, to permit that which would offend her. Secondly, these losses are a hundred and a hundred million times executed daily by herself; nightly pollutions, the inutility of seed during woman's childbearing, are not these losses authorized by her laws? proving to us that, but little sensible of what may result from this liquor to which we have the folly of attaching so high a price, she permits us the loss with the same indifference as she proceeds thereby every day; that she tolerates the propogation, but that the propogation is far from being in her views; that she is most "willing we should multiply, but that, gaining no more from one of these acts than from the other which is opposed to them, the choice we make is all the same to her; that, leaving us the masters to create or not to create or to destroy, we shall neither contend nor offend her any more by choosing, among either of these parties, the one which will suit us best; and that the one we shall select being only the result of her power and action over us, sad position, were we in the midst of society, . . . were it will be always well pleasing to her the more surely as it will run no risk of offending her. Whatsoever be the temple in which we sacrifice, when she permits incense to be burnt therein, it is because the homage does not offend her; the refusals of producing, the losses of the seed which serves for production, the extinction of this seed, when it has taken root, the annihilation of this germ even a long while after its formation, all these, *Therese*, are imaginary crimes which nowise interest Nature, and at which she amuses herself as at all our other institutions, which often outrage her instead of serving her."

*Cœur-de-Fer* grew warm in explaining his perfidious maxims, and I soon beheld him in the state he had so greatly frightened me on the eve; he wanted, in order to give more force to the lesson, to at once add the practice to the precept; and his hand, in spite of my resistance, strayed towards the altar into which the traitor wished to penetrate. . . . Should I confess it to you, Madam? blinded by the seductions of this nasty man, pleased, in somewhat yielding, to save what appeared the most essential; reflecting neither on the incongruity of his sophisms, nor on what I was about to risk myself since this dishonest man, possessing huge proportions, was not even in the possibility of seeing a woman in the most permitted spot, and that led on by his natural wickedness, he certainly had no other end than that of maiming me; with my eyes fascinated over all that, I say, I was going to give myself up, and through virtue to become a criminal; my resistance was calming down; being already master of the throne, this insolent vanquisher no longer busied himself except to fix himself thereon, when the jolting of a car was heard on the high-road. *Cœur-de-Fer* quits on the instant his pleasures for his duties; he assembles his men and flys to fresh crimes. Shortly afterwads we hear cries, and these bloody scoundrels return triumphantly loaded with spoils. "Let us quickly decamp," said *Cœur-de-Fer* ; "there is no longer any safety for us here." The booty is divided, *Cœur-de-Fer* wants me to have my share; it amounted to twenty *louis;* I am obliged to accept them; I quaked under the obligation of harbouring a like money: we are however hurried on, each one loads himself and we leave.

We found ourselves next day safely in the forest of Chantilly; our men were counting, during supper, how much their last operation had brought them, and not valuing at two hundred *louis* the totality of the prize:— "Indeed," said one of them, "it was not worth while committing three murders for so small a sum!" — "Not so fast, my friends," replied *la Dubois*, "it is not for the sum that I myself exhorted you to give these travellers no quarter, it is for our mere safety; these crimes are the fault of the laws and not ours: so long as robbers' lives are taken away as murderers', thefts will never be committed without assassinations. The both crimes are equally punished: why deny one's self the latter from the moment it may cover the former? To what do you attribute in other respects," continued this horrible creature, "that two hundred *louis* are not worth three murders? You should never calculate things except by the relation they have with our interests. The cessation of the existence of each of the three sacrificed beings, is nothing in respect to us. Surely we would not give an *obole* whether these individuals be alive or in the tomb; consequently, if the slightest interest accrues to us, from one of these cases, we ought without any remorse determine it by preference in our own favor; for in a thing wholly indifferent, we ought, if we are wise and masters of that thing, undoubtedly to make it turn to the side wherein it is profitable to us, abstraction made of all the adversary may lose thereby; because there is no reasonable proportion between that which concerns us, and that which concerns others. We feel the one physically, the other comes to us only morally, and moral sensations are deceitful; the only real ones are physical sensations; thus not only two hundred *louis* suffice for three murders, but even thirty *sous* would have done, for thirty *sous* would have procured us a satisfaction which, though a very slight one, ought nevertheless to affect us much more keenly than the three murders could have done, which are nothing for us, and from the wrong of which not even a scratch overtakes us. The weakness of our organs, the lack of reflection, the cursed prejudices in which we have been bred, the vain terrors of Religion or of laws, that is what stops fools in the career of crime, that is what hinders them from doing great things; but every individual full of strength and vigor, endowed with an energetically organised soul, who preferring himself, as he ought, to others, will know how to weigh their interest in the scales of his own, mock God and men, brave death and despise the laws, thoroughly convinced that it is to himself alone he ought to refer everything, will feel that the greatest multitude of wrongs on others, of which he ought to be nowise physically sensible, can not be laid down as a compensation for the slightest of enjoyments, purchased by this uncommon union of forfeits. Enjoyment flatters him; it is part of him; now, I ask what reasonable man will not prefer that which affords him delight to that which is strange to him, and who will not consent to commit this strange thing from which he will experience nothing troublesome, in order to procure himself the one by which he is agreeably affected?"

— "Oh! Madam," said I to *la Dubois*, in asking her leave to reply to her execrable sophisms, "do you not then feel your condemnation written in that which has just fallen from your lips? Such principles could at most become the being powerful enough to have nothing to fear from others; but we, Madam, perpetually in dread and humiliation; we, banished from all honest men, condemned by every law, ought we to admit systems which can only sharpen the sword hung over our heads? Might we not even find ourselves in this we where we ought to be, without our misconduct or misfortunes, do you imagine such maxims could become us better? How will you have it that he who, through a blind selfishness, wishes to struggle along against the combined interest of others, should not perish? Is not society authorized never to suffer within its bosom him who declares himself against it? And can the individual who isolates himself struggle against all? Can he flatter himself with being happy and tranquil, if, not accepting the social pact, he agrees not to yield a trifle of his happiness in order to secure the rest thereof? Society is merely sustained by the perpetual exchanges of benefits, these are the ties which keep it together; such a one who, instead of these benefits, will offer but crimes, much needs be dreaded henceforth, and will necessarily be attacked if he is the strongest, sacrificed by the former whom he will offend, if he is the weakest; but destroyed in every manner of the powerful reason which obliges man to secure his rest and hurt those that wish to trouble him; such is the cause that renders the duration of criminal associations impossible; opposing only sharp daggers to the interest of others, all ought to promptly unite in order to blunt the edges thereof. Even amongst ourselves, Madam, need I add, how can you flatter yourself with maintaining concord, when you counsel everyone to listen only to his sole interest? Shall you have from this moment anything meet to reproach any of us who is willing to stab the others, who may do so, in order to annex to himself alone his fellow's portion? Ah! what finer eulogy of Virtue than the proof of our necessity, even in a criminal society, . . . than the certainty that this society could not be kept together a moment without Virtue!"

— "What you reproach us with, *Therese*, are sophisms," said *Cœur-de-Fer*, "and not what *la Dubois* had asserted. It is not Virtue that keeps our criminal associations together; it is interest, selfishness; that eulogy of Virtue which you have drawn from a chimerical hypothesis drops therefore into the water; it is nowise through virtue that believing myself, I suppose, the strongest in the gang, I do not stab my comrades to have their share, it is because, finding myself then alone, I should deprive myself of the means which may secure the fortune I expect from their assistance; this motive is the only one which likewise keeps back their arms from me. Now, this motive, you see, *Therese*, is but a selfish one, it has not the slightest appearance of Virtue. He who wishes to struggle alone against the interest of society ought, you say, expect to perish: will he not perish far more certainly, if he has for existing therein only his wretchedness and the renouncement of others? What they style the interest of society is merely the mass of private interests united together, but it is never except in yielding that this private interest can agree and be attached to general interests; now, what will you have him yield who has nothing? If he does so, you will confess to me that he is so much the more mistaken, as he finds himself bestowing then infinitely more than he receives, and in this case the inequality of the bargain ought to prevent him from making it; caught in this trap, the best thing such a man has to do, is not to retire from this unjust society in order to grant rights only to a different society, which, placed in the same position as himself, has for interest to combat, through the re-union of its slender powers, the more extensive sway which wanted to force the unfortunate wretch to give up the little he had in order to get nothing from the others? But there will spring from this, you will say, a state of perpetual war. Be it so! is it not that of Nature? Is it not the only one which really suits us? Men were all born isolated, envious, cruel and despotic; wishing to have everything and give up nothing, and incessantly fighting to maintain either their ambition or rights, the legislator came and said: Cease from fighting thus; in yielding a little on both sides, tranquillity is about to spring up again. I do not blame the proposition of this pact, but I hold that two classes of individuals ought never to submit to it: those who, feeling themselves the strongest, and no need of parting with anything in order to be happy, and those who, being the weakest, found themselves parting with infinitely more than was secured for them. Yet, society is merely composed of weak and strong beings; now, if the pact was to displease the strong and the weak, it was very far therefore from becoming society, and the state of war which existed before, ought to be found infinitely preferable, since it left every one of the free to exercise of his forces and industry of which he found himself deprived by the unjust pact of society, always taking too much from the one and never granting enough to the other; hence the truly wise being is he who, at the risk of beginning again the state of war which reigned previous to the pact, sets himself irrevocably up against this pact, violates it as much as he can, certain that what he will profit by these damages will be always superior to what he may lose, if he finds himself the weakest; for he was so all the same in respecting the pact, he may become the strongest in violating it; and if the laws bring him back to the class which he wanted to leave, the worst that can happen him is to lose his life, which is an infinitely less greater misfortune than that of existing in opprobrium and misery. These are therefore two positions for us: either crime which renders us happy, or the scaffold which hinders us from being unhappy. I ask, is there anything to hesitate at, lovely *Therese*, and will your mind find a reasoning which can combat that one?"

— "Oh! Sir," I answered with that vehemence which the good cause gives, "there are a thousand; but ought this life be in other respects, therefore, the sole object of man? Is he in it otherwise than on a way, as it were, every step of which he traverses ought, if he is reasonable, but to lead him towards that eternal happiness, the assured reward of Virtue? I suppose with you (which is however rare, which is however against the lights of reason, but never mind), I grant you for an instant that crime may render the wretch who gives himself up to it happy here below: do you fancy the justice of God awaits not this dishonest man in another world to take vengeance for this one! . . . Ah! believe not the contrary, Sir, believe it not," I added with tears, "this is the only consolation of the unfortunate one, take it not away from us; when men abandon us, who will avenge us if it be not God?"

— "Who? nobody, *Therese*, absolutely nobody; it is in nowise necessary that misfortune should be avenged; it flatters itself because it would have it so, this idea consoles it, but it is nevertheless false: nay more, it is essential that misfortune should suffer; its humiliation, its pains are among the number of Nature's laws, and its existence is useful to the general plan, as that of prosperity which crushes it; such is the truth that ought to stifle remorse in the soul of the tyrant or malefactor; let him not hold back; let him blindly deliver himself up to all the wrongs the idea of which arises within him; it is the voice alone of Nature that suggests this idea to him; it is the only way in which she makes us the agents of her laws. When her secret inspirations dispose us for evil, it is because the evil is necessary for her, it is because she wishes it, because she requires it, because the amount of crimes being incomplete, insufficient for the laws of equilibrium, the only laws by which she is ruled, she requires the former moreover for the completion of the balance; let him not therefore be frightened, or stopped, he whose soul is carried on to evil; let him commit it without fear, as soon as he has felt its compulsion: it is only by resisting it that he would outrage Nature. But let us lay aside the moral for an instant, since you will have theology. Learn then, young innocent girl, that religion on which you throw yourself, being but the relation of man with God, the worship which the creature thought it ought to render his creator, is annihilated as soon as the existence of this creator is itself shown to be chimerical.

The first men, frightened by phenomena which struck them, must necessarily have thought that a sublime being and unknown to them had directed their march and influence. It is natural to weakness to suppose or dread force; the mind of man, still too much in childhood to search, to find in the bosom of Nature the laws of movement, the only spring of the whole mechanism at which he was astonished, thought it simpler to suppose a mover for this Nature than to consider herself as mover, and, without reflecting how he would have still more difficulty to invent, to define this gigantic master, than to find in the study of Nature the cause of that which surprised him, he admitted this sovereign being, he set up worships to him. From this moment, every Nation composed some analogous to its morals, knowledge and climate; there were soon over the earth as many religions as nations, as many gods as families; under all these idols it was easy nevertheless to recognise this absurd phantom, the first fruit of human blindness. They dressed it up differently, but it was always the same thing. Now, say, *Therese*, must it follow from this, because idiots talk nonsense about the erection of an unworthy chimera and the manner of serving it, that the wise man ought to renounce the certain and present happiness of his life? ought he, like that dog of an Æsop, leave the bone for the shadow, and give over real enjoyments for illusions? No, *Therese*, no, there is no God; Nature suffices for herself; she has no earthly need of an author, this supposed author is only a decomposition of her own forces, is only what we call in the schools *petitio principii*. A God supposes a creation, viz., an instant when there was nothing, or an instant when all was chaos. If either of these states was bad, why did your God allow it to exist? Was it a good one, why then change? But if everything is all-right now, your God has nothing more to do: now, if he is useless, can he be powerful, can he be God? If Nature moves herself, of what use is the mover? And if the mover acts upon the matter in moving it, how is it he is not matter himself? Can you conceive the effect of the mind on matter, and the matter receiving the movement of the mind which has itself no movement? Examine cooly for an instant all the ridiculous and contradictory qualities, with which the fabricators of the execrable chimera are obliged to invest it; observe how they destroy one another, how they mutually absorb one another, and you will acknowledge that this deistic phantom, sprung from the dread of some and the ignorance of all, is merely a revolting nonsense which deserves of us neither an instant's belief nor a minute's examination; a woeful extravagance which is repugnant to the mind, revolts the heart, and which must have issued from the darkness only to return into it again for ever.

Let not the hope or fear of a future world, the fruit of those first lies, therefore trouble you, *Therese*; cease especially from trying to make us halters out of it. We the feeble particles of a vile and raw matter, shall, at our death, viz., at the re-union of the elements which compose us to the elements of the general mass, pass, annihilated forever, whatever may have been our conduct, an instant in the crucible of Nature, to issue forth under other forms, and that without there being further prerogatives for him who foolishly extolled virtue, as for him who abandoned himself to the most shameful excesses, because Nature is offended by nothing, and because all men have sprung alike out of her bosom, having acted during their lives only according to her impulses, will all find therein, after their existence, both the same end and same destiny."

I was going to answer these awful blasphemies, when the sound of a man on horseback reached us. "To arms!" cried *Cœur-de-Fer*, eager to put his systems into action to consolidate their basis. They are off . . . and in an instant they convey an unfortunate traveller into the under-wood where we pitched our camp.

Questioned on the motive which caused him to travel alone and so early, along a by-way, on his age and profession, the horseman replied that his name was *Saint-Florent*, one of the first business men of Lyons; that he was thirty-six years old, that he was returning from Flanders about business connected with his trade, that he had but little money about him though many papers. He added that his footman had left him on the eve, and that, in order to avoid the heat, he travelled by night with the intention of reaching Paris on the same day, where he would hire a new servant, and conclude a part of his business; that, moreover, if he was following a solitary path, he must have apparently gone astray while falling asleep on his horse. And having said this, he sued for his life, offering himself all he possessed. They examined his pocket-book, counted his money, the prize could not be a better one. *Saint-Florent* had nearly half a million payable at sight on the Capital, a few jewels and about one hundred *louis*. . . . "Friend," said *Cœur-de-Fer* to him, holding the barrel of a pistol under his nose, "you understand that after such a robbery we can not leave you your life." — "Oh, Sir," I cried in throwing myself at this wretch's feet, "I do conjure you, do not offer me, on my reception into your gang, the horrible spectacle of this unfortunate man's death; spare his life, do not refuse me the first favor I ask of you." And, having at once thought of a pretty strange stratagem, in order to legitimate the interest I appeared to take in this man: "The name which the Gentleman has just given," I warmly added, "causes me to believe that I am closely related to him. Do not be astonished, Sir," I continued in addressing myself to the traveller, "be not surprised at finding a relative in this situation; I shall explain to you all this. Under those rights," I began by again imploring our Chief, "under those rights, Sir, grant me this wretched man's life; I shall acknowledge this favor by the most complete devotedness to all that can serve your interests." — "You know on what conditions I can grant you the favor you ask of me, *Therese*," *Cœur-de-Fer* answered me; "you know what I request of you. . . ." — "Ah! good Sir, I shall do everything," I cried in casting myself between this unhappy man and our Chief ever-ready to slay him. . . . "Yes, I shall do everything, Sir, I shall do everything, save him." — "Let him live," said *Cœur-de-Fer*, "but let him become one of our number; this last clause is indispensable, I can do nothing without it, my comrades would be opposed to it."

The merchant, being surprised at hearing nothing about this relationship which I established, but seeing his life saved, if he ceded to the proposals, did not think he should waver a moment. They made him refresh himself, and as our men did not wish to depart from that place except in the day-time: "*Therese*," said *Cœur-de-Fer* to

me, "I claim your promise; but as I am over-jaded this e·
repose quietly near *la Dubois*; I shall call you about day-bre..
that scoundrel's life, should you waver, will avenge me for your
roguery." — "Sleep, Sir, sleep," answered I, "and know that she
whom you have loaded with gratitude, has no other desire than of
discharging it." That was however very far from being my scheme,
but if ever I believed dissimulation permitted, it was indeed on this
occasion. Our knaves, filled with too great a confidence, drink
more and fall asleep, leaving me perfectly free, near *la Dubois*, who,
drunk like the rest, also closed her eyes.

Then sprightly taking advantage of the first moment's sleep of
the profligates who are about us: — "Sir," said I to the young *Lyonnese*, "the most dreadful catastrophy has thrown me among these
robbers; I detest both of them and the fatal instant which led me
into their band; likely I have not the honor of being related to you,
I have made use of this stratagem to save you and escape myself,
with you, should you think well, out of the hands of these wretches.
The moment is a propitious one," I added, "let us flee away; I perceive your pocket-book, let us take it back; let us bid adieu to the
cash, it is in their pockets; we should not take it out of them without
danger. Let us depart, Sir, let us depart; you see what I am doing
for you, I place myself in your hands; pity my lot; be not especially
crueler than those fellows; deign to respect my honor, I do entrust
it to you, it is my sole treasure, leave it with me, they have not ravished me of it."

One would but badly express the pretended gratitude of *Saint-
Florent*. He knew not what terms to employ in order to paint it for
me; but we had no time for talking; the question was to fly. I cleverly
steal the pocket-book, hand it over to him, and speedily clearing
the under-wood, leaving the horse behind for fear the noise he
would have made should waken our heroes, we make towards, in
the greatest haste, the path which was to lead us out of the forest.
We were fortunate enough to be out of it by day-break, and without
having been pursued by anybody; before ten o'clock in the morning
we entered Luzarches, where, free from all fear, we thought no
longer except of resting ourselves.

There are moments in life when we find ourselves very rich without having however the means of living: such was the case of *Saint-Florent*. He had five hundred thousand francs in his pocket, and not a single crown-piece in his purse; this reflection stopped him before going into the inn. — "Be not uneasy, Sir," said I to him on seeing his embarrassment, "the robbers who I am quitting did not leave me without money; there are twenty *louis,* take them, I do entreat you, make use of them, give the remainder to the poor; I should not for anything in the world keep gold obtained by murders."

*Saint-Florent,* who was showing his delicateness, but who was very far from the one I was to suppose, did not wish to absolutely take what I was offering him; he enquired what were my intentions, told me he would make himself a law to fulfil them, and that he only desired he would be able to acquit himself towards me: — "It is from you I hold my fortune and life, *Therese,*" he added, in kissing my hands, "can I do better than in offering you both? Accept them, I do conjure you, and allow the God of hymen to bind tighter the knots of friendship."

I know not, but whether foresight or indifference, I was so far from thinking that what I had done for this young man could attract such feelings on his part, that I let him read in my countenance the refusal which I dared not express; he understood it, insisted no further, and confined himself to ask me only what he could do for me. — "Sir," said I to him, "if really my proceeding is not without value in your eyes, I ask you for sole reward but to lead me with you to Lyons, and place me there in some respectable house, where my chastity may have no more to suffer." — "You could not do better," said *Saint-Florent,* "nobody is in a nicer position than I am to render you this service: I have twenty relations in this town;" and the young Merchant then begged me to relate to him the reasons which determined me to go away from Paris, where I had told him I was born. — "Oh! if it is only that," said the young man, "I can be useful to you before being at Lyons; fear nothing, *Therese,* your trial is at an end; they will not look for you again, and certainly less in the retreat I wish to place than elsewhere. I have a lady relation near Bondy; she lives in a charming country-seat about here; she will consider it a pleasure, I am sure, to have you close to her. I shall introduce you to her tomorrow." I, filled with gratitude in my turn, accept the proposal which suits me so nicely. We repose ourselves during the remainder of the day at Luzarches, and proposed to reach on the following day Bondy, which is but six leagues from there. "It is fine weather," said *Saint-Florent*; "if you take my advice, *Therese*, we shall go on foot to my relation's Castle; we shall there relate our adventure, and this mode of travelling will, it seems, attach still greater interest to us." Being very far from suspecting that there was to be less safety for me with him than in the infamous company I was leaving, I accept everything without fear or repugnance. We take dinner and supper together; he is not at all opposed to my having a separate room from his for the night; and having let the great heat pass by, being sure of what he told me, viz., that four or five hours suffice for us to go to his relation's place, we set out from Luzarches and make our way on foot towards Bondy.

It was about five o'clock in the evening when we entered the forest. *Saint-Florent* had not as yet belied himself for an instant: still the same honesty, still the same desire of showing his good feelings towards me. I should not have thought myself safer, had I been with my father. The shades of night began to spread over the forest that sort of religious awe, which at the same time causes fear to spring up in timorous souls, and the project of crime in ferocious hearts. We were following only by-ways; I was walking ahead, I turn round to inquire of *Saint-Florent* whether those by-ways are really those we should take, if he is not by chance going astray, if he thought, in fine, we should soon arrive. — "We are there, harlot," replied this rascal, in knocking me down with a blow of a stick on my head, which leaves me senseless. . . .

Oh! Madam, I no longer know what this man said or did; but the state I found myself in only too well allowed me to recognise how much I had been his victim. It was completely night when I came to my senses; I was at the foot of a tree out of every route, benumbed, all besmeared with blood . . . dishonored, Madam. Such had been the reward of all I had just done for this wretched man;

and carrying his infamy to the highest pitch, the rascal, after having done with me everything he desired, after having abused me in all taken away my purse, . . . that same money I had so manners, even in that which outrages Nature most, had generously offered him. He had torn my clothes, the greater part of which lay in rags around me; I was almost naked, and bruised in several parts of the body. You may judge of my situation: in the midst of darkness, without resource, without honor, without hope, exposed to every danger, I wished to end my days. Had a weapon been offered me, I would have seized it, and with it I would have shortened this unhappy life which afforded me only plagues. . . . The monster! what have I then done against him, said I to myself, to have thus deserved from him so cruel a treatment? I save his life for him, I hand him over his fortune, he snatches from me what I hold most dear! A ferocious beast would have been less cruel! O man, there thou art then when thou listenest only to thy passions! Tigers in the depths of the most savage deserts would hold thy forfeits in horror. . . . A few moments of discouragement succeeded these first vents of my sorrow; my eyes filled with tears turn mechanically towards heaven; my heart rushes to the feet of the Master who inhabits it. . . . This pure and brilliant vault . . . this imposing stillness of night . . . this fright which froze my senses . . . this image of Nature in peace, beside this disorder of my lost soul, all spread a dark horror over me, whence soon springs the need of prayer. I cast myself at the knees of this Almighty God, denied by the impious, the hope of the poor and afflicted. "Holy and majestic Being," I cried in tears, "thou who deignest in this awful moment to fill my soul with a heavenly joy, who has undoubtedly prevented me from making an attempt on my days; O my protector and guide, I aspire to thy goodness, I implore thy clemency: do behold my wretchedness and my sorrows, my resignation and my vows. Almighty God! thou knowest I am innocent and weak; I am betrayed and ill-used; I have wished to do good after thy example, and thy will punishes me for it. Let it be accomplished, O my God! all those sacred effects are dear to me; I respect them and cease to complain of them. But if I am, however, to find herebelow only thorns, is it to offend thee, O my Sovereign Master, to beseech thy power to call me to thee, that I may bless thee without fear, adore thee far from those perverse men who have caused me, alas! to meet only with evils, and whose bloody and perfidious hands drown at their pleasure my sad days in torrents of tears and the abyss of sorrows?"

Prayer is the sweetest consolation of the unhappy one. It becomes the more efficacious when he has discharged his duties. I rise full of courage, I gather up the rags which the rascal left me, and I penetrate into the brush-wood to spend the night therein with less risk. The safety in which I fancied myself, the satisfaction I had just tasted in drawing nigh God, all, all contributed to make me repose a few hours; the sun was already high when my eyes opened again. The moment of awakening is terrible for the unfortunate; the imagination, refreshed by the sweetness of slumbers, is much more quickly and dolefully filled with the evils, the remembrance of which those instants of deceitful repose have caused it to forget.

Well, said I to myself then on examining myself, it is therefore true that there are human creatures, whom Nature abases down to the same lot as that of ferocious beasts! Hid in this cover, fleeing from men after their example, what difference is there now between them and me? Is it then worth while to be born for so woeful a destiny?. . . And my tears flowed abundantly on making these sad reflections; I scarcely finished them, when I heard a noise about me; gradually I distinguish two men. I give heed: — "Come, dear friend," says one of them, "we shall be admirably well off here; the cruel and fatal presence of an aunt whom I detest will not prevent me from tasting for a moment with you, the pleasures which are so sweet to me." They draw nigh, they plant themselves in such a way before me, that none of their propositions, none of their movements, can escape me, and I see . . . Good Heavens! Madam, said *Therese* in interrupting herself, is it possible that destiny never placed me except in such critical situations, that it becomes as difficult for virtue to hear their recitals, as for chastity to paint them! This horrible crime which equally outrages both Nature and the social conventions, this forfeit, in fine, upon which the hand of God was so often laid heavy, rendered lawful by *Cœur-de-Fer*, proposed by him to the unfortunate *Therese*, involuntarily consummated on her by the butcher who has just immolated her; finally this shocking execration, I saw it accomplished under my eyes with all the impure researches, all the frightful episodes, that the most reflected depravity can place in it. One of these men, he who lent himself, was about twenty-four years old, well enough dressed to give an idea of the elevation of his rank; the other, of about the same age, looked like one of his servants. The act was scandalous and a long one. Leaning on his hands at the top of a small hill in front of the under-wood where I was, the young master laid bare for his companion of debauchery the impure altar of sacrifice, and the latter, fired at this spectacle, caressed the idol thereof, quite ready to immolate it with a far more frightful and huge dagger than that by which I was threatened by the chief of the brigands of Bondy; but the young master, in nowise fearful, seems to brave with impunity the bait which is offered to him; he teases it, he excites it, he covers it with kisses; is seized by it, is penetrated with it himself, delights in swal-lowing it up; enthusiastic with his criminal caresses, the infamous wretch wreathes under the iron and seems to regret it is not still more frightful; he braves the blows, he meets them, he wards them off. . . . Two tender and lawful spouses would caress each other with less ardour. . . . Their mouths press together, their sighs are con-founded, their tongues entwine, and I see them both, drunk with lust, finding in the midst of their delights the completion of their perfidious horrors. The homage is renewed, and to kindle the incense thereof, nothing is spared by him who requires it; kisses, handlings, pollutions, subtilities of the most notorious debauchery, all are employed to restore the strength which is extinguished, and all succeed in re-animating it five consecutive times; but without either of them changing his role. The young master was always the woman, and although the possibility of being a man in his turn might be discovered in him, yet he had not even the appearance of conceiving for an instant the desire of it. If he visited the altar sim-ilar to the one on which one used to sacrifice with him, it was to the other idol's profit, and no attack ever seemed to threaten that one.

Oh! how this time appeared long to me! I dared not stir, for fear of being perceived. At last the criminal actors of this indecent scene, satiated no doubt, rose to continue the way which was to lead them home, when the master approaches the bush which conceals me; my bonnet betrays me. . . . He perceives it. . . . — "Jasmin," said he to his footman, "we are discovered. . . . A girl has witnessed our mysteries. . . . Draw up, let us make this whore come from there, and know why she is there."

I did not give them the trouble of dragging me out of my refuge; immediately tearing myself out of it, and falling at their feet. . . . "Oh, Gentlemen!" I cried, on holding out my arms to them, "deign to take compassion on an unfortunate girl whose lot is more to be pitied than you think; but few reverses can equal mine, let not the situation in which you find me give rise to any suspicion about me: it is the consequence of my misery, much rather than of my wrongs. Far from increasing the evils which overwhelm me, be pleased to lessen them by facilitating for me the means of escaping the plagues which pursue me."

The Count of *Bressac* (this was the young man's name), into whose hands I fell, with a great deal of wickedness and libertinism in his mind, was not provided with a very abundant supply of pity in his heart. It is unfortunately only too common to see libertinism extinguishing pity in men; its ordinary effect is to harden the heart: whether the greater part of his errings necessitates the apathy of the soul, or the violent outburst which this passion imprints on the mass of nerves, diminishes the force of their action, it always holds good that a libertine is seldom a sensible man. But to this natural hardness of heart in the kind of men whose character I am sketching, was still joined in *Mr. de Bressac* so inveterate a disgust for our sex, so implacable a hatred for all that characterized it, that it was very difficult for me to succeed in stiring in his soul the sentiments with which I wished to touch it.

— "Wooden turtle-dove," said the count to me with severity, "if thou art looking for dupes, hit the mark better; neither my friend nor I ever sacrifice to the impure temple of thy sex; if it be alms thou askest, seek the persons that are fond of good works, we never do anything of this kind. . . . But speak, wretch, hast thou seen what has passed between this Gentleman and me? — I saw you talking on the grass," replied I, "nothing further, Sir, I assure you." — "I will believe so," said the young Count, "and that for thy own sake; if I thought thou couldst have seen anything else, thou wouldst never leave this thicket. . . . Jasmin, it is early, we have time to hear this girl's adventures; and we shall see afterwards what can be done for her."

These young men sit down; they bid me place myself near them, and then I ingeniously relate to them all the misfortunes which overwhelm me since I came into the world. — "Come, Jasmin," said *Mister de Bressac*, on rising up, when I had ended, "let us be just once. The upright Themis has condemned this creature; let us not suffer the views of the Goddess to be so cruelly frustrated; let us make the delinquent undergo the sentence of death which she would have encured. This petty murder, very far from being a crime, will become a reparation in the moral order; since we have the misfortune of sometimes putting it out of place, let us establish it courageously at least when the occasion presents itself. . . ." And the hardhearted fellows, having removed me from my place, are already dragging me to the wood, laughing at my tears and cries. "Let us bind her up by the four limbs, to four trees forming a long square," said *Bressac*, on stripping me naked. Then by means of their neckties, handkerchiefs and garters they make cords with which I am instantly bound, as they purpose, namely, in the cruelest and most painful attitude that is possible to be imagined. One can not describe what I suffered: it seems as if they tore asunder my limbs, and that my stomach, which miscarried, inclined by its weight towards the ground, had to gape at every instant. The sweat streamed down from my brow. I existed no further than by the violence of the pain; had this ceased to press my nerves together, the pangs of death would have set upon me. The wicked wretches were amused at this posture; they viewed me in it while hugging each other. "That is enough of it," said *Bressac* at last "I am willing that this time she gets off for her fear. *Therese*," continued he while loosing my bonds and ordering me to dress, "be discreet, and follow us: if you become attached to me, you shall have no reason to repent of it. My aunt wants a second women, I am going to present you to her, on the faith of your recitals: I am going to take the responsibility of your conduct; but if you abuse my goodness, if you betray my confidence, or if you do not submit to my intentions, look at those four trees, *Therese*; look at the ground they encompass, and which is to be your grave. Remember that this fatal spot is only a league from the castle to which I am taking you, and for the slightest fault you will be instantly conveyed hither."

On the instant I forget my misfortunes. I cast myself at the Count's knees. I swear to him in tears, an oath for my good conduct; but, as insensible of my joy as of my sorrow: — "Let us go," said *Bressac*, "it is this conduct that will speak in your behalf, it alone will regulate your destiny."

We advance. Jasmin and his master were talking together in a whispering voice. I humbly followed them without saying a word. In a short hour we arrive at the *Marchioness de Bressac*'s castle, the magnificence of which and the host of servants it contains, cause me to see that, whatever post I am to fill in the house, it will surely be more advantageous to me than that of being *Mr. du Harpin*'s head governess. They make me wait in an office where Jasmin kindly offers me all that can serve to comfort me. The young Count goes into his aunt; he gives her notice, and comes himself for me half an hour afterwards to present me to the Marchioness.

*Madam de Bressac* was a woman of forty-sx years old, being still very handsome; she appeared to me to be honest and sensible, although she mixed a little severity in her principles and discourses. Since two years she was left a widow by the young Count's uncle, who had married her without any other fortune than the fine name which he bestowed upon her. All the wealth that *Mr. de Bressac* could hope for depended on this aunt; what he had got from his father hardly afforded him enough for his pleasures; *Madam de Bressac* added thereto a considerable pension, but that did not suffice. Nothing dear like the Count's voluptuousnesses; perhaps these are paid less than the others, but multiply much more. There was a revenue of fifty thousand crowns in the house, and *Mister de Bressac* was alone. He could never be prevailed upon to enter the service; everything that removed him from his libertinism was so intolerable to him, that he could not adopt its bondage. The Marchioness inhabited this land three months in the year. She spent the remainder of her time in Paris. And these three months which she required of her nephew to pass with her, were a kind of punishment for a man detesting his aunt and considering as lost every moment he spent away from the city where his centre of pleasures lay.

The young Count ordered me to relate to the Marchioness the things of which I had informed him, and when I had done: — "do not permit me to doubt about your being truthful. I shall seek no further information about you, if it be not to find out whether you really are the man's daughter you mention to me. If this is so, I knew your father, and this is a further reason why I should be interested in you. As to the affair at the *du Harpin*'s, I undertake to settle it in two visits to my old friend, the Chancellor. He is the most upright man in the world; the mere question is to prove to him your innocence in order to undo all that has been done against you. But consider well, *Therese*, that what I promise you is only at the price of a spotless conduct; so you see that the effects of the knowledge which I require will always turn to your profit." I cast myself at the Marchioness' feet, assured her that she would be pleased with me: she kindly lifted me up and directly put me in possession of the second chambermaid's place in her own service.

At the end of three days, the inquiries that *Madam de Bressac* had made in Paris arrived; they were such as I could have desired. The Marchioness praised me for not having imposed upon her, and all the ideas of misfortune vanished at last from my mind, to be no longer replaced except by the hope of the sweetest consolations that it would be allowed me to expect. But it was not arrangd in Heaven that poor *Therese* should be happy; and if a few moments of calm haply dawned for her, it was but to render those of horror which were about to ensue still more bitter for her.

We were scarcely in Paris, when *Madam de Bressac* hastened to work in my behalf. The first President wished to see me; he listened with interest to the recitals of my misfortunes; the calumnies of the *du Harpin*s were known, but people vainly sought to punish him for them: *du Harpin*, having succeeded in a transaction of false notes by which he ruined three or four families, and by which he gained nearly two millions, had just escaped to England. Concerning the burning of the Palace prisons, people were convinced that, if I had profited by this event, I had at least no hand in it; and my process fell to the ground, I was assured, without the magistrates, who were employed in it, thinking they should use other formalities about it. I knew no more about it; I contented myself with what I was told: you shall shortly see whether I was wrong.

It is easy to imagine how much such proceedings attached me to *Madam de Bressac*; had she not had, moreover, all sorts of goodnesses towards me, how would not such steps have bound me forever to so powerful a protectress? The young Count's intention was however very far from seeing me so closely linked to his aunt. . . . But now is the time to paint this monster for you.

*Mr. de Bressac* united to the charms of youth the most bewitching face; if his waist or features had any defects, it was because they somewhat approached that negligence, that slothfulness which belong to women; it seemed that, in lending him the attributes of this sex, Nature had likewise inspired him with their tastes. . . . Yet what a soul was hid under those womanish charms! You meet there with all the vices which characterise that of rascals; nobody ever surpassed him in wickedness, vengeance, cruelty, atheism, debauchery, contempt of every duty and especially of those which Nature seems to form our delights. In the midst of all these errings, *Mr. de Bressac* had especially that of hating his aunt. The Marchioness did everything in the world to bring her nephew back to the paths of Virtue; perhaps she did so with too much rigour; the result of it was that the Count, inflamed the more by the very effects of this severity, gave himself up with still greater impetuosity to his tastes, and the poor Marchioness had by her persecutions only to get herself hated the more.

"Do not imagine," the Count often said to me, "that my aunt acts of herself in all that concerns you, *Therese*; know that, if I did not persecute her at every instant, she would hardly recall the cares she promised you. She lays great stress upon what she does for you, whereas it is but my work. Yes, *Therese*, yes, it is to me alone that you owe gratitude, and what I require of you, ought to appear to you so much the more disinterested as, however pretty you may be, you are well aware that I do not aspire to your favors. No, *Therese*; the services I expect from you are of quite another kind, and when you are thoroughly convinced of what I have done in your behalf, I hope I may find in your soul what I have a right to expect."

This discourse appeared to me so obscure that I knew not how to reply to it; I did so however at random, and perhaps with too much facility. Must I confess it to you? Alas, yes; to disguise you from my wrongs would be to betray your confidence and badly to answer the interest with which my misfortunes have inspired you. Hear, then, Madame, the only voluntarily fault I have to reproach myself with. . . . What do I say, a fault? a folly, an extravagance . . . which never had anything like it, but it is at least no crime, it is a mere mistake, which punished only myself, and of which it does not appear that the just hand of heaven should have made use to plunge me into the abyss which yawns under my steps. Whatever had been the unworthy proceedings of the *Count de Bressac* in my regard on the first day I had become acquainted with him, it had been however impossible for me to look on him without feeling myself attracted towards him by a fit of tenderness that nothing had been able to overcome. Notwithstanding all my reflections on his cruelty, his aversion for women, the depravity of his tastes, the moral distances which separated us, nothing in the world could extinguish that rising passion; and if the Count had requested my life from me, I would have sacrificed it for him a thousand times. He was far from conjecturing my feelings. . . . He was far, the ungrateful fellow, from discovering the cause of the tears I used to shed daily; but still it was impossible for him not to have an inkling of the desire I had of anticipating everything that could please him, it could not be that he had not a glimpse of my readiness to serve him. This readiness, too blind no doubt, was carried to such a degree of serving his errors, as decency could permit of me, and of always disguising it from his aunt. This conduct had in some way gained over to me his confidence, and everything that came from him was so precious in my eyes, I grew so blind about the trifle his heart offered to me, that I sometimes had the weakness to believe I was not indifferent to him. But how the excess of his disorders speedily undeceived me! these were such that even his health was impaired by them. I sometimes took the liberty of picturing to him the inconveniences of his conduct; he used to listen to me without reluctance, then end by telling me how nobody ever corrected himself of the kind of vice which he cherished.

'Ah! *Therese*," cried he one day enthusiastically, "if thou knewest the charms of this fantasy, if thou couldst understand what one experiences in the sweet illusion of being no longer but a woman! Incredible erring of the mind! We abhor this sex and we wish to imitate it! Ah! how sweet it is to succeed therein, *Therese*! how delightful it is to be the wanton of all those who desire you, and bringing to bear on this point, to the highest pitch, delirium and prostitution; to be successively on the same day the mistress of a Porter, a Marquis, a Valet, a Monk; to be by turns loved, caressed, grown jealous of, threatened, browbeaten, now between their victorious arms, and now a victim at their feet, soothing them by caresses, re-inflaming them by fits! . . . Oh! no, no, *Therese*, thou dost not comprehend what this pleasure is for a head organised like mine. . . . But, laying aside the moral, if thou didst represent thyself what the physical sensations of this divine taste are! it is impossible to resist them; it is a tickling so keen, titillations of a voluptuousness so quick . . . one loses his wits . . . one talks nonsense; a thousand kisses the one tenderer than the other exalt not yet with enough of ardor the intoxication into which the agent plunges us: rolled up in his arms, both our mouths stuck together, we would that our whole existence might become incorporated with his; we should like to form with him but one sole being; if we dare complain, it is of being neglected. We should like that, more robust than Hercules, he would split us open, penetrate into us; that this precious seed, cast burning into the depths of our bowels, might, through its heat and force, spirt ours up into his hands. . . . Do not imagine, *Therese,* that we are made like other men; it is quite a different construction, and that ticklish membrane which decks in you the temple of Venus, Heaven in creating us adorned with it the altars whereon our Celadons[5] do sacrifice: we are as truly women there as you are in the sanctuary of generation. There is not a single one of your pleasures that is not known to us; not a single one but we know how to enjoy, but we have, besides, our own, and this delightful blending which turns us into the most sensible men of voluptuousness on the earth, the best created for feeling it. This enchanting blending makes the correction of our tastes impossible; it would turn us into enthusiasts and madmen, if anybody had still the stupidity of punishing us, . . . it causes us to adore at last, up to the coffin, the charming of God that captivates us!"

Thus the Count expressed himself, in extolling his oddities. Did I try to speak to him about the being to whom he owed everything, and of the sorrows which like disorders were causing this respectable aunt, I perceived no more in him than vexation and bad humour, and especially impatience to see so long in such hand riches, which, he used to say, ought to be already his. I saw no more in him than the most inveterate hatred against this so honest a woman, the openest revolt against the feeling of Nature. Would it be therefore true that, where one has succeeded in so formally transgressing in the tastes the sacred instinct of this law, the necessary consequence of this first crime would be a fearful inclination to commit all the others afterwards?

Sometimes I made use of the means of Religion; being nearly always consoled through it, I tried to make its sweetness pass into the pervert's soul, almost sure of keeping him within bounds by these ties if I succeeded in getting him to partake of its charms. But the Count did not allow me to apply these arms long. A declared enemy of our most holy mysteries, a stubborn stickler against the purity of our dogmas, an enraged antagonist of the existence of a Supreme Being, *Mr. de Bressac,* instead of letting himself be converted by me, sought much rather to corrupt me.

"All Religions spring from a false principle, *Therese*," he used to say to me; "they also suppose the worship of a Being creator as necessary; but this creator never existed. Recollect on this heading the sound precepts of that *Cœur-de-Fer* who, thou toldest me, *Therese*, had, as I do, worked up thy mind; nothing is juster than this man's principles, and the abasement, in which people have the folly of holding him, does not deprive him of the right of reasoning well.

If all the productions of Nature are the resultative effects of the laws which control her; if her action and perpetual reaction suppose the necessary movement of her essence, what becomes of the sovereign master whom fools gratuitously lend her? That is what thy wise teacher told thee, dear girl. What are then Religions according to this, if they be not the curb by which the tyranny of the strongest man wished to inthral the weakest man? Full of this design, he dared tell him over whom he pretended to domineer, that a God forged the irons with which his cruelty surrounded him; and the latter brutalized by his misery, indistinctly believed everything the other wished. Can Religions therefore, sprung from these impostures, deserve any respect? Is there a single one of them, *Therese*, but bears the emblem of imposture and stupidity? What do I behold in them all? Mysteries which cause reason to quake, dogmas outraging Nature, and grotesque ceremonies which inspire only derision and disgust. But if, out of them all, there be one which more especially deserves our contempt and hatred, O *Therese*, is it not that barbarous law of Christianity in which we were both born? Is there one of them more odious?. . . one at which both heart and mind so much revolt?

How can reasonable men have still any belief in the obscure words, she pretended miracles of the vile founder of this frightful worship? Did there ever exist a juggler better calculated to raise public indignation? What is a leprous Jew who, born of a wanton and a soldier in the meanest corner of the Universe, dares make himself pass for the mouth-piece of him who, they say, created the world? With such lofty pretentions, thou wilt own, *Therese*, a few titles were at least wanted. What are those of this ridiculous

Ambassador? What is he going to do in order to prove his mission? Is the face of the earth going to be changed? Are the plagues which afflict it going to be done away with? Is the sun going to brighten it day and night? Will vices no longer sully it? Are we going in fine to behold but happiness reigning?. . . No it is through juggler's tricks, through puns[6] that the messenger of God announces himself to the universe; it is in the respectable society of labourers, artisans and merry girls, that the minister of Heaven comes to manifest his greatness; it is in getting drunk with the one, sleeping with the other, that the friend of a God, a God himself, comes to submit the hardened sinner to his laws; it is inventing for his farces only what can satisfy either his lust or his gluttony, that the scoundrel proves his mission. Be that as it may, he makes his fortune; a few low satellites join in with this rogue; a sect is formed; the dogmas of this rabble succeed in seducing a few Jews: being slaves under the Roman sway, they were to joyfully embrace a religion which, freeing them from their bonds, only trained them up to the religious curb. Their motive is guessed, their indocility is unveiled; the seditious are arrested; their chief perishes, but of a death undoubtedly much too mild for his kind of crime, and, through an unpardonable fault of reflection, the disciples of this pitiful wretch are allowed to disperse themselves about, instead of being slain with him. Fanaticism seizes upon the minds, women bawl, fools beat themselves, idiots believe, and lo the most despicable of beings, the most awkward knave, the weightiest imposter that had ever appeared, behold him God, behold him the son of God, equal to his father; behold all his raves consecrated, all his words become dogmas, and his absurdities, mysteries! The bosom of his fabulous father opens to receive him, and this Creator, single of old, behold him grown three-fold in order to comply with this son so worthy of his greatness. But will this holy God stop there? No, indeed; it is to much greater favours that his heavenly power is about to lend itself. At the will of the priest, namely, of a droll covered with lies and crimes, this great God, the Creator of all we behold, is about to abase himself in descending ten or twelve million times every morning in a bit of paste, which, having to be digested by the faithful, is going to be immediately changed, in the bottom of their bowels, into the vilest excrements, and that for the satisfaction of this very son, the odious inventor of this monstrous impiety, at a public house supper. He said so, that must be so. He said: This bread which you behold shall be my flesh; you shall digest it as such; now I am God, therefore God will be digested by you; therefore the Creator of Heaven and earth will be changed, because I have said so, into the vilest matter that can be exhaled from man's body, and man will eat his God, because that God is good and almighty. Yet these fooleries scatter abroad; their increasing is attributed to their reality, grandour, sublimity, to the power of him who introduced them, whilst the simplest causes double their existence, whilst the credit acquired through error never proved but swindlers on the one hand and idiots on the other. This infamous religion arrives at last upon the throne, and it is a feeble, cruel, ignorant and fanatic Emperor that, covering it with the royal diadem, thus sullies with it both ends of the earth. O *Therese*, of what weight ought these reasons to be over a scrutinizing and philosophical mind? Can the wise man see, in this heap of marvellous fables, anything else but the disgusting fruit of the imposture of a few men and the false credulity of a greater number? Had God wished us to have any religion, and was he really powerful; or, still better, if there really was a God, would it be by such absurd means that he would have communicated his orders to us? Would it be through the mouth-piece of a despicable bandit, that he would have shown us how it was necessary to serve him? If this God, of whom you speak to me, is supreme, powerful, just, good, will it be enigmas and farces that he will teach me how to serve and know him? Sovereign mover of the stars and of man's heart, can he not instruct us in making use of the one, or convince us by engraving himself in the other? Let him imprint one day in fiery characters, in the centre of the Sun, the law which may please him and which he wishes to give us; from one end of the universe to the other, all men reading it, seeing it at the same time, will then become guilty if they do not follow it. But not to indicate his desires except in an ignored nook of Asia; to choose as spectator the craftiest and most visionary people; as substitute the vilest artisan, the most absurd and greatest rogue; to entangle the doctrine so well, that it is impossible to comprehend it; to absorb its knowledge among a small number of individuals; to leave the others in error and punish them for having remained in it. . . . Ah! no, *Therese*, no, no; all those atrocities are not framed to guide us: I should rather die a thousand times than believe them. When atheism will have martyrs, let it designate them, and my blood is quite ready. Let us detest those horrors, *Therese*; let the worst kind of outrages cement the contempt that is justly due to them. . . . Scarcely were my eyes opened than I detested those gross raves; I framed for myself since that time a law to trample them under foot, an oath never to return to them; imitate me, if thou wishest to be happy; detest, abjure, profane as well as I both the hateful object of this frightful worship, and this worship itself, created for chimeras, formed, as they, to be despised by everybody who pretends to wisdom."

— "Oh! Sir," replied I in weeping, "you would deprive an unfortunate girl of her sweetest hope, if you mangled within her heart this religion which consoles her. Firmly attached to what it teaches; wholly convinced that all the blows levelled at it are merely the effects of libertinism and of passions, shall I go and sacrifice to blasphemies, to sophisms which cause me horror, the dearest idea of my mind, the sweetest food of my heart?" To this I added a thousand other reasonings at which the Count only laughed, and his captious principles, nourished by a more manly eloquence, sustained by lectures that I had fortunately never read, used to daily attack mine, but without shaking them. *Madam de Bressac*, full of virtue and piety, did not ignore that her nephew maintained his errings by all the paradoxes of the day; she often shuddered at them with me; and, she condescended to find a little more good sense in me than in her other women, she liked to entrust me with her chagrins.

There were however no further limits to her nephew's proceedings towards her; the Count was on the point of no longer concealing them from her. He had not only surrounded his aunt with all that dangerous rabble serving his pleasures, but he had also borne the audacity so far as to declare to her before me, that if she again thought of thwarting his tastes, he would convince her of what charms they were, in delivering himself up to them under her very eyes.

I wept; this conduct caused me horror. I tried to find therein personal motives in order to stifle in my soul the unfortunate passion with which it was burnt, but is love an evil which one can cure? Everything I sought to oppose to it only stirred up its flame the more keenly, and the perfidious Count never appeared to me more amiable than when I had united before me all that should prompt me to hate him.

I was four years in this house, ever persecuted by the same chagrins, ever consoled by the same coaxing expressions, when this abominable man, thinking himself at last sure of me, dared to unveil to me his infamous designs. We were at the time in the country; I was alone with the Countess: her first maid had obtained leave to stay in Paris during the summer on account of some business of her husband. One evening, shortly after I had retired, respiring on the balcony of my room, and being unable, owing to the excessive heat, to decide on going to bed, all of a sudden the Count knocks, and begs me to allow him to talk with me. Alas! every instant this cruel author of my woes granted me seemed to me too precious that I should refuse any of them; he enters, carefully shuts the door, and throwing himself into an arm-chair at my side: — "Listen, *Therese*," he said to me with some embarrassment, . . . "I have things of the greatest consequence to tell you; swear to me that you will never reveal anything about them." — "Oh! Sir," answered I, "could you believe me capable of abusing your confidence? — Thou knowest not what thou wouldst risk, if thou didst happen to prove to me that I am mistaken in according it to thee! — The most dreadful of all my sorrows would be to have lost it, I need no greater threats. . . ." — "Well, *Therese,* I have condemned my aunt to death . . . and it is thy hand which is to serve me. . . ." — "My hand!" I cried in reeling backwards with fright. . . . "Oh! Sir, have you been able to conceive the like projects?. . . No, no; dispose of my life, if you want it, but never imagine that you will obtain from me the horror you propose to me." — "Listen, *Therese*," said the Count to me in pulling me with tranquillity; "I well doubted of thy repugnances, but as thou hast some wit, I flattered myself with vanquishing them . . . with proving to thee that this crime, which appears to thee so enormous, is after all but a very simple thing.

Two forfeits here present themselves, *Therese*, to thy but scanty philosophical eyes: the destruction of a creature which resembles us, and the evil with which this destruction increases, when this creature is closely connected with us. Concerning the crime of the destruction of one's likeness, be assured, dear girl, it is purely chimerical; the power of destroying is not granted to man; he has at the most that of varying the forms; but he has not that of annihilating them: now every form is equal in the eyes of Nature; nothing is lost in the immense crucible in which her variations are executed; every portion of matter that falls therein springs forth therefrom incessantly under other forms, and whatever be our proceedings upon this, no doubt none outrages her, none could offend her. Our destructions re-animate her power; they maintain her energy, but none attenuates her; she is vexed by none. . . . Ah! what does it matter to her ever creating hand, whether this matter of flesh forming to-day a two-footed individual be reproduced to-morrow under the form of a thousand different insects? Will anybody dare state that the construction of this two-footed animal costs her more than that of a little worm, and that she ought to take therein a more lively interest? If therefore this degree of attachment, or rather of indifference is the same, what is it to her, whether by the sword of one man another be changed into a fly or grass? When it will have been proved to me that it is of such importance to Nature, that her laws are necessarily irritated by this transmutation, I shall be then able to believe that murder is a crime; but when the most profound study will have shown me that everything which vegetates on this globe, the most imperfect of Nature's works, is of an equal price in her eyes, I shall never admit that the changing of one of these creatures into a thousand others can in anywise disturb her views. I will say to myself: all men, all animals, all growing plants,

nourishing themselves, destroying themselves, producing themselves by the same means, never receiving a real death, but a simple
variation in that which modifies them; all, I say, appearing to-day
under one form, and in a few years under another, may, by the will
of the being who wishes to move them, change thousands and
thousands of times in one day, without a single law of Nature being
for an instant affected thereby, what do I say? without this
transmuter's having done anything else but good, since in decom-
posing individuals whose basis become again necessary for Nature,
he does but render her, through this action improperly styled criminal, the creating energy of which he necessarily deprives her, who,
by a stupid indifference, dares not to undertake any overthrowing.
O *Therese*, it is man's pride alone which established murder as a
crime. This vain creature, fancying himself to be the sublimest on
the Globe, thinking himself the most essential, set off from this false
principle in order to assure that the action which destroyed him
could be but infamous; but his vanity, his madness, change nothing
in Nature's laws; there is no being that does not experience, in the
bottom of his heart, the most ardent desire of being rid of those
who annoy him, or whose death may bring some profit; and from
this desire to the effect, dost thou imagine, *Therese*, that the difference is very great? Now if these impressions come to us from
Nature, it is presumable that they irritate her? Would she inspire
us with what would degrade her? Ah! grow quiet dear girl, we experience nothing but what serves her; every movement she places in
us is the mouth-piece of her laws; the passions of men are only the
means which she employs to arrive at her designs. Does she need
individuals? she inspires us with love, there are creations; do
destructions become necessary for her? she plants in our hearts,
vengeance, lust, ambition, there are murders; she has always
worked for herself and we have become, without suspecting it, the
credulous agents of her caprices.

Ah! no, no, *Therese*, no; Nature leaves not within our reach the
possibility of crimes which could disturb her economy; can it come
under the senses that the weakest man can really offend the
strongest man? What are we with relation to her? Can she have, in

creating us, placed in us what might be capable of hurting her? Can this stupid supposition accord with the sublime and sure manner by which we behold her arriving at her ends? Ah! if murder was not one of man's actions which best fulfills her intentions, would she permit it to be operated? Can imitating her therefore hurt her? Can she be offended to see man committing on his likeness what she herself commit on him every day? Since it is proved that she can reproduce only by destructions, is it not to act according to her views the incessant multiplying of them? In this case the man, who shall deliver himself up to them with most ardour, will therefore be incontestably he that will serve her best, since he will be the one who will most co-operate with the designs she manifests every instant. The first and finest quality of Nature, is the movement which incessantly agitates her; but this movement is only a perpetual sequel of crimes, it is only through crimes that she conserves it: the being that best resembles her, and consequently the most perfect being will therefore necessarily be the one whose most active agitation will become the cause of many crimes; whereas, I repeat, the inactive or indolent being, namely, the virtuous being, ought to be in her eyes the least perfect no doubt, since he tends only towards apathy, tranquillity which would instantly plunge every thing again into chaos, if its ascendancy became victorious. Equilibrium must be conserved; this can be only so through crimes; crimes therefore serve Nature; if they serve her, if she requires them, if she desires them, can they offend her? and who can be offended, if she is not?

But the creature whom I destroy is my aunt. . . . Oh! *Therese,* how frivolous are those links in the eyes of a Philosopher! Permit me not even to speak to thee of them, they are so useless. Can these despicable chains, fruits of our laws and public institutions, be anything in Nature's eyes?"

"Leave aside then thy prejudices, *Therese,* and serve me; thy fortune is made."

"— Oh! Sir," replied I quite terrified to the *Count de Bressac,* "that indifference which you suppose in Nature is still here only the work of the sophisms of your mind. Condescend rather to listen to your

heart, and you shall hear how it will condemn all those false reasonings of libertinism; this heart, to the tribunal of which I refer
you, is it not then the sanctuary in which that Nature you outrage
wishes us to listen to, and respect, her? If she engraves therein the
greatest horror of the crime which you are meditating, will you
grant me that it is guilty? Passions, I know, blind you at present, but
as soon as they are dead, to what a pitch will your remorse torture
you! The greater is your sensibility, the more their sting will torment you. . . . Oh! Sir, conserve, respect the days of this tender and
precious friend; do not sacrifice her, you should die of despair for
it! Every day, at every instant, you would behold her before your
eyes, this darling aunt whom your blind fury would have hurled into
the tomb; you would hear her plaintive voice pronouncing those
gentle names which caused the joy of your infancy; she would
appear in your awakenings and torment you in your dreams; she
would open with her gory fingers the wounds you made on her; not
a happy moment would ever thenceforward shine for you on the
earth; all your pleasures would be sullied, all your ideas troubled;
a heavenly hand, whose power you forget, would avenge for the
days you would have cut away, by empoisoning all yours; and without having enjoyed your forfeits, you would die of mortal regret for
having dared accomplish them."

I was bathed in tears while uttering these words, I was at the
Count's feet; I conjured him by everything he could hold most
sacred, to forget an infamous erring which I swore to him that I
would conceal all my life. . . . But I knew not the man with whom I
had to do; I was not aware to what degree passions had established
crime in this perverse soul. The Count rose cooly. — "I clearly see
that I was mistaken, *Therese,*" said he to me; "I am perhaps as sorry
for it on your account as on my own; never mind, I shall find other
means, and you shall have lost a great deal without your mistress'
gaining anything by it."

This threat changed all my ideas: in not undertaking the crime
proposed to me, I hazarded very much, and my mistress infallibly
perished; in consenting to the complicity, I placed myself under
shelter from the Count's wrath, and I assuredly saved his aunt. This

reflection, which was in me the work of an instant, decided me on accepting everything. But as so speedy a change might have appeared suspected, I managed my defeat for some time. I placed the Count in the necessity of repeating his sophisms often to me. I gradually looked as if I no longer knew what to reply to them; *Bressac* believed I was overcome. I rendered my weakness lawful through the power of his art, at last I surrendered. The Count rushed into my arms. How this impulse would have filled me with joy, had it had another cause! . . . What do I say? it was no longer time: his horrible conduct, his barbarous designs had killed all the sentiments that my weak heart dared conceive, and I no longer beheld in him but a monster. . . . — "Thou art the first woman I embraced," said the Count to me, "and in deed, it is with all my heart. . . . Thou art delightful, my child; a ray of wisdom has then traversed thy mind! Is it possible this charming head has so long remained in darkness!" And then we agreed about our facts. In two or three days, more or less, according to the facility I should find for it, I was to slip a small package of poison, which *Bressac* handed me, into the cup of chocolate which Madam was accustomed to drink in the morning. The Count went guarantee for the consequences, and delivered up to me a contract for a revenue of two thousand crowns, the very day of the execution. He signed these promises, without characterising what was to make me enjoy them, and we parted.

There happened during these transactions something too extraordinary, too well suited to unveil for you the atrocious soul of the monster with whom I had to deal, that I should not interrupt for a while, in order to tell it to you, the recital, of which you are no doubt awaiting the discovery of the plot of the adventure in which I had engaged myself.

Two days after our criminal pact, the Count learned that an uncle, on whose succession he was not counting, had just left him an income of eighty thousand livres. . . . Oh! Heavens, said I to myself, on hearing the news, is this the way that celestial justice punishes the plot of forfeits! . . . And soon repenting on this blasphemy against Providence, I throw myself on my knees, I ask pardon for it, and flatter myself because this unexpected event is at least about to change the Count's projects. . . . What was my mistake! "Oh! my dear *Therese*," he says to me on running into my room the same evening, "how prosperities are raining down on me! I often told thee so, the idea of a crime or its execution is the surest means of attracting happiness; there is no longer any except for the wicked." — "Ah! what, Sir," answered I, "this fortune on which you were not counting, does not decide you to await patiently the death you wish to hasten?" — "To await?" the Count hastily replied; "I would not wait two minutes, *Therese*; dost thou bear in mind that I am twenty-eight years old, and it is hard to wait at my age?. . . No, let this change nothing in our schemes, I pray thee, and grant me the consolation of seeing everything done, before the time of our return to Paris. . . . To-morow, the day after to-morrow at the latest. . . . I already long to count thee down a quarter of thy revenues . . . to put thee in possession of the act which fixes them on thee. . . ." I did my utmost in order to disguise the fright that this violent propensity put into my head, and I again took my resolutions of the eve, being thoroughly convinced that if I did not execute the horrible crime with which I was entrusted, the Count would soon find out that I was mocking him, and that if I warned *Madam de Bressac*, whatever party the revelation of this project would make her espouse, the young Count, on seeing himself still deceived, would speedily adopt the surest means, which, while equally causing the aunt's death, would expose me to the whole vengeance of the nephew. The way of Justice lay open to me, but nothing in the world would have prevailed on me to take it. I therefore determined to warn the Marchioness; of all possible parties, that seemed to me the best, so I yielded to it.

"Madam," said I to her the day after my last interview with the Count, "I have something of the utmost importance to reveal to you, but to whatever extent it may interest you, I am decided to keep silent, unless you first promise me your word of honor to bear no resentment against your nephew for what he has the impudence of projecting. . . . You will act, Madam, you will employ the best means; but you will not say one word. Condescend to promise me so, or I hold my tongue." *Madam de Bressac*, who fancied it was all about some of her nephew's usual follies, bound herself by an oath which I exacted, and I revealed everything. This unhappy woman burst into tears on learning this infamy. . . . — "The monster!" she exclaimed, "what have I ever done except for his welfare? If I have wished to prevent his vices, or to correct him for them, what other motive but his happiness could force me to this severity? And this succession which has just fallen to him, does he not owe it to my cares? Ah, *Therese*, prove clearly to me the truth of this scheme . . . put me into the situation of being unable to doubt of it; I need everything that may completely extinguish in me the feelings which my blinded heart dares still conserve for this monster. . . ." And then I let her see the package of poison; it was difficult to furnish a better proof. The Marchioness wished to make some trails of it; we made a dog which we locked up swalllow a slight dose of it, and it died at the end of two hours in terrible convulsions. *Madam de Bressac*, no longer doubting, made up her mind; she ordered me to give her the remainder of the poison, and at once wrote through a messenger to the *Duke de Sonzeval*, her relative, to betake himself to the Minister's, to unfold to him the atrocity of a nephew whose victim she was on the eve of falling; to provide himself with a "lettre de cachet"; to hasten to her lands and deliver her as soon as possible from the wretch who was so cruelly conspiring against her days.

But this abominable crime was to be perpetuated; it was necessary that, through an incomprehensible permission from Heaven, virtue should yield to the efforts of wickedness. The animal on which we had made our experiment, discovered the whole thing to the Count; he heard it howling; knowing that this dog was beloved by his aunt, he asked what had been done to it; those to whom he applied, ignoring all, answered him nothing distinctly. From this moment he formed suspicions; he said not a word, but I saw him troubled. I informed the Marchioness about this state, she grew the more uneasy about it, without being able notwithstanding to imagine anything else but to hasten the messenger, and to conceal still better, if it was possible, the object of his mission. She told her nephew that she was sending in all speed to Paris, to beg the *Duke de Sonzeval* to put himself directly at the head of the succession of the uncle from whom they had just inherited, because, if nobody appeared, there were processes to be feared. She added that she enjoined on the *Duke* to come and give her an account of everything, that she might decide to set out herself with her nephew, should business require it. The Count, being too good a physiognomist not to see the embarrassment in his aunt's face, not to observe a little confusion in mine, feigned to believe all of it and was only the better on the alert. He removes from the castle, under the pretext of taking a walk; he lies in wait for the messenger in a spot by which he was inevitably to pass. This man, being much more attached to him than to his aunt, made no ado about handing him the letters, and *Bressac*, convinced of what he no doubt calls my treason, gives the messenger a hundred *louis* with injunctions never to appear again at his aunt's. He returns to the castle, the rage in his heart, but silent; he meets me, he fawns upon me as usual; he asks me if it is to be the next day, makes me observe that it is essential it should be before the *Duke*'s arrival, then goes to bed with a tranquil look and without taking notice of anything. I knew nothing then, I was the dupe of everything. If this awful crime was perpetrated, as the Count informed me of it afterwards, he committed it himself no doubt, but I know not how. I made several conjectures; of what good would it be to mention them to you? Let us rather come to the cruel manner in which I was punished for not having been willing to undertake it. On the day after the messenger's arrest, Madam drank her chocolate as usual, she rose, made her toilet, appeared to me agitated, and sat down at table; we were scarcely outside, when the Count accosts me: — "*Therese,*" he says to me with the greatest phlegm, "I have found a safer means than the one I had proposed to thee, in order to accomplish our schemes; but this requires explanations, I dare not go so often into thy room; be at five o'clock exactly in the corner of the park, I shall meet thee there, and we shall go and take a walk in the wood, during which I shall explain everything to thee."

I confess to you, Madam, whether it was the permission of Providence, an excess of candor, or blindness, nothing forboded to me the dreadful misfortune which was awaiting me; I fancied myself so sure of the secret and arrangements of the Marchioness, that I never imagined the Count could have discovered them. There was however embarrassment within me:

Perjury is a virtue when we promise crime,

said one of our tragical Poets; but perjury is ever hate-ful for a delicate and sensible soul which finds itself obliged to have recourse to it. My role was embarrassing me.

Whatever might come of it, I was off to the rendezvous; the Count was not long about putting in an appearance there, he comes to me with a free and gay countenance, and we proceed into the forest without there being question of anything else but laughing and joking, as was his custom with me. When I wanted to turn the conversation on the object which caused him to desire our discourse, he always told me to wait, that he was afraid we were observed, and that we were not yet in safety. We insensibly arrived at the four trees to which I had been so cruelly attached. I started up on again seeing these places; all the horror of my destiny then presents itself to my eyes, and judge whether my fright redoubled, when I beheld the dispositions of this fatal spot. Ropes were hanging from one of the trees; three monstrous English dogs were tied to the other tree, and appeared to be waiting only for me, to abandon themselves at need to eating, as their frothy and wide open mouths foreboded; one of the Count's favorites was guarding them.

Then the perfidious villian, no longer using with me but low epithets: "Wench," he says to me; "dost thou recognise this bush from which I dragged thee like a wild beast to restore thee to the life which thou hadst deserved to lose?. . . Dost thou recognise these trees where I threatened to replace thee, if thou ever gavest me a reason to repent of my goodness? Why didst thou accept the services which I asked of thee against my aunt, if thou hadst the intention of betraying, and how hast thou imagined to serve Virtue, in risking the liberty of him to whom thou owest happiness? Necessarily placed between two crimes, why hast thee chosen the most abominable? — Alas! did I not choose the least? — Thou shouldst have refused," continued the Count, in a rage, seizing me by one arm and violently shaking me: "Yes, undoubtedly refuse, and not accept in order to betray me." Then *Mr. de Bressac* told me all he had done to take Madam's despatches unawares, and how the suspicion arose which had persuaded him to intercept them. "What hast thou done by thy falsehood, unworthy creature?" continued he. "Thou hast risked thy days without conserving my aunt's; the blow is dealt, my return to the castle will offer me its fruits, but thou must die, thou must learn, before expiring, that the way of virtue is not always the safest, and that there are circumstances in the world in which the complicity of a crime is preferable to its formation." And without giving me time to answer, without showing the least pity for the cruel state in which I was, he drags me towards the tree which was destined to me and where his favorite was waiting. "There she is," said he to him, "she that wanted to poison my aunt, and that perhaps has already perpetrated this awful crime, inspite my cares to prevent it; I would have done better no doubt by placing her in the hands of Justice, but she would have lost her life on that account, and I wish to leave it with her that she may have longer to suffer."

Then the two wretches seize upon me, they strip me naked in an instant. "The lovely buttocks!" said the Count in the most ironical tone and touching these objects with brutality; "superb flesh! . . . an excellent breakfast for my dogs!" As soon as no robe was left me, they bind me to the tree by a rope which goes round my loins, leaving my arms free that I might defend myself as best I could, and through the freedom they allowed the rope, I may go forwards or backwards about six feet. Once there, the Count, greatly moved, has just observed my countenance; he turns about and goes round me; in the rough way he feels me, it seems his sanguinary hands wanted to dispute it in rage with the dog's sharp teeth. . . . "Come," said he to his assistant, "set these animals free, it is time."

They unchain them, the Count excites them, the whole three rush upon my unfortunate body, you would say they divided it between them so that none of its parts should be exempt from their furious attacks; I vainly tried to repulse them, they only tore me with greater fury, and during this horrible scene, *Bressac*, the unworthy *Bressac*, as if my sufferings had kindled his perfidious lust . . . the infamous villian! lent himself on examining me to the criminal caresses of his favorite. "That is enough of it," said he, at the end of a few minutes, "tie up the dogs and let us abandon this unfortunate girl to her evil lot."

— "Well, *Therese*!" he softly says to me on breaking my bonds, "virtue often costs very dear, as thou seest; dost thou imagine that a pension of two thousand crowns were not worth more than the bites with which thou art covered?" But in the frightful state I was, I could hardly hear him; I drop at the foot of the tree, and am ready to lose my senses. "I am very kind to spare thy life," says the traitor whom my woes irritate; "take care at least of the use thou makest of that favor. . . ." Then he orders me to get up, regain my clothes and quit this place as soon as possible. As my blood is flowing from all parts, that my clothes, the only ones I had left, may not be stained with it, I pull up some grass to cool myself, to wipe myself, and *Bressac* walks about, much more occupied with his own ideas than with me.

The swelling of my flesh, the blood still oozing from my wounds, excruciating pains I endure, all render the operation of dressing myself almost impossible without ever the dishonest man who has just reduced me to this cruel state . . . he, for whose sake I would have formerly sacrificed my life, condescended to show me the slightest token of pity. As soon as I was ready: — "Go whereever you like," he says to me, "you must have some money left; I do not deprive you of it; but take good care never to appear again at any of my houses in town or country; two weighty reasons are opposed to it. It is well that you should know in the first place that the process which you thought was ended, is not so at all. You were told that it no longer existed, you were led into error; the sentence has not been purged; you were left in this situation to see how you would behave yourself; in the second place you are going to pass as the Marchioness's murderer; if she still breathes, I am going to make her carry this idea to the tomb, the whole world shall know it. There are two condemnations against you instead of one, and in place of the vile usurer for opponent, a rich and powerful man, determined to prosecute you as far as Hell, if you abuse the life which his pity leaves you."

— "Oh! Sir," I reply, "whatever may have been your severities towards me, fear nothing from my proceedings; I thought it my duty to take some against you when there was question of your aunt's life. I shall never undertake any when there will be question only of the unhappy *Therese*. Farewell, Sir, may your crimes render you as happy as your cruelties cause me sufferings! and whatever be the lot it may Heaven to place me in, so long as it will conserve my deplorable days, I shall employ them only in praying for you." The Count raised his head; he could not help gazing upon me at these words, and as he saw me staggering and covered with tears, in the fear of being moved no doubt, the cruel fellow went away, and I saw him no more.

Being entirely abandoned to my woe, I let myself drop down at the foot of the tree, and there, giving it full vent, I made the forest resound with my groans; I pressed the ground with my unhappy body, and I bedewed the grass with my tears.

"O my God," I cried, "you have willed it; it was in your eternal decrees that the innocent one should become the prey of the guilty. Dispose of me, O Lord, I am still far from the ills which you suffered for us; may those that I endure in adoring you, make me one day worthy of the rewards you promised to the weak one, when she has you for her object in her tribulations, and when she glorifies you in her pains!"

The night fell: it was impossible for me to go farther; I could barely keep myself together; I cast my eyes on the bush where I had slept four years before, in almost as unfortunate a situation. I dragged myself to it as best I could, and having put myself in the same spot, annoyed by my still bleeding wounds, overwhelmed by the ills of my mind and the sorrows of my heart, I passed the cruelest night it is possible to imagine.

The vigour of my age and constitution having restored me a little strength at day-break, being too much afraid of the neighbourhood of this cruel castle, I speedily made away from it. I left the forest, and resolved to reach at random the first dwelling that presented itself to me, I entered the Borough of Saint-Marcel, about five leagues distant from Paris. I inquired for the Surgeon's house, they pointed it out to me; I begged him to bind up my wounds; I told him that, while flying on account of a love matter from my mother's house in Paris, I had been met during the night by bandits in the forest who, in order to avenge themselves for the resistances I had offered their desires, and had me thus treated by their dogs. *Rodin,* such was this artist's name, examined me with the greatest attention, he discovered nothing dangerous in my sores; he would have, said he, undertaken to restore me in less than fifteen days as fresh as before my adventure, and I arrived at his house on the same instant; but the night and annoyance had envenomed my wounds, and I could be cured only in a month. *Rodin* gave me lodging in his house, took all possible care of me, and on the thirtieth day, there no longer existed on my person any vestige of *Mister de Bressac*'s cruelties.

As soon as the state I was in permitted me to take the air, my first eagerness was to try and find in the Borough a young girl clever and intelligent enough to go to the Marchioness's castle and inquire of everything new that had taken place there since my departure. Curiosity was not the real motive which determined me to this step; this likely dangerous curiosity would have certainly been much out of place; but what I had earned at the Marchioness's had remained in my room; I had scarcely six *louis* about me, and I possessed more than forty at the Castle. I did not imagine that the Count was cruel enough to refuse me what so lawfully belonged to me. Being persuaded that, his first fury having passed, he would not do me such an injustice, I wrote as moving a letter as I could. I carefully concealed from him the place I lived, and begged him to send him my clothes with the trifle of money which belonged to me in my room. A smart and witty country lass of twenty-five took charge of my letter and promised me to make inquiries enough underhand, in order to satisfy me on her return about the different objects of which I let her see a clear explication was necessary for me. I recommended her especially to conceal the name of the place I was in, not to speak about me on any account, and to state that she had the letter from a man who carried it from more than ten leagues off. *Jeannette* set out and, twenty-four hours after, she brought me back the answer; it still exists, there it is, Madam, but deign, before reading it, to listen to what passed at the Count's since I was away from him.

The *Marchioness de Bressac*, having fallen dangerously ill, on the very day of my going away from the castle, had died the next day in the most awful pains and convulsions; the relatives had come running, and the nephew, who appeared in the greatest desolation, pretended that his aunt had been poisoned by a chamber-maid who had stolen away on the same day. Researches were made, and the intention was to put that unfortunate wretch to death should she be discovered: besides, the Count found himself much richer by this succession than he had fancied; the safe, pocket-book, and jewels of the Marchioness, all objects of which nobody had any knowledge, placed her nephew, independently of his revenues, in possession of more than six hundred thousand francs of value or ready cash. This young man had, they say, through his affected grief, great difficulty in concealing his joy, and the relations, convoked for the opening of the body exacted by the Count, after having deplored the lot of the unfortunate Marchioness and sworn to avenge her if the guilty one fell into their hands, had left the young man in full and peaceful possession of the fruit of his wickedness. *Mister de Bressac* had spoken in person to Jeannette, and had set her different questions, to which the young girl had replied with so much frankness and firmness, that he had resolved to give her his answer without urging her further. There it is, this fatal letter, says *Therese* on handing it to *Madam de Lorsange*, yes there it is, Madam, it is sometimes necessary for my heart, and I shall keep it until death; read it, if you can, without shuddering.

*Madame de Lorsange* having taken the note from the hands of our fair adventurer, read therein the following words:

*"A wicked wretch, capable of having poisoned my aunt, is very daring to attempt to write to me after this execrable crime; what she has best to do is to carefully conceal her retreats she may be sure that she will be troubled in it, if she is discovered. What dares she claim? What does she say about money? Is what she may have left equivalent to the thefts she made, either during her stay in the house, or in perpetrating her last crime? Let her avoid a second message like this one, for it is hereby declared to her that her erand-boy will be arrested, until the place which conceals the guilty one be known to the Justice."*

"Continue, my dear child," says *Madam de Lorsange* on giving back the note to *Therese*, "these are proceedings which cause horror; to float in gold and refuse an unfortunate girl who did not wish to commit a crime, what she lawfully earned, is a gratuitous infamy which has no example."

Alas! Madam, continued *Therese*, on taking up the sequel of her story, I wept two days over this unfortunate letter; I lamented far more for the horrible proceeding it proved, than for the refusals it contained. "There I am therefore guilty!" I cried, "behold me then a second time denounced to the Justice for having too well known how to respect her laws! Be it so, I do not repent for it; whatever may befall me, I shall not at least feel the stings of remorse so long as my soul will be pure, and so long as I shall have done no other evil than to have listened to the just and virtuous sentiments which will never forsake me."

It was still impossible for me to think that the researches of which the Count spoke to me, were really true; they had so little likelihood, it was so dangerous for him to make me appear in Justice, that I imagined he ought within himself be much more frightened to see me than I had reason to tremble in his menaces. These reflections decided me to stop where I was, and to take service even there if it was possible, until my funds should be somewhat increased to allow me to go farther. I communicated my project to

*Rodin*, who approved of it, and even proposed to me to stay in his house; but before telling you of the party I took, it is necessary to give you an idea of this man and his suroundings.

*Rodin*, was a man of forty, dark, heavy eye-brows, quick eye, a strong and healthy aspect, partaking at the same time of libertinism. Very far above his state, and possessing an income of from ten to twelve thousand livres, *Rodin* exercised the surgical art only from taste; he had a very fine house in Saint-Marcel, which he merely occupied, having lost his wife a few years ago, with two girls to wait on him, and his daughter. This young person called *Rosalie,* had just attained her fourteenth year; she united all the charms best calculated to cause sensation: a nymph-like waist, a round, fresh and extraordinary animated face, delicate and pleasing features, the prettiest mouth possible, large black eyes full of soul and sentiment, chestnut-color hair falling to the bottom of the girdle, skin of a brightness . . . of an incredible smoothness, already the loveliest bosom in the world: besides the wit, liveliness, and one of the fairest souls that Nature had as yet created. Concerning the fellow maid-servants with whom I was to serve in this house, they were two peasants, one of whom was the governess and the other the cook. The one that filled the first office might be about twenty-five years old, the other about nineteen or twenty, and the both extremely pretty; this choice gave rise to some suspicions in me about the eagerness *Rodin* had in keeping me. What need has he of a third woman, said I to myself, and why does he want them good-looking? Surely, continued I, there is something in all this but little conform to the regular morals from which I never wish to deviate; let us examine.

Consequently, I begged *Mr. Rodin* to allow me to regain my strength another week in his house, assuring him that before the end of this time he would have my answer on what he kindly wished to propose me.

I profited by this interval to become more closely bound to *Rosalie,* determined to settled down at her father's only in as much as there would be nothing in his house that could cause me suspicion. In this intent bringing my observations to bear on everything, I perceived from the following day how this man had an arrangement, which since that time caused me furious suspicions about his behaviour.

*Mr. Rodin* kept in his house a children's school for both sexes; he had the privilege of it during his wife's lifetime, and nobody had thought of depriving him of it when he had lost her. *Mr. Rodin's* pupils were not numerous, but chosen; he had in all only fourteen girls and fourteen boys. He never took them under twelve years old, they were always sent away at sixteen; nothing was so handsome as the subjects whom *Rodin* admitted. If he was presented with one that had any bodily defects, or no face, he had the craft of refusing him under twenty pretexts always tinged with sophisms to which nobody could reply; thus, either the number of his boarders was incomplete, or what he had was always charming. These children did not eat at his house, but they came to it twice a day from seven o'clock until eleven in the morning, from four to eight in the evening. If up to then I had not yet seen all this little retinue, it is because I arrived at this man's house during the holidays, and the scholars were not coming any longer; they re-appeared there towards my recovery.

*Rodin* himself kept the schools; his governess cared that of the girls, into which he passed as soon as he had finished the boys' instruction; he taught these young pupils how to write, arithmetic, a smattering of history, drawing, music, and employed for all that no other masters than himself.

I expressed at first my astonishment to *Rosalie*, because her father, exercising the function of Surgeon, could at the same time discharge that of school-master; I told her that it appeared to me strange, that, being able to live at his ease without professing either of these states, he should give himself so much trouble to attend to them. *Rosalie*, with whom I was already on good footing, began to laugh at my reflection; the way in which she took what I was saying to her only afforded me the greater curiosity, and I begged her to lay herself wholly open to me. "Listen," said this charming girl to me, with all the candour of her age and all the simplicity of her amiable character; "listen, *Therese*, I am going to tell thee everything, I clearly see thou art an honest girl . . . incapable of betraying the secret I am about to confide to thee.

Surely, dear friend, my father could do without all this, and if he exercises either of these trades which thou seest him perform, two motives which I am going to reveal to thee are the cause thereof. He exercises the surgery from taste, for the sole pleasure of making fresh discoveries in art; he has so greatly multiplied them, he has given out on his part works so relished, that he generally passes for the most skilful man there is now in France; he worked twenty years in Paris, and it is on account of his pleasure that he retired into this country place. The true Surgeon of Saint-Marcel is one named *Rombeau*, whom he has taken under his protection, and whom he admits to his experiments. Thou wishest to know now, *Therese*, what entices him to hold a school?. . . libertinism, my child, mere libertinism, a passion carried to the extreme in him. My father finds in his scholars of both sexes, objects which dependency submits to his propensities, and he profits by them. . . . But hold . . . follow me," says *Rosalie* to me, "it is precisely to-day, Friday, one of three days in the week that he corrects those who have made mistakes; it is in this kind of correction that my father finds his pleasures; follow me, I tell thee, thou art going to see how he comes about it. We can observe all from a cabinet in my room, next to that of his expeditions; let us betake ourselves to it without noise, and take good care especially never to say a word, either of what I told thee, or of what thou art going to behold."

It was so important of me to know the morals of the new personage who offered me an asylum, that I should neglect anything that could unveil them to me. I follow in *Rosalie's* steps; she places me near a partition-wall badly enough joined to leave, between the boards which form it, several slits sufficing to distinguish all that passed in the next room.

We are hardly planted when *Rodin* enters, leading with him a young girl of fourteen, as fair and handsome as Venus; the poor creature, all in tears, too well acquainted unfortunately with what is awaiting her, follows only in moaning her hard teacher; she throws herself at his feet, she implores for pardon; but *Rodin*, inflexible, kindles in this very severity the first sparks of his pleasure, they already rush from his heart, through the ferocious looks. . . . "Oh, no, no," he cries, "no, no, that is too often this happens to you, *Julie;* I repent of my goodnesses, they have served only to plunge you into fresh faults, but can the gravity of this one even allow me to use clemency, supposing I wished it?. . . A note given to a boy on coming into class?" — "Sir, I protest to you no!" — "Oh! I saw it, I saw it," — "Believe nothing of the sort," said *Rosalie* to me at this stage, "these are faults that he concocts in order to strengthen his pretexts; this little creature is an Angel, it is because she resists him that he is treating her severely." And during this time, *Rodin*, being very excited, seizes the little girl by the hands, ties them up to a ring of a post placed in the middle of the correction room. Julie has no other defence . . . no other . . . except her fair head turned wistfully towards her tormentor, her beautiful hair all dishevelled, and her tears bathing the handsomest face in the world . . . the sweetest . . . the most interesting. *Rodin* gazes on this picture, he is inflamed with it; he blind-folds those eyes which are imploring him, his mouth closes up to them, he dares not kiss them. Julie holds no longer anything. *Rodin* the more easily undoes the veils of chastity, the chemise tucked up under the bodice is raised as far as her loins. . . . How much whiteness! How many beauties! these are roses grafted on to lilies by the very hand of the *Graces*. What is he then, the being hard-hearted enough to doom charms so delicate, so pleasing to torments? What monster can seek pleasure in the bosom of tears and sorrow? *Rodin* contemplates . . . his wandering eye runs over his hands and dare profane the flowers his cruelties are about to tarnish. Being right in front, no stir can escape us; at one while the libertine rather opens, at another while squeezes these delicate charms which are bewitching him; he presents them to us under every shape, but keeps to these alone. Although the true temple of Love is within his reach, *Rodin*, being steadfast to his worship, does not even cast a glance at it, he can not bear even its very sight; if the posture exposes it, he cloaks it; the

slightest erring would disturb his homage, he will have nothing dis-
tract him. . . . His fury at last has no bounds; he expresses it at first
by invectives; he loads with menaces and evil proposals this unfortunate little girl writhing under the lashes by which she sees herself
ready to be mangled; *Rodin* is no longer himself, he snatches up a
fistful of rods out of a great tub, where they acquired in the vinegar
which steeps them, more verdure and suppleness. . . . "Come,"
said he on approaching his victim, "get ready, you must suffer." And
the hard-hearted wretch letting these rods fall perpendicularly with
a vigorous arm on the parts which are exposed to him, lays on at
first twenty-five lashes which soon change the tender carnation of
this so delicate a skin into vermillion.

Julie fetched cries . . . shrill cries that pierced my soul, . . . tears
are flowing down under her bandage, and dropping in pearls on
her lovely cheeks; *Rodin* only becomes the more furious at them. . . .
He runs his hands over the molested parts, feels, presses them,
seeming to prepare them for fresh assaults; these closely follow the
former, *Rodin* is in raptures; he delights in contemplating these
eloquent proofs of ferocity. He is no longer able to retain himself, the most indecent state manifests his flame; he is not afraid to
expose everything: Julie can not see him . . . for an instant he
presents himself at the breach; he would feign ascend it as a vanquisher, but dares not. Recommencing fresh tyrannies, *Rodin*
lashes with all the force of his arm; by dint of stripes he succeeded in somewhat opening this sanctuary of the *Graces* and voluptuousness. . . . He no longer knows where to stop; his intoxication
is at the pitch of depriving him of the further use of reason; he
swears, blasphemes, revels, nothing is secure from his barbarous
blows, every visible thing is treated with the same rigour. But the
wretch stops nevertheless; he feels himself in the impossibility of
going farther, without spending the force needful for fresh operations. "Dress yourself," he says to Julie, on setting her free, and
fixing himself up, "and should a similar thing happen you again,
know that you will not get over it so lightly." Julie enters her school-
room, *Rodin* goes into the boys'; he immediately brings out a young
scholar of fifteen years old, handsome as the day; *Rodin* scolds him;
being more at home with him, he kisses him while preaching to

him: "You have deserved to be punished," he says to him, "and you are going to be punished. . . ." At these words he outsteps all the bounds of pudicity with this child; but everything interests him now, nothing is excluded, the veils are lifted, everything is handled without distinction. *Rodin* threatens, caresses, kisses, inveighs; his impious fingers try to cause voluptuous sentiments rise in this boy, sentiments which he exacts from him. "Well!" says the satyr to him on seeing his success, "there you are in the state which I forbade you. . . . I bet that with two more motions, the whole thing will be over me. . . ." Too sure of the titillations he produces, the libertine steps forward to receive their homage, and his mouth is the temple offered to this sweet incense; he himself is quite ready to let go, but he wishes to prolong it until the end. "Ah! I am going to punish you for this folly," he says on rising. He takes the young man by both hands, masters him, presents to himself the whole altar on which his fury wants to sacrifice. He opens it a little, his kisses run over it, his tongue sticks into it, and loses itself therein. *Rodin*, being drunk with love and ferocity, mingles the expressions and sentiments of both. . . . "Ah! thou little rascal," he cries, "I must be avenged of the illusion thou causest me!" The rods are picked up, *Rodin* lashes; being more excited no doubt than with the vestal, his strokes become heavier and more numerous, the child weeps, *Rodin* is enraptured, but fresh pleasures call him, he frees the child and flees to other sacrifices. A little girl of twelve years old succeeds the boy, and succeeds another boy followed by a little girl. *Rodin* flogs nine of them, five boys and four girls. The last is a little boy of fourteen, with a very handsome face. *Rodin* wants to enjoy him, the scholar defends himself; being out of his wits with lust, he flogs him, and the wretch, having no longer any control over himself, pours frothy jets of his flame over the molested parts of his young pupil, he drenches him with it from the loins to the heels. Our reformer, being furious for not having strength enough to forbear at least until the end, liberates in a surly mood the child, whom he sends back to the school-room, assuring him that it is not all over with him yet. These are the discourses I heard, these are the pictures that struck me.

— "Oh! Heavens," said I to *Rosalie* when these frightful scenes were over, "how can anyone abandon himself to such excesses? How can anyone find pleasures in the torments he causes?" — "Ah! thou knowest not all," *Rosalie* answers me; "listen," she says to me on returning into her room with me, "what thou hast seen may have made thee understand that when my father finds any facilities in these young pupils, he carries his horrors much farther; he seduces the little girls in the same manner as the little boys." *Rosalie* made me understand thereby that criminal manner in which I myself had been near falling a victim with the head of the bandits, into whose hands I had been cast after my escape from Jail, and in which I had been stained from the Merchant from Lyons. "By this means," continued this young slip, "the little girls are not dishonored, no childbearing is to be feared, and nothing hinders them from finding husbands; there is hardly a year passes without his corrupting all the boys, and at least one half of the other children. But the fourteen girls thou hast seen, eight are already stained in this way, and he has enjoyed nine boys. The two women that wait on him are submitted to the same horrors. . . . O *Therese*," added *Rosalie* on throwing herself into my arms, "O my dear girl, and myself also, and myself he seduced me from my earliest childhood; I was hardly eleven years old when I was already his victim . . . that I was, alas! without being able to defend myself from him." — "But, Miss," I interrupted terrified . . . "and Religion? you had at least this path left you. . . . Could you not consult a Director and confess everything to him? — Ah! art thou not then aware that accordingly as he corrupts us, he stifles with us all the seeds of Religion, and that he prohibits all its acts?. . . and besides could I do so? He has scarcely educated me. The little he taught me about these matters was merely from fear lest my ignorance might betray his impiety. But I have never been to confession, I never made my first Communion; he knows so well how to turn these things into ridicule, efface even the slightest ideas about them in us, that he removes those whom he has seduced for ever from their duties; or if they are obliged to discharge them on account of their families, it is with so thorough an indifference and lukewarmness, that he has nothing to fear from their indiscretion. But convince thyself, *Therese*, convince thyself with thy own eyes," she continues on pushing me very quickly into the closet out of which we were going; "come, that room where he corrects his scholars is the same one as that in which he makes use of us. Now the school time is over; it is the hour that, heated up by the preliminaries, he is about to come and pay himself off for the constraint which his prudence sometimes imposes on him; place thyself again where thou wast, dear girl, and thy eyes are going to behold everything."

However slightly curious I was of these fresh horrors, it was nevertheless better for me to thrust myself into the closet, than to allow myself to be taken unawares with *Rosalie* during school hours; *Rodin* would have infallibly conceived some suspicion about it. I therefore take my place of stand; I am barely there when *Rodin* comes into his daughter's room; he takes her into the one already mentioned, the two women of the house repair to it. And there, the lascivious *Rodin*, having no longer to keep within limits, abandons himself at his ease and without any veil to all the irregularities of his debauchery. The two peasants, being stark-naked, are lashed with all the might of his arm; while he is acting upon one, the other pays it back to him, and during the intervals, he loads with the filthiest, the most moderate, the most disgusting caresses the same altar in *Rosalie*, who, raised upon an arm-chair, presents it to him, somewhat bent downwards. This unfortunate girl's turn comes next: *Rodin* attaches her to the post as his pupils, and while his women, one after the other and sometimes both together, are tearing himself, he lashes his daughter, striping her from the middle of her loins to the bottom of her thighs, on falling into raptures of pleasure. Extreme is his excitement, he yells, blasphemes, scourges; he stamps his rods nowhere that his lips are not at once stuck there. Both the inside of the altar, and the victim's mouth . . . all, except the front, all is devoured by eager kisses; soon, without varying the posture, contenting himself with rendering it more propitious, *Rodin* penetrates into the narrow sanctuary of pleasures. His governess offers the same throne to his kisses during this time; the other girl lashes him as long as she has strength; *Rodin* is in his glory, he divides in two, he tears; a thousand kisses the one warmer than the other express his heat, on what is presented to his lust; the shell explodes, and the drunken libertine dares taste of the sweetest pleasures in the bosom of incest and infamy.

*Rodin* went and placed himself at table: he was in need of repairing his forces after such exploits. There were again class and correction in the evening; I might observe fresh scenes and I desired, but I had quite enough of them to be convinced and to prepare my answer for the offers of this wretch. The time I was to give it was drawing nigh. Two days after these events, he came himself into my room for it. He took me by surprise in bed. The pretext of seeing if there remained any traces of my wounds, gave him, without my being able to oppose it, the right of examining me naked; and as he did as much twice a day for a month, without my having as yet perceived anything in him that could offend chastity, I did not think I should resist. But *Rodin* had other schemes, this time; when he arrived at the object of his worship, he passes one of his thighs around my loins, and presses it so strong, that I find myself, as it were, beyond defence. "*Therese*," said he to me then on passing his hands so as to leave me no further doubt, "there you are cured, my dear; you may now prove me the gratitude with which I have seen your heart filled; the manner is easy, all that is wanted is this," continued the traitor on placing me in a position with all the force he could muster up.... "Yes, merely this, that is my reward, I never exact more than this from women. . . . But," continued he, "this is one of the finest I have seen in my life. . . . How round! what suppleness! . . . how smooth the skin is! . . . Oh! I absolutely wish to enjoy it. . . ." *Rodin* on saying this, being apparently ready for the execution of his schemes, in order to succeed in accomplishing them is obliged to let me loose a moment; I take advantage of the means he grants me, and freeing myself from his arms; — "Sir," said I to him, "I beg you to be thoroughly convinced that there is nothing in the whole world, that could entice me into the horrors you seem to require. My gratitude is due to you, I admit, but I shall not pay it off at the expense of a crime. I am poor and very unhappy no

doubt; never mind, there is the trifle of money I possess," I continue
on offering him my mean purse; "take what you think fit, and let
me quit this house, I beg you, since I am in a way to do so."

*Rodin*, confounded by a resistance he was but little expecting
from a girl deprived of resources, and whom, according to the
usual injustices of men, he supposed to be honest from the fact of
her being in misery; *Rodin*, I say, looks at me attentively. —
"*Therese*," he began again at the end of an instant, "it is pretty wrong
out of season for thee to act the Vestal with me; I had, it seems to
me, some rights to complacencies from thee; no matter, keep thy
money, but do not leave me. I am very glad to have a good girl in
my house, those that surround me are but so little so! . . . Since
thou showest thyself so virtuous in this case, thou wilt be so, I hope,
likewise in all. My interests will be found therein; my daughter loves
thee, she has just now besought me to prevail upon thee not to
leave us; remain therefore with us, I invite thee." — "Sir," I replied,
"I would not be happy here; the two women who wait on you aspire
to all the sentiments that it is in your power to grant them; they
will not behold me without being jealous, and I shall be forced
sooner or later to leave you." — "Do not apprehend it," replied
*Rodin* to me, "fear none of the effects of these women's jealousy; I
shall know how to keep them in their place while maintaining
thine, and thou alone shalt possess my confidence without the
resulting therefrom of any risk for thee. But in order to continue
worthy of it, it is well that thou shouldst know the first quality I
require of thee, *Therese*, is a discretion against every proof. Many
things take place here, very many which will annoy thy principles
of virtue; thou must see everything and never say anything. . . . Ah!
stay with me, *Therese*, stay here, my child, I gladly keep thee; in the
midst of a lot of vices into which a fiery temper, an unbridled mind
and a very spoiled heart carry me, I shall at least have the
consolation of possessing one virtuous being near me, and into
whose lap I shall cast myself as at the feet of God, when I am satiated
with my debaucheries. . . ." Oh! Heavens . . ., thought I on this
moment, virtue is therefore necessary, it is therefore indispensable
for man, since the vicious man himself is obliged to be re-assured

by it, and to make use of it as of a cover? Recalling to my mind next the prayers *Rosalie* had made me not to leave her, and fancying that I recognised some good principles in *Rodin*, I decidedly hired in his service. "*Therese*," *Rodin* said to me, at the end of a few days, "it is with my daughter I am going to put thee; in this way, thou wilt have no meddling with my two other women, and I give thee three hundred livres for wages." Such a place was a kind of fortune in my position; inflamed with the desire to bring *Rosalie* back to the good, and perhaps her father himself, if I gained any influence over him, I did not repent for what I had just done. . . . *Rodin* having made me dress myself, led me on the very instant to his daughter, on announcing to her that he was giving me to her; *Rosalie* received me with the greatest transports of joy, and I was speedily installed.

Eight days had not passed without my beginning to work at the conversions I desired, but *Rodin*'s obduracy spoiled all my schemes.

— "Do not fancy," he used to reply to my wise counsels, "that the kind of homage I have rendered to virtue, in thee, is a proof, that I either esteem virtue, or have a mind to prefer it to vice. Do not imagine it, *Therese*, thou wouldst deceive thyself; those who, starting from what I have done with regard to thee, would maintain, according to this proceeding, the importance of the necessity of virtue, would fall into a great error, and I would be very sorry that thou shouldst believe such is my way of thinking. The hut which serves me as a shelter in hunting, when the two scorching rays of the sun dart perpendicularly on my person, is certainly not a useful monument, its necessity is only of circumstance: I expose myself to a sort of danger, I find something that saves me, I make use of it, but is this something nevertheless useless? can it be less despicable? In wholly vicious society, virtue would be good for nothing: ours not being of this kind, it is absolutely necessary either to play upon it, or to make use of it, in order to have less to fear from those who follow it. Let nobody adopt it, it will become useless. I am not therefore wrong when I assert that its necessity is only of opinion, or of circumstance; virtue is not a fashion of an incontestable price, it is but a manner of conducting one's self, which varies according to each climate and which consequently has nothing real: that alone proves its uselessness. That only which is constant is really good; that which perpetually changes could not pretend to the character of goodness. That is why they have placed immutability in the rank of the perfections of the Eternal; but virtue is wholly deprived of this character: there are not two nations, on the face of the globe, which are virtuous in the same way, therefore virtue has nothing real, nothing intrinsically good, and nowise deserves our worship; it is necessary to use it as a stay, to politically adopt that of the country in which one lives, in order that those who practice it from taste, or who ought to revere it from state, may leave you in peace, and in order that this virtue, respected where you are, guarantee you by its preponderance of *convention,* against the attempts of those who profess vice. But again: all this is of circumstances, and nothing of all that assigns one real merit to virtue. There is such a virtue, moreover, impossible to certain men; now, how can you persuade me that a virtue which combats or which annoys the passions, can be found in Nature? And if it is not herein, how can it be good? Surely there will be among the men of whom there is question, the vices opposed to these virtues, which will become preferable, since these are only the modes, . . . the only ways of being which will arrange themselves best to their physic or their organs; there will be then some very useful vices in this hypothesis: now how will virtue be so, if you prove to me that its contraries may be so? As to this you are told: virtue is useful to others, and in this sense it is good; for if it is admitted to merely do to others what is good, I shall in my turn receive only good. This reasoning is merely a sophism: for the little good I receive from others, by means of their practicing virtue through the obligation of practicing it in my turn, I make a million sacrifices which in no way repay me. Receiving less than I bestow, I therefore make a very bad bargain; I experience much more evil from the privations I endure for being virtuous, than the good I receive from those that are so; the arrangement being unequal, I ought not therefore submit to it, and sure, being virtuous, of not doing so much good to others as the troubles I should gain in forcing myself to be so, would not be therefore better for me to give over procuring them a happiness which is to cost me so much ill? There now remains the wrong I could do others being vicious, and the evil I will receive in my turn, if everybody is like me. In admitting a whole circulation of vices, I assuredly risk, I grant; but the chagrin experienced by what I risk is compensated by the pleasure of what I make others risk; behold thenceforward equality established, henceforth everybody is almost equally happy: which is not nor could be in a society in which some are good, others wicked, because there results from this mixture perpetual snares which do not exist in the other case. In the mixed society, all the interests are diverse: behold the source of an infinity of woes; in the other association, all the interests are equal, each individual that composes it is endowed with the same tastes, the same propensities, all march towards the same end; all are happy. But fools tell you, evil does not render one happy. No, when one has agreed on praising the good; but depreciate, abase what you call the good, you will no longer reverence except what you had the folly of calling the evil; and all men will have pleasure in committing it, not because it will be permitted (this would be sometimes a reason for diminishing its charm), but it is because they lessen, through the fear they inspire, the pleasure which Nature has placed in crime. I suppose a society in which it is understood that incest let us admit this crime as any other), that incest, I say, is a crime: those that abandon themselves to it will be unhappy, because opinions, laws, worship, all will come to freeze up their pleasures; those who will desire to commit this evil, and who will not attempt it, according to the curbs, will be equally unhappy; thus the law which will prescribe incest will have only made unfortunate ones. In the next society let incest be not a crime: those who will not desire it will not be unhappy, and those who will desire it will be happy. Therefore the society which will have permitted this action will suit men better than that one which will have raised this same action to a crime. It is the same with all the other actions wrongly considered as criminal: on examining them under this point of view, you make a crowd of unhappy people; in permitting them, nobody complains; for he who likes this action whatever it be delivers himself up to it in peace, and he who does not care about it, either remains in a sort of indifference which is nowise painful, or pays himself for the wrong he may have received, by a host of other wrongs by which he aggrieves in his turn those of whom he has had to complain. Therefore everybody in a criminal society finds himself either very unhappy, or in a state of carelessness which has nothing painful; consequently, nothing good, nothing respectable, nothing done to render happy in what they call virtue. Let those who follow it not swell with pride then at this kind of homage, that the constitution of our societies forces us to render it; it is purely an affair of circumstances, of convention; but in fact, this worship is chimerical, and the virtue which obtains it an instant is not any fairer on that account."

Such was the infernal logic of *Rodin*'s unfortunate passions; but *Rosalie*, milder and much less corrupted, *Rosalie*, detesting the horrors to which she was subjected, ceded with greater docility to my advice: I ardently longed to get her to discharge her first duties of Religion. It would have been necessary for this to get a priest into the confidence, and *Rodin* would not have one of them in his house, he held them in horror as well as the worship they professed: he would not for anything in the world have suffered any of them near his daughter. It was equally impossible to take this young slip to a Director: *Rodin* never allowed *Rosalie* to go out without her being accompanied. It was therefore necessary to wait until some opportunity presented itself; and during these delays, I used to instruct her; in giving her a taste for virtues, I inspired her with that of Religion, I unveiled to her the holy dogmas and the sublime mysteries, I united these two sentiments so closely in her young heart, that I rendered them indispensable for the happiness of her life.

"O Miss," said I to her one day on reaping the tears of her compunction, "can man be blinded to so great an extent as not to think himself destined to a better end? Is it not enough for him to be endowed with the power and faculty of knowing his God, to be assured that this favor has been only granted him that he may discharge the duties it imposes? Now, what may be the base of the worship due to the Eternal, if it is not the virtue of which he himself is the example? Can the Creator of so many wonders have any other laws but the good? And can our hearts please him if the good is not their element? It seems to me that with sensible souls, no other motive of love towards this Supreme Being should be used except those that gratitude inspires. Is it not a favor to have made us to enjoy the beauties of the Universe, and do we not owe him some gratitude for such a benefit? But a stronger reason still establishes, proves the universal chain of our duties: why should we refuse to discharge those that his law requires, since they are the same as those which consolidate our happiness with men? Is it not sweet to feel that we render ourselves worthy of the Supreme Being, simply on exercising the virtues which ought to effect our contentment on earth, and that the means which make us worthy of living with our likenesses, are the same as those which give us after this life the assurance of being regenerated near the throne of God? Ah! *Rosalie,* how blinded are those that would wish to despoil us of this hope! Deceived, seduced by their horrible passions, they prefer to deny the eternal truths, than to abandon that which can render them worthy of them. They choose to say: *People deceive us,* rather than acknowledge that they deceive themselves; the idea of the losses they prepare for themselves would trouble their unworthy voluptuousnesses; it seems less frightful to them to destroy the hope of Heaven, than to deprive themselves of what ought to acquire it for them! But when those tyrannical passions grow dim in them, when the veil is rent asunder, when nothing wavers any longer in their corrupted hearts that imperious voice of the God whom their delirium disregarded, how this recoiling, O *Rosalie,* on themselves must be cruel! and how the remorse which attends it must make them pay dearly for the instant error that blinded them! That is the state in which man must be judged that we regulate our own conduct: it is neither in the intoxication, nor in the transport of a burning fever that we should believe what he states; it is when his reason being calmed down, enjoying the full force of his energy, seeks the truth, divines and beholds it. We then desire of ourselves this holy Being formerly disregarded; we implore him, he consoles us; we pray to him, he hears us. Ah, why then should I deny him? Why disregard him, that object so necessary for happiness? Why should I prefer to say with the lost man: *There is no God,* whilst the heart of the reasonable man offers me every instant proofs of this Divine Being's existence? Is it then better to rave with fools, than to think rightly with wise men? Nevertheless all flows from this first principle: since there exists a God, this God deserves a worship, and the first base of this worship is incontestably Virtue."

From the first truths I easily deduced others, and *Rosalie*, once deist, was soon a Christian. But what means, I repeat, of joining a little practice with the morals? *Rosalie*, being obliged to obey her father, could not show for it but disgust at most, and with a man like *Rodin*, might this not become dangerous? He was untractable; none of my systems held out against him; but if I did not succeed in convincing him, he did not at least shake my faith.

Yet, such a school, so constant dangers, so real, caused me to quake for *Rosalie*, to such a degree that I did not think myself at all guilty in persuading her to flee this perverse house. It seemed to me there was less harm in tearing her from her incestuous father's bosom, than to leave her there running the chance of all the risks that might befall her there. I had already lightly touched on this question, and I was not perhaps far from succeeding in it, when all of a sudden *Rosalie* disappeared from the house, without its being possible to know where she was. Did I interrogate the women at *Rodin*'s, or *Rodin* himself, they assured me that she had gone to pass the fine season at a relation's place, ten miles off. Did I inquire in the neghborhood, the people were at first astonished at a like question set by one of the house, then they answered me like *Rodin* and his servants: people had seen her, embraced her on the eve, even on the day of her departure; and I got the same answers everywhere. When I asked *Rodin* why this departure had been concealed from me, why I had not followed my mistress, he assured me the sole reason had been to prevent a painful scene for both of us, and that I would certainly see her again whom I loved. It was necessary to be satisfied with these replies, but to be convinced by them was more difficult. Was it presumable that *Rosalie*, *Rosalie* who loved me so dearly! would have consented to leave me without mentioning a word to me? And, according to what I knew of *Rodin*'s character, was there not very much to apprehend for the destiny of this unfortunate girl? I therefore resolved to put everything into practice to find out what had become of her, and to arrive thereat, all means seemed good to me.

On the following day, being alone in the house, I carefully ran through all its nooks; I fancy I hear some moans from the bottom of a very dark cellar. . . . I draw nigh, a heap of wood appeared to block up a narrow and remote doorway; I advance on removing all obstacles . . . fresh sounds become heard; I fancy I recognize the voice. . . . I lend an ear. . . . I no longer doubt. "*Therese,*" do I hear at last, "O *Therese,* is it you?" — "Yes, dear and loving friend," I cried, on recognizing the voice of *Rosalie.* . . . "Yes, it is *Therese* whom heaven sends to relieve thee; . . ." and my flood of questions hardly leaves this interesting girl time to answer me. I learn at last that a few hours previous to her disappearing, *Rombeau,* the friend and colleague of *Rodin,* had examined her naked, and that she had received the order from her father to lend herself with this *Rombeau* for the same horrors as *Rodin* exacted from her every day; that she had resisted, but *Rodin,* being furious, had seized and presented her himself to his colleague's lewd attempts; that the two friends had then whispered a very long while together, leaving her still naked, and coming occasionally to examine her again, to still enjoy her in this same criminal manner, or to ill-use her in a hundred different ways; that finally, after four or five hours of this meeting, *Rodin* had told her that he was going to send her to the country to one of his relative's houses, but that she could set out at once and without speaking to *Therese,* for reasons he would explain to her himself next day in this country seat where he would immediately go and meet her. He had made *Rosalie* understand that it was about marriage for her, and that it was owing to this that his friend *Rombeau* had examined her, in order to see whether she was in a state of becoming a mother. *Rosalie* had really departed under the care of an old woman; she had traversed the borough, bade farewell on her way to several acquaintances; but as soon as night had come on, her guide had led her back to her father's house, where she had entered at midnight. *Rodin,* who was awaiting her, had seized her, and with his hand stopped up her mouth, and had without saying a word cast her into this cellar, where they had however fed and cared for her pretty well ever since her being there.

"I fear everything," added this poor girl; "my father's behaviour since then, his conversations, that which had preceded *Rombeau*'s examination, everything proves that those monsters are about to make use of me for some of their experiments, and it is all over with thy poor *Rosalie*." After the tears which flowed abundantly from my eyes, I asked this poor girl if she knew where they used to put the key of this cellar; she did not know, but she did not think however that they used to carry it away. I looked for it on all sides, it was in vain; and the hour for re-appearing arrived without my being able to afford this dear child any other helps than consolations, some hopes and tears. She made me swear that I would come next day; I promised her I would, even assuring her that if I had not then discovered anything satisfactory about what concerned her, I should at once leave the house, I would lodge my complaints before the Justice, and would set her free, cost whatever it might, from the horrible destiny which was menacing her.

I go upstairs again; *Rombeau* was taking supper that evening with *Rodin*. Being fully up to everything, in order to get an insight into my mistress's destiny, I hide myself near the apartment where the two friends were, and their topics only too well convince me of the awful scheme which was occupying both of them.

"Never," said *Rodin*, "will anatomy be at its latest degree of perfection, until the examination of the arteries is made on a child of fourteen or fifteen years old, having died a cruel death; it is only from this contraction that we can obtain a complete analysis of so interesting a party." — "It is the same," replied *Rombeau*, "for the membrane which guarantees virginity; we necessarily want a little girl for this experiment. What do we observe in the age of puberty? nothing; woman's monthly terms mangle hymen, and all the researches remain inaccurate. Thy daughter is precisely what we want; although she is fifteen, she has not had her flowers; the way in which we have enjoyed her does not in any manner harm this membrane, and we shall handle her at our ease. I am delighted that thou hast at last made up thy mind."

— "Of course I have," replied *Rodin*; "it is hateful that absurd consideration should stop thus the progress of the sciences; have great men allowed themselves to be captivated by such despicable ties? And when *Michael Angelo* wanted to paint a Christ after nature, did he make it a case of conscience to crucify a young man, and copy him in agonies? But when there is question of our art, of what necessity ought not these same means to be! And how much less evil is there to be allowed them! It is one subject sacrificed to save a million; should we waver at this price? If the murder operated through the laws of any other kind save that which we are going to effect, and is not the object of these laws, which people find wise, the sacrifice of one in order to save a thousand?" — "This is the only way of instructing ourselves," said *Rombeau*; "and I have witnessed in the hospitals where I worked during my early age, a thousand similar experiments; I was afraid that, owing to the ties which endear thee to that creature, I do confess, thou mightest waver."

— "Why! because she is my daughter? A fine reason!" cried *Rodin*; "and what rank dost thou imagine then that this title ought to have in my heart? I look upon a trifle of engendered seed, with the same eye (allowance made for the weight) as that which it pleases me to lose in my pleasures. I never made more ado about the one than about the other. One is the master to take back what he has given; the right of disposing of one's children, has never been disputed among any nation on the earth. The Persians, Medes, Armenians, Greeks enjoyed it in its whole extent. The laws of *Lycurgus,* the model of Legislators, not only left to the fathers all rights over their children, but also condemned to death those that the parents did not wish to bring up, or those that were deformed. A great party of Savages kill their children as soon as they are born. Nearly all the women of Asia, Africa and America cause themselves to miscarry without incurring any blame; *Cook* found this custom throughout all the South-Sea islands. *Romulus* permitted infanticide; the laws of the Twelve Tables likewise tolerated it, and up to *Constantine,* the Romans exposed or killed their children with impunity. *Aristotle* advises this pretended crime; the sect of Stoics looked on it as praiseworthy; it is still in vigour among the Chinese. Every day are to be found both in the streets and canals of Pekin, more than ten thousand individuals immolated or abandoned by their parents, and whatever be a child's age in this wise Empire, a father needs only, in order to get rid of it, to place it in the hands of the Judge. According to the laws of Parthes, people used to kill their sons, daughters or brothers, even at a marriageable age; Caesar found this custom general among the Galls; several passages of the *Pentateuch* prove that it was permitted to kill one's children among God's people; and finally God himself exacted it from *Abraham*. It was for a long time thought, says a celebrated modern author, that the prosperity of empires depended on the servitude of children; this opinion had for basis the principles of the soundest reason. Well! a monarch will fancy himself authorized to sacrifice twenty or thirty thousand of his subjects in one sole day for his own cause, and father can not, when he thinks fit become master of the life of his children! What absurdity! What incongruity and what weakness in those who are held back by such ties. The authority of the father over his children, being the only real one, the only one which has served as bases for all the others, is dictated to us by the very voice of Nature, and the profound study of her operations at every instant offers us examples of it. The *Czar Peter* did not at all doubt of this right; he made use of it, and addressed a public declaration to all the Order of his Empire, by which he said that, according to the divine and human laws, a father had entire and absolute right of judging his children to death, without appeal and without taking the advice of whomsoever. It is only in our barbarous France where a false and ridiculous pity fancied that this right should be enchained. No," continued *Rodin* warmly, "no, my friend, I shall never understand how a father, who was eager to bestow life, is not free to bestow death. It is the ridiculous price that was set on this life, which everlastingly causes us to talk nonsense about the kind of action which engages one man to rid himself of his fellow-man. Thinking that existence is the greatest of goods, we stupidly imagine that we are committing a crime on doing away with those who are enjoying it; but the ceasing of this existence, or at least what follows it, is no more an evil than life is a good; or rather if nothing dies, if nothing is destroyed, if nothing is lost in Nature, if all the decomposed parts of any body only await the dissolution to re-appear immediately under fresh forms, what indifference will there not be in the action of murder, and how will people have the bold-ness of finding any harm in it? Were there therefore only question here of my own fantasy, I should consider the thing as quite simple, a *fortiori* when it becomes necessary for an art so useful to men. . . . When it may supply such important lights, it is henceforth no longer an evil, my friend it is no longer a forfeit; it is the best, wisest, the most useful of all actions, and it would be only in depriving one's self of it that there could exist any crime."

— "Ah!" said *Rombeau*, filled with enthusiasm for such frightful maxims, "I approve of thee, my dear; thy wisdom enchants me, but thy indifference astonishes me, I thought thou wast amorous. — I! in love with a girl?. . . Ah! *Rombeau*, I fancied thou knewest me bet-ter; I make use of those creatures when I have nothing better: the extreme proclivity I have for pleasures of the kind of which thou beholdest me taste, renders all the temples, where this sort of incense may be offered, precious to me; and, in order to increase them, I sometimes assimulate a little girl to a fine boy. But when one of these female individuals has unfortunately fed ever so little my illusion too long, the disgust declares itself energetically, and I never knew but one means of deliciously satisfying it. . . . Thou understanest me, *Rombeau*; *Chilperic*, the most voluptuous of the Kings of France, was of the same opinion. He used to boldly assert that one could, when the worst comes to the worst, make use of a woman, but on the express condition of doing away with her as soon as one had enjoyed her[(7)]. This little play-thing has served for my pleasures these five years: it is time she should pay for the ceasing of my intoxication by that of her existence."

The repast was drawing to a close; I clearly saw by the gait of these two furious villains, by their talk, their actions, their prepa-rations, in fine by their state which partook of delirium, that there was not a moment to be lost, and that the time for the destruction of this unhappy *Rosalie* was fixed for the same evening. I fly to the cellar, being resolved to die or set her free. — "O dear friend," I cried to her, "not a moment to be lost . . . the monsters! . . . it is for this evening . . . they are going to come. . . ." And on saying this, I make the most violent efforts to burst in the door. One of my shakes causes something to fall down, I put my hand to it, it is the key; I pick it up, I hasten to open. . . . I embrace *Rosalie*, I urge her to fly, I answer her that I shall follow her steps, she rushes off. . . . Good Heavens! it was again stated that Virtue should succumb, and that the tenderest sentiments of compassion were about to be severely punished. . . . *Rodin* and *Rombeau*, being informed by the governess, appear on a sudden; the former seizes his daughter the moment she is clearing the threshold of the door, beyond which she had only a few more steps to take to be free. — "Where art thou going, unfortunate thing?" cried *Rodin* on stopping her, whilst *Rombeau* lays hold of me. . . . "Ah!" continues he on staring me, "it is that jade that assists her flight! *Therese*, that is then the effect of your mighty principles of virtue . . . to rob a father of his daughter!" — "Certainly" I firmly replied, "and I ought to do so, when this father is barbarous enough to plot against the life of his daughter." — "Ah! ah! eavesdropper and seducer," continued *Rodin*; "all the most dangerous vices in a servant! let us go upstairs, we must consider this business." *Rosalie* and I being dragged by these two villains, reach the apartments; the doors are shut. The unhappy girl is tied to the bed-posts, and the whole rage of these frantic fellows is turned on me; I am loaded with the most abusive invectives, and the most dreadful sentences are pronounced; there was question of nothing less than to dissect me all alive, in order to examine the heart-beating, and make on this party observations impracticable on a dead body. During this time they undress me, and I become a prey to the most unchaste handlings. — "Before all," said *Rombeau*, "I am of opinion to boldly attack the fortress which thy kind proceedings respected. . . . Why, it is delightful; admire then the mellowness, the whiteness of these two half-moons which bar its entrance: never was a virgin fresher." — "Virgin! but she is almost one," said *Rodin*. . . . "She was violated once alone in spite of her, and not the slightest thing since. Yield the post to me for an instant. . . ." And the wretch mingles the homage of these cruel and fierce caresses which degrade the idol instead of honoring it. Had there been there any rods, I would have been harshly treated. They spoke of them, but none were to be had, they contented themselves with what thy could do with their hands; I was stormed. . . . The more I defended myself, the faster I was held; when I saw however that they were about to decide on more serious steps, I flung myself at the feet of my ravishers, I offered them my life, and begged them for honor. — "But, since thou art not a maiden," said *Rombeau*, "what matter does it make? thou wilt be guilty of nothing; we are going to violate thee as thou has been already, and henceforth not the slightest sin on thy conscience; it will be force which shall have ravished thee of everything. . . ." And the infamous villain, while consoling me in this hard hearted manner, was already laying me upon the sofa. — "No," said *Rodin* on stopping the effervescence of his colleague whose victim I was on the point of becoming, "no, let us not waste our forces with that creature, remember how we can not defer any longer the proposed operations on *Rosalie*, and our strength is necessary for us in order to come at them: let us punish the unfortunate girl in some other way." On saying this, *Rodin* puts an iron-bar into the fire. "Yes," continues he, "let us punish her a thousand times more than if we took away her life, let us brand her, let us tatoo her; this abasement, together with all the bad things she has to her account, will have her hanged or starved; she will suffer at least until then, and our vengeance, being the further prolonged, will become the more delightful on this account," he spoke; *Rombeau* seizes me, and the abominable *Rodin* applies behind my shoulder the red iron with which robbers are branded. "Let her dare show herself now, the jade," continues this monster, "let her dare do so, and on showing this ignominious letter, I shall sufficiently legitimate the reasons which caused me to send her away so secretly and promptly."

They dress my wounds, they put on my clothes, they fortify me with a few drops of liquor, and taking advantage of the darkness of the night, the two friends convey me to the skirts of the forest, and cruelly abandon me there, after having further made me see the danger of a recrimination, if I dare undertake it in the state of abasement I was in.

Any other but myself would have cared very little about this menace; from the moment it was possible for me to prove that the treatment I had just suffered was the work of no tribunals, what had I to fear? But my weakness, my natural bashfulness, the dread of my misfortunes in Paris, and those of the *Castle de Bressac*, all, all astounded me, all frightened me; I thought only of flying away, far more affected by the grief of forsaking an innocent victim in the hands of these two villains ready to immolate her no doubt, than grieved for my own ills. More annoyed, more afflicted than physically ill-used, I set out on the same instant; but not considering where I was, inquiring after nothing, I only went round Paris, and on my fourth day's journey, I was merely at Lieusaint. Knowing that this route could lead me towards the southern provinces, I then resolved to follow it, and so to reach, as best I could those distant regions, fancying that peace and rest, so cruelly denied to me in my own land, were perhaps awaiting me at the end of France. Fatal mistake! how many chagrins there still remained for me to experience!

Whatever may have been my pains until then, I had at least my innocence left me. Solely the victim of the attempts of a few monsters, I could, nevertheless, still consider myself as being almost in the class of honest girls. In fact, I had only been truly stained by a rape committed five years ago, the traces of which were closed up again . . . a rape consummated in an instant when my stunned senses had not even left me the faculty of feeling it. What had I besides to reproach myself with? Nothing, oh! undoubtedly nothing, and my heart was pure; I was too glorious, my presumption was to be punished, and the outrages which were awaiting me were about to become such as it soon be no longer possible for me, however slightly I participated in them, to form in the bottom of my heart the same subjects of consolation.

I had all my fortune about me this time: namely, about one hundred crown-pieces, amount resulting from what I had saved up at *Bressac*'s, and from what I had earned with *Rodin*. In the excess of my misfortune, I still found myself happy because these helps had not been taken away from me; I was flattering my self that with the frugality, temperance, economy to which I was accustomed, this money would suffice for me at least until I was in a situation of being able to procure some place. The execration that they had caused me did not appear to view; I fancied I could always conceal it, and that this blemish would not hinder me from earning my bread. I was twenty-six years old, of good health, of a shape which, for my misfortune, people only praised too much; a few virtues which, although they had always done me harm, yet consoled me, as I have just told you, and caused me to hope that at least Heaven would bestow on them if not rewards, at least some respite from the ills which they had drawn on me. Filled with hope and courage, I continued my way as far as Sens, where I rested myself a couple of days. In one week I was completely recovered, perhaps I might have found some place in this town, but, impressed by the necessity of going away, I set out with the intention of seeking my fortune in Dauphiny; I had heard much about this country, I fancied happiness was there. We are going to see how I succeeded in it.

The sentiments of Religion had, in no circumstances of my life, abandoned me. Despising the vain sophisms of free-thinkers, believing them all the outcome of libertinism much rather than from a firm persuasion, I opposed to them my conscience and heart, and found by means of both all that was necessary to answer them. Being often times obliged through my misfortunes to neglect my acts of piety, I repaired for these wrongs as soon as I had an opportunity.

I had just departed from Auxerre on the 7th August: I shall never forget this date; I had gone about two leagues, and the heat beginning to trouble me, I ascended a little height covered with a wood-grove, not far from the road, with the intention of refreshing myself and of sleeping a couple of hours in it, for less expense than at an inn, and in better safety than on the highway; I pitched my tent at the foot of an oak, and after a frugal breakfast, I indulge in a short nap. I had enjoyed it for a long while in peace, when opening my eyes, I take pleasure in contemplating the landscape which presents itself to me in the distance. From the midst of a forest, which stretched away to the right, I thought I beheld at nearly three or four leagues from me, a small belfry modestly rising in the air. . . . Lovely solitude, say I to myself how thy abode causes me envy! thou must be the refuge of some mild and virtuous cloistered nuns who busy themselves only about God . . . their duties; or of some holy Hermits solely consecrated to Religion. . . . Removed from that pernicious Society in which crime, incessantly on the lookout for innocence, degrades and destroys it . . . ah! all the virtues must dwell there, I am sure, and when the crimes of man banish them from off the earth, it is there, it is within this lonely retreat they go to be buried in the bosoms of fortunate beings who cherish and cultivate them every day.

I was lost in these thoughts, when a girl of my own age, herding sheep on this woodland height, all at once presents herself to my view; I interrogate her about this dwelling, she tells me that what I am looking at is a Benedictine Convent, occupied by four anchorites whose religion, chastity and sobriety nothing equals. "People go there," this girl tells me, "once a year on pilgrimage to a miraculous Virgin, from whom pious folks obtain everything they wish." Being strangely touched by the desire of going at once and implore some assistance at this Holy Mother of God, I ask this young girl whether she wishes to come there and pray with me; she answers me how that is impossible for her, how her mother is waiting for her; but that the way is easy. She points it out to me, she assures me that the Superior of this house, being the most respectable and holy of men, will recieve me admirably well, and will offer me all the assistance which may be needful for me: "They call him *Dom Severino*," continued this girl; "is an Italian a near relation of the Pope's, who loads him with gifts; he is mild, honest, serviceable, fifty-five years old, more than the two-thirds of which he has spent in France. . . . You will be pleased with him, Miss," continued the shepherdess; "go and be edified in that saintly solitude, and you will come back from it only better."

This recital inflaming still more my zeal, it became impossible for me to resist the longing desire I had to go and visit this holy church, and repair therein by some pious acts for the negligence of which I was guilty. Whatever need I had myself of charity, I give a crown-piece to this girl, and here I am on the road to *Sainte-Marie-des-Bois:* such was the name of the Convent towards which I directed my steps.

As soon as I had gone down into the plain, I no longer perceived the belfry; I had but the forest to guide me, and then I began to think that the distance, of which I had forgotten to inquire, was quite different from the estimate I had taken of it; but nothing discourages me, I arrive at the end of the forest, and seeing I have still day-light enough left me, I resolve to enter it, still imagining that I can reach the Convent before night. Yet no human trace presents itself to my eyes. . . . Not a house, and the only route a path but slightly trodden which I followed at random. I had already made at least five leagues, and as yet I saw nothing offering itself to view, when the sun having wholly ceased to brighten the universe, it seemed to me I heard the sound of a bell. . . . I listen, I advance towards the noise, I make haste, the path becomes somewhat larger, I behold at least a few hedges, and shortly afterwards the Convent. Nothing wilder looking than this solitude: no dwelling near it, the nearest was six leagues off, and immense woods encompassed the mansion; it was situated in a hollow, I had to descend a great deal to come to it, and such was the reason of my having lost sight of the belfry, when I was in the plain. A gardener's cottage was adjacent to the Convent walls; it was there people applied previous to entering. I ask this kind of a porter whether it is permitted to speak to the Superior; he inquires what I want with him; I give him to understand that a religious duty attracts me to this pious retreat, and that I would be thoroughly consoled for all the hardships I had taken in order to arrive, if I could cast myself an instant at the feet of the miraculous Virgin and holy Clergyman in whose house this divine image is kept. The gardner rings and goes into the Convent; but as it was late and the fathers were at supper, he is sometime before coming back. He at last re-appears with one of the Monks.

— "Miss," he says to me, "there is *Dom Clement,* the procurator of the house; he comes to see if what you want is worth the trouble of disturbing the superior."

*Clement,* whose name did not in the least accord with his person, was a man of forty-eight years old, of a huge bulk, of a gigantic size, with dark and savage looks, expressing himself only in rough, sharp words through a hoarse voice, a true figure of a satyr, the exterior of a tyrant; he caused me to shudder. . . . Then, without its being possible for me to defend myself from him, the remembrance of my former woes rushed back to my troubled mind in gory darts. . . . — "What do you want?" says the Monk to me, with the sourest countenance, "is this the time to come into a church?. . . You look very like an adventuress." — "Holy man," said I on casting myself at his feet, "I thought it was always time for presenting ourselves at God's house; I ran from afar to come to it, filled with fervor and devotion; I beg to be confessed if it is possible, and when the interior of my conscience will be known to you, you shall see whether I am worthy or not to throw myself at the feet of the holy Image." — "But this is not the time to confess," said the Monk on softening down, "where shall you spend the night? We have no night refuge . . . it was better for you to come in the morning." To this I gave him the reasons which had hindered me from doing so, and, without answering me *Clement* went off to render an account of them to the Superior. A gew minutes after, the church is opened; *Dom Severino* comes himself, towards the Gardener's cottage, and invites me to enter the temple with him.

*Dom Severino,* of whom it is well to give you an idea at once, was a man of fifty-five years old, as I had been told, but of very handsome appearance, his countenance still fresh, shaped into a vigorous man, as strong as Hercules, and all that without harshness; a sort of elegance and grace reigned throughout all his parts, and let one see that he must have possessed, in his youth, all the attractions which form a fine man. He had the prettiest eyes in the world, nobleness in his features, and the most upright, comely, polite tone. A sort of pleasing accent, of which not a single one of his words was corrupted, caused one however to recognise his country, and, I acknowledge, all the exterior charms of this monk recovered me somewhat from the fright the other had given me.

— "My dear girl," he kindly says to me, "although it is an unreasonable hour, and we are not accustomed to receive so late, I shall nevertheless hear your confession, and shall advise you afterwards about the means of getting you to pass the night decently, until the moment when you can kneel tomorrow to the holy Image which attracts you here." We are entering the church; the doors are closed; a lamp near the confessional box is lit. *Severino* bids me take my place; he sits down, and persuades me to confess myself to him with all confidence.

Being thoroughly encouraged with a man who appeared to me so gentle, after having humbled myself, I hide nothing from him. I confess him all my faults. I inform him of all my misfortunes; I disclose to him even to the shameful brand with which the barbarous *Rodin* stained me. *Severino* listens to everything with the greatest attention, he even makes me repeat some particulars with a look of pity and interest; but a few motions, a few words nevertheless betray him. Alas! it was only afterwards, when I reflected better on it; when I was cooler about this event, it was impossible for me not to remember how the Monk had allowed himself several times many gests on himself which proved that his passion had much to do with the questions he was putting to me, and that these questions not only stopped complaisantly at the obscene details, but also complaisantly insisted on the five following points:

1st If it was really true that I was an orphan and born in Paris. 2nd If it was sure that I had no longer either relations, friends, protection or finally anybody to whom I might write. 3rd If I had entrusted only to the shepherdess who had spoken to me of the Convent the intention I had of coming there, and if I had not given her a rendezvous at my return. 4th If it was certain that I had seen nobody since my rape, and if I was quite sure that the man who had seduced me had done so equally with the side which Nature condemns, as with the one she permits. 5th If I thought I had not been followed, and that nobody had seen me entering the Convent.

After having these questions answered, with the most modest, sincere and natural look: "Well!" says the Monk to me on rising and taking me by the hand, "come, my child, I shall grant you the sweet satisfaction of receiving the communion to-morrow at the feet of the Image which you come to visit: let us begin by providing for your first wants;" and he leads me towards the bottom of the church. . . . — "What!" said I to him then with a sort of uneasiness of which I did not feel myself mistress. . . . "What! my father, in the inside?" — "And where then, charming pilgrim," replied the Monk to me, on introducing me into the sacristy. . . . "What! you are afraid to pass the night with four holy Hermits?. . . Oh! you shall see that we will find the means of recreating you, dear angel: and if we do not afford you very great pleasures, you will at least serve ours to their most extreme extent." Their words cause me to bounce; a cold sweat comes over me, I stagger; it was night, no light guided our steps; my frighted imagination presented to me the spectre of death poising his sithe over my head; my knees bend. . . . At this time the Monk's language suddenly changes, he props me up, on upbraiding me:— "Wench," he says to me, "you must walk; try here neither complaint, nor resistance, it will be all useless." These dire words restore me my forces, I feel I am lost, if I waver; I rise. . . . — "O Heavens!" I cry to this traitor, "must I then be still the victim of my good sentiments, and must the desire of my approaching what Religion holds as the most venerable, go to be again punished as a crime! . . ." We go on walking, and we get entangled in blind windings of which nothing can make known to me either the local or outlets. I was going before *Dom Severino*; his breathing was heavy, he was uttering inconsequent words; you would have thought him drunk; from time to time he stopped me with his left arm round my waist, whilst his right hand, slipping behind under my petticoats, impudently ran over that dishonest part which, while assimilating us to men, forms the sole object of the homages of those who prefer this sex in their shameful pleasures. This libertine's mouth even dares several times pass over these spots, in their most secret recess; then we began again to walk. A staircase presents itself; at the end of thirty or forty steps, a door opens, glimpses of light strike our eyes, we enter a splendid and magnificently lit up hall. There, I see three Monks and four girls round a table served by four women stark naked: this spectacle makes me quake; *Severino* pushes me, and behold me in the hall with him. — "Gentlemen," said he on entering, "allow me to introduce to you a real phenomenon: here is a Lucretia who at the same time bears on her shoulders the brand of bad-lived girls, and in her conscience all the frankness, all the simplicity of a maiden. . . . Only one attack of rape, my friends, and that one six years ago; she is therefore almost a Vestal . . . indeed I give her to you as such . . . besides the loveliest. . . . Oh! *Clement*, how thou art going to cheer thyself up on these fine lumps! . . . what elasticity, my friend, what carnation!" — "Ah! strum pet!" said *Clement*, half drunk, on rising and coming towards me; "the meeting is a pleasant one, and I wish to verify the facts."

I shall leave you the least possible time in suspense about my situation, Madam, said *Therese*; but the necessity I am in describing the new folks with whom I find myself, obliges me to break off for an instant the thread of my recital. You are acquainted with *Dom Severino*, you guess his tastes; alas! his depravity of this kind was such that he had never tasted any other pleasures; and yet what inconsistency in the operations of Nature, since with the strange fantasy of choosing only by-ways, this monster was supplied with faculties so huge, that even the most beaten down routes would have still appeared too narrow for him!

As to *Clement*, his sketch is already known. Add to the exterior I have described, ferocity, sordidness, the most dangerous roguery, intemperance in every way, a sarcastic and biting mind, a corrupted heart, the inhuman relishes of *Rodin* with his scholars, no sentiments, no delicacy, no religion, a temper so worn out that he was for the past five years beyond the state of procuring himself any other enjoyments but those for which his barbarity afforded him the liking, and you shall have the most complete image of this nasty man.

*Antonin,* the third actor of these detestable orgies, was forty years of age; low, thin-spared, very vigorous, as formidably organised as *Severino* and almost as bad as *Clement*; an enthusiast of the pleasures of this colleague, but delivering himself up to them at least in a less fierce intention; for if *Clement,* making use of this strange mania, had for objects only to annoy, tyrannise over women, without being able to enjoy them otherwise, *Antonin,* in using them with pleasure in all the purity of Nature, was wont to put the whipping episode into practice only to give her whom he honored with his favors, greater flame and energy.

*Jerome,* the oldest of those four anchorites, was also the most debauched of them; all tastes, all passions, all the most monstrous irregularities were found united in the soul of this Monk; he joined to the whims of the others, that of loving to receive upon himself what his colleagues used to distribute to the girls, and if he bestowed (which frequently happened to him), it was always on the conditions of being treated likewise in his turn; all the temples of enus were moreover equal to him, but his strength beginning to weaken, he would nevertheless prefer these few years the one, which requiring nothing from the agent, left to the other the care of awaking the sensations and of producing the ecstasy. The mouth was his favorite temple, and while he abandoned himself to those chosen pleasures, he employed a second woman to heat him up by aid of rods. This man's character was besides quite as sullen, quite as bad as that of the others, and under whatever form vice can be shown, it was sure of immediately finding followers and temples in this infernal house. You will understand it more easily, Madam, by explaining to you how it was formed. Prodigious funds had been got up to fix for the Order this obscene retreat existing over a hundred years, and was always inhabited by the four richest Monks, the most knowing of the Order, of the highest descent, and of a libertinism important enough to require to be buried in this dark den, the secret of which went no further, as you shall see by the sequel of the explanations which remain for me to make. Let us go back to the portraits.

The eight girls who found themselves for the time at supper were so remote by their ages, that it would be impossible for me to sketch them for you in a block; I am necessarily forced to a few particulars. This singularity astonished me. Let us begin by the youngest, I shall paint in this order.

This youngest one of the girls was scarcely ten years old: a rumpled face, pretty features, look humbled at her destiny, fearful, fretful and trembling.

The second was fourteen years of age: the same embarrassment in her looks, aspect of abased chastity, but a bewitching form, a deal of interest on the whole.

The third was twenty years of age: made to be painted, fair, the prettiest of hair, delicate features, regular and mild; appearing more tamed.

The fourth was thirty years old: she was one of the finest women it was possible to behold, frankness uprightness, decency of bearing and all the virtues of a gentle soul.

The fifth was a girl of thirty-six years old, being these three months in the family-way; dark, very lively, with pretty eyes; but having as it seemed to me, lost all remorse, all decency, all modesty.

The sixth was of the same age: stout as a block, tall in proportion, handsome features, a real colossus the shape of which was spoiled by the good plight of the belly; she was naked when I saw her, and I easily distinguished that there was not an inch of her huge body that did not bear the stamp of the brutality of the villians whose pleasures her evil luck caused her to serve.

The seventh and eighth were two very handsome women of about forty years old.

Let us now continue the story of my arrival in this filthy place.

I told you how I had hardly entered, when each one advanced towards me; *Clement* was the boldest, his polluted mouth was soon stuck to mine. I turn round with horror; but they make me understand that all these resistances are only apish tricks which become useless, and what I have best to do is to imitate my companions.

— "You easily imagine," says *Dom Severino* to me, "that it would be of no avail to try resistances in the inaccessible retreat in which you find yourself. You have, you say, experienced many misfor-

tunes; the greatest of all, for a virtuous girl, was however still lacking
on the list of your mishaps. Was it not time that this haughty virtue
should become wrecked, and can one still be almost a maiden at
twenty-two! You behold companions who, like you, on entering,
wished to resist and who, as you are wisely going to do, finished by
yielding, when he saw that their defence could but bring bad treatment on them. For it is well to make it known to you, *Therese*,"
continued the Superior, on showing me the disciples, rods, ferules,
switches, ropes and a thousand other kinds of tools of
punishment . . . "yes, it is well that you should know it: there is what
we use with rebellious girls; see if you have a mind to be convinced
of it. And besides, what would you claim here? equity? we know it
not; humanity? our only pleasures is to violate its laws; Religion? it
is null in our eyes, our contempt of it increases in proportion as we
know it the more; relations, . . . friends, . . . Judges? there is nothing
of all that in these quarters, dear girl; you will find here only selfishness, cruelty, debauchery and the best sustained impiety. The
most complete submission is therefore your only lot; cast your eyes
on the inaccessible refuge you are in; no mortal ever showed his
face in these places; let the Convent be taken, plundered, burnt
down, this retreat would all the same remain undiscovered; it is an
insulated, interred pavilion, which six walls of an incredible thickness encompass on all sides, and you are within it, my girl, in the
midst of four libertines, who certainly have not a mind to spare you,
and whom your entreaties, tears, proposals, genuflections or your
cries will but inflame the more. To whom then will you have
recourse? Will it be to that God whom you had just implored so
zealously, and who, in order to reward you for this fervour, only
precipitates you somewhat more certainly into the trap? To that
chimerical God whom we ourselves outrage here every day by
insulting his vain laws?. . . You comprehend how it is then,
*Therese*; there is no power, of whatever nature you may suppose it,
that can succeed in tearing you from our hands, and there is neither
in the class of possible things, nor in that of miracles, no kind of
means which can succeed in making you conserve any longer that
virtue of which you are so proud; which can in fine prevent you
from becoming in every sense and manner, a prey to the lewd fits

to which we are all four going to abandon ourselves with you. . . . Undress thyself then, wench, offer thy person to our lusts, that it may be polluted by them in an instant, or the cruellest treatments are about to prove to you the risks which a wretch like thee runs in in disobeying us."

This discourse . . . this terrible order left me no further recourses, I felt it; but would I not have been guilty for not employing that which my heart indicated to me and which my situation still left me? I then cast myself *Dom Severino*'s feet, I make use of all the eloquence of a soul in despair, to beg him not to take advantage of my state; the most bitter tears abundantly flow over his knees, and everything I imagine the strongest, everything I fancy the most pathetic, I dare try it with this man. . . . What was the good of it all, great God! was I to ignore that tears have an additional attraction in the libertine's eyes? had I to doubt that all that I was undertaking to soften these barbarians was to succeed in simply inflaming them?. . . — "Take this harlot," says *Severino* in a rage, "take hold of her, *Clement*, let her be naked in a minute, and let her learn that it is not with folks like us, compassion stifles Nature." *Clement* frothed; my resistances had animated him; he seizes me with a lean and brawny arm; underlining his proposals and actions by frightful curses, in one minute, he peels off my clothes." — "There is a lovely creature," says the Superior on running his fingers over my loins; "may God strike me dead if ever I saw a better made one! Friends," continued this Monk, "let us put order in our proceedings; you know our formulas of reception, let her undergo them all without accepting a single one; let the other eight women during the while keep round us, to supply the wants or to excite them." Immediately a ring is formed, and I am placed in the centre, and there, for more than two hours, I am examined, viewed, handled by these four Monks, receiving from each in his turn, either elogiums or criticisms.

You will allow me, Madam, says our comely prisoner on blushing, to conceal a part of the obscene particulars of this detestable ceremony; let your imagination picture to itself all that debauchery

can in a similar case dictate to ruffians; let it behold them successively pass from my companions to me, compare, bring us together,
confront, discourse, and it will likely have as yet but a slight idea of
what took place in these first orgies, very insignificant no doubt, in
comparison with all the horrors I was shortly to experience.

— "Come!" says *Severino,* whose prodigiously exalted desires can
no longer retain themselves, and who, in this frightful state, gives
an idea of a tiger ready to devour its victim; "let us make her feel
his favorite enjoyment." And the infamous fellows, placing me on
a sofa in the posture suitable to his execrable schemes, himself with
me in that criminal and perverse manner which causes us to resemble the sex which we do not possess, simply by degrading the one
we have. But, getting me held by two of his Monks, tries to satisfy
whether this lascivious scoundrel is too stoutly fitted, or Nature
revolted in me at the mere suspicion of these pleasures, he can not
surmount the obstacles; he scarcely presents himself, when he is at
once repulsed. . . . He scatters, he squeezes, he tears, all his endeav-
ours are superfluous; this monster's fury is brought to bear upon
the altar where his vows can not reach; he strikes it, he pinches it,
he bites it; fresh trial spring from the bosom of these brutalities.
The softened flesh adapts itself, the path gapes, the battering-ram
enters. I fetch awful cries; the whole bulk is swallowed up, and the
adder, forthwith casting out a poison which robs it of its force, yields
at last, on weeping with rage, at the motions I make to rid myself
of it. I never suffered so much in my life.

*Clement* comes up; he is armed with rods; his treacherous designs
sparkle in his eyes. — "It is I," he says to *Severino,* "it is I who am
going to take vengeance for you, my father; it is I who am going to
correct this beast for her resistances to your pleasures." Nobody
needs hold me; one of his arms twists and presses me on one of his
knees which, pushing against my belly, exposes more barely to him
what is about to serve his whims. He at first tries his lashes, it seems
he has merely the intention of preluding; being soon fired with lust,
the heartless ruffian strikes with all his might; nothing escapes his
ferocity. From the centre of the loins to the calves of the legs is all
gone over by this traitor. Attempting to blend love at these cruel
moments, its mouth sticks itself up to mine and wants to inhale the

sighs which my sufferings are tearing from me. . . . My tears are flowing down, he drinks them up, by fits he kisses, menaces, but continues to strike; while he is at work, one of the women is exciting him; on her knees before him, she labours variously at him with each of her hands; the better she succeeds in it, the more violence are in the strokes which reach me. I am ready to be torn, when nothing as yet tells the end of my ills: they have in vain to waste themselves on all sides, he is null; this end which I am expecting will be but the work of his delirium; a fresh cruelty decides him. My breast is at the mercy of this brute, it inflames him, he brings his teeth to bear on it, the cannibal bites it: this fit determines the crisis, the incense escapes. Frightful yells, dreadful curses characterized its pitches, and the enfeebled Monk abandons me to *Jerome.*

— "I shall not be more dangerous for your virtue than *Clement,*" says this libertine to me on caressing the bloody altar where this Monk had just sacrificed, "but I wish to kiss those furrows; I am so worthy of opening them a little also, that I owe them some honor; I want much more," continued this old satyr on introducing one of his fingers where *Severino* placed himself, "I wish the hen to lay, and I wish to eat up her egg . . . does it exist?. . . Yes, by Jove! . . . Oh! my child, how tender it is! . . ." His mouth replaces his fingers. . . . I am told what I must do, I perform it with disgust. In the situation I am in, alas! is it permitted me to refuse? The unworthy wretch is glad . . . he swallows; then, making me go down on my knees before him, he sticks himself unto me in this posture; his ignominious passion spends itself in a spot which bars me every complaint. While he is acting thus, the stout woman flogs him; another, placed on a level with his mouth, discharges for him the same duty to which I have just been submitted. — "It is not enough," says the infamous fellow; "it is necessary that each of my hands . . . one can not multiply those things too much. . . ." The two prettiest girls come up; they obey: there are the excesses to which satiety has brought *Jerome.* However it is, he is by dint of impurities happy, and my mouth, at the end of half an hour receives at last, with a repugnance which is easy for you to guess, the disgusting homage of this nasty man.

*Antonin* appears: — "Let us see then," says he, "this so pure a virtue; being damaged by a single assault, it ought hardly be visible in it." His arms are pointed, he would willingly make use of *Clement's* episodes. I told you the active floging pleased him quite as much as this Monk; but as he is in a hurry, the state in which his colleague put me becomes sufficient for him; he examines this state, he enjoys it, and leaving me in the so favorite a posture of the whole of them, he strikes an instant on the two half-moons which defend the entrance; he shakes in a fury the porticos of the temple, he is soon within the sanctuary; the assault, though as violent as *Severino's*, made in a less narrow path is not however so dude to injure. The strong athlete seizes my two haunches, and supplying for the bounces I am able to make, he tosses me unto himself with vivacity. You would say, by the redoubled efforts of this Hercules, that not content with being master of the place, he wishes to reduce it to powder. Such terrible attacks, so new to me, are about making me succumb; but, without any uneasiness for my pains, the cruel vanquisher only thinks of doubling his pleasures; all around him, all excite him, all concur to his voluptuousnesses; in front of him, raised upon my loins, the girl of fifteen years old, with her legs spread out, offers to his mouth the altar on which he is sacrificing with me; he leisurely pumps into it this precious juice of Nature, the ejection of which is scarcely allowed by her to this young child. One of the old lasses, on her knees before the loins of my van-quisher, agitates them, and her polluted tongue animating his desires, she brings on their ecstasy, whilst to inflame himself still better, the lewd fellow excites a woman with each of his hands. There is not a single one of his senses is but tickled, not a single one which does not concur in the perfection of his delirium; he is touching on it, but my constant horror for all these infamies hin-ders me from partaking of it. . . . He arrives at it alone, his jerks, his cries, everything announces it, and I am drenched, inspite of me, with the proofs of a flame which I kindle only in a sixth part. At last I fall again on the throne where I have been just immolated, no longer feeling my existence except through my grief and tears . . . my despair and remorse.

Yet *Dom Severino* bids the women make me eat; but, very far from giving heed to these attentions, a fit of sorrow comes to assail my soul. I who was wont to place all my glory, all my happiness in my virtue, I, who used to console myself for all the ills of fortune, provided I was always good, I can not lay hold of the horrible idea of seeing myself so cruelly stained by those from whom I ought to expect most help and consolation. My tears flow in abundance, my cries make the vault ring; I roll on the ground, I bruise my breasts, I tear my hair, I invoke my tormentors, I beseech them to slay me. . . . Will you believe me, Madam, this frightful spectacle irritates them still more. — "Ah!" says *Severino*, "I never enjoyed a finer scene: see, my friends, the state it puts me in; it is extraordinary, what womanish griefs obtain from me! — Let us take her again," says *Clement*, "and in order to teach her how to howl thus, let the rogue be more harshly treated in this second assault." This project is scarcely conceived when it is executed; *Severino* comes up, but let him say what he liked, his desires being in need of a further degree of irritation, it is only after having made use of *Clement*'s cruel means that he succeeds in finding the necessary force for the accomplishment of his fresh crime. What a fit of ferocity, great God! Could it be that these monsters carried it to the degree of choosing the moment of a crisis of moral suffering, so violent as the one I felt, as to make me undergo so barbarous a physical one! — "It would be unmeet of me not to employ in the main point, with this novice, what serves you so nicely as episode," says *Clement* on beginning to act, "and I go bail to you that I shall not treat her better than you." — "A moment!" cries *Antonin* to the Superior whom he saw ready to seize me again; "while your zeal is going to be exhaled in the hind parts of this lovely girl, I may, it seems to me, incense the contrary God; we shall lay her between us both." The posture is so arranged that I can still offer my mouth to *Jerome*; they require: *Clement* places himself in my hands; I am obliged to excite him. All the priestesses surround this frightful group. Each lends to the actors what she knows ought to excite them most; yet I bear all; the whole weight is on me alone. *Severino* gives the alert, the other three follow him closely, and here I am, for the second time, shamefully stained with the proofs of the disgusting lust of those notorious rascals.

— "That's enough of it for a first day," says the Superior; "we must now let her see that her companions are no better treated than she." They set me in a high arm-chair, whence I am forced to look on the fresh horrors which are about to end the orgies.

The Monks are in line; all the sisters file off before them, and receive the whip of each one; they are next obliged to excite their butchers with their mouths while the latter torment and inveigh them.

The youngest, she of ten years old, places herself on the sofa, and each Monk comes to make her undergo a torment according to his choice. Near her, is the girl of fifteen, whom he who has just caused the pain to be endured, is to forthwith enjoy as he pleases; she is the target. The oldest ought to follow the Monk who is acting, in order upon him either in this operation, or in the act which is about to terminate. *Severino* employs but his hand to tease her who offers herself to him, and flies to be absorbed in the sanctuary which enchants him and which she whom they placed hard-by presents to him; the old hag, being armed with a fistful of nettles, gives him back what he had just performed. It was from the bosom of these painful titillations that this libertine's intoxication springs. . . . Consult him, will he acknowledge himself cruel? He has done nothing which he does not endure himself.

*Clement* slightly pinches the little girl's flesh: the enjoyment offered beside him becomes forbidden to him; but they treat him as he has treated, and he lays at the idol's feet the incense which he has no longer the strength of casting as far as the sanctuary.

*Antonin* amuses himself at vigorously kneading the fleshy parts of his victim's body; being fired by the bounces she makes, he rushes into the part offered to his chosen pleasures. He is in his turn kneaded, beaten, and his intoxication is the fruit of the pains.

Old *Jerome* only uses his teeth, but every bite leaves a trace from which the blood directly spouts out; after a dozen, the plastron presents him her mouth; he appeases his rage therein, whilst he is himself bitten as hard as he has done.

The Monks drink and retrieve their strength.

The woman of thirty-six, being as I have said, six months in the family-way, hoisted by them upon a pedestal eight feet high; being able to place but one leg on it, she is obliged to keep the other in the air; there are about her mattresses trimmed with briars, holms, thorns three feet thick; they give her a long flexible pole to bear her up: it is easy to see on the one hand the interest she has for not falling down, on the other the impossibility of observing an equilibrium; this alternative diverts the Monks. The whole four ranged round her, each has one or two women to variously excite him during this spectacle; all bulky as she is, the unfortunate woman remains in position nearly a quarter of an hour; her strength fails her at last, she falls on the thorns, and our villains, drunk with lust, are going to offer for the last time the abominable homage of their ferocity on her person. . . . They withdraw.

The Superior placed me in the hands of the one of these girls, aged thirty, of whom I have spoken to you; they called her *Omphale*. She was charged to instruct me, to install me in my new home; but I neither saw nor heard anything this first night; being fagged, past hopes, I thought only of taking a little rest. I perceived, in the room where they placed me, fresh women who were not at supper; I postponed to the next day the examining of all these new objects, and occupied myself but in seeking a little repose. *Omphale* let me alone; she too went to bed. I was scarcely in mine, when all the horror of my lot presents itself still more vividly: I could recover neither from the execrations I had suffered, nor from those of which I had been made a witness. Alas! if my imagination had sometimes wandered over these pleasures, I believed them chaste as the God who inspired them; being given by Nature to serve as consolation for mankind, I fancied they were sprung from love and delicacy. I was far from believeing that man, after the example of ferocious beasts, could enjoy only in causing his companion to shudder. . . . Then, coming back to the fatality of my destiny. . . . O good Heavens! said I to myself, it is then quite certain that no act of virtue will proceed from my heart, without its being directly followed by pain! And what harm was I doing, great God! in desiring to come and discharge in this convent a few duties of religion? Do I offend heaven in wishing to pray to it? Incomprehensible decrees of Providence, vouchsafe then, I continued, to make known your will to me, if you wish me not to revolt against you! Bitter tears followed these reflections, and I was still drenched with them, when day appeared; *Omphale* then approached my bed.

"Dear companion," she says to me, "I come to exhort thee to have courage; I wept like thee on the first days, and now I have got accustomed to it; thou wilt accustom thyself to it as I have done; beginnings are awful. It is not only the necessity of glutting the passions of these debauched men that causes the torment of our lives, it is also the loss of our freedom, it is the cruel way in which we are led into this frigtful house."

The unhappy fellows console themselves in seeing others near them. However keen my sorrows were, I appeased them an instant, in order to beg my companion to give me a true notion of the evils I was to expect.

— "Wait a moment," my instructress says to me, "get up, let me first run through our retreat, observe thy new companions; we shall talk afterwards." On consenting to *Omphale*'s counsels, I saw that I was in a very large room where there were eight pretty clean little printed calico beds; there was a closet near each bed; but all the windows which gave light to either these closets or room, were raised five feet from the ground and provided with an iron-grating inside and outside. There was in the middle of the principal room a large table fixed in the ground, for eating or working; three iron-clad doors closed this room in; there were no locks on our side; enormous bolts on the other. — "There is now our prison?" said I to *Omphale*.

— "Alas! yes, my dear," she answered me; such is "our only dwelling; the other eight girls have a similar room hard-by, and we never communicate with one another." I went into the closet which was laid out for me; it was about eight square feet; the daylight entered it as in the other room, through a window very high up and all set off with a grating. The only furniture were a biddy, a toilet and a broken-bottomed chair. I return; my companions being eager to see me, surrounded me; they were seven: I made the eighth. *Omphale*, living in the other room, was in this one only to instruct me; she would remain in it if I wished, and the one of those whom I saw would replace her in her room; I requested this arrangement, so it was granted. But before coming to *Omphale's* recital about them, it seems to me essential to describe to you the seven new companions whom destiny gave me; I shall proceed herein by order of age, as I have done for the others.

The youngest was twelve years old, of a very lively and witty physiognomy, the loveliest hair and prettiest mouth.

The second was sixteen; she was one of the handsomest fair girls that it was possible to behold, of truly delightful features, and all the graces, pretty ways of her age, mingled with a sort of interest, the fruit of her sadness, which rendered her a thousand times still more beautiful.

The third was twenty-three; very pretty, but too much effrontery, too much impudence degraded, according to my opinion, in her, the charms with which Nature had adorned her.

The fourth was twenty-six; she was formed like Venus; the outlines being however rather too pronounced; of a dazzling whiteness, her physiognomy being mild, open and smiling, with beautiful eyes, her mouth somewhat large, but admirably well furnished, and superb fair-hair.

The fifth was thirty-two; she was gone four months in the family way; of an oval face, of delicate health, a tender voice, and of little bloom, naturally a libertine: I am told she wears herself away in person.

The sixth was thirty-three; a tall woman, a well-set, the prettiest face in the world, lovely skin.

The seventh was thirty-eight; a true model of a waist and beauty; she was the Senior of my room. *Omphale* warned me of her mischeviousness, and especially of the liking she had for women. — "To yield to her is the true way of pleasing her," says my companion to me; "resist her is to accumulate on one's head all the evils that may afflict us in this house. Thou wilt think over it."

*Omphale* asked *Ursule* (this was the Senior's name) for leave to instruct me; *Ursule* consented to it under the condition that I should go and kiss her. I approached her: her polluted tongue wanted to be united with mine, whilst her fingers were at work to bring on sensations which she was very far from obtaining. I was obliged in spite of me nevertheless to adapt myself to everything, and when she thought she had triumphed, she sent me off to my closet, where *Omphale* spoke to me thus:

"All the women thou sawest yesterday, my dear *Therese*, and those thou hast just seen, are divided into four classes of four girls each. The first is called the child's class; it is composed of girls from the tenderest age up to twelve; a white attire distinguishes them.

The second class, the color of which is green, is called the youthful class; it is composed of girls from sixteen up to twenty-one years old.

The third class is the rational age; it is dressed in blue; they are in it from twenty-one to thirty, it is the one we are both in.

The fourth class, dressed in a purple gown, is destined for the ripe age; it is made up of all that passes thirty.

These girls either mix up indiscriminately at the Reverend Father's suppers, or they appear there by class: it all depends on the whims of the Monks; but outside of the suppers, they mix up in the two rooms, as thou mayst judge by those who live in ours."

"The instruction I have to give thee," says *Omphale* to me, "ought to be embraced under four principle articles: we shall treat in the first of what concerns the house; in the second, we shall place what relates to the demeanour of the girls, their punishment, their diet, etc., etc., etc.; the third article will instruct thee about plan of those Monk's pleasures, about the manner in which the girls serve them; the fourth will explain for thee the history of reforms and changes.

I shall not describe to thee, *Therese*, the accesses of this frightful house, thou knowest them as well as I do; I shall speak to thee only of the inside; they have shown it to me that I may be able to give a picture of it to me that I may be able to give a picture of it to the new comers, with whose education I am entrusted, and to remove from them by this description all notion of stealing away. *Severino* explained a part of it for thee yesterday, he did not deceive thee, my dear. The church and the pavilion which is contiguous to it form what they properly call the Convent; but thou ignorest how the apartment in which we live is situated, how one gets to it; here it is. At the end of the sacristy, behind the altar, there is a door disguised in the wains-cotting which a spring opens; this door is the entry into a trench, as dark as long, the windings of which thy fright on coming in hindered thee, no doubt, from perceiving; at first this trench descends, because it must pass under a moat thirty feet deep, then it ascends when the breadth of this moat is passed, and runs no more than six feet under ground; thus it reaches the subterraneous passages of our pavilion, at about a quarter of a league distant from the other. Six thick enclosures hinder its being possible to perceive this lodging, had you even gone upon the church-belfry; the reason of this is simple: the pavilion is very low, it is not twenty-five feet, and the enclosures composed, some of walls, others of bushy hedges very close to one another, are each of them more than fifty feet high: from whatever side you view this part, it can be then taken only for a coppice of the forest, but never for a dwelling; it is therefore, as I have just told thee, by a trap-door leading into the subterraneous places, that the way out from the dark corridor, of which I have given thee an idea, is situated, and which it is impossible for thee to remember owing to the state thou must be in on traversing it. This pavilion, my dear, has in only subterranes, one ground-floor, an under-story and a first story; the roof is a very thick vault adorned with a leaden cistern, full of clay, in which ever-green shrubs are planted, which, while matching with the hedges that surround it, gives the whole an aspect of a still truer thicket. The subterraneous places form a large hall in the middle and eight closets around, two of which are used as dungeons for the girls who have deserved this punishment, and the other six, as cellars; over head is the supper hall, kitchens, offices, and two closets where the Monks pass when they wish to isolate their pleasures and taste them with us, out of their colleague's sight. The under-story comprises eight rooms, four which have a closet: these are the cells where the Monks sleep and fetch us, when their lubricity dooms us to partake of their beds; the four other rooms are those of the Lay-Brothers, one of whom is our goaler, another the Monks' lackey, the third, the surgeon, having in his cell all that is necessary for urgent needs, and the fourth, the cook; these four Brothers are deaf and dumb; with great pains one therefore expect from them, as thou seest, any consolations or helps; besides, they never stop with us, and we are totally forbidden to speak to them. The upper parts of those under-stories form therefore the seraglios; they exactly resemble each other: it is, as thou seest, a large room to which eight closets are contiguous. Thus thou comprehendest, dear girl, that, supposing one broke the bars of our casements, and descended by the window, one would still be very far from stealing away, since there would remain five bushy hedges, a strong wall, and a large moat to be got over; even were these obstacles surmounted, where would one fall again, moreover? Into the yard of the Convent which, being itself carefully closed up, would not yet afford, from the first moment, a very secure way out. A less dangerous way of escape perhaps would be, I grant, to find in our subterraneous places the mouth of the trench which leads to it; but how arrive in these excavations, perpetually locked up as we are? even one was there, this opening would not yet be discovered: it leads into a hidden nook, ignored by us, and is itself barricaded by gratings of which they alone have the key. Yet were all these drawbacks got the better of, were one in the trench, its route would be still no safer for us; it is secured by traps which only themselves know, and in which the persons who should wish to run through it without them, would be inevitably caught. It is therefore necessary to give over the idea of escaping, such is impossible, *Therese*; believe that if it was feasible, I would have fled this detestable abode long ago, but this can not be. Those who are in it leave it only at death; and hence spring that impudence, cruelty, tyranny which those villains use with us; nothing inflames them, nothing exalts their imagination like the impunity which this inaccessible retreat affords them; being certain of never having for witnesses of their excesses but the victims that satisfy them, being quite sure that their escapades will never be revealed, they carry them to the most odious extremes; being freed from the curb of the laws, having violated those of religion, disregarding those of remorse, there is no atrocity which they do not allow themselves, and in this criminal apathy, their abominable passions find themselves so much the more voluptuously provoked, that nothing, they say, fires them like solitude and silence, as weakness on the one hand and impunity on the other. The Monks sleep regularly every night in this pavilion; they come to it at five o'clock in the evening and go back to the Convent about nine in the morning, except one who by turn spends the day here: he is styled the *Guard-Regent*. We shall shortly see his office. As to the four Brothers, they never stir. We have in each room a bell which communicates with the goaler's cell; the Senior alone has the right of ringing it, but when she does so, according to her wants or ours, they run directly; the Fathers themselves bring on returning, every day, the necessary supplies, and hand them to the cook who employs them after their orders; there is a fountain in the subterraneous places and abundance of wines of all kinds in the cellars. Let us pass to the second article, which treats about the girl's dress, diet, punishment, etc.

Our number is always equal; steps are taken so that we are always sixteen, eight in each room, and, as thou seest, always in the uniform of our classes; the day will not pass by without their giving thee the habits of that into which thou enterest; we are every day in home dress of the color which belongs to us; in the evening, in a long frockcoat of this same color, our hair dressed as best we can. The Senior of the room has all power over us; to disobey her is a crime; she is entrusted with the care of inspecting us, before we betake ourselves to the orgies, and if things are not in the desired state, she is punished as well as we. The faults we may commit are of several sorts. Every one has her particular punishment, the list of which is posted up in both rooms; the *Day-Regent*, he who comes, as I shall presently explain for thee, to notify to us the orders, name the supper girls, visit our dwellings, and receive the complaints from the Senior, this Monk, I say, is the one who distributes in the evening the punishment that each has deserved; here is the state of these punishments besides the crimes which bring them on us:

Not to be up in the morning at the prescribed hour: thirty lashes (for it is nearly by this torture that we are punished; it was simple enough that an episode of these libertines' pleasures should become their chosen correction.) To present either through misunderstanding, or through whatever cause there might be, a part of the body, in the act of pleasures, instead of the one which is desired: fifty lashes. To be badly clad or have the hair badly dressed: twenty lashes. Not to have given notice when one has the monthly terms: sixty lashes. The day on which the Surgeon has proved your being with child: a hundred lashes. Negligence, impossibility or refusal in the lustful propositions: two hundred lashes. And how often their hellish wickedness takes us falling short of this, without our being the least in the wrong! How often one of them suddenly requests what he knows very well that one has just bestowed on another, and which can not be done again at once! The correction must nevertheless be undergone; our advices, our complaints are never listened to; we must obey or be corrected. Want of conduct in the room, or disobedience towards the Senior: sixty lashes. Tokens of tears, sorrow, remorse, even a look of the slightest return to religion: two hundred lashes. If a Monk chooses you in order to taste with you the last crisis of pleasure and that he can not arrive at it, whether it be of his fault, which is very common, or whether it be of yours: forthwith, three hundred lashes. The merest look of repugnance to the Monk's propositions, of whatever nature these propositions may be: two hundred lashes. An undertaking to escape, revolt: nine days of the dungeon, stark naked, and three hundred lashes with a whip daily. Cabals, evil counsels, bad proposals with one's self, as soon as this is discovered: three hundred lashes. Schemes of suicide, refusals to nourish one's self as it behooves: two hundred lashes. To be wanting in respect towards the Monks: one hundred and eighty lashes. These are our sole crimes; we can, however, do what we like, sleep together, quarrel with one another, fight, run into the last excesses of drunkenness and gluttony, swear, blaspheme: that is all one, they do not say a word to us for those faults; we are checked only for those I have just told thee, but the Seniors can spare us many of these troubles, if they like. Unfortunately, this protection is simply purchased by condescensions oftentimes more burdensome than the pains warranted by them; they are of the same taste in both halls and it is only in granting them favors that one succeeds in captivating them. If one refuses them, they multiply without reason the sum of your wrong-doings, and the Monks whom one serves, in doubling the amount of them, very far from scolding them for their injustice, incessantly encourage them to it; they are themselves subjected to all these rules, and besides are very severely punished, if they are suspected of being indulgent. It is not that these libertines need all this, in order to misuse us, but they are exceedingly glad to have pretexts; this aspect of nature lends charms to their voluptuousness, it is increased by it. We have every one of us a small supply of linen on entering here; they give us everything by the half-dozen, and they renew it every year, but we must give up what we bring; we are not allowed to keep the least thing of it; the complaints of the four Brothers, of whom I have spoken to thee, are listened to as the Seniors; we are punished on their simple information, but the former require nothing from us at least, and there is not so much to be apprehended as with the very exacting and dangerous Seniors, when caprice or vengeance directs their proceedings. Our diet is very good and always in great abundance; if they did not reap therefrom branches of voluptuousness, perhaps this article would not be so good, but as their filthy debaucheries gain thereby, they neglect nothing to cram us with food: those who like flogging us have us plumper, fatter, and those who, as *Jerome* told thee yesterday, like to see the hen laying, are sure by means of an abundant nourishment, of a greater quantity of eggs. Consequently, we are fed three times a day; they give us for breakfast, between nine and ten o'clock, always a fowl with rice, raw or stewed fruits, tea, coffee or chocolate; at one o'clock dinner is served up; each table of eight is served the same: a very good pottage, four courses of dishes, a dish of roast meat, and four dainty dishes; dessert in every season. At half-past five, luncheon is served up: pastries or fruits; the supper is undoubtedly excellent, if it is that of the Monks; if we do not assist at it, as we are then only four per room, they serve us up at the same time three dishes of roast meats and four dainty dishes; we have each one bottle of white wine, one of claret, and half a bottle of liquor daily; those who do not drink so much are free to give to the others. There are some amongst us very greedy who drink astonishingly, who get drunk, and all that without being rebuked for it; there are likewise some for whom these four meals do not yet suffice; these have only to ring, they are immediately brought what they request.

The Seniors oblige eating at meals, and should one persist in not wishing to do so, through whatever motive it might be, at the third time, one would be severely punished. The Monk's supper is composed of three dishes of roast meats, six courses of dishes taken away in order to serve up a cold piece and eight dainty dishes, fruit, three kinds of wine, coffee and liquors. Sometimes we are all eight at table with them; other times they compel four of us to wait upon them, and these sup afterwards; it also happens, from time to time, that they take only four girls to supper; these are usually then of entire classes; when we are eight at it, there are always two of each class. It is useless to tell thee that nobody in the world never visits us; no stranger, under any pretext whatsoever, is introduced into this pavilion.

Should we fall ill, the Brother Surgeon alone cares us, and if we die, it is without any religious assistance; they cast us into gullies formed by the hedges, and all is over; but by a singular cruelty, if the sickness becomes too serious or if they fear the contagion, they do not wait until we are dead in order to bury us: they carry us away and throw us where I have told thee, still all alive; for the eighteen years I have been here, I have seen more than ten examples of this notorious ferocity. To this they say that it is better to lose one, than to risk sixteen; that, besides, a girl is so trifling a loss, so easily recovered, one should have but little regret for her. Let us pass to the plan of the Monk's pleasures and everything that concerns this subject.

We rise here exactly at nine o'clock in the morning, in all seasons; we lie down more or less late, owing to the Monks' supper. As soon as we are up, the *Day-Regent* comes to pay his visit; he seats himself in a big arm-chair, and there, each of us is obliged to go and place herself before him, with her petticoats lifted up on the side he likes; he handles, he kisses, he examines, and when all have discharged this duty, he names those who are to be of the supper-party; he prescribes for them the state in which they must be, he takes the complaints from the Senior's hands, and the punishments are imposed. They seldom go out without a scene of lust, at which we are all eight commonly employed. The Senior directs these lecherous acts, and the most complete submission on our part reigns thereat. It often happens, before breakfast, that one of the Reverend Fathers gets one of us asked into his bed; the Brother goaler fetches a card with the name of her who is required. Should the *Day-Regent* occupy her then, he has not even the right to detain her: she passes, and comes back when she is sent away. The first ceremony being over, we breakfast: from this time until evening, we have nothing more to do; but at seven o'clock in summer, at six in winter, they send for those who have been named; the Brother goaler conducts them in person, and after supper, those who are not detained for the night return to the seraglio. Often none remains; they are fresh ones they send to take for the night; and these are likewise warned, several hours beforehand, of the dress in which they must go; sometimes there is only the *Guard-Girl* who goes to bed." — "The *Guard-Girl?* "

I interrupted, "which is then this new office?" — "Here it is," my historian replies to me.

"The first of every month, each Monk adopts a girl who is during this interval to fulfil for him both the place of a servant and plastron in his unhallowed desires; the Seniors alone are exempted on account of the duty of their room. They can neither change them in the course of the month, nor make them perform two consecutive months; nothing is cruel, nothing is hard like the mean jobs of this service, and I know not how they wilt go about it. The moment it strikes five in the evening, the *Guard-Girl* goes down to the Monk she serves, and she no longer leaves him until next day, at the time when he passes again to the Convent. She takes him again as soon as he comes back; she employs these few hours in eating and resting herself, for she must keep awake during the nights which she spends with her master; I repeat to thee, this unfortunate girl is there to serve as plastron all the whims which may pass through this libertine's head: cuffs, floggings, evil proposals, enjoyments, she must suffer everything; she is to be on foot all the night in her governor's room and ever ready to offer herself to the passions which may agitate this tyrant; but the cruelest, the most ignominious of these bondages, is the terrible obligation she is under of presenting her mouth or breast to either of this monster's needs; he never uses any other vase; she must receive all, and the slightest repugnance is directly punished by the most barbarous tortures. In all the scenes of lust, these are the girls who favor the pleasures, who care them, and who clean everything that may be polluted: is a Monk so on having just enjoyed a woman? it is the business of the servant's mouth to redress this disorder; does he want to be excited? this is the care of that unhappy girl. She accompanies him everywhere, dresses him, undresses him, in a word waits on him in every case, is always wrong, and is always beaten; at the suppers her place is either behind her master's chair, or like a dog at his feet, under the table, or on her knees, between his thighs, exciting him with her mouth; sometimes, she serves him as a seat or a flambeau; at other times, they are all four about the table in the most lustful attitudes, but at the same time the most annoying.

If they lose their equilibrium, they risk, either to fall upon thorns which are placed hard-by, or to break a limb, or even kill themselves, which is not without example; and during this time, the villains rejoice, perform debauchery, get drunk at leisure over dishes, wines, lust and cruelty." — "Oh Heavens!" said I to my companion in shuddering with horror, "Can one bring himself to such excesses! What a hell!" — "Listen, *Therese*, listen, my child, thou art still far from knowing all," says *Omphale*. "The state of child-bearing, revered in the world, is a certainty of reprobation among these infamous wretches; it dispenses neither with punishments, nor guards; it is on the contrary a vehicle to pains, humiliations, sorrows. How often is it by force of strokes that they cause those to miscarry, whose fruit they are decided not to receive! and if they do receive it, it is to enjoy it: what I am telling you here should suffice for thee in order to persuade thee to preserve thyself from this state as long as possible. — But can one do so? — Undoubtedly, there are certain spunges. . . .

But if *Antonin* perceives, one escapes not from his wrath; the safest is to stifle the impression of Nature on dismounting the imagination, and with such villains, this is not difficult."

"Moreover," continued my instructress, "there are here relationships and kindreds which thou dost not suspect, and which it is well to explain to thee; but this comes into the fourth article, viz., into that of our recruits, our reforms and changes: I am going to enter upon it in order to include this short particular therein.

Thou ignorest not, *Therese*, that the four Monks who compose this Convent are at the head of the Order, are all four of illustrious families, and all four very rich of themselves. Independent of the immense funds formed by the Order of Benedictines for the keeping of this voluptuous retreat where all have the hope of passing in their turn, those who are in it still add to these funds a large portion of their wealth; these two objects united amount to more than one hundred thousand crowns a year, which are used only in recruitings or in the expenses of the house; they have twelve sure and confidential women, solely entrusted with the care of bringing them a subject every month, between the age of twelve and thirty, neither under, nor over. The subject must be exempt from every defect and endowed with the most qualities possible, but especially with an illustrious birth. These well-paid rapes, always executed very far from here, entail no drawback; I never saw any complaints resulting from them. Their extreme precautions secure them from everything; they do not absolutely confine themselves to the first flowers: a girl already seduced or a married woman equally pleases them; but rape must take place, it must be proved; this circumstance inflames them; they want to be certain that their crimes cost tears; they would send away a girl that would willingly give herself up to them. If thou hadst not defended thyself wonderfully, had they not recognized a real fund of virtue in thee, and consequently the certainty of a crime, they would not have kept thee twenty-four hours. All that is here, *Therese*, is then of the best breeding. Such as thou beholdest me, dear friend, I am sole daughter of the Count***, carried away in Paris at twelve years old, and destined one day to have a dowry of one hundred thousand crowns; I was snatched from my governess's arms who was taking me alone in a car, from a county-seat of my father's, to the *Abbaye de Panthemount,* where I was brought up; my governess disappeared; she was likely bought over; I was conveyed hither by mail. Such is the case with all the others. The girl of twenty years old belongs to one of the most distinguished families of the Poitou. The one of sixteen is the daughter of the *Baron de\*\*\**, one of the greatest Seigniors of Lorraine; Counts, *Dukes* and *Marquises* are the fathers of our twenty-three, of her of twelve, of her of thirty-two; not one, in fine, but can claim the finest titles, and not one but is treated with the last ignominy. But these dishonest fellows have not contented themselves with those horrors, they have wished to dishonor the very bosom of their own families. The young person of twenty-six, undoubtedly one of our handsomest, is *Clement's* daughter; she of thirty-six is *Jerome's* niece.

As soon as a fresh girl has arrived at this polluted sink, as soon as she is in it for ever withdrawn from the universe, they directly reform one of them, and lo, dear girl, lo the completion of our sorrows; the cruelest of our evils is to ignore what happens us, in these awful and perplexing reforms. It is wholly impossible to say what becomes of one on leaving these places. We have as many proofs as our solitude permits us to acquire of it, that the girls reformed by the Monks never appear again; themselves warn us of it, they do not conceal from us that this retreat is our tomb; but do they assassinate us? Good Heavens! Would murder then, the most execrable of crimes be for them, as for that famous *Mareschal de Retz*[8], a sort of enjoyment, the cruelty of which, by exalting their perfidious imagination, could plunge their senses into a more living intoxication? Being accustomed to enjoy only through suffering, to revel only through tortures and torments, would it be possible for them to lose themselves so far as to believe that, on improving the first cause of the delirium, they must inevitably make it more perfect, and then without principles, as without faith, without morals, as without virtues, the rascals, misusing the misfortunes into which their first forfeits hurled us, should satiate themselves by other crimes which might take our life away? I know not. . . . If they are questioned about it, they stammer, now answer negatively, and now affirmatively; what is certain, is, that none of those who went out, whatever promises they had made us lodging complaints againts these fellows, and of working at our release, none, I say, has ever kept word with us. . . . Nay more, do they appease our complaints, or do they place us out of state of making them? When we inquire of those who arrive about those who have left us, they never know any of them. What then becomes of those unfortunate women? That is what torments us, *Therese*, that is the fatal uncertainity which forms the misfortune of our days. I am in this house these eighteen years, more than two hundred girls do I see going out of it. . . . Where are they? Why, all having sworn to serve us, have none kept word?

Nothing moreover legitimates our retreat; age, change of faces, nothing prevails in it; whimsy is their only rule. They will reform today her whom they caressed yesterday, and they will keep for ten years those of whom they have most glutted; such is the history of the Senior of this hall: she is in the house these twelve years, they will feast on her, and I have seen, in order to conserve her, children of fifteen reformed, whose beauty would have made the *Graces* jealous. She who left eight days ago, was not yet sixteen years old; beautiful as Venus herself, they enjoyed her merely for one year, but she became pregnant, and I have told thee, *Therese*, this is a great mistake in this house. Last month, they reformed one of seventeen years old. A year ago, one of twenty, being eight months with child; and lately one at the moment when she felt the first pains in labour. Do not fancy that conduct has any hand in it: I have seen some who wish to anticipate their desires, and who departed at the end of six months; others, slovenly and whimsical, whom they kept a great many years. It is then useless to prescribe any kind of conduct for our new comers; the fantasy of these monsters infringes on all bounds, and becomes the sole law of their actions.

When we are to be reformed, we are advised about it in the morning, never sooner. *The Day-Regent* puts in an appearance at nine o'clock as usual, and he says, I suppose: "*Omphale, the Convent reforms you, I shall come for you this evening.*" Then he continues his business. But at the examination you no longer offer yourself to him, then he walks off; the reformed one embraces her fellows, she promises them a thousand times over to be of service to them, to lodge complaints, to divulge what takes place; the hour strikes, the Monk appears, the girl departs, and nobody hears of her more. Yet the supper begins as usual; the only remarks we made on those days, are that the Monks seldom arrive at the last episodes of pleasure: one would say they are taking care of themselves; still they drink far more, sometimes even to intoxication; they send us off much earlier; no woman stays behind to go to bed, and the Guard-Girls retire to the seraglio." — "Good, good," say I to my companion, "if nobody has been of service to you, it is because you have had to do only with weak, intimidated creatures, or with children who have attempted nothing for you. I am not afraid if they do kill us, at least I do not think so; it is impossible that reasonable beings could carry crime to that pitch. . . . I am well aware that. . . . According to what I have seen, perhaps I ought not to justify men as I do; but it is impossible, my dear, that they can perform horrors the very idea of which is not to be conceived. Oh! dear companion," I warmly continued, "wilt thou make me this promise in which I swear I shall not fail?. . . " "Dost thou wish so?" — "Yes." — "Well! I swear to thee by all I hold most sacred, by the God who loves me and whom alone I adore, . . . I solemnly promise thee either to die in the performance, or do away with those infamies; dost thou promise me as much?" — "Dost thou doubt it?" *Omphale* answers me; "but be certain of the inanity of these promises; others more angry than thee, more resolute, better backed up, in fine, perfect friends who would have shed their blood for us, have failed in the same oaths; allow therefore, dear *Therese*, allow my dire experience to look upon ours as vain, and to reckon no farther on them."

"— And the Monks," said I to my companion, "do they also change? do fresh ones often come?" — "No," she answered me, "*Antonin* is here these ten years; *Clement* eighteen; *Jerome* is here those thirty years, and *Severino* for the past twenty-five years. This Superior, being born in Italy, is a near relative of the Pope's with whom he is on the best of terms; it is only since his time that the pretended miracles of the Virgin assure the reputation of the Convent, and keep backbiters from too closely observing what is going on here; but the house was got up as thou seest it, when he came to it; for more than a hundred years it stands on the same footing, and all the Superiors who came to it have conserved an order so advantageous to their pleasures. *Severino*, the most lustful man of his time, had himself placed in it simply to lead a life appropropriate to his likings. His intention is to maintain the secret privileges of this Abbey as long as he can. We belong to the Diocese of Auxerre, but be the Bishop informed or not, we never see him put in an appearance, he never sets foot in the Convent. Very few people generally do come here, except towards the festival time, which is that of our Lady of August. There do not appear, as the Monks tell us, ten persons per year in this house; yet it is likely that when any strangers do present themselves here, the Superior takes care to receive them kindly; he imposes on them through the appearances of religion and austerity, they go away contented, they make the elogium of the Monastery, and the impunity of these villains is thus established on the people's sincerity and on the credulity of the devout."

*Omphale* was hardly finishing her instruction, when it struck nine; the Senior very speedily called us, the *Day-Regent* in fact appeared. It was *Antonin*; we formed in line according to the custom. He cast a precursory glance over the whole, counted us, then sits down; we next went one after another lifting up our petticoats before him, on one side as far as the navel; on the other to the middle of the loins. *Antonin* received this homage with the indifference of satiety; he was not affected by it; then, in looking at me, he asked me how I felt after the adventure? Seeing me answer only by tears. . . . — "She will make herself used to it," said he in laughing; "there is not a house in France where girls are better trained than in this one." He takes the list of the guilty ones from the Senior's hands; then, addressing himself again to me, he made me shudder; every gest, every movement which seemed about to refer me to these libertines, was for me like the sentence of death. *Antonin* bids me sit down on the side of a bed, and in this posture, he tells the Senior to come and bare my bosom, and lift up my petticoats as far as the pit of my stomach; himself places my legs as far asunder as possible; he seats himself in front of this perspective, one of my companions comes and lays herself upon me in the same posture, so that it is the altar of generation which offers itself to *Antonin* instead of my face, and which, if he enjoys it, he will have these attractions on a level with his mouth. A third girl, on her knees before him, comes to excite him with her hand, and a fourth, quite naked, points out to him with her fingers, on my body, where he is to strike. This girl insensibly excites me myself, and what she does to me, *Antonin* likewise does with each of his hands at right and left to two other girls. One does not imagine the evil proposals, the obscene discourses by which this lewd man provokes himself; he is at last in the state he desires, they lead him to me. But everybody follows him, everybody seeks to inflame him while he is going to enjoy: stripping stark naked all his hinder parts. *Omphale*, who takes hold of them, omits nothing in order to irritate them: rubbings, kisses, pollutions, she makes use of everything; *Antonin* on fire rushes upon me. . . . "I will have her pregnant this time," says he in a rage. . . . These wanderings determine the physic. *Antonin*, whose custom was to fetch terrible cries in the last moment of his intoxication, utters some awful ones; everybody surrounds him, everybody waits on him, everybody is at work to double his ecstasy, and the libertine attains to it in the midst of the strangest episodes of lust and depravity.

These sorts of groups were often put into practice. It was the rule that, when a Monk was enjoying in whatsoever way it might be, all the girls should encompass him then, in order to inflame his senses on all sides, that voluptuousness might, if it is permitted to express one's self thus, penetrate him then more surely through everyone of his pores.

*Antonin* walked out, they served up breakfast; my companions forced me to eat, I did so in order to please them. We had hardly finished when the Superior entered: seeing us still at table, he dispensed us with the ceremonies which were to be the same for him as those we had just performed for *Antonin.* "It is high time to think of dressing her," said he looking at me. At the same time he opens a closet and throws on my bed several gowns of the color suited to my class, and a few parcels of linen. — "Fit on all this," he says to me, "and give me up what belongs to you." I execute, but, doubting of the fact, I had wisely removed my money during the night, and had hid it in my hair. At every garment I take off, the burning eyes of *Severino* are fixed on the uncovered attraction, his hands wander to it directly. At last, being half naked, the Monk seizes me; he puts me into the posture suitable to his pleasures, namely, in a position quite contrary to the one in which *Antonin* had just placed me; I wish to beg forgiveness, but, seeing the fury already in his eyes, I fancy that obedience is the safest; I set myself, they surround him, he beholds no longer round him but this obscene altar which delights him; his hands squeeze it, his mouth sticks to it, his looks devour it . . . he is at the height of pleasure.

Should you think fit, Madam, said lovely *Therese,* I am going to confine myself to explaining here for you the abridged story of the first month I spent in this Convent, namely, the principal anecdotes of this interval; the remainder would be a repetition; the monotony of this sojourn would interland some of them in my recitals, and I ought immediately after to pass, it seems to me, to the event which brought me at last out of this polluted sink.

I was not of the supper-party this first day: they had simply named me to go and spend the night with *Dom Clement;* I betook myself, according to custom, to his cell a few moments before he was to enter it; the Brother goaler led me to it, and locked me in it.

He arrives as heated up with wine as with lust, followed by the girl of twenty-six who was for the time being guard near him; informed of what I had to do, I go on my knees as soon as I hear him. He comes to me, examines me in this humiliation, then orders me to rise, and to kiss him on the mouth; he relishes this kiss several minutes and gives it all the expression . . . all the extent that it is possible to conceive in it. During this time, *Armande* (this was the name of her who was waiting on him) was undressing me in particular parts; when the lower portion of the loins, by which she had begun, is laid bare, she hastens to turn me about, and expose to her uncle the side beloved of her likings. *Clement* examines it, he feels it; then; seating himself in an arm-chair, he bids me come and get him to kiss it; *Armande* is at his knees, she is exciting him with her mouth; *Clement* plants his in the sanctuary of the temple which I offer him, and his tongue wanders into the path that one finds at the centre. His hands were pressing the same altars with *Armande*, but as the garments which this girl still had were embarrassing him, he orders her to quit them, which was speedily done; and this docile creature came and resumed close to her uncle an attitude by which, no further exciting him but with her hand, she found herself more in the reach of *Clement*'s. The filthy Monk, still occupied in the same manner with me, then bids me give into his mouth the freest course to the winds with which my bowels might be affected; this whim appeared shocking to me, but I was as yet far from being acquainted with all the irregularities of debauchery; I obey and soon feel the effect of this excess. The Monk, being the better excited, becomes more ardent; he suddenly bites, in six places, the fleshy globes that I present to him; I screech and jump forward; he gets up, advances towards me, wrath in his eyes, and asks me if I know what I have risked in disturbing him; I make him a thousand apologies, he seizes me by my bodice on my stomach, and tears it off as well as my chemise in less time than it takes me to tell it to you. . . . He ferociously grasps my breast, and inveighs against it on squeezing it; *Armande* undresses him, and there we are all three naked. For an instant *Armande* occupies him, he gives her furious slaps of his hand; he kisses her on the mouth, he gnaws her tongue and lips, she screams; sometimes the pain forces involuntary tears from this girl's eyes; he makes her go upon a chair, and requires of her that same episode which he desired with me. *Armande* satisfies him, I excite him with one hand; during this lust, I slightly whip him with the other; he equally bites *Armande*, but she contains herself, and dares not stir. This monster's teeth have been however imprinted in the flesh of this pretty girl. They are seen there in several places. Then turning himself hastily round: — "*Therese*," he says to me, "you are going to suffer cruelly." He had no need of telling it, his eyes only too well foreboded it. "You shall be whipped everywhere," he says to me; "I except nothing." And so saying, he had taken me again by the windpipe, which he brutally handled; he bruised its extremities with the end of his fingers and caused me very keen pains; I dared say nothing, for fear of irritating him still more; but the sweat covered my forehead, and my eyes were in spite of me filled with tears. He wheels me round, makes me kneel on the edge of a chair, the back of which my hands were to hold, under the most grievous sufferings, without disturbing himself for a minute. Seeing me at last there, right in his reach, he orders *Armande* to fetch him rods; she hands him a fistful of long slender ones; *Clement* seizes them, and, recommending me not to stir, he begins by a score of stripes on my shoulders and hips; he quits me for an instant, comes back to *Armande* and places her six feet from me, likewise on her knees, on the edge of a chair. He declares to us that he is going to scourge us both together, and that the first of the two who will let go the chair, utter a cry, or shed a tear, will be immediately subjected by him to such torture as will see fit to him. He administers *Armande* the same number of stripes as he had just laid unto me, and positively on the same places; he takes me again; he kisses everything he has just molested, and lifting up his rods: — "Hold thyself properly, wench" he says to me, "thou art going to be treated as the worst of wretches." At these words I receive fifty lashes, but these embrace only from the middle of the shoulders to the hollow of the hips exclusively. He flies to my comrade and treats her in the same manner. We do not utter a word; one merely heard a few hollow and refrained groans, and we had force enough to keep back our tears.

To whatever degree the Monk's passions were inflamed, we nevertheless perceived as yet any sign of them; he greatly excited himself occasionally, without anything rising up. On approaching me, he eyes for a few moments these two fleshy and still entire globes which were going in their turn to endure the torture; he handles them, he can not forbear from opening them a little, from tickling them, from kissing them a thousand times over. — "Come," says he, "courage. . . ." A shower of strokes fall at once upon these lumps, and bruise them as far as the thighs. Being exceedingly animated with the rebounds, skippings, the grinding of teeth, the writhings which the pain forces from me, he, on examining them, seizing on them with delight, comes to wring out of them, upon my mouth which he ardently kisses, the sensations with which he is agitated. . . . "This girl pleases me," he cries, "I have never whipped any that has given me so much pleasure." And he turns round to his niece, whom he treats with the same barbarity. There remained the lower part, from above the thighs to the calves, and he strikes upon one and the other with the same ardour. — "Come," he says again, on turning me round, "let us change hand, and visit this." He gives me a score of stripes from the middle of the belly to the bottom of the thighs; then, making me spread them out, he smote rudely in the interior of the cave which I opened for him through my posture. — "That is," says he, "the bird I wish to pluck." A few strokes having, by the precautions he took, penetrated very far in, I could not retain my cries. — "Ah! ah!" says the villain, "I have then found out the sensible spot; soon, soon we shall visit it somewhat better." Yet, his niece is put into the same posture and treated in the same manner; he likewise reaches the most delicate places of a woman's body; but whether habit, courage, or the fear of incurring severer treatments, she has the force of containing herself, and one perceives of her only quakings and a few involuntary contortions. There was however a slight change in the physical state of this libertine, and although things had as yet but little consistency, by dint of shakes they incessantly announced some. — "Go on your knees," the Monk says to me, "I am going to whip you on your breast." — "On my breast, father!" — "Yes, on these two lecherous lumps which never excited me except for this purpose." And he squeezed them, he violently pressed them in saying that. — "Oh! my father! this part is so tender you will make me die." — "What matter? provided I am satisfied." And he applies five or six blows which I ward off with my hands. Seeing this, he ties them behind my back; I have no longer anything but the motions of my countenance and tears to implore my pardon, for he had severely ordered me to hold my tongue. I try then to soften him . . . but in vain. He vigorously brings to bear a dozen lashes on my two breasts, which nothing further secures; frightful welts are forthwith stamped in gory streaks; the pain wrung from me tears which fell anew over the marks of this monster's rage, and made them, he said, a thousand times more interesting; . . . he kissed them, he devoured them and returned from time to time to my mouth, to my eyes flooded with tears, which he likewise sucked with lubricity. *Armande* places herself, her hands are joined together, she offers an alabaster-like bosom and of the finest roundness; *Clement* pretends to kiss it, but it is to bite it. . . . He strikes at last, and this lovely skin so white, so plump, in a short time no longer presents to the eyes of their butcher but bruises and bloody streaks. "— An instant!" said the Monk in wrath, "I wish to whip at the same time the most beautiful of the hinder parts and the softest of the breasts." He leaves me on my knees, and placing *Armande* upon me, he makes her spread out her legs, in such a manner that my mouth is on a level with her lower belly, and my breast between her thighs, under her backside. By this means, the Monk has what he wants in his reach, he has under the same point of view *Armande*'s buttocks and my breasts; he furiously strikes both, but my companion, in order to spare me the blows which become far more dangerous for me than for her, has the goodness to stoop and thus secure me, in receiving herself the lashes which would have inevitable wounded me. *Clement* perceives the trick, he alters the posture: — "She will gain nothing by it," he says in a rage, "and if I am willing to spare that part to-day, it will be only to molest another as tender at least." In rising, I then saw that so many infamies were not committed in vain: the debauched fellow was in the most brilliant state. He is only the more furious for it; he changes tools, he opens a closet, in which are several hammers, he takes out one of them with iron claws, which causes me to shudder. — "Hold, *Therese*," he says to me in showing it to me, "see how delightful it is to lash with that. . . . Thou shalt feel it . . . thou shalt feel it, strut, but, for the moment, I am willing to use only this one. . . ." It was of knotted cords of twelve thongs; at the bottom of each one, there was a stronger knot than the others and about the size of a plum-stone. — "Come, for the Calvacade! . . . for the Calvacade!" he says to his niece. She, who was aware of what it was about, gets on her hands and feet, with her loins raised as high as possible, in telling me to imitate her; I do so. *Clement* bestrides my loins, with his head towards my rump; *Armande*, with hers presented, is in front of him. The villain, then seeing us both quite within his reach, hurls furious blows on the charms which we are offering him; but as, through this posture, we lay open as wide as possible that delicate part which distinguishes our sex from men's, the barbarian directs his blows thereat; the long and pliant branches of the whip he uses, penetrating into the interior with much greater facility than the twigs, leave therein deep traces of his rage; now he strikes on the one, now his strokes rush on the other: being as good a jockey as dauntless whipper, he changes his steed several times; we are outstripped, and the titillations of the pain are of such violence, that it is hardly possible to bear them any longer. — "Get up," he then says to us on taking the rods again, "yes, get up and fear me." His eyes sparkle, he foams. Being equally menaced over the whole body, we avoid him . . . we run like lost people throughout the room, he pursues us, striking indiscriminately both on one and the other; the wretch gores us; he drives us at last against the bedside. The blows redouble: the unfortunate *Armande* receives one of them on her breast which makes her stagger; this last horror brings on the ecstasy, and while my back receives its cruel effects, my loins are flooded with the proofs of a delirium the results of which are so dangerous.

"Let us lie down," *Clement* finally says to me; "that is perhaps too much of it for thee, *Therese*, and certainly not enough for me; one does not get tired of this mania, although it be but a very imperfect image of what one would really like to do. Ah! dear girl, thou know-est not how far this depravity drags us, the intoxication into which it casts us, the violent commotion which results, in the electric fluid, from the irritation produced from the pain upon the object which serves our passions; how one is tickled by one's evils! The desire of increasing them . . . that's the stumbling-block of this fantasy, I know it, but is this stumbling-block to be feared by him who mocks every-thing?" Although *Clement's* mind was still in the enthusiasm, seeing nevertheless his senses calmer, I attempted, answering what he had just said, to reproach him with the depravity of his likings; and the manner in which this libertine justified them, deserves, it seems to me, to find space in the avowals which you require of me.

— "The most ridiculous thing in the world no doubt, my dear *Therese,*" says *Clement* to me, "is to want to dispute about man's tastes, to thwart them, blame or punish them, if they are not in conformity either with the laws of the country which we inhabit, or with social conventions. What! men will never understand that there is no kind of tastes, however odd, even however criminal one may suppose them to be, but depends on the sort of organisation which we have received from Nature? This being laid down, I ask, with what right will one man dare require of another man, either to reform his tastes, or model them after the social order? With what right even will the laws, which are merely formed for man's happiness, attemp to punish him who can not correct himself, or who would succeed to do so only at the expense of that happiness which the laws should conserve for him? But should one even wish to change tastes, could one do so? Is it in our power to undo ourselves? Can we become others than we are? Would you require it of a counterfeited man, and is this incongruity of our tastes anything else in the moral than the imperfection of a counterfeited man is in the physical?

Let us go into a few particulars, I consent to it: the mind which I recognise in thee, *Therese,* affords thee the capacity of compre-hending them. Two irregularities have, I perceive, already stricken thee among us: thou are astonished at the poignant sensation felt by some of our fellows for things usually known as fetid or polluted,

141

and thou art likewise surprised because our voluptuous faculties may be shaken by actions which, according to thee, bear only the emblem of ferocity. Let us analyse each of these tastes, and try, if possible, to convince thee that there is nothing simpler in the world than the pleasures which result therefrom.

It is strange, dost thou pretend, that dirty and intemperate things could produce in our senses the irritation essential for the completion of their delirium; but previous to being astonished at this, it would be necessary to feel, dear *Therese*, that objects have no value in our eyes except the one which our imagination sets upon them; it is therefore quite possible, according to this constant truth, that not only the oddest things, but also the vilest and most shocking, may effect us very sensibly. The imagination of man is a faculty of his mind in which, through the organ of senses, objects go to be painted, to be modified and next his thoughts to be formed, by reason of the first perception of these objects. But this imagination, being itself the result of the species of organisation with which man is endowed, adopts the received objects only in such or such a manner, and next creates thoughts simply according to the effects produced by the shock of the objects perceived. Let a comparison facilitate for thy eyes what I am explaining. Hast thou not seen, *Therese*, mirrors of different shapes? Some which diminish the objects, others which magnify them; the latter make them frightful looking; the former lend them charms? Dost thou now fancy that if each of these looking-glasses united the creative faculty with the objective faculty, it would not give, of the same man who would have viewed himself in it, quite a different portrait? and would not this portrait be in consideration of the manner in which it would have perceived the object? If to the two faculties which we have just lent to this looking-glass, it now added that of sensibility, would it not have for this man seen by it, in such or such a manner, the kind of sentiment which would be possible for it to conceive in behalf of the sort of being that it would have perceived? The looking-glass that would have seen him handsome, would love him; the one which would have seen him hideous looking, would hate him; and yet it would be still the same individual.

Such is man's imagination, *Therese* : the same object represents itself to it under as many shapes as it has different modes, and according to the effect received upon the object, whatever it be, it is determined to love or hate it. If the shock of the object perceived strikes it agreeably, it likes it, it prefers it, although this object has no real charm in itself; and if this object, though of a certain value in the eyes of another, has stricken the imagination of which there is question, only in a disagreeable manner, it will be estranged from it, because none of our sentiments is formed, is realised except by reason of the produce of different objects on the imagination. It is not at all surprising, according to this, that what really pleases some, may displease others, and, *vice-versa,* and the most extraordinary thing finds nevertheless sectarians. . . . The counterfeited man also finds mirrors to make him handsome.

Now if we grant that the enjoyment of the senses is always dependent on the imagination, we should be no longer astonished at the numerous variations which the imagination will suggest in these enjoyments, at the host of tastes and various passions that the different wanderings of this imagination will produce. These tastes, although lustful, ought not to strike more than those of a simple kind; there is no reason for finding a table-fantasy less extraordinary than a bed-fantasy; and in either kind, it is not more wonderful to dote upon a thing which the common of men looks on as detestable, than it is to be fond of one generally recognized as good. Common consent proves conformity in the organs, but nothing in favor of the thing liked. Three fourths of the Universe may find the smell of a rose delicious, without its serving as a proof, either to condemn the fourth part that might think it bad, or to show that this smell is truly agreeable.

If there exist, therefore, in the world beings whose tastes are opposed to the admitted prejudices, we must not only be not astonished at them, we must not only not find fault with them, nor punish them; but we must render them services, content them, destroy all the curbs which vex them, and afford them, if you will be just, every means of satisfying themselves without risk; because it no more depended on them to have this strange taste, than it depended on you to be witty or stupid, to be well shaped or hunchbacked. It is in the mother's womb that are formed the organs which are to make us susceptible of such a fantasy; the first objects presented, the first discourses heard, finish by determining the spring; the tastes are formed, and nothing in the world can henceforth destroy them. In vain, education sets to work, it no further alters anything, and he is to become a villain becomes one, however sound be the education he has received, quite as certainly, as he whose organs are fitted out for the good assuredly hastens towards virtue, although he lacked the teacher. Both have acted according to their organization, according to the impressions they had received from Nature, and the one is not more deserving of punishment, than the other of reward.

What is very strange, is, that, so long as there is simple question of trivial things, we are not astonished at the difference of tastes; but the moment it treats about lust, behold all in uproar! the women, ever watching after their rights, the women, whom their weakness and worthlessness persuade to lose nothing, are at every instant fretting lest anything be taken away from them, and if anybody unfortunately makes use of, in enjoyment, any proceedings contrary to their worship, behold crimes deserving the gallows! And yet what injustice! Is the pleasure of the senses therefore to render a man better than the other pleasures of life? In fine, is the temple of generation to fix our propensities better, awaken our desires more surely, than the part of the body, the most contrary to, or the farthest away from it, than the most fetid or disgusting emanation of this body? It ought not, it seems to me, to appear more wonderful to behold a man carrying singularity into the pleasures of libertinism, than in seeing him using it in the other functions of life! Again, his singularity is, in each case, the outcome of his organs: is it his fault, if what effects you is null for him, or if he is moved only by that which is repugnant to you? Who is the man that would not instantly reform his tastes, affections, propensities according to the general plan, and would not rather be as everybody else, than to be singular, were he master of them? To which to punish such a man is the silliest and most barbarous intolerance; he is no guiltier with respect to society, whatever be his errings, than he who, as I have just stated, would have come into the world one eyed or lame. And it is as unjust to punish or mock the latter, as it would be to afflict or ridicule the former. The man endowed with strange tastes is a sickly man; he is, if you will, a hysterical vapoured woman. Has it ever occurred to our minds to punish or vex either of these? Let us be equally just towards the man whose whims are astonishing; being not at all unlike the sick man or the vaporous woman, he is to be pitied as they are and not blamed. Such in the moral is the plea of persons about whom there is question; it would undoubtedly be found, with the same facility, in the physical, and when anatomy is brought to perfection, the relation of man's organization with the tastes which will have affected him, will be easily shown through it. Pendants, Tormentors, Turn-keys, Legislators, Tonsured rascality, what shall ye do, when this is proved? What will become of your laws, ethics, religion, gibbets, paradise, Gods, hell, when it shall be proven that such or such a course of liquors, such a sort of fibres, such a degree of sourness in the blood or in the animal spirits suffices to make a man the object of your pains or recompenses? Let us continue. Cruel tastes amaze thee!

What is the object of the man who enjoys? Is it not to afford his senses all the irritation of which they are susceptible, in order the better and more speedily to arrive, by means of this, at the last crisis . . . the precious crisis which characterizes the good or bad enjoyment, by reason of the greater or less activity in which this crisis happens to be? Now is it not an unwarrantable sophism to dare state that it is necessary, in order to improve it, that it be shared by the woman? Is it not therefore evident that the woman can partake of nothing with us if it be not to take away from us, and that all she robs ought necessarily to be at our expense? And of what necessity is it then, I ask, that a woman should enjoy when we are enjoying? Is there any other sentiment to be flattered in this proceeding, than pride? And shall you not find far more pleasantly the sensation of this proud sentiment, by firmly forcing, on the contrary, that woman to cease enjoying to allow your enjoying alone, in order that nothing may hinder her from being occupied with your enjoyment? Does not tyranny flatter pride far more keenly than benevolence? Finally, is not he who imposes much more certainly master than he who shares? But how can it come into a reasonable man's head that delicacy should be of any value in enjoyment? It is absurd to try and hold that it is necessary for it; never does it add anything to the pleasures of the senses, I state further, it is noxious to it; it is quite a different thing that of loving or that of enjoying; the proof of it is, people love every day without enjoying, and people enjoy without loving. Everything that is combined with delicacy in the pleasures of which there is question, can be granted to the woman's enjoyment only at the expense of the man's, and so long as the latter is occupied with getting enjoyed, he certainly does not enjoy, or his enjoyment is merely intellectual, namely, chimerical and far below that of the senses. No, *Therese*, no, I shall not give over repeating it, it is utterly useless that an enjoyment should be shared in order to be vivid, and render this sort of pleasure as agreeable as it is susceptible of being; on the contrary, it is most essential that man should merely enjoy at the woman's expense, taking from her (whatever sensation she feels by it) all that may afford any increase of the voluptuousness which he wishes to enjoy, without the slightest respect for the effects which may result from it for the woman because these respects will trouble him: he will either have the woman to partake, then he no longer enjoys; or he will fear lest she should suffer, and there he is disturbed. If selfishness is the first law of Nature, it is most certainly more in the pleasures of lubricity than elsewhere, that this heavenly Mother desires it should be our sole mover. It is a very slight misfortune that, on account of the increase of the man's voluptuousness, he must either neglect, or trouble that of the woman; for if this trouble causes him to gain anything, what the object which serves him loses, nowise concerns him; it ought to be indifferent to him whether this object is happy or unhappy, provided he himself is delighted; indeed, there is no kind of relation between this object and him. He would be therefore mad to occupy himself about the sensation of this object at the expense of his own; a thorough simpleton if, in order to modify these alien sensations, he renounces the improvement of his own. This being taken for granted, if the individual of whom there is question, is unfortunately so organized as to be moved only by producing, in the object which serves him, painful sensations, you will admit he ought to abandon himself to it without remorse, since he is up to enjoy, abstraction made of all that may accrue therefrom for this object. . . . We shall return to it: let us continue proceeding by order.

Isolated enjoyments possess therefore charms, they may have more of them than any others; ah! if it was not so, how would so many old men, so many counterfeited or defective folks enjoy? They are perfectly sure they are not loved; thoroughly certain that it is impossible for anyone to partake of what they feel: have they less voluptuousness on this account? Do they merely desire the illusion? Being entirely selfish in their pleasures, you see them occupied only with taking some of them, sacrificing everything in order to receive some, and never suspecting, in the object which serves them, any other properties, except passive ones. It is therefore nowise necessary to bestow pleasures in order to receive some of them; the happy or the unhappy situation of the victim of our debauchery is then absolutely the same to the satisfaction of our senses; there is by no means question of the state in which its heart or spirit may be; this object may indiscriminately be pleased or suffer according to what you are doing to it, love or detest you: all these considerations are null from the moment it treats of the senses. The women, I grant, may establish contrary maxims; but the women, who are simply the engines of voluptuousness, who ought to be only its targets, are suspected every time it is necessary to establish a real system upon this sort of pleasure. Is there a single reasonable man who is envious of having his enjoyment shared by fast girls? And yet are there not millions of men who take great pleasures with these creatures? There are then so many individuals persuaded of what I establish, who put it into practice, without suspecting it, and who ridiculously blame those who legitimate their actions by sound principles, and that, because the Universe is full of organized statues which go, come, act, eat, digest, without ever rendering an account of anything.

Isolated pleasures, being proved as delightful as the others, and certainly much more so, it therefore becomes quite simple then that this enjoyment, taken independently of the object which serves us, is not only very far from what may please it, but is also found contrary to its pleasures: I go further, it may become an imposed pain, a vexation, a torture, without there being anything extraordinary, without anything else resulting from it but the increase of a much surer pleasure for the despot who torments or vexes. Let us try and prove it.

The emotion of voluptuousness is no other upon our soul than a kind of vibration, produced by means of the shakes which the imagination, inflamed by the remembrance of a wanton object, causes our senses to experience, or by means of the presence of this object, or still better by the irritation which this object feels in the kind which moves us the most strongly. Thus our voluptuousness, this inexpressible tickling which misleads us, which transports us to the highest pinnacle of happiness to which man can go, will never be kindled except by two causes: either in perceiving truly or falsely, in the object which serves us, the kind of beauty which flatters us most, or in seeing this object feeling the greatest possible sensation. Now there is no sort of sensation more quickening than that of suffering; its impressions are certain, they do not deceive as those of pleasure, everlastingly played out by the women and hardly ever felt by them; besides, what a deal of self-love, youth, strength, health must there not be in order to be sure of producing in a woman this doubtful and slightly satisfactory impression of pleasure! That of pain, on the contrary, does not require the least thing: the more defects a man has, the older he is, the least amiable he is, the better he will succeed. As to the end, it will be more surely attained, since we establish that one never reaches it, I mean that one never irritates his senses better than when one has produced in the object which serves us the greatest possible impression, no matter by what way. Therefore, he who will cause the most tumultuous impression to spring up in a woman, he who will best turn the whole organization of this woman up-side down, will have decidedly succeeded in procuring himself the greatest possible dose of voluptuousness, because the shock resulting from the impressions of others upon us, to be in proportion to the produced impression, will be necessarily more active, if the impression of others has been painful, than if it has been only mild or pithy; and according to this, the voluptuous egotist who is persuaded that his pleasures will be keen only in as much as they will be whole, will therefore impose, when he is master of it, the strongest possible dose of pain upon the object which serves him, being thorough-certain that what he will reap from voluptuousness will be but in proportion to the most violent impression he will have produced. — These are horrible systems, my father," said I to *Clement*, they lead "to cruel tastes, to terrible tastes. — And what does it matter?" replied the barbarian; "again, are we masters of our tastes? Ought we not to yield to the sway of those we have received from Nature, as the proud head of the oak bends beneath the storm which buffets it about? If Nature was offended by these tastes, she would inspire us with them; it is impossible that we could receive from her a sentiment formed to outrage her, and, in this extreme certainty, we may give ourselves up to our passions, of whatever kind, of whatever violence they may be, quite certain that all the drawbacks which their shock entails are merely designs of Nature whose unwilling organs we are. And what are the consequences of these passions to us? When anyone wishes to delight himself by any action, there is no question about consequences." — "I am not speaking to you of consequences," I hastily interrupted, "the question is about the thing itself; surely if you are not the stronger, and that by atrocious principles of cruelty you liked only to enjoy through pain, in view of increasing your sensations, you will insensibly succeed in producing them upon the object which serves you, to the degree of violence capable of snatching away its life. — Be it so; that is to say, that by the tastes bestowed by Nature, I shall have served the designs of Nature who, working out her creations only through destructions, never inspires me with the idea of the latter but when she needs the former; that is to say, out of an oblong portion of matter I shall have formed three or four thousand round of square ones. Oh! *Therese*, are those crimes?

Can one so name that which serves Nature? Has man the power of committing crimes? And when, preferring his own happiness to that of others, he overthrows or destroys all he finds in his way, has he done anything else but serve Nature whose first and surest inspirations prompt him to make himself happy, no matter at whose expense? The system of the neighbor's love is a chimera we owe to Christianity and not to Nature; the follower of the Nazarean, plagued, unhappy and consequently in the state of weakness which was to have toleration, humanity cried out, was necessarily to establish this fabulous relation of one being with another; he preserved his life in getting it to succeed. But the philosopher does not admit these huge relations; beholding, considering but himself alone in the universe, it is to himself alone that he reports everything. If for an instant he coaxes or caresses others, it is never except relatively to the profit he thinks he will get out of them. Has he no further need of them, does he prevail by his strength, he then everlastingly abjures all those fine systems of humanity and beneficence to which he simply submitted for policy-sake; he no longer fears to give back all to himself, to bring back to himself everything that surrounds him, and whatever thing his enjoyments may cost others, he satisfies them without examination, as without remorse.

— But the man of whom you are speaking is a monster! — The man of whom I am speaking is that one of Nature. — He is a ferocious beast! — Well, the tiger, the leopard, of which this man is, if thou wilt, the image, is it not as he created by Nature and created to fulfill the intentions of Nature? The wolf which devours the lamb accomplishes the views of this common mother, as the malefactor who destroys the object of his vengeance of lubricity. — Oh! you may talk ever so much, my father, I shall never admit of this destructive lubricity. — Because thou art afraid of becoming the object of it, there is selfishness; let us change roles and thou wilt understand it; interrogate the lamb, it will not understand either that the wolf can devour it; ask the wolf what is the good of the lamb: To feed me, he will answer. Wolves which eat lambs, lambs devoured by wolves, the strong one which sacrifices the weak one, the weak one victim of the strong one, that is Nature, those are her views, those are her plans; perpetual action and reaction, a host of vices and virtues, a perfect equilibrium, in fine, resulting from the equality of the good and evil over the earth; an equilibrium essential for the maintenance of the planets, vegetation and without which everything would be instantly destroyed. O *Therese*! this Nature would be greatly astonished, if she could for a moment reason with us, and we told her that those crimes which serve her, that those forfeits which she requires and with which she inspires us, are punished by laws we are assured that they are the image of hers. Dunce, she would answer us, sleep, drink, eat and fearlessly commit such crimes when it will seem good to thee: all these pretended infamies please me, and I desire them since I inspire thee with them. It becomes thee indeed to regulate what irritates me, or what delights me! learn that thou hast nothing in thee but belongs to me, nothing but what I have placed there for reasons which it does not fit thee to know; that the most abominable of thy actions is, as the most virtuous of another, simply one of the ways of serving me. Hold not thyself back therefore, scorn thy laws, thy social conventions and thy Gods; only listen to me alone, and know that if there exists a crime in my eyes, it is the opposition thou placest to what I inspire thee, by the resistance or sophisms." — "Oh good heavens!" I cried, "you make me shudder. If there were no crimes against Nature, whence, therefore, comes to us that invincible repugnance which we feel for certain offences?" — "This repugnance is not dictated by Nature," this rascal hastily replied; "it has its source only in the want of habit; is it not the same with certain dishes? Although excellent, are we not opposed to them simply for want of custom? Should one dare state according to this that these dishes are not good? Let us try and overcome ourselves, and we shall soon agree about their savour. We are loath to take medicines, although they are however wholesome for us; let us in like manner accustom ourselves to the evil, we shall soon no longer meet in it but charms; this momentary repugnance is much rather a craftiness, a coquetry of Nature, than a warning that the thing outrages her: she thus prepares for us the pleasures of triumph; she increases thereby those of action itself. Nay more: it is because, the more the action seems dreadful to us, the more it thwarts our customs and morals, the more bonds it severs, the more it clashes with our social conventions, the more it hurts what we believe to be laws of Nature, so much the more, on the contrary, is it useful to this same Nature. It is never except through crimes that she enters into the rights which Virtue incessantly robs her of. If the crime is slight in differing less from Virtue, it will establish more slowly the equilibrium requisite for Nature; but the more capital it is, the more it equalizes the weights, so much the more does it counterpoise the empire of Virtue, which, without this, would destroy everything. Let him who meditates a forfeit, or him who has just committed it, cease therefore from being frightened: the more extent his crime will have, the better he will have served Nature."

These horrible systems soon brought back my ideas to the sentiments of *Omphale* about the manner in which we left this frightful house. It was therefore from that time I adopted the projects which you shall see me executing afterwards. Nevertheless, in order to finish my enlightenment, I could not forbear asking *Father Clement* a few questions. "At least." said I to him, "you do not keep forever the unhappy victims of your passions? You send them away, no doubt, when you are tired of them?" — "Of course, *Therese*," the Monk answered me, "thou hast entered this only to go out of it, when we four have agreed to grant thee thy retreat. Thou shalt have it most certainly." — "But are you not afraid," I continued, "that younger and less discreet girls do not go sometimes and reveal what takes place with you? — It is impossible. — Impossible? — Utterly. — Could you explain for me?. . . . — No, that is our secret; but all that I can assure you, is, that discreet or not, it will be wholly impossible for thee ever to tell, when thou art out of here, one word of what passes in it. So thou seest, *Therese,* I impose no discretion upon thee; a restrained policy in nowise bridles my desires. . . ." And the Monk fell asleep at these words. From this moment it was no longer possible for me not to see that the most violent measures were being taken against the unfortunate reformed girls, and that this terrible security of which one boasted was simply the fruit of death. I persisted only the more in my resolution; we shall shortly see the effect of it.

As soon as *Clement* was asleep, *Armande* came to me: "He is going to waken up directly as a madman," she said to me; "Nature lulls his senses to sleep merely to lend them, after a brief repose, a much greater energy; one more scene, and we shall be quiet until tomorrow." — "But thou," said I to my companion, "why dost thou not sleep a few moments?" — "Can I do so?" *Armande* answered me; "if I did not watch on foot about his bed, and my neglect was discovered, he would be the man to stab me." — "Oh! Heavens!" said I, "what! even while sleeping, this rascal wishes that what encompasses him be in a state of suffering?" — "Yes," my companion answered me, "it is the barbarity of this idea which procures him that furious awaking which thou art about to see in him; he is thereupon as those perverse writers, whose corruption is so dangerous, so active, that they have for end in printing their frightful systems, but to extend beyond their lives the amount of their crimes; they can perpetrate no more of them, but their cursed writings will cause them to be committed, and this sweet idea which they carry to the tomb consoles them for the obligation in which death puts them on renouncing evil." — "The monsters!" I cried . . . *Armande*, who was a very gentle creature, kissed me in shedding tears, then began again to tramp round the bed of this wicked man.

At the end of a few hours, the Monk really did wake up, in a prodigious agitation, and seized me with such force that I thought he was going to choke me; his respiration was quick and hurried; his eyes sparkled, he uttered broken sentences, which were nothing else but blasphemies or wanton words. He calls *Armande*, he requests her for rods, and begins to whip us both, but more vigorously than he had done previous to falling asleep. It is by me he appears that he wishes to end, I scream; in order to shorten my pains, *Armande* violently excites him, he is bewildered, and the monster, at last determined by the most violent sensations, loses with the burning floods of his seed his ardour and desires.

All was still the rest of the night. The Monk on rising contented himself with handling and examining us both; and as he was going to say his Mass, we entered the seraglio. The Senior could not keep from lusting after me in the state of inflammation she pretended I must be; being ruined as I was, could I defend myself? She did as she liked, sufficiently to convince me that even a woman, at such a school, soon losing all the delicacy and bearing of her sex, could, after the example of her tyrants, become only smutty or cruel.

Two nights afterwards, I slept with *Jerome*; I shall not describe his horrors to you, they were still more frightful. What a school, great God! In short, at the end of a week all my rounds were taken. Then *Omphale* asked me if it was not true that of them all, *Clement* was the one of whom I had most to complain? —"Alas" I answered, "in the midst of a host of horrors and filth which now disgust and now shock, it is very hard for me to pass my judgment on the most odious of the villains; I am abused by them all, and I should like to see myself already outside, whatever be the destiny that awaits me." — "It might be possible for thee to be shortly satisfied," my companion answered me; "we are drawing nigh the festival; this circumstance seldom takes place without fetching them victims; or they seduce young girls by means of confession, or they filch them, if they can: so many fresh recruits that suppose reforms."

This famous festival arrived. . . . Can you believe, Madam, into what monstrous impiety the Monks ran on this event? They imagined that a visible miracle would double the lustre of their reputation. Consequently they dressed up *Florette,* the youngest of the girls, with all the Virgin's attire; they bound her to a niche in the wall by chords which were not seen, and ordered her to raise all of a sudden her arms with compunction towards Heaven, when the host would be elevated to it. As this little creature was threatened with the cruelest chastisements, should she attempt to utter a single word, or fail in her role, she got through it admirably well, and the fraud had all the success one could expect from it. The people cried miracle, left rich offerings to the Virgin, and returned hence more convinced than ever of the efficacity of this heavenly mother's graces. Our libertines wished, in order to double their impieties, that *Florette* should appear at the evening orgies in the same robes which had attracted her so much homage, and each of them inflamed his odious desires by subjecting her, under this costume, to the irregularity of his whims. Being provoked by this first crime, the sacrilegious men do not stop at that: they get this child stripped naked, they stretch her flat upon a large table, they light wax candles, they place the image of our Saviour in the middle of the loins of the young girl and dare consummate on her buttocks the most awful of our mysteries. I fainted at this horrible sight, it was impossible for me to bear it. *Severino*, seeing me in this state, said that in order to familiarize me to it I should serve as altar in my turn. They seize me; they put me in the same place as *Florette*; the sacrifice is consummated, and the host . . . this sacred symbol of our august Religion. . . . *Severino* lays hold of it, he thrusts it into the obscene local of his Sodomite enjoyments . . . stamps upon it upbraidingly . . . crushes it ignominiously beneath the redoubled sallies of his huge dart, and dashes, in blaspheming, over the body of his Saviour, the polluted floods of the torrent of his lubricity! . . .

I was taken motionless out of their hands; I had two days over the horrible crime for which I had served in spite of me. This remembrance still breaks my soul, I do not think of it without horror. . . . Religion is in me the effect of sentiment: everything that offends or outrages it causes the blood of my heart to spirt up.

The time for the month's repetition was going to arrive, when *Severino* enters our room one morning, about nine o'clock. He appeared greatly inflamed; a sort of bewilderment was painted in his eyes. He examines us, sets us one after another in his beloved posture, and stops especially at *Omphale*; he remains several minutes to contemplate her in this attitude, he excites himself privately, he kisses what is presented to him, pretends he is in course of consummating, and consummates nothing. Getting her next lifted up, he casts upon her glances in which rage and wickedness are depicted; then giving her with all the force of his loins a strong kick in the bottom of the belly, sends her reeling twenty paces off. — "The Society reforms thee, wench" he says to her, "it is tired of thee; be ready by night fall, I myself shall come for thee." And he walks away.

When he had gone away, *Omphale* rises. She throws herself weeping into my arms: — "Well!" she says to me, "at the infamy, the cruelty of the preliminaries, canst thou be still blind about the consequences? What is going to become of me, great God!" — "Grow quiet," said I to this unhappy girl, I am now bent on "everything; I am waiting only the opportunity; perhaps it may present itself sooner than thou thinkest; I shall divulge these horrors; if it is true that their proceedings are as cruel as we have reason to believe, try and obtain some delay, and I shall tear thee out of their hands." In case *Omphale* would be released, she swore likewise to be of service to me, and we both wept. The day passed without incident. About five o'clock, *Severino* himself came up. — "Come," he hastily said to *Omphale*, "art thou ready?" — "Yes, my Father," she replied in sobbing; "allow me to embrace my companions." — "That is needless," said the Monk; "we have no time to perform a weeping scene; they are waiting for us, let us depart." Then she asked whether she should take away her goods. —"No," said the Superior, "does it not all belong to the house? You have no further need of it." Then correcting himself, as one who has said too much about it: "Those goods become useless to thee; you will get some made to measure, which will fit you better; content yourself therefore with carrying away only what you have on." I inquired of the Monk whether he would be willing to allow me to accompany *Omphale* only as far as the house-door. . . . He answered me by a look which caused me to recoil with fright. . . . *Omphale* leaves, she casts wistful glances at us full of trouble and tears, and as soon as she is outside, I toss myself upon the bed in despair.

My companions, being accustomed to these events or blinded of their consequences, took less share in it than I, and the Superior stepped in at the end of an hour; he came for those of the supper-party. I was of the number; there were to be but four women at it, the girl of twelve, the one of sixteen, the one of twenty-three and I. Everything passed off nearly as the other days; I simply remarked that the guard-girls were not there, that the Monks often whispered, that they drunk very much, that they contented themselves with violently exciting their desires, without ever allowing themselves to consummate them, and that they sent us away much earlier, without keeping back any to go to bed. . . . What conclusions to be drawn from these remarks? I drew them, because one pays attention to everything in similar circumstances, but what to conjecture therefrom? Ah! such was perplexity, that no idea presented itself to my mind, but it was directly combatted by another. On recollecting the conversations of *Clement*, I had undoubtedly everything to fear; and then, the hope . . . this deceitful hope which consoles us, which blinds us and thus does us almost as much good as evil, in fine, hope came to reassure me. . . . So many horrors were so far from me, that it was impossible for me to suppose them! I lay down in this terrible state; now and then persuaded that *Omphale* would not fail in the oath; convinced immediately after that the cruel means they would take with her would deprive her of all power to be of use to us. And such was my last opinion, when I saw the third day closing without having as yet heard anything spoken of.

On the fourth I was again at the supper-party; it was numerous and select. On that day, the finest eight women assisted at it; they had done me the favor of taking me to it; the guard-girls were there also. From the moment we were entering we saw our new companion. — "There she is whom the society destines to replace *Omphale*, Ladies," *Severino* says to us. And so saying, he tore from the girl's bust the mantlets, the gauzes with which she was covered, and we beheld a young person of fifteen, of the most pleasing and delicate form. She gracefully raised her lovely eyes towards each of us; they were still wet with tears, but of the liveliest interest; her waist was nimble and small, her skin of dazzling whiteness, the prettiest hair in the world, and something so bewitching on the whole that it was impossible to see without feeling one's self involuntarily attracted towards her. They called her *Octavie*. We soon learned that she was a girl of the first quality, born in Paris and coming out of a Convent to wed the Count of***: She had been carried away by force in her carriage with two governesses and three lackeys; she ignored what had become of her retinue; she was taken alone about nightfall, and her eyes having been blindfolded, she was conveyed to where we saw her, without its becoming possible for her to know more about it.

Nobody had as yet spoken a word to her. Our four libertines, a moment in ecstasy before so many charms, had only strength to admire them. The empire of beauty forces respect; the most corrupted rascal renders it, in spite of his heart, a kind of worship which he never infringes without remorse: but monsters such as those we had to do with, languish but little under like curbs. — "Come, fair child," says the superior in impudently pulling her towards the arm-chair in which he was seated, "come, let us see if the rest of your charms correspond to those which Nature has placed with so much confusion over your face." And as this lovely girl was getting confused, as she was blushing, and was trying to get away, *Severino,* hastily seizing her across the body: — "Understand," he says to her, "little Agnes, understand that what one wishes to tell you is to strip yourself instantly stark naked." And the libertine, at these words, slips one hand under her petticoats while holding her with the other; *Clement* steps up, he raises *Octavie's* clothes above her groins, and by means of this manoeuvre exposes the sweetest, the most enticing attractions that it is possible to behold; *Severino,* who handles, but who does not perceive, stoops to look, and there they are all four agreeing that they have never seen anything so beautiful. Yet the modest *Octavie,* but little formed for such outrages, replies by tears and defends herself. — "Let us undress, let us undress," says *Antonin;* "nothing can be seen in this way." He helps *Severino,* and on the instant the little girl's attractions appear unveiled to our eyes. There never was undoubtedly a whiter skin, never happier proportions. . . . God, what a crime! . . . Were so much beauty, freshness, innocence and delicacy to become prey of these barbarians! *Octavie,* ashamed, knows not where to flee in order to conceal her charms, everywhere she meets only with eyes which devour them, with brutal hands which rummage them; the ring is formed round her, and, as I had done, she runs through it in every direction. The brutal *Antonin* has not the force of resisting; a cruel attempt brings on the homage, and the incense smokes at the feet of the God. *Jerome* compares her to our young comrade of sixteen, undoubtedly the handsomest in the seraglio; he places the two altars of his worship near each other. — "Ah! what a lot of whiteness and graces!" he cried in feeling *Octavie*; "but what a deal of gentility and bloom is likewise in this one! Indeed," continued the Monk on fire, "I am undecided." Then imprinting his mouth upon the attractions which his eyes confront: "*Octavie*," he cried, "thou shalt have the apple, it solely depends on thee, give me the precious fruit of this beloved tree of my heart. . . . Oh! yes, yes, let either of you give it to me, and I everlastingly assure the prize of beauty to whoever will have served me sooner." *Severino* sees it is time to think of more serious things: wholly out of patience, he lays hold of this unfortunate girl, he places her according to his desires; not yet replying sufficiently on his own cares, he calls *Clement* to his aid. *Octavie* weeps and is not heard; the fire shines in the lecherous Monk's looks; being master of the place, one would say he is considering the avenues thereof only to attack it the more securely; no crafts, no preparations are employed; would he gather the roses with so many charms, if he removed their thorns? However enormous the inequality is between the conquest and the assailant, the latter nevertheless undertakes the combat; a shrill cry announces victory, but nothing affects the enemy; the more the captive implores quarter, the more she is vigorously squeezed, and the unhappy girl vainly struggles, she is soon sacrificed. — "Never was laurel harder," said *Severino* on withdrawing; "I fancied that, for the first time in my life, I would miscarry near harbour. . . . Ah! how much narrowness and heat! She is the Ganymede of the Gods."

— "I must restore her to the sex which thou hast just sullied," said *Antonin*, seizing her thence, and without wishing to let her get up; "there is more than one breach in the rampart," said he. And proudly approaching, he is in an instant at the sanctuary. Fresh cries are heard: "God be praised!" said the dishonest man; "I should have doubted of my success without the victim's groans, but my triumph is assured, for there are blood and tears."

— "Indeed," said *Clement* closing up, rods in hand, "I shall not disturb this sweet attitude either, it is too favorable for my desires." *Jerome*'s guard-girl and the one of thirty were holding *Octavie*; *Clement* examines, handles; the little girl, frightened, implores him but does not affect him.

— "Oh! my friends," said the exalted Monk, "why not flog the novice who shows us so beautiful an arse?" The air directly resounds with the whizzing of the rods and the deaf sound of their blows upon this lovely flesh; *Octavie*'s cries are mingled with them, the blasphemies of the Monk reply to them: what a scene for those libertines given up, in the midst of us all, to a thousand obscenities! They applaud it, they encourage it; yet *Octavie*'s skin changes color, the tints of the liveliest carnation are blended with the glow of lilies; but that which would perhaps amuse Love an instant, if moderation directed the sacrifice, becomes by dint of rigor a frightful crime against its laws; nothing stops the perfidious Monk; the more the young pupil complains, the more the Regent's severity breaks out; from the middle of the loins to the bottom of the thighs, all is treated in the same way, and it is at last upon the gory vestiges of his barbarous pleasures, that the base wretch appeases his flames. — "I shall be less fierce than all that," said *Jerome* in taking the beautiful one and applying himself to her coral lips; "this is the temple in which I am going to sacrifice . . . and within this bewitching mouth. . . ." I hold my tongue. . . . It is the polluted reptile tarnishing a rose, my comparison tells you all.

The remainder of the evening became similar to all you know: if it is only the beauty, the touching age of this youthful girl, inflaming still more those rascals, all their infamies redoubled, and satiety rather than pity, in sending away this unhappy girl into her room, restored her at least for a few hours the calm of which she was in need.

I should have liked very much to be able to console her this first night; but being obliged to spend it with *Severino*, it had been, on the contrary, myself who was in the necessity of having great need of help. I had had the misfortune, not of pleasing, the word would not be appropriate, but of exciting more keenly than another the infamous desires of this Sodomite. He now longed for me almost every night; being exhausted by the latter, he had need of refinements; fearing no doubt lest he should not yet do me harm enough with the dreadful sword with which he was gifted, he imagined this time to perforate me by one of those Nun's moveables which decency does not permit me to name and which was of a huge size; it was necessary to consent to everything. He himself caused the weapon to penetrate into his beloved temple; by dint of jerking it entered very far in; I scream, the Monk is amused thereat; after a few going backwards and forwards, all of a sudden he violently withdraws the tool and consumes himself in the gulf which he has just opened a little. . . . What a whim! Is not that contrary to what men may desire? But who can define a libertine's soul? It is a long while ago since people are aware that this is the enigma of Nature, she has not yet given us its meaning.

In the morning, finding himself somewhat refreshed, he wanted to try another torture, he showed me a still much larger engine: this was hollow and set off with a piston squirting water with an incredible stiffness through an opening which afforded the spout more than three inches in circumference; this huge tool was itself nine inches round by twelve in length. *Severino* had it filled with very warm water and wanted to thrust it into my forepart; being frightened at a like project, I cast myself at his knees to beg forgiveness, but he is in one of those cursed moods in which pity is no longer understood, in which the passions, far more eloquent, put instead of it, a cruelty oftentimes very dangerous. The Monk threatens me with all his wrath, if I do not consent; I must obey. The perfidious machine penetrated two thirds, and the tearing which it causes me, together with the extreme heat of it, is about to take away from me the use of my senses. During this time, the Superior, not ceasing to inveigh against the parts he molests, gets himself excited by his waiting maid; after a quarter of an hour of this rubbing which is lacerating me, he lets loose the piston which makes the scalding water jut up into the death of the womb. . . . I fainted. *Severino* was enraptured. . . . He was in a delirium at least equal to my pain. — "It is merely that," said the traitor, when I had recovered my senses; "we treat those attractions much harder sometimes here. . . . A thorn salad, zounds! well peppered, well seasoned with vinegar, thrust inside with the blade of a knife, in order to cheer them up; at the first fault thou shalt make, I do doom thee to it," said the villain while still handling the sole object of his worship. But two or three homages, after the debaucheries of the eve, had exhausted him: I was discharged.

I found, on entering, my new companion in tears; I did what I could to calm her down, but it is not easy to be readily resolved upon a change of so frightful a situation; this little girl had besides a great fund of religion, virtue and sensibility: her state appeared to her only the more terrible on this account. *Omphale* was right in telling me that seniority had no influence over the reforms; that merely dictated by the Monks' fantasy, or by their fear of any farther researches, one might undergo it at the end of eight days, as at the end of twenty years. *Octavie* was not four months with us, when *Jerome* came to announce to her, her departure; although it was he who had most enjoyed her during her stay in the Convent, who moreover appeared to love and seek her, the poor child left, making us the same promises as *Omphale*; she kept them quite as little.

I no longer occupied myself, from that time, but with the project I had conceived since *Omphale*'s departure; up to everything in order to flee this savage den, nothing frightened me from succeeding in it. What could I apprehend in executing this design? Death. Of what was I sure in remaining? Of death. And in succeeding, I saved myself. I had not therefore to waver; but it beloved, previous to this enterprise, that the fatal examples of rewarded vice should be again reproduced under my eyes; it was written in the great book of the Fates, in this dark book of which no mortal has knowledge, it was engraved therein, I say that all those who had tormented, humbled me, bound in irons, should unceasingly receive before my eyes the price of their forfeits, as if Providence had made it a duty to show me the uselessness of virtue. . . . Fatal lessons which did not however correct me, and which, should I escape again from the sword hung over my head, will not prevent me from being ever the slave of this Divinity of my heart.

One morning, without expecting it, *Antonin* put in an appearance in our room and announced to us that the Reverend *Father Severino*, a relative and protege of the Pope, had been just nominatd by His Holiness, General of the Benedictine Order. On the next day, this Monk really did set out without seeing us; there was expected, we were told, another far superior for debauchery to all those who remained: fresh motives for hastening my steps.

The day after *Severino's* departure, the Monks had decided on reforming another of our companions. I chose, for my escape, the very day they came to announce this wretch's judgment, that the Monks being busier might pay less attention to me.

We were at the beginning of Spring; the length of the nights still somewhat favored my steps. I was preparing them for two months without anybody's suspecting them; I used to gradually saw, with an old pair of scissors I had found, the gratings of my cabinet; already my head easily passed through it, and, with the linen which used to serve me, I had formed a rope more than sufficient to get over the twenty or twenty-five feet of which *Omphale* had told me the building was. When they had taken away my clothes, I was careful, as I have told you, to retire from them my little fortune amounting to nearly six louis, I had always diligently hid it; in departing I put it back in my hair, and almost the whole of our room being of the supper-party that evening, alone with one of my companions who went to bed as soon as the others had gone down, I passed into my cabinet; there, freeing the hole I had taken care to stop up every day, I fastened my rope to one of the bars which was not damaged, then, letting myself slide down by this means, I had soon touched the ground. This is not what had puzzled me the most: the six enclosures of walls or thick fir hedges, of which my companion had spoken to me, puzzled me quite otherwise.

Once there, I recognized that every space or circular alley left from one hedge to the other was not more than eight feet wide, and it is this nearness which caused the view to imagine, that all within this place was simply an under-wood. The night was pitchy dark; while going round this circular alley to reconnoitre whether I should not discover an opening in the hedge, I passed under the supper-room. There was no longer anybody in it; my uneasiness redoubled on this account; I nevertheless continued my researches, I thus reached to the height of the window of the great subterraneous hall which is beneath that of the usual orgies. I perceived much light in it, I was bold enough to approach it; owing to my position I peeped into it. My unhappy companion was stretched upon a rack, her hair in disorder, and destined no doubt to some frightful torture in which she was going to find, for liberty the eternal end of her woes. . . . I quaked, but what my looks had just surprised soon astonished one more: *Omphale*, either had not known all, or she had not told me all; I beheld four naked girls in this underground place, who appear to me very handsome and young, and who were certainly none of ours; there were in this frightful refuge other victims of these monsters' lubricity . . . other unfortunate girls unknown to us. . . . I hastened to flee, and went on turning until I was at the side opposed to the underground-room: not having as yet discovered any breach, I resolved to make one; I had, without anyone's perceiving, supplied myself with a long knife; I worked; in spite of my gloves, my hands were soon torn. Nothing stopped me; the hedge was more than two feet thick, I opened it a little, and behold me in the second alley; there, I was surprisd at feeling under my feet but soft, boggy clay into which I was sinking to the ankle: the further I advanced into this thick brush-wood, the darker it grew. Being curious to know whence came the change of ground. I grope with my hands. . . . O good Heavens! I seize the head of a corpse! Great God! thought I terrified, such is here undoubtedly, I was indeed told so, the grave-yard where those butchers throw their victims; scarcely do they take the trouble of covering them with clay! . . . This skull is perhaps that of my dear *Omphale*, or that of unhappy *Octavie*, so handsome, so mild, so kind, and who appeared on earth but as the roses of which her charms were the image! Myself, alas! this had been my place, why not undergo my lot? what shall I gain in going to seek fresh reverses? Have I not committed enough of evil in it? Have I not become in it the motive of a pretty large number of crimes? Ah! let us fill up my destiny! O earth, open to swallow me up! It is well worth while, when one is so forsaken, so poor, so abandoned as I am, to give one's self so many pains to vegetate a few instant's longer, among monsters! . . . But, no, I ought to avenge Virtue in irons. . . . She expects it from my courage. . . . Let us not suffer ourselves to be cast down . . . let us advance: it is essential for the universe to be rid of villains so dangerous as these. Ought I fear losing three or four men in order to save a million of individuals whom their policy or ferocity sacrifices?

I therefore pierce the hedge where I am; this one was thicker than the other: the farther I advanced, the stronger I found it. The hole is nevertheless effected, but a solid ground beyond . . . nothing further announced me the same horrors as I had just met. So arrive at the brink of the ditch, without having found the wall of which *Omphale* had told me; there certainly was none, and it is likely the Monks said so merely to frighten us the more. Being less enclosed beyond this six-fold surrounding, I distinguished objects better; the church and the building which was adjacent to it forthwith presented themselves to my eyes; the ditch hemmed in both; I took good care from trying to climb over it at this side; I walked along the sides, and seeing myself at last in front of one of the routes of the forest, I resolved to cross it there and throw myself in this route when I should have got upon the other side. This ditch was very deep, but dry, for my good luck; as the lining was of brick, there was no means of slipping on it, I therefore precipitated myself: somewhat stunned by my fall, I was a few moments before getting up. . . . I went on, I reached the other bank without obstacle; but how climb it? By force of looking for a convenient spot, I find one at last where a few demolished bricks afforded me at the same time both the facility of serving me with others as stiles, and that of sticking, in order to bear me up, the tip of my foot in the ground; I was already nearly upon the top, when all giving way under my weight, I fell back into the ditch beneath the rubbish I had dragged; I thought I was dead; this fall, involuntarily made, had been ruder than the other; I was besides all covered over with the materials which had followed me; a few having knocked me on the head, I was quite bruised. . . . O God! said I to myself in despair, let us go no farther; let us stay there; it is a warning from Heaven; it does not wish me to go on: my ideas are no doubt deceiving me; evil is perhaps useful on earth, and when the hand of God desires it, perhaps it is wrong to be opposed to it! But being soon stirred up against a system, the too unlucky a fruit of the corruption which had surrounded me, I free myself from the rubbish with which I am covered, and finding greater ease in re-ascending by the breach I have just formed, owing to the fresh holes effected therein, I try again, I stir myself up, in an instant I find myself on the top. All this had removed me from the path I had perceived, but having taken particular notice of it, I come across it again, and set to flee at a good rate. Before the day was over, I found myself outside the forest, and shortly upon that hill from which I had six months ago, for my misfortune, spied this frightful Convent. I rest myself a few minutes, I was all in a sweat; my first care is to cast myself on my knees and beg God for fresh pardons for the involuntary faults I had committed in that odious receptacle of crime and pollutions; tears of sorrow soon flowed from my eyes. Alas! said I to myself, I was much less criminal, when I left last year this same path, guided by a principle of devotion so fatally deceived! O God! In what a state can I now look upon myself! These fatal reflections somewhat calmed down by the pleasure of seeing myself free, I pursued my way towards Dijon, imagining that it could be only in this Capital my complaints were to be lawfully received. . . .

Here *Madam de Lorsange* wished to oblige *Therese* to take breath, at least for a few minutes; she was in need of it; the heat she threw into her narration, the sores these fatal recitals opened anew in her soul, in short, everything invited her to a few moments rest. *Mr. de Corville* had refreshments brought, and after a brief repose, our Heroine continued, as you are going to see, the particulars of her deplorable adventures.

**END OF PART FIRST**

# JUSTINE, OR THE MISFORTUNES OF VIRTUE

## PART II

# JUSTINE, OR THE MISFORTUNES OF VIRTUE

## PART II

I was on my second day's journey, perfectly calm about the fears I had had at first of being pursued; it was extremely warm, and according to my economical custom, I had wandered from the road to find shelter where I might make a slight repast which would put me in a way of waiting for the evening. A small grove on the right of the road, through the midst of which a limpid stream meandered, appeared to me suitable for refreshing me. My thirst being quenched with this pure and fresh water, nourished with a little bread, my back propped against a tree, I allowed a wholesome and serene breeze to circulate in my veins; it refreshed me, it tranquillized my senses. There I reflected on that almost unexampled fatality which, notwithstanding the thorns with which I was surrounded in the career of virtue, always brought me back, whatever might become of it, to the worship of that Divinity, and to acts of love and resignation towards the Supreme Being from whom it proceeds, and whose likeness it is. A sort of enthusiasm had just set upon me: Alas! said I to myself, he does not abandon me, this good God whom I adore, since I have just found on this very instant the means of repairing my strength. It is not to him I owe this favor? And are there not on earth beings to whom it is refused? I am not therefore wholly unhappy, since there are still others more to be pitied than I am. . . . Ah! am I not less so than the unfortunate girls whom I am leaving in this den of vice, out of which God's goodness has caused me to go as by a kind of miracle?. . . And full of gratitude, I threw myself upon my knees; fixing the sun as the finest work of

168

the Divinity, as the one which best manifests his grandeur, I drew from the sublimity of this planet fresh motives for prayer and thanks-giving, when all of a sudden I feel myself seized by two men who, having enveloped my head to prevent me from seeing and crying, hand-cuff me as a criminal, and drag me without uttering a word.

We march thus almost two hours without its being possible for me to see what route we are taking, when one of my conductors, hearing me breathe with difficulty, proposes to his comrade to rid me of the veil which is incommoding my head; he agrees to it, I breathe and perceive at last that we are in the midst of a forest following a pretty large route, although but little frequented. A thousand fatal ideas present themselves then to my mind, I fear I am taken again by the agents of those shameful Monks. . . . I fear I am being brought back to their hateful convent. "Ah!" said I to one of my guides, "Sir, may I not beseech you to tell me where I am led to? May I not ask you what they pretend to do with me?" — "Soothe yourself, my child," this man said to me, "and let not the precautions that we are obliged to take cause you any fear: we are bringing you to a good master's; weighty reasons force him to take a chamber-maid for his spouse, only with this glow of mystery; but you will be all-right there." "—Alas! Gentlemen," I replied, "if it is my happiness you are causing, it is needless to oblige me by force: I am a poor orphan, greatly to be pitied no doubt; I ask only a place: as soon as you give it to me, why are you afraid of my running away?" "—She is right," said one of the guides, "let us set her more at ease, let us merely hold but her hands." They do so, and our march is continued. Seeing me tranquil, they even reply to my inquiries; I at last learn from them, that the master to whom I am destined is called the *Count de Gernande*, born in Paris, but possessing great wealth in this country, and rich in all with over five hundred thousand livres a year, which he spends alone, said one of my guides to me. — "Alone?" — "Yes, he is a solitary man, a philosopher: he never sees anybody; in return, he is one of the greatest gluttons in Europe; there is not an eater in the world fit to cope with him. I say nothing to you about him, you shall see him. — But what do these precautions signify, Sir? — Here it is. Our master has the misfortune of having a wife whose head became deranged; she must be kept within sight, she does not go out of her room, nobody wishes to wait upon her; we should have vainly proposed it to you: had you been warned, you would never have accepted. We are obliged to carry away girls by force, to fulfill this fatal service." — "What! I shall be a captive near this Lady?" — "Yes, indeed, that is why we hold you thus. You will be well off there . . . soothe yourself, perfectly well off; save this inconvenience, you shall want for nothing." — "Ah! good Heavens! what a constraint!" — "Come, come, my child, courage, you will get out of it one day, and your fortune will be made." My guide had not achieved these words, when we beheld the castle. It was a superb and vast isolated building in the midst of the forest, but this great edifice was far from being se peopled as it appeared built to be so. I saw merely a little movement, a scanty resort of people towards the kitchens situated in the cellars under the middle of the house. All the rest was as solitary as the site of the castle. Nobody took notice of us when we entered; one of my guides went into the kitchen, the other introduced me to the Count. He was at the end of a vast and superb apartment, he was rolled up in a morning-gown of Indian satin, stretched on an ottoman, and near him two young men so indecently, or rather so ridiculously dressed, coifed with so much elegance and skill, that I took them at first for girls; a little further examination finally made me recognize them for boys, one of whom might be fifteen years old, and the other sixteen. They appeared to me to be of very pretty faces, but in such a state of effeminacy and prostration that I at first thought they were ill.

"Here is a girl, *Monseigneur*," said my guide; "she appears to us to be what suits you: she is mild, she is honest, and asks but a place; we hope you will be pleased with her." — "All-right," said the Count, while scarcely looking at me; "you will shut the doors after you, *Saint-Louis,* and you shall see that nobody is to come in until I ring." Next the Count rose, and came to examine me. While he is scrutinizing me, I can depict him for you: the singularity of the portrait deserves your attention for an instant. *Mister de Gernande* was then a man of fifty years old, being almost six feet high, and of a huge size. Nothing is so frightful as his face: the length of his nose, the thick obscurity of his eyebrows, his black and wicked eyes, his big mouth badly supplied, his tenebrous and bald brow, the sound of his voice terrible and hoarse, his enormous arms and hands, all contribute to form a gigantic fellow of him, whose access inspires much greater fear than assurance. We shall shortly see whether the moral and the actions of this kind of Centaur were in conformity with his frightful caricature. After a most rapid and blunt examination, the Count asked me my age. — "Twenty-three years, Sir," I replied; and he added to this first inquiry a few questions about my personal self. I acquainted him with everything that concerned me. I do not even forget the stain I had received from *Rodin* ; and when I had described to him my misery, when I had proved to him that misfortune had constantly pursued me: — "So much the better!" the nasty man cruelly said to me, "so much the better! you will be only the more docile for it in my house; it is a very slight drawback that bad luck pursues this abject race of people whom Nature dooms to crawl near us on the same soil: it is the more active and the less insolent for it, discharges on this account its duty much better towards us." — "But, Sir, I have told you of my birth, it is not abject." — "Yes, yes, I am aware of all that; people always make themselves pass off as being mighty when they are nothing, or in misery. The illusions of pride must indeed come to console the wrongs of fortune; it next involves upon us to believe what we please about those births broken down by mere destiny. Besides, it is all the same to me; I find you looking like, and in the attire of a servant; I shall therefore take you on this footing, if you think fit. Yet," continued this stern man, "it depends but on yourself to be happy: some patience, discretion, and in a few years I shall discharge you from here, in a way of your being able to live on your own account."

Then he took my arms one after the other, and tucking up my sleeves to the elbow, he attentively examined them in asking me how often I had been bled? "Twice, Sir," I said to him, pretty much surprised at this inquiry, and I mentioned the occasions on informing him of the circumstances of my life when it had taken place. He pressed his fingers upon the veins as when one wishes to swell them in order to proceed to this operation, and when they are at the degree he requires, he puts his mouth to them while sucking them. From that moment, I no further doubted that libertinism was still mixed up with this nasty man's proceedings, and the stings of uneasiness awoke in my heart. "I must know how you are formed," continued the Count, in staring me with a look which caused me to tremble; "there must be no bodily defect for the place you have to fill; show therefore all you bear." I defended myself; but the Count, angerly working up all the muscles of his frightful face, rudely tells me that he does not advise me to act the prude with him, because he has sure means of getting the upper hand of women. "What you have related to me," he says to me, "does not forebode a very lofty virtue; thus your resistances would be as much out of place as ridiculous."

At these words, he beckons to his young waiters, who, directly approaching me, set to undress me. With such worn-out, such decayed fellows as those that surround me, defence is certainly not hard; but of what use would it be? The Cannibal who set them at me, would have, had he wished, reduced me to powder with a blow of his fist. I therefore understood it was necessary to give in: I was undressed in an instant; this is hardly performed, than I perceive I am exciting still more the merriment of these two Ganymedes. "My friend," said the younger to the other, "what a beautiful thing a girl is! . . . But what a pity that it is empty there." — "Oh!" said the other, "there is nothing more infamous than this void; I should not have to do with a woman when there would be question of my fortune." And while my forepart was so ridiculously the subject of their sarcasms, the Count, close partisan of the back-side (unfortunately, alas! like all libertines), was a scrutinizing mine, he handled it roughly, kneaded it forcibly; and taking pinches of flesh between his five fingers, he soften it even to bruise it. He next made me take a few steps forward, and return backwards towards him, in order not to lose sight of the perspective he had offered to himself. When I got back to him, he made me bend down, keep erect, squeeze, separate. He often went on his knees before that place which alone busied him. He imprinted kisses in several different spots, even several on the most sacred orifice; but all these kisses were the image of sucking, he gave not one which had not this action for end. He appeared to suck every one of the places where his lips were carried. It was during this examination that he asked me many particulars about what had been done to me at the convent of *Sainte-Marie-des-Bois*; and without taking heed that I was doubly stirring up his passions by these recitals, I had the frankness of making them all to him with simplicity. He got one of his young men to draw up, and setting beside me, he loosed the running knot of a great flood of pink ribbon, which was holding the white gauze breeches, and laid bare to view the whole attractions veiled by this garb. After a few slight caresses upon the same altar as the Count sacrificed with me, he changed the object all of a sudden, and began sucking this child at the place which marks his sex. He went on feeling me: whether it was the young man's custom, or dexterity on the part of this Satyr, in a very few minutes, vanquished Nature caused what she shot out of the member of the one to flow into the other's mouth. That is how this libertine wore out the unfortunate children he had in his house, the number of whom we shall shortly see; this is the way he enervated them, and hence the state of languor in which I had found them. Let us now see how he went about putting the women in the same state, and what was the true reason of the retreat in which he kept his wife.

The homage the Count had paid me was long; but not the merest infidelity to the temple he had selected: neither his hands, looks, kisses, nor desires wandered from it an instant. After having likewise sucked the other young man, gathered, devoured in like manner his seed: "Come," he said to me, on pulling me into a neighboring closet, without permitting me to regain my clothes; "come, I am going to let you see what it is about." I could not dissemble my confusion, it was awful; but there was no means of causing my destiny to wear another appearance, it was necessary to swallow to the dregs the chalice which was presented to me.

Two other young boys of sixteen, quite as handsome, quite as debilitated as the two former ones we had left behind in the drawing-room, were working at tapestry in the closet. They rose when we entered. "*Narcisse,*" said the count to one of them, "here is the Countess's new chamber-maid, I must try her; hand me my lancets." Narcisse opens a press, and forthwith takes out of it all that is needed for bleeding. I leave it to you to think what I became; my butcher saw my embarrassment, he simply laughed at it. "Place her, *Zephire,*" said *Mr. de Gernande* to the other young man; and this child, coming up to me, said to me in smiling: — "Be not afraid, Miss, this can only do you the greatest good. Place yourself so." The question was to be slightly propped upon the knees, at the side of stool laid in the middle of the room, the arms sustained by two black ribbons attached to the ceiling.

I am hardly in position, when the Count approaches me, lancet in hand: he scarcely breathed, his eyes were sparkling, his figure caused fear; he ties both my arms, and in less than the twinkling of an eye he pricks the both. He heaves a yell escorted by two or three blasphemes, as soon as he beholds the blood; he goes and sits down six feet away, opposite to me. The light gown with which he is covered is soon spread out; *Zephire* goes on his knees between his legs, he sucks him; and Narcisse, with both his feet upon his master's arm-chair, presents to him the same object for sucking as he himself offers to the other to be pumped. *Gernande* grasps *Zephire*'s groins, he squeezes him, he presses him against himself, but left him nevertheless to cast his burning eyes upon me. Still my blood escaped in floods, and fell again into two white bowls placed under my arms. I soon felt myself growing weak: — "Sir! Sir!" I shouted; "have pity on me, I am fainting." And I staggered; being stopped by the ribbons, I could not fall; but my arms faltering, and my head floating upon my shoulders, my face was besmeared with blood. The Count was in drunkenness. . . . I did not however see the end of his operation, I swooned before he got to the end; perhaps he was only to attain it on beholding me in this state, perhaps his supreme ecstasy depended on this image of death? Be that as it may, when I recovered my senses, I found myself in an excellent bed, and a pair of old women near me. As soon as they saw my eyes open, they presented me broth, and every three hours exquisite pottages until the third day. By this time, *Mr. de Gernande* had me told to get up, and come and speak with him in the same drawing-room where he had received me on my arrival. I was led into it: I was still somewhat weak, but, however, pretty well; I arrived.

"*Therese*," says the Count to me, on making me sit down, "I shall seldom renew such experiments on you, your person is useful to me for other objects; but it was essential that I should make you acquainted with my tastes, and the way in which you shall one day end in my house, should you betray me, should you unfortunately let yourself be suborned by the woman near whom you are going to be placed.

This woman is mine, *Therese*, and this title is undoubtedly the most fatal she can have, since it obliges her to lend herself to the whimsical passion of which you have just been the victim. Do not fancy I treat her thus through vengeance, contempt, through any feeling of hatred; it is the mere history of the passions. Nothing equals the pleasure I feel in shedding her blood. . . . I am intoxicated when it is flowing; I have never enjoyed this woman in any other way. It is three years ago since I espoused her, and since she exactly undergoes every four days the treatment which you have experienced. Her blooming youth (she is not twenty), the particular cares taken of her, all this sustains her; and as reparations are being made in her by reason of what she is forced to lose, she has been pretty well ever since. With a similar subjection you are perfectly aware that I can neither let her out, nor allow her to see anybody. I therefore pass her off as mad, and her mother, the only relation she has left, living in her castle six leagues from here, is so convinced of it, that she dares not even come to see her. The Countess very often craves her forgivness, there is nothing she would not do to soften me; but she will never succeed in it. My lust has dictated her sentence, it is immutable, she will go on in this way as long as she can: she shall want for nothing during her lifetime, and as I like to waste her away, I shall sustain her as long as possible; when she can hold out no longer, God speed her! She is my fourth;

I shall shortly have a fifth, nothing troubles me less than a woman's lot; there are so many of them in the world, and it is so sweet to change them!

Be this as it may, *Therese*, your office is to care for her: she loses regularly two *porringers* of blood every four days, she no longer swoons now; habit lend her force, her faintness lasts twenty-four hours, she is all-right the other three days. But you easily understand this life displeases her; there is nothing she would not do to be released from it, nothing she would not undertake to make known her true state to her mother. She has already corrupted two of her women, whose manoeuvres were discovered time enough to put an end to their success; she has been the cause of those two unfortunate women's deaths, she repents of it today, and recognizing the constancy of her fate, she accepts her lot, and promises to no further try to seduce the persons with whom I shall surround her. But this secret, what becomes of one if I am betrayed, all this, *Therese*, obliges me to place near her only persons taken away by force as you have been, in order to avoid thereby lawsuits. Not having taken you at anybody's house, not having to render an account of you to whomsoever, I am moreover in a position to punish you, should you deserve it, in a manner which, although it should take away your life, could not however bring on me either researches, or any troublesome affairs. Henceforth, you are therefore no longer of this world, since you may disappear from it at the slightest act of my will: such is your lot, my child, you see; happy if you conduct yourself well, dead if you sought to betray me. In any other case, I should ask you for your answer: I have no need of it in the situation you are; I hold you, you must obey me, *Therese*. . . . Let us go in to my wife."

Having nothing to object to so distinct a conversation, I followed my master. We passed through a long gallery, as dark, as lonely as the rest of this castle; a door opens, we enter an antechamber where I behold the two old women who had waited upon me during my swoon. They rose and introduced us into a superb apartment, where we found the unhappy Countess embroidering at the frame upon a long chair; she stood up when she beheld her husband: — "Be seated," the Count says to her, "I allow you to listen to me so. There is at last a chamber-maid I have found for you, Madam," he continued; "I hope you will remember the fate which you have caused the others to experience, and that you will not try to hurl this one into the same misfortunes." — "That would be needless," said I then, full of eagerness to wait upon this unfortunate lady, and wanting to cloak my intentions; "yes, Madam, I dare certify in your presence, this would be needless, you shall not say a word to me that I do not directly relate to your spouse, and indeed I shall not risk my life in order to serve you." — "I shall undertake nothing that may place you in this exigency, Miss," said this poor woman, who did not yet comprehend the motives which caused me to speak thus; "be not uneasy: I require only your cares." — "They will be wholly yours. Madam," I replied, "but nothing further." And the Count, delighted with me, shook my hand in whispering in my ear: — "Good, *Therese*, thy fortune is made, if thou behavest as thou sayest." Then the Count showed me my room adjacent to that of the Countess, and he made me observe that the whole of this apartment, closed in by excellent doors, and encompassed by double gratings at all its openings, left no hope of escape. "There is a terrace-walk," continued *Mr. de Gernande*, on leading me into a little garden which was on a level with this apartment, "but its height does not give you, I think, a mind to measure its walls; the Countess may come here and breathe the fresh air as much as she likes, you will keep her company . . . farewell."

I returned to my mistress, and as we examined each other at first without speaking, I understood her well enough on this first moment to be able to describe her to you.

*Madam de Gernande*, nineteen and a half years old, was of the finest, the noblest, the most majestic size it was possible to behold; not one of her gests, not one of her movements but was a grace, not one of her looks but was a sentiment. Her eyes were of the prettiest jet, although she was fair; nothing equalled their expression, but a sort of languor, the sequel of her misfortunes, in tempering their brightness rendered them a thousand times more engaging; her skin was very white, and the loveliest hair, a very small mouth, too much so perhaps, I should have been little surprised that one would have found this defect in her. It was a pretty rose not sufficiently blown: but the teeth of a freshness . . . the lips of a carnation! . . . one would have said that Love had colored her with tints borrowed from the Goddess of flowers. Her nose was aquiline, narrow, close at the bridge, and crowned by a pair of ebony eyebrows; the chin truly handsome; in a word, a face of the most beautiful oval, over the whole of which there reigned a kind of charm, simplicity, frankness, which would have much rather caused this bewitching figure to be taken for an Angel, than for the physiognomy of a mortal. Her arms, breast, buttocks were of a glow . . . of a roundness formed to serve artists as a model; a light and black moss covered the temple of Venus, sustained by two moulded thighs; and what astonished me, in spite of the slenderness of the Countess's waist, in spite of her misfortunes, nothing altered her stoutness: her round and plump buttocks were as fleshy, fat, solid, as if her waist had been stouter and she always lived in the bosom of happiness. There were however on all this frightful marks of her spouse's libertinism, but, I repeat, nothing altered . . . the image of a beautiful lily in which the bee has made some stains. To so many gifts, *Madam de Gernande* joined a mild character, a romantic and tender mind, a heart of sensibility! . . . instructed talents . . . a natural art for seduction against which there could only be her infamous spouse who was able to resist a charming accent and very much piety: such was the unhappy wife of the *Count de Gernande,* she was the angelical creature against whom he had plotted; it seemed the more things she inspired, the more she inflamed his ferocity, and the abundance of the gifts she had received from Nature, merely became further motives for this rascal's cruelties.

"On what day were you bled, Madam?" I asked her, in order to let her see that I was acquainted with everything.

— "Three days ago," she says to me, "and it is tomorrow . . ." then, with a sigh, "yes tomorrow. . . . Miss, tomorrow . . . you shall be witness of this fine scene. — And you do not grow weak?" — "Oh!

good Heavens! I am not twenty, and I am sure one is not weaker at seventy. But that will end, I flatter myself; it is wholly impossible that I live long thus; I shall go and find my father, I shall go and seek in the arms of the Supreme Being a repose which men have so cruelly refused me in the world." These words burst my heart; wishing to uphold my character, I concealed my pain, but I clearly promised myself inwardly, from that moment, to rather lose a thousand times my life, if it was necessary, than not to tear from misfortune this unhappy victim of a monster's debauchery.

It was the time of the Countess's dinner. The two old women came to advise me to get her into her cabinet: I told her about it; she was used to all that. She walked out immediately, and the two old women informed me that they would not stir from the antechamber in order to be within reach of receiving Madam's orders about everything she might desire. I told the Countess, she seated herself, and invited me to do the same with a look of friend-ship, kindness, which achieved the gaining over of my soul. There were at least twenty dishes upon the table.

"With respect to this portion, you see they take care of me, Miss," she says to me. — "Yes, Madam," I answer, "and I know that the Count's good will is that you may want for nothing." — "Oh! yes, but as the motives of these attentions are only cruelties, they little concern me.

*Madam de Gernande*, exhausted, and sharply urged by Nature to perpetual reparations, ate very much. She desired partridges and a young duck from Rouen, which were at once brought to her. After meal, she went to take an airing on the terrace, but in tending me her hand: it would have been possible for her to go ten paces with-out this help. It was during this time she let me see all the parts of her body which I have just described to you; she showed me her arms, they were covered with scars. — "Ah! he does not stop there," she says to me; "there is not a spot of my unhappy person from which he is not pleased to see the blood flow." And she let me see her feet, neck, the pit of her stomach and several other fleshy places likewise covered with scars. I confined myself the first day to a few slight complaints, and we retired to bed.

179

The following day was the Countess's fatal day. *Mister de Gernande*, who set about this operation only on coming out from dinner, always taken before his wife's, had told me to come and sit down at the table with him; and it was there, Madam, that I witnessed this ogre operating in so frightful a manner, that I had, in spite of my eyes, difficulty in conceiving it. Four valets, among whom were the two who had led me to the castle, were serving up this wonderful repast. It is worth giving an account of: I am going to do so without exaggeration; they had certainly put nothing extra for me. What I therefore saw was every day's story.

Two pottages were served up, the one of paste and saffron, the other a bisque with ham-dripping; in the middle a short rib of beef in the English fashion, eight side-dishes, five courses of coarse meats, five mock and lighter coarses, a wild boar's head in the middle of eight dishes of roast meats, which they took away in order to serve up two courses of dainty dishes, and sixteen dishes of fruit; ices, six kinds of wine, four sorts of liquor and coffee. *Mister de Gernande* began with all the dishes, he left some of them wholly bare; he drank twelve bottles of wine, four of Burgondy on commencing, four of Champagne at the roast meats; the Tokai, Mulseau, Hermitage and Madera were swallowed down at the fruit. He finished by two of liquor from the Islands and ten cups of coffee.

As fresh on stepping out from the table as if he had just woke up, *Mister de Gernande* says to me: — "Let us go and bleed thy mistress; thou wilt tell me, I pray thee, whether I am going about it as well with her as with thee. "Two young boys whom I had not yet seen, of the same age as the former ones, were waiting for us at the door of the Countess's apartment; it was there the Count informed me he had twelve of them whom they changed for him every year. These appeared to me still handsomer than any of those I had previously seen: they were less extenuated than the others. We entered. . . . All the ceremonies of which I am going to give you an account here, Madam, were those required by the Count: they were regularly observed every day, nothing was changed in them at most except the bleeding places.

The Countess, simply surrounded by a floating muslin gown, went upon her knees as soon as the Count came in. — "Are you ready?" her spouse asked her. — "For everything, Sir," she humbly answered; "you know very well I am your victim, and it depends but on yourself to command." Then *Mr. de Gernande* bade me undress his wife and lead her to him. Whatever reluctancy I felt at all these horrors, you know, Madam, I had no other side than the most entire resignation.

Never look upon me, I do not conjure you, except as a bondswoman in all I have related, and all that remains for me to tell you: I only lent myself when I could not do otherwise, but I acted not of my own free will in anything whatsoever.

I therefore lifted up the simar to my mistress, and led her naked to her husband, already seated in a large arm-chair. Fully acquainted with the ceremony, she stood upon this arm-chair, and went of her own accord to present him that favorite spot to be kissed, which he had so much feasted on with me, and which appeared to me to equally affect him with all beings and sexes. — "Spread out then, Madam," the Count brutally says to her . . . and he feasted a long while on what he desired to see, causing different positions to be successively taken. He opened a little, he squeezed; with the end of his finger, or the tip of his tongue, he tickled the narrow orifice; and soon, carried away by the ferocity of his passions, he took a piece of flesh, pressed and scratched it. Accordingly as the slight wound was made, his mouth was at once brought to bear upon it. During these cruel preliminaries, I was holding his unhappy victim, and the two young boys stark naked relieved each other near him; on their knees, each in his turn between his legs, they made use of their mouths in order to excite him. It was then I saw, not without strange surprise, that this giant, these species of monster, whose aspect alone frightened, was, however, hardly a man; the slenderest, the feeblest fleshy excrescence, or, that the comparison may be more correct, what one would behold with a three-years old child, was at most what one noticed with this fellow so huge and corpulent every place else; but his sensations were not less quick on this account, and every vibration of pleasure was a spasmodic attack in him. After this first performance, he stretched himself upon the sofa and desired that his wife, astraddle on him, should continue to have her backside laid upon his face, while with her mouth she should render him, by means of sucking, the same services as he had just received from the young Ganymedes, whom he excited right and left with his hands; during the while mine were at work upon his backside: I was tickling him, I polluted him in all directions. This posture, being kept for more than a quarter of an hour, produced nothing as yet, it had to be changed: I stretched the Countess, by order of her husband, upon a long chair, couched on her back, her thighs as far asunder as possible. The sight of what she then opened a little set the Count into a sort of madness; he gazes upon . . . his looks flash fire, he blasphemes; he casts himself like a fury upon his wife, pricks her with his lancet in five or six parts of her body; but all these sores were light, one or two drops of blood hardly issued from them. These first cruelties at last ceased to make room for others. The Count sat down again, he lets his wife breathe an instant; and busying himself with his two minions, he obliged them to suck each other mutually, or else he arranged them in such a way that while he was sucking one of them, the other was sucking him, and that the one he was sucking went from his mouth to render the same service to him by whom he was sucked: the Count received a great deal, but gave nothing. His satiety, impotency were such, that the greatest efforts did not succeed in drawing him out of his numbness: he appeared to feel very violent titillations, but nothing showed itself; he sometimes ordered me to suck myself his Wantons, and come directly to give back into his mouth the incense I should gather. At last he sets them one after the other towards the unlucky Countess. These young men approach her, they insult her; and the more they molest her, so much the more are they praised, encouraged by the Count.

*Gernande* then busied himself with me; I was before him, my groins on a level with his face, and he rendered homage to his God; but he did not touch me; I know not why he did not annoy his Ganymedes, either, he had simply a design upon the Countess alone. Perhaps the honor of being his became a title for being ill-used by him; perhaps he was only really moved by cruelty on account of the ties which lent force to outrages. One may suppose everything in such heads, nearly always bet that what will look most a crime, will be what will inflame them the more. He places us at last, his young men and me, at the sides of his wife, mixed up all together: here a man, there a woman, and all four present the backside to him; he examines at first in front somewhat in the distance, then he closes up, he feels, he compares, he caresses; the young men and I had nothing to suffer, but every time he came to his wife, he used to plague, vex her in one way or another. The scene changes again: he gets the Countess put on her belly upon a sofa, and taking each of the young men one after the other, he introduces them himself into the narrow route offered by *Madam de Gernande*'s posture: he allows them to warm themselves in it, but it is only within his mouth that the sacrifice is to be consummated; he sucks them likewise accordingly as they come out. While the one is acting, he gets himself sucked by the other, and his tongue wanders to the throne of voluptuousness which the agent presents to him. This act is a long one, the Count is annoyed at it, he stands up and wants me to replace the Countess; I beseech him not to request it, there is no speaking to him. He places his wife upon her back along the sofa, gets me stuck upon her, my loins turned towards him, and there, he orders his minions to sound me through the forbidden route: he presents them to me, they are introduced merely guided by his hands; I must then excite the Countess with my fingers, and kiss her on the mouth. For him, his offering is the same; as each of his minions can only act in showing one of the sweetest objects of his worship, he profits by it as best he can, and as with the Countess, it is necessary that he who is boring me, after a few going backwards and forwards, proceed to make the incense kindled for me flow into his mouth. When the young men have done, he sticks himself upon my loins, and seemingly wishes to make amends for them. — "Superfluous efforts!" he cries . . . "that is not what I want! . . . to the business! . . . however pitiful my state appears. . . . I can't resist any longer. . . . Come, Countess, your arms," He then seizes her with ferocity, he places her as he had done with me, her arms supported with two black ribbons from the ceiling. I am entrusted with the care of laying on the bands; he inspects the bindings: not finding them tight enough, he squeezes

them, in order, said he, that the blood may rush more forcibly out:
he feels the veins, and pricks them both almost at the same time.
The blood juts very far: he falls into an ecstasy; and, returning to
place himself in front, while these two fountains are flowing, he
makes me go on my knees between his legs, to suck him; he gets
each of his Wantons to do as much, by turns, without ceasing to
carry his eyes upon these two spouts of blood which are inflaming
him. As for me, being sure that the moment the crisis he is expecting will take place, will be the time of the ceasing of the Countess's
tortures, I exert all my cares to bring on this crisis, and I become,
as you see, Madam, a harlot through beneficence, and a libertine
through virtue. This so expected an issue comes on at last; I knew
neither its dangers nor violence: the last time it had taken place, I
was in a swoon. . . . Oh! Madam, what erring! *Gernande* was nearly
ten minutes in the delirium, in struggling with himself, like a man
who falls from epilepsy, and heaving cries which would have been
heard a league away; his oaths were awful, and, striking all that surrounded him, he made frightful efforts. The two minions are upset;
he wants to rush upon his wife, I hold him back; I finish pumping
him, the need he has of me causes him to respect me; I at last bring
him back to his senses, by freeing him of that burning fluid of which
the heat, thickness and especially the abundance put him in such
a state of madness, that I thought he was going to die, seven or eight
spoons would have scarcely held the dose, and the thickest pap
would badly represent its consistence; with that no erection, the
very look of exhaustion: these are some of those contrarieties which
persons of the art will explain better than I. The Count used to eat
excessively, and wasted thus only every time he was wont to bleed
his wife, viz., every fourth day. Was that the cause of this phenomenon? I know not, and not venturing to give a reason for what
I do understand, I shall content myself with telling what I have seen.

However I fly to the Countess, I stop her blood, I untie her and
place her upon a sofa in a very weak state; but the Count, without
troubling himself, without vouch-safing to cast even a glance on this
unhappy victim of his rage, walks out hastily with his minions, leaving me to put everything in order as I please. Such is the fatal
indifference which marks, better than anything else, the soul of a

true libertine: is he simply carried off by the heat of his passions? remorse will be depicted upon his face, when he calmly sees the direful effects of delirium; is his soul wholly corrupted? such consequences will not frighten him; he will consider them without pain as without regret, nay more with emotions of the infamous voluptuousness which produced them.

I made *Madam de Gernande* lie down. She had, according to what she told me, lost a good deal more this time than usual; but so much care, so many restoratives were lavished upon her, that nothing further appeared next day. On the same evening, as soon as I had nothing more to do with the Countess, *Gernande* sent me word to come and speak to him. He was at supper; at this meal, taken by him with still far greater intemperance than the dinner, I had to wait upon him; four of his minions sat down at the table with him, and there, the libertine drank, regularly every evening, even to intoxication; but twenty bottles of the most excellent wines barely sufficed to succeed in it, and I often saw him empty thirty of them. Supported by his minions, the debauched rascal was wont to go afterwards to bed every evening with two of them. But he used to put nothing of his own in, and all this was no more than vehicles which prepared him for the great scene.

Yet I had discovered the secret of getting myself, as much as possible, in this man's favor: he of course acknowledged that few women had pleased him so much. Hence I acquired rights to his trust, of which I took advantage only to serve my mistress.

One morning, as *Gernande* had called me into his closet to inform me about some fresh schemes of libertinism, after having listened very attentively to him, loudly applauded, I wished, seeing him pretty calm, to try and soften him on his unlucky wife's fate: "Is it possible, Sir, said I to him, that one could treat a woman in this manner, independent of all her ties with you? Vouchsafe therefore to reflect on the moving charms of her sex."

— "Oh! *Therese* ! with judgment," the Count answered me, "is it possible to cite to me for reasons of quietness, those which positively annoy me best? Listen to me, dear girl," he went on while placing me near him, "and whatever be the invectives which thou art about to hear me uttering against thy sex, no anger; reasons, I shall give in to them, if they are good.

By what right, I pray thee, dost thou pretend, *Therese*, that a husband is obliged to form the happiness of his wife? and what titles dares this wife quote in order to exact it from her husband? The necessity of rendering themselves mutually such, can only lawfully exist between two beings alike provided with the faculty of hurting each other, and consequently between two beings of one and the same force: such an association could not take place, unless a pact be at once formed between these two being to perform, each in respect to the other, only the sort of use of their strength as may injure neither of the two; but this ridiculous convention could not certainly exist between the strong one and the weak one. By what right will this latter exact that the former should spare him? and by what stupidity would the former bind himself to it? I may agree not to make use of my forces with him who may cause himself to be feared by his own; but through what motive should I lessen their effects with the being that Nature renders subservient to me? You will answer me: *for pity-sake?* This feeling is only compatible with the being who resembles me, and as it is a selfish one, its effect but takes place on the tacit conditions that the individual who will inspire me with compassion, will have of it likewise concerning me; but if I constantly prevail over him by my superiority, his commiseration becoming needless to me, I ought never, in order to have it, consent to any sacrifice. Should I not be a ninny to take pity on the chicken which is slaughtered for my dinner? That individual too far below me, deprived of no relation with me, can never inspire me with any feeling; now, the relations of the wife with the husband are not of a consequence different from that of the chicken with me; both are household beasts of which we must make use, which must be employed to the purpose indicated by Nature, without distinguishing them in whatsoever. But, I ask, if the intention of Nature was that your sex should be created for the happiness of ours, and *vice versa,* would this blind Nature have made so many silly things in the construction of both of these sexes? Would she have lent them mutually such serious wrongs, that estrangement and mutual antipathy must infallibly result therefrom? Without going farther to seek examples, with the organization which thou knowest I have, tell me, I pray thee *Therese,* what woman is there I could make happy, and *vice versa* what man can find the enjoyment of a woman sweet, when he is not supplied with huge proportions necessary for satisfying her? Will these be, in thy opinion, the moral qualities which will make amends for physical defects? And what rational being, on thoroughly knowing a woman, will not cry out with *Euripides* : *He who of the Gods has placed woman in the world, may boast of having, produced the worst of all creatures, and the most troublesome for man?* If it is therefore proved that two sexes do not at all mutually suit each other, and that there is not a grounded complaint, made by the one, but directly suits the other, it is therefore false, henceforth, that Nature created them for their reciprocal happiness. She may have permitted them the desire of drawing nearer each other to concur in the aim of propagation, but nowise that of purposely binding themselves to find their happiness in each other. The weaker, having therefore no title to claim in order to obtain pity from the stronger, being no longer able to object to him that he can find his happiness in him, has no other side but submission; and as, notwithstanding the difficulty of this natural happiness, it is in the individuals of both sexes to work only to procure it for themselves, the weakest one ought to unite in himself, through this submission, the sole dose of felicity possible for him to reap, and the strongest one ought to work at his own, by such a way of oppression as he chooses to adopt, since it is proved that the very happiness of force is in the exercise of the faculties of the strong, viz., in the most complete oppression. Thus, this happiness which the two sexes can not find with one another, they will find it, the one by his blind obedience, the other by the most thorough energy of his sway. Ah! if it was not the intention of Nature that one of these sexes should tyrannize over the other, would she not have created them of an equal force? In making the one inferior to the other in every respect, has she not sufficiently indicated that her will was the strongest one should use the rights she gave him? The more the latter extends his authority, the more unhappy he renders, thereby, the woman, bound to his destiny and the better he discharges the vows of Nature; it is not on the complaints of the feeble being the process must be judged; such judgements could only be vicious, since you would borrow, while forming them, merely ideas from the feeble: the action must be judged on the power of the strong, on the extent he has given to his power, and when the effects of this force are extended to a woman, then examine what a woman is, the way in which this despicable sex has been viewed be it in antiquity, be it nowadays, by three fourths of the Nations upon the Earth.

Now, what do I behold in proceeding coolly to this examination? A mean creature, ever inferior to man, infinitely less than he, less ingenious, less wise, constituted in a disgusting manner, wholly opposed to what can please man, to what can delight him . . . a sickly being three fourth of her lifetime, unable to satisfy her husband every time that Nature forces her to child-bearing, of a sour, pee-vish, haughty mood; a tyrant, if she is entrusted with rights, low and crouching if she is captivated; but ever false, ever wicked, ever dangerous; finally, so perverse a creature, that it was very seriously controverted in the Council of Macon, during several sittings, whether this strange individual, as distinct from man as is the monkey of the woods, could pretend to the title of human creature, and whether it could be reasonably accorded to her. But would this be an error of the century, and is woman better viewed in preceding ones? Used the Persians, Medes, Babylonians, Greeks, Romans honor this hateful sex of which we form our ideal nowadays? Alas! I see it crushed everywhere, everywhere rigorously removed from affairs, everywhere despised, scorned, locked up; in short, women everywhere treated like beasts of which people make use in the hour of need, and which are directly put back in the fold. Stop I a moment in Rome, I hear the Sage Cato crying out to me from the midst of the ancient Capital of the world: *If men were without women, they would still converse with the Gods.* I hear a Roman Censor beginning his harangue by these words: *Gentlemen, if it were possible for us to live without women, we should henceforth know true happiness.* I hear the poets singing in the theatres of Greece: *O Jupiter! what reason could oblige thee to create women? Couldst thou not bestow being on men by better, wiser ways, in fine, by means which would have spared us the plague of women?* I behold these same Nations, the Greeks, holding this sex in such contempt, that laws are necessary to compel a Spartiate to propagation, and that one of the punishments of those wise Republics is to force a felon to dress in woman's attire, namely, to dress himself like the vilest and most contemptible being that they know.

But without going to look for examples in centuries so far back from us, with what an eye is this unlucky sex viewed even still over the surface of the globe? How is it dealt with here? I see it, shut in throughout the whole of Asia, serving there in slavery the barbarous whims of despot who teases, torments it, and who makes himself a play of its sufferings. In America, I see nations naturally humane, the Eskimaux, using among men all possible acts of benevolence, and treating the women with all imaginable roughness; I behold them humilated, prostituted to foreigners in one port of the Universe, serving as money in another. In Africa, being undoubtedly far more abased, I behold them performing the office of beasts of burden, ploughing the earth, sowing it, and waiting on their husbands only upon their knees. Shall I follow Captain Cook throughout his fresh discoveries? Will the charming Isle of Otaiti, where pregnancy is a crime which sometimes costs the mother's death, and nearly always the child's offer me happier women? In other Islands discovered by this same seaman, I behold them beaten, tormented by their own children, and the husband himself joining in with his family to torture them more rigorously.

Oh! *Therese* ! be not amazed at all this, be not surprised either at the general right which husbands had, in all times, over their wives: the nearer Nations are to Nature, the better they observe her laws; the wife can have no other relations with her husband than that of the slave with his master; she decidedly has no right to pretend to dearer titles. You must not confound with rights, ridiculous abuses, which while debasing our sex, raised yours for an instant: it is necessary to seek the cause of those abuses, to name it, and return from it only the more steadfastly after, to the wise counsels of reason. Now here it is, *Therese*, that cause of momentary respect which your sex obtained formerly, and which still abuses nowadays, without their suspecting it, those who prolong this respect.

Among the Galls of old, namely, in this sole part of the world which did not wholly treat the women as slaves, they were in the habit of prophesying, telling fortunes. The people imagined that they succeeded in this craft simply by reason of the close traffic they undoubtedly had with the Gods; hence they were so to say affiliated to the priesthood, had enjoyed a part of the consideration attached to priests. Knighthood was established in France upon these prejudices, and, finding them favorable to its spirit, it adopted them; but it was with this as with everything: the causes died out and the effects were handed down; Knighthood disappeared, and the prejudices it had fondly increased. This ancient respect granted to airy titles, could not be even done away with, when that which founded these titles vanished: witches were no longer respected, but whores were venerated; and what was worse, people continued to slaughter one another for them. Let such nonsense cease to have an influence over the mind of philosophers, and putting the women back in their true place, let them behold in them, as Nature indicates, as the wisest Nations admit, mere individuals created for their pleasures, subjected to their caprices, whose weakness and wickedness should deserve from them only contempt!

"But, *Therese*, not only all the Nations of the earth enjoyed the most expansive rights over their women, there were even some which doomed them to death as soon as they came into the world, absolutely conserving merely the small number requisite for the reproduction of the species. The Arabs, known under the name of Koreihs, used to bury their daughters from the seventh year, upon a mountain near Mecca, because so vile a sex appeared to them, they were wont to say, unworthy of beholding the light of day. In the seraglio of the King of Achem, for the mere suspicion of infidelity, for the slightest disobedience in the service of the Prince's voluptuousnesses, or as soon as ever they inspire disgust, the most frightful tortures instantly await them as punishment. On the banks of the Ganges, they are compelled to immolate themselves over the ashes of their spouse, as being useless in the world, since their masters can no longer enjoy them. Elsewhere they are hunted like wild beasts, it is an honor to simply kill a great many of them; in Egypt they are immolated to the Gods; at Formosa they are trampled under foot, if they become pregnant. The German laws used to condemn only to a fine of ten crown-pieces the one who killed a strange woman, nothing if she was his wife, or a courtesan. Everywhere in fine, I repeat, everywhere I behold the women humiliated, molested, everywhere sacrificed to priest's superstition, to husbands' barbarity, or to the caprices of libertines. And because I have the bad luck to live among a people still clownish enough as not to dare abolish the most ridiculous of prejudices, I would deprive myself of the rights which Nature grants me over this sex! I would resign all the pleasures which spring from these rights! . . . No, no, *Therese*, that is not fair: I shall hide my behaviour since it is necessary, but I shall make amends in silence, in the retreat I exile myself in, for the absurd chains to which the law condemns me, and there, I shall treat my wife as I think fit, as I find the right thereof in all the codes of the Universe, in my heart and in Nature."

— "Oh! Sir," I said to him, "your conversion is impossible." — "Indeed I advise thee not to undertake it, *Therese*," *Gernande* answered me; "the tree is too old to be bent; one may take at my age a few paces more in the career of evil, but not a single one in that of good. My principles and tastes formed my happiness since my childhood, they were always the sole basis of my conduct and actions: perhaps I shall go farther, I feel it is possible, but to return, no; I have too much horror for men's prejudices, I hate their civilisation, their virtues and their Gods too sincerely, to ever sacrifice my proclivities for them."

For this moment I clearly saw I had no other side to espouse, whether to get myself out of this house or to free the Countess, except to use craft, and concert with her.

For the year that I was in her house, I had let her read too well in my heart not to be convinced of the desire I had of serving her, and not to guess what had caused me consented. We agreed upon our plans: the question was at first to act differently. I let her into the secret, she to instruct her mother, to open her eyes concerning the infamies of the Count. *Madam de Gernande* doubted not but this unfortunate Lady would at once run to break her daughter's chains; but how come about it? We were so well locked in, so well kept within sight! Accustomed to clear forts, I surveyed those of the terrace: they were hardly thirty feet; no enclosure appeared to my eyes, I thought that once at the bottom of these walls I would be on the way to the wood; but the Countess, having come by night to this apartment, and having never gone out of it, could not test my ideas. I consented to try scaling. *Madam de Gernande* wrote to her mother the best calculated letter in the world to affect and determine her to come to the help of so unhappy a daughter; I put the letter into my bosom, I embraced this dear and interesting woman; then, aided by our sheets, as soon as it was night, I let myself slip down to the foot of this fortress. What became of me, O Heavens! when I recognized that very much was wanted before I could be outside the enclosure! I was only in the park, and in a park surrounded by walls the sight of which had been hidden from me by the density and quantity of the trees: these walls were more than forty feet high, all protectd by glass on the top, and of wonderful breadth. . . . What was going to become of me? The day was ready to dawn: what would people think of me in seeing me in this place where I could only be with the certain scheme of escape? Could I free myself from the Count's fury? What appearance was there that this ogre would not drink my blood plentifully in order to punish me for such a fault? To return was impossible, the Countess had drawn in the sheets; to knock at the doors was to betray myself still more securely. A little more then and my head had been totally deranged, and I had violently yielded to the effects of my despair. Had I known any pity in the Count's soul, hope perhaps would have for an instant deceived me; but a tyrant, a barbarian, a man who detested women, and who, he said, was on the lookout this long while for an opportunity of immolating one, by causing her to lose her blood drop by drop, in order to see how many hours she could live thus! . . . I was going most certainly to serve as a proof. Not knowing therefore what was to become of me, meeting with perils everywhere, I cast myself at the foot of a tree, bent on awaiting my fate, and resigning myself in silence to the will of the Eternal. . . . The day dawned at last; good Heavens! the first object that presents itself to me . . . is the Count in person: it was excessively warm during the night; he had gone out for an airing. H thinks he is mistaken, he believes he beholds a ghost, he draws back: courage is seldom the virtue of traitors. I rise trembling, I throw myself at his knees. "What are you doing there, *Therese*?" he says to me. — "Oh! Sir, punish me," I replied, "I am guilty, and have nothing to answer." Unluckily I had forgotten in my fright to tear the letter of the Countess: he conjectures it, he requests it of me, I am willing to deny; but *Gernande*, beholding this fatal letter peering under the kerchief upon my breast, snatches it, reads it over hastily and greedily, and bids me follow him.

We go back into the castle by a hidden stairs landing under the vaults: dead silence still reigned there. After a few windings, the Count opens a dungeon, and throws me into it. — "Unwise girl," he then says to me, "I had advised you that the crime you have just committed was here punished by death: get ready therefore to undergo the chastisement which you have been pleased to incur. On coming out from the table tomorrow, I will be here to dispatch you." I rushed anew to his knees, but seizing me by the hair, he drags me along the ground, makes me take thus two or three rounds of my prison, and ends by dashing me against the walls so as to crush me thereby — "Thou wouldst deserve thy four veins to be instantly opened," he says on shutting the door, "and if I delay thy torture, be thoroughly certain that it is only to make it the more horrible."

He is without, and I in the most violent agitation. I do not describe the night I passed: the torments of the imagination, joined to the physical ills which this monsters first cruelties had just caused me to feel, rendered it one of the most dreadful in my life. One does not imagine the anguishes of an ill-fated being who at every hour is awaiting his execution, whose hope is removed, and who knows not whether the minute he breathes will not be the last of his days. Uncertain of his torture, he represents it to himself under a thousand forms the one more ghastly than the other; the slightest noise he hears seems to him to be that of his executioners; his blood curdles, his heart dies within him, and the sword which is about to end his days is less cruel than those direful moments when death is menacing him.

It is very likely the Count began by avenging himself on his wife; the event which saved is about to convince you of it as me. I was thirty-six hours in the crisis I have just told you of, without anyone's bringing me relief, when the door opened and the Count put in an appearance. He was alone, wrath sparkled in his eyes. — "You ought to have a clear inkling," he says to me, "of the kind of death you are going to suffer: this perverse blood must flow in all parts; you shall be bled three times a day, I want to see how long you can live in this way. It was an experiment I was longing to make, you know; I thank you for having afforded me the means." And the monster, without busying himself for the time being about any other passions than his vengeance, gets me to stretch out my arm, pricks me, and binds up the wound after two porringers of blood. He had barely finished, when screams were heard. — "Sir! . . . Sir!" said one of the old women who used to wait on us, while running . . . "come as speedy as possible, Madam is dying, she wishes to speak to you before giving up the ghost." And the old one flies back to her mistress.

However accustomed one be to crime, it is rare that the tidings of its fulfillment do not frighten the one who has just perpetrated it. This awe avenges Virtue: such is the moment that her rights are retrieved. *Gernande* goes out bewildered, he forgets to shut the doors. I take advantage of the occasion, however spent I am by a fast of more than forty hours, and by a bleeding; I rush out of my dungeon. All is open, I traverse the yards, and behold me in the forest without my being noticed. Let us march, said I to myself, let us march courageously; if the strong one despises the weak, there is an Almighty God who protects the latter, and who never forsakes him. Big with these ideas, I boldly advance, and before nightfall, I find, myself in a hut four leagues from the castle. I had some money left: I get myself cared as best I can; a few hours set me right. I start at day-break, and having the way pointed out to me, giving over all projects of complaint, whether former or recent, I get directed towards Lyons, where I arrived on the eighth day, exceedingly fagged, suffering a great deal, but luckily without being pursued. There, I thought only of recovering myself previous to reaching *Grenoble*, where I had always fostered in my idea that good luck was awaiting me.

One day as I chanced to glance over a foreign gazette, what was my surprise to behold in it again crime rewarded, and one of the principal authors of my ills in the highest position! *Rodin*, that surgeon of Saint-Marcel, that infamous man who had so cruelly punished me for having been willing to spare him his daughter's murder, had just been, said the newspaper, named Head Surgeon to the Empress of Russia, with immense salaries. Let him be fortunate, the wretch, said I to myself, let him be so, since Providence will have it so! and thou, suffer, unlucky creature, suffer without complaining, since it is stated that tribulations and pains are to be the frightful share of Virtue; never mind, I shall never grow weary of her.

I was not at the end of these striking instances of the triumph of vices, instances so discouraging to Virtue, and the prosperity of the fellow I was about to find again should vex and surprise me more than any other, no doubt, since it was that of one of the men from whom I had received the most bloody outrages. I occupied myself only with my departure, when one evening I got a note which was handed me by a lackey dressed in gray, wholly unknown to me; on giving it to me, he told me he was entrusted by his master to obtain without fail an answer from me. The following were the terms of this note:

*"A man who did you some wrongs, who thinks he recognized you in Bellecour-place, is longing to see you, and to make amends for his conduct; make haste and come to him: he has tidings to impart to you, which will perhaps clear him of all he owes you."*

This note was not signed, and the lackey did not explain himelf. Having informed him that I was decided not to answer till I knew who his master was: — "He is *Mister de Saint-Florent*, Miss," he tells me; he has had the honor of being acquainted with you formerly in the environs of Paris; he pretends you did him services which he is patiently longing to discharge. Being now at the head of the commerce in this town, he enjoys here at once a consideration and wealth which enable him to prove to you his gratitude. He is waiting for you."

My reflections were soon made. If this man had not good intentions towards me, I said to myself, would it be likely he would write to me, that he would have me addressed to in this way? He has remorse for his past infamies, he recollects with fright having snatched from me what I held most dear, and having reduced me, by the concatenation of his horrors, to the most grisly state a woman can be in. . . . Yes, yes, let us not doubt about it, these are remorses; I should be guilty towards the Supreme Being if I did not consent to appease them. Am I in a position besides to reject the help which presents itself? Ought I not rather too eagerly to seize every thing that is afforded to relieve me? It is in his hotel that this man wants to see me: his fortune must surround him with folks in whose presence he will respect himself too much to dare do amiss again, and in the state I am in, Great God! can I inspire anything else but pity? I therefore assured the lackey of *Saint-Florent* that next day, about eleven o'clock, I would have the honor of going to pay my respects to his master; that I congratulated him on the favors he had received from Fortune, and that she was very far from dealing with me as with him.

I went into my room, but so taken up with what this man wanted to say to me, that I did not close an eye the whole night. I finally arrived at the address mentioned; a superb palace, a crowd of valets, the scornful looks of this rich rabble on the misfortune it despises, all imposes upon me, and I am ready to retire, when the same lackey as had spoken to me on the eve, accosts me and leads me, on encouraging me, into a sumptuous cabinet where I quite readily recognized my butcher, although then forty-five years old, and it being nearly nine since I saw him. He does not rise, but he orders us to be left alone, and beckons to me to come and place myself on a chair beside the huge arm-chair which contains him.

— "I wished to see you, my child," said he with the mortifying tone of superiority, "not that I fancy I am greatly in the wrong with respect to you, not that a troublesome remembrance forces me to reparations beyond which I believe myself; but I remember that during the little while we knew each other, you let me see some genius: it is necessary for what I have to propose to you, and if you accept it, the need I shall then have you, will cause you to find in my fortune the resources which you require, and upon which you would vainly rely otherwise." I wanted to reply by a few rebukes to the levity of this debut; *Saint-Florent* imposed silence upon me. — "Let us lay aside what is passed," he says to me; "it is the history of the passions, and my principles incline me to think that no curb ought to stop their impetuosity; when they speak, they must be waited upon: it is my law. When I was captured by the robbers with whom you were, did you see the complain of my lot? To console one's self and act by one's wits, if one is the weakest; to enjoy all one's rights; if the strongest, such is my system. You were young and pretty, *Therese*; we were in the depths of a forest; there is no volup-tuousness in the world which kindles my senses as the rape of a maiden: you were such, I ravished you; perhaps I would have done worse with you, if what I ventured had not had success, and should you have offered me any resistance. But I robbed you. I left you without resources in the middle of the night, a dangerous route; two motives caused this fresh offence: I wanted money, I had none; as to the other reason which was able to induce me to this proceeding, I should vainly explain it for you, *Therese*, you would not understand it. The beings alone who know man's heart, who have studied its recesses, who have disentangled the most impenetrable nooks of this dark maze, might expound to you this sort of error." — "What! Sir, money which I had offered you . . . the service I had just done you . . . to be paid for what I had wrought in your behalf by base treachery . . . that may, you say, be comprehended, that may be legalized?" — "Ay! *Therese*, ay; the proof that this may be explained is that in having just plundered, just molested you . . . (for I beat you, *Therese*), well! at twenty paces from there, thinkof the state I was leaving you in, I directly found in these ideas strength for fresh outrages, which I should perhaps have never committed on you otherwise. You had lost only one of your first fruits. . . . I was going away, I retraced my steps, and I made you lose the other. . . . It is therefore true that in certain souls voluptuousness may spring up in the heart of crime! What am I saying? it is therefore true that crime alone rouses and decides it, and that there is not a single voluptuousness in the world but it inflames and improves. . . ." — "Oh! Sir, what a horror! — Could I not commit a greater one? . . . I was very near it, I confess to you, but I strongly suspected that you were about being reduced to the last extremities: this idea satisfied me, I left you. Let us pass over that, *Therese*, and come to the point which made me wish to see you."

"That incredible taste I have for either maidenhead of a little girl, has not forsaken me, *Therese*," continued *Saint-Florent* ; "it is with this as with all the other errors of libertinism: the older one grows, the more sway they obtain; former offences spring from fresh desires, and new crimes from these desires. All this would be nothing, my dear, if what one employs to succeed was not itself very guilty. But as the want of evil is the first mover of our caprices, the more that which guides us is criminal, the better we are excited. Once at this point, one no longer complains except of the mediocrity of the means: the more their atrocity extends itself, the more pleasing our voluptuousness becomes, and one thus sinks in the mire without the least mind to get out of it.

It is my history, *Therese*; two young children are every day necessary for my sacrifices. Have I enjoyed? not only I see again no more the objects thereof, but it even becomes essential for the entire satisfaction of my fantasies, that these objects do at once go forth from the town: I should badly relish the next day's pleasures, if I thought the victims still breathed the same air as I. The means of ridding myself of them is easy. Wouldst thou believe it, *Therese* ? Those are my debaucheries that people Languedoc and Provence with the host of objects of libertinism which their bosom enclose[1]: one hour after these little girls have served me, trusty emissaries ship and sell them to bawds at Nimes, Montpellier, Toulouse, Aix and Marseilles. This trade, of which I have two thirds of the benefit, largely indemnifies me for what the subjects cost me, and I thus satisfy two of my dearest passions, both my lust and cupidity; but the discoveries, seductions give me pain. Moreover, the species of subjects infinitely concerns my lubricity: I wish them all to be taken in those abodes of misery, where the lack of food and the impossibility of thriving in them absorb courage, pride, delicacy, in short, enervating the soul, decide, in the hope of an indispensable sustenance, upon all that appears needful to assure it. I get all those nooks unmercifully searched: one does not imagine what they yield me. I go farther, *Therese* : activity, industry, a little ease, in struggling against my subordinations, would rob me of a great part of subjects: I oppose to these stumbling blocks the influence I enjoy in this town, I excite *oscillations* in trade, or dearth of provisions, which, by multiplying the classes of the poor, removing from them on the one hand the means of work, and on the other rendering those of life hard for them, increase in equal ratio the sum of the subjects that misery delivers up to me. The trick is well known, *Therese* : this scarcity of wood, corn and other provisions, from which Paris suffered so many years, had no other aims than those which animate me; avarice, libertinism, such are passions which, from the midst of gilt ceilings, stretch out host of nets up to the humble roof of the poor man. But whatever dexterity I employ to press on one side, if skilful hands do not quickly heave up on the other, I gain only my pains, and the machine quite as badly as if I did not tire out my imagination in resources, and my influence in operations. I therefore want an intelligent spruce young woman who, having herself passed through the thorny paths of misery, should know better than anyone else the means of debauching those who are in it; a woman whose penetrating eyes divine adversity in its most obscure garrets, and whose corrupting mind determines the victims thereof to retire from oppression through the means I offer; in fine, a witty woman, without scruple as without pity, who neglects nothing in order to succeed, even to the cutting away of the slender resources which, by still keeping up the hope of those unfortunate people, prevent them from being resolved. I had an excellent and trusty one: she has just died. One does not imagine how far that intelligent creature was wont to carry effrontery; she not only isolated these wretches to such a degree as to force them to come and implore her on their knees, but if those means did not succeed soon enough to hasten their downfall, the strumpet used to go even to rob them. She was a treasure; I merely want two subjects a day: she would have given me six of them, had I wished for them. Hence it resulted that I could make better choices, and the superabundance of the first matter of my operations indemnified me for the workmanship. It is necessary to replace these women, my dear; thou shalt have four of them at your orders, and two thousand crowns salary. I have spoken; answer, *Therese*, and especially let not chimeras hinder thee from accepting thy good luck, when hasard and my hand offer it to thee."

— "Oh! Sir," said I to this dishonest man, on quaking with horror at his discourse, "is it possible that you could conceive such voluptuousnesses, and that you dare propose me to serve them! What a lot of horrors you have just let me hear! Cruel man, if you were unfortunate for two days only, you would see how these systems of inhumanity would be soon destroyed within your heart: prosperity blinds and hardens you; you are surfeited with the view of ills from which you fancy yourself in security, and because you hope never to feel them, you suppose yourself justified to inflict them; may good luck never come near me, from the moment it can corrupt to such a degree! O good Heavens! not to content one's self with abusing misfortune! to urge audacity and ferocity even to increase it, even to prolong it for the sole satisfaction of one's desires! What cruelty, Sir! the most ferocious beasts set us no examples of a like barbarity." — "Thou are mistaken, *Therese*, there is no roguery the wolf does not contrive to attract the lamb into his snares: these wiles are in Nature, and benevolence is not in her; it is simply a mark of weakness, cried up by the slave in order to affect his master and incline him to greater leniency; it never declares itself in man except in two cases: if he is either the weakest, or if he is afraid of becoming so. The proof that this pretended virtue is not in Nature, is because it is ignored by the man nearest to her. The Savage, in despising it, unmercifully kills his equal, either through vengeance or covetousness . . . would he not respect this virtue, if it was written his heart? But it never appeared therein, it will never be found every place where men will be equal. Civilization, in refining individuals, in distinguishing ranks, in offering a poor man to the eyes of the rich man, in causing the latter to dread a change of state which might hurl him into the other's nothingness, forthwith placed in his mind the desire of relieving the unfortunate one to be relieved in his turn, should he lose his riches. Then sprang up benevolence, fruit of civilization and fear: it is therefore only a virtue of circumstances, but nowise a sentiment of Nature, which never placed in us any other desire than that of satisfying ourselves, at what price soever. It is in confounding thus all sentiments, in never analyzing anything, that people are blinded about everything, and that they deprive themselves of all enjoyments. — "Ah! Sir," I warmly interrupted, "can there be a sweeter one than that of relieving misfortune? Let us lay aside the fear of suffering one's self, is there a truer satisfaction than that of obliging?. . . To enjoy the tears of gratitude, to partake of the well-being one has just spread among the unhappy who, although your fellow-creatures, stood in need of the things of which you form your first wants, to hear them sing your praises and call you their father, to replace serenity on brows darkened through failure, neglect and despair; no, Sir, no voluptuousness in the world can equal this: it is that of the Divinity himself, and the happiness it promises to those who will have served it on Earth, will be merely the possibility of seeing or making happy beings in Heaven. All virtues spring from it, Sir; one is a better father, better son, better spouse, when one knows the charm of soothing misfortune. As the rays of the sun, one would say the presence of the charitable man scatters over all that surrounds him fertility, sweetness and joy, and the miracle of Nature, after this hearth of celestial light, is the honest, tender and sensible soul whose supreme felicity is to work at that of others."

— "That's all bosh, *Therese*! the enjoyments of man are in ratio to the sort of organs he has received from Nature; those of the weak individual, and consequently of all women, ought to convey, for such beings, to moral voluptuousnesses, sharper ones than those which would only have influence over a physic wholly destitute of energy: the contrary is the history of strong souls, who, being much more delighted with the vigorous shocks imprinted on that which surrounds them, than they would be with the delicate impressions felt by these same beings existing near them, inevitably prefer, according to this constitution, what affects the others in painful senses, to what would only touch in a milder manner. Such is the sole difference between cruel people and kind people: both are endowed with sensibility, but they are each so in his own way. I do not deny of there being enjoyments in both classes, but I hold with many philosophers, no doubt, that those of the individual organized in the most vigorous manner, will be unquestionably keener than all those of his adversary; and these systems being granted, there can be and there ought to be a kind of men who find as much pleasure in all that cruelty inspires, as the others taste of it in benevolence. But the latter will be mild pleasures, and the former very keen pleasures: some will be undoubtedly surer, realer, since they characterize the propensities of all men still in the cradle of Nature, and even children, previous to their knowing the sway of civilization; others will be only the effect of civilization, and, consequently of deceitful voluptuousness and without any salt. And besides, my child, as we are here less for philosophizing than for consolidating a determination, kindly let me know your final answer. . . . Do you accept, or not the offer I make you?" — "I certainly do refuse it,

Sir," I answered in standing up. . . . I am very poor . . . "oh! yes, exceedingly poor, Sir, but richer in the sentiments of my heart than in the gifts of fortune, never shall I sacrifice the former to possess the latter: I shall know how to die in penury, but I will not betray virtue." — "Be off," this detestable man cooly says to me, "and let me especially not have to fear any indiscretions from you: you would be soon put in a place whence I should have no longer to dread them." Nothing encourages virtue like the apprehensions of vice: much less fearful than I would have thought, I dared, while promising him he would have nothing to dread from me, remind him of the robbery he had committed on me in the forest of Bondy, and make him feel that, in the circumstance I was, this money became necessary for me. The monster then harshly answered me that it depended upon myself to earn some, and that I refused to do so. — "No, Sir," I replied firmly, "no I repeat to you, I should die a thousand times rather than save my days at this price." — "And I," said Saint-Folrent, "there is in like manner nothing that I should not prefer to the grief of giving my money without its being earned; notwithstanding the refusal you have the insolence of making me, I am quite willing to still spend a quarter of an hour with you; come therefore into this study, and a few moments of obedience will set your funds right." — "I have no greater mind to serve your debaucheries in one sense than in another, Sir," I resolutely replied; "I do not ask for alms, cruel man; no, I do not procure you that enjoyment; I claim only what is due to me: what you stole from me in the most shameful manner. . . . Keep it, hard-heart, keep it, if you think fit; behold, without pity, my tears; hear if thou canst, without being moved, the sad notes of need, but remember if thou perpetratest this fresh infamy, I shall have at the price of what it costs me, purchased the right of despising thee for ever."

*Saint-Florent*, being furious, bade me go out, and I could read in his frightful countenance that, without the secrets he had entrusted to me, and the publishing of which he feared I should have perhaps paid by some brutality from him the boldness of having spoken too truly to him. . . . I do walk out. At the same instant, one of these unlucky victims of his sordid debauchery was brought to him. One of the women, whose horrible state he proposed me to share, was leading to his house a poor little girl of about nine years old, in all the attributes of misfortune and weakness: she appeared to have scarcely strength to stand upon her legs. . . . Oh Heavens! thought I on seeing this, can it be that such objects inspire any other sentiments but those of pity! Woe to the depraved being who can suspect pleasures in a breast which want is wasting away; who will wish to gather kisses upon a mouth which famine withers, and which opens only to curse him!

My tears flowed down: I should have liked to rob this victim from the tiger that was awaiting it, I dared not. Could I have done so? I speedily betook myself to my inn, as mortified by a misfortune which brought upon me such proposals, as revolted against the opulence which ventured to make them.

I departed from Lyons next day to take the route for Dauphiny, ever big with the foolish hope that some good luck was awaiting me in this province. I was hardly two leagues from Lyons, on foot, as usual, with a couple of chemises and a few handkerchiefs in my pocket, when I met an old women who accosted me with a look of suffering, and who besought me to give her alms. Far from the hard heartedness of which I had just received such cruel examples, knowing no happiness in the world but that of obliging an unfortunate person, I instantly pulled out my purse on purpose to take out of it a crown, and give it to this woman; but the base creature, being much smarter than I, although I had at first deemed her old and broken down, nicely jumps at my purse, snatches it, lays me low with a strong box of her fist in the stomach, and appears again to view only a hundred paces away, surrounded by four scoundrels who threaten me if I dare advance.

Great God! I bitterly cried, it is therefore impossible for my soul to open itself to any virtuous motion without my instantly being punished by the severest chastisements! In this fatal moment all my courage forsook me; I most sincerely crave pardon for it to-day from Heaven, but I was blinded by despair. I felt ready to quit the career in which so many thorns presented themselves; two choices presented themselves, that of going and joining in with the knaves who had just robbed me, or that of returning to *Lyons* to there accept *Saint-Florent*'s proposal. God spared me from yielding, and although the hope he kindled anew in me was deceitful, since so many adversities were still in store for me, I thank him nevertheless for having sustained me: the ill-fated star which leads me, though innocent, to the scaffold, will never procure me but death; other choices would have procured me infamy; and the latter is much less cruel than the rest.

I go on directing my steps towards the town of Vienne, decided on selling there what I had left, in order to reach *Grenoble.* I was marching along sadly, when at a quarter of a league from that town, I perceive in the plain, on the right side of the road, two cavaliers who were trampling a man under their horses' feet, and who, after having left him for dead, galloped off at full speed; this dreadful spectacle affected me to tears. Alas! said I to myeslf, there is a man more to be pitied than I am; my health and strength at least still remain, I can earn my bread, and if this unhappy man is not rich, what is going to become of him?

To whatever degree I should have been on my guard against the motions of compassion, however unlucky it was for me to yield to them, I could not overcome the extreme desire I felt of going up to this man, and of lavishing my cares on him. I flee to him; he breathes in through my solicitude a little spirituous water I kept about me; he at last opens his eyes, and his first accents are those of gratitude. Being still more eager to be useful to him, I tear up one of my chemises to bind his wounds, to stanch his blood; one of the only effects I have left, I sacrifice for this unhappy man. Having fulfilled these first cares, I give him a little wine to drink. This unfortunate man quite recovered his senses; I observe and distinguish him more clearly. Although on foot, and in pretty nice attire, he did not however appear in mediocrity; he had some valuable effects, rings, a watch, boxes, but all this greatly damaged by his adventure. He asks me, as soon as he is able to speak, who is the kind of angel that brings him assistance, and what can he do to show his gratitude to her for it. Having still the foolishness to believe that a soul linked through acknowledgment should be mine everlastingly, I fancy I can safely enjoy the sweet pleasure of getting him, who has just shed them within my arms, to partake of my tears: I inform him of my reverses, he listens to them with interest, and when I have ended by the last catastrophe which has befallen me, the recital of which shows him the wretched state I am in: — "How happy I am," he cries "to be at least able to acknowledge all that you have just done for me! My name is *Roland*," continues this adventurer; "I possess a very fine castle in the mountains, fifteen leagues hence, I invite you to follow me there; and that this proposal may not alarm your delicacy, I am going to explain for you at once of what use you will be to me. I am a bachelor, but I have a sister whom I passionately love, who is devoted to my solitude, and who shares it with me: I want a subject to wait on her; we have just lost her who used to discharge this duty, I offer you her place." I thanked my protector, and took the liberty of asking him by what hazard a man like him exposed himself to travel without attendance, and as it had just happened to him, to be molested by rogues? — "Somewhat burly, young and strong, I am these several years," *Roland* says to me, "in the habit of coming from my place to Vienne in this way. My health and purse gain by it: not indeed that I am in need of paying attention to the expense, for I am rich: you shall shortly see the proof of it, if you do me the kindness of coming to my house; but parsimony never spoils anything. As to the men who have just in-me, they are two shabby gents of the district, from whom I won one hundred louis last week, in a house at Vienne; I contented myself with their word of honor, I meet them today, I request my rights from them, and that is how they serve me."

I was deploring with this man the two-fold misfortune of which he was the victim, when he proposed to me to set out. "I feel rather better, thanks to your cares," *Roland* says to me; "night is coming on, let us reach a house which must be two leagues from here; by means of the horses we shall take there to-morrow, we can arrive at my home on the same evening."

Wholly bent on profiting by the helps which Heaven seemed to send me, I aid *Roland* to set out, I bear him up on the way, and we really do find at two leagues off, the inn he had mentioned. We take supper in it honestly together. After meal, *Roland* recommends me to the mistress of the house, and next day, on two hired mules which the valet of the inn escorted, we reach the borders of Dauphiny, still steering our course towards the mountains. The journey being to long to make in one day, we pulled up at Virieu, where I experienced the same cares, the same consideration from my master, and the following day, we continued our way, still in the same direction. About four in the evening, we arrived at the foot of the mountains: there the road becoming almost unpassable, *Roland* charges the muleteer not to leave me for fear of accident, and we penetrated into the narrow passages. We did but simply wind, ascend and descend for more than four leagues, and we had then so forsaken every dwelling and every beaten way, that I fancied I was at the end of the Universe. A little uneasiness came upon me in spite of me; *Roland* could not help seeing it, but he said nothing, and his silence frightened me still more. At last we beheld a castle perched upon the top of a mountain at the brink of a frightful precipice, into which it seemed ready to sink: no route appeared to lead to it; the one we were following, only made by goats, filled with stones from all sides, arrived at this horrible resembling much rather a refuge of robbers than the abode of virtuous people.

"There is my house," said *Roland* to me, as soon as he thought the castle had met my looks. And upon my expressing to him my surprise to see him inhabiting such a wild: — "It is what suits me," he hastily replies to me. This reply redoubled my fears: nothing escapes in misfortune; a word, a modulation more or less accentuated in those on whom we depend, stifles or re-animates hope; but being no longer in a position to take a different course, I kept silent. By dint of winding, this antique ruin stood all of a sudden before us: a quarter of a league at most still separated from it. *Roland* alighted from his mule, and having told me to do the same, he gave the both to the valet, paid him and ordered him to return with them. The fresh procedure again displeased me; *Roland* noticed it.

— "What ails you, *Therese*?" he says to me, while making our way towards his dwelling; "you are not out of France; this castle is upon the borders of Dauphiny, and dependent upon *Grenoble*." — "Be it so, Sir." I replied; "but how has it come into your mind to settle down in such a dangerous place?" — "It is because those who inhabit it are not very honest folks," said *Roland*; "it might be quite possible that thou wouldst not be edified at their conduct." — "Ah! Sir," said I to him in trembling, "you cause me to quake, where are you leading me to, then?" — "I am fetching thee to wait upon false-coiners whose chief I am," says *Roland* to me, on seizing me by the arm and making me cross by force a little bridge which was lowered at our arrival, and raised immediately after. "Dost thou see this well?" he continued, as soon as we had entered, on showing me a great, deep grotto at the bottom of the yard, where four naked and chained women were making a wheel turn; "there are thy fellows, and this is thy work; providest thou workest ten hours daily in turn- ing this wheel, and that thou satifiest as those women all the caprices to which it may please me to submit thee, six ounces of black bread and a plate of beans a day will be allowed thee; as to thy freedom, give it over: thou shalt never have it. When thou art dead at the toil, thou wilt be thrown into this hole which thou beholdest beside the well, with sixty or eighty other wenches of thy kind who are awaiting thee in it, and thou shalt be replaced by a fresh one."

— "Oh! Great God!" I cried on throwing myself at *Roland*'s feet, "vouchsafe to recollect, Sir, how I have saved your life; how for an instant, moved by acknowledgement, you seemed to offer me hap- piness, and how it is in casting me into an eternal abyss of ills that you require my services! Is what you are doing meet, and is not remorse already coming to avenge me in the depths of your heart?" — "What dost thou understand, I pray thee, by that senti- ment of acknowledgement with which thou imaginest thou hast captivated me?" said *Roland*. "Reason better, thou mean creature; what wast thou doing, when thou camest to my relief? Between the possibility of continuing thy way and that of coming to me, didst thou not choose the latter as a movement inspired by thy heart? Thou gavest thyself therefore up to an enjoyment? How the dickens dost thou pretend that I am obliged to reward thee for the pleasures thou bestowest upon thyself? And how did it ever occur to thy mind that a man who, as I am, is floating in gold and wealth, deigns to stoop to be anything indebted to a wretch of thy kind? Hadst thou restored me life, I would owe thee nothing, since thou didst act only in thy behalf. To work, slave, to work! learn that civilization, in overthrowing the principles of Nature does not however remove from her her rights: she created in the origin strong and weak beings, with the intention that the latter should be always subordinate to the former; the dexterity, the intelligence of man diversified the position of individuals; it was no longer physical force that determined ranks, it was that of gold; the richest man became the strongest man, the poorest became the weakest; save the motives which founded the power, the priority of the strong man was always within the laws of Nature, to which it became all one whether the chain which captivated the weak man was held by the richest or by the strongest man, and whether it should crush the weakest or else the poorest. But those fits of acknowledgment of which thou wishest to compose links for me, she disregards them, *Therese*; it was never within her laws that the pleasure to which one yielded in obliging should become a motive, for him who received, to forego his rights over the other. Dost thou see, among the animals which serve us as examples, those sentiments thou claimest? When I bear sway over thee by my riches of force, is it natural for me to yield thee up my rights, either because thou hast enjoyed in obliging me, or because being misfortunate, thou didst imagine that thou wouldst gain something by thy action? Even were the service rendered from an equal to an equal, the pride of an elevated soul will never allowed itself to be bowed down through acknowledgment; is not he who receives always humiliated? And does not this humiliation which he feels sufficiently pay the benefactor who, by that alone, finds himself above the other? It is not an enjoyment for pride to raise one's self above the equal? Does he who obliges need any other? And if the obligation, in humbling him who receives, becomes a burden to him, by what right force him to keep it? What must I consent to let myself be humiliated every time the looks of him who has obliged me strike me? Ingratitude, instead of being a vice, is therefore the virtue of proud souls, as truly as acknowledgment is that of weak souls: let people oblige me as much as they like, but let them require nothing for having enjoyed!"

At these words, to which *Roland* did not give me time to reply, two valets seize upon me by his orders, strip me, and chain me with my companions, whom I am obliged to help at once, without its being simply permitted me to rest myself after the tiresome journey I have just made. *Roland* approaches me then; he brutally handles me on all the places which chastity forbids me to name, loads me with sarcasms and impertinences about the scandalous and but little deserved brand that *Rodin* had laid on me; then, arming himself with a bull's pizzle ever at hand, he saluted me with twenty stripes on the backside. — "This is how thou shalt be dealt with, wench," he says to me, when thou art wanting in thy duty; I do not do this for any fault already committed by thee, but merely to show thee how I act with those who do make them." I scream loudly in struggling under my irons; my writhings, yells, tears, the cruelest expressions of my suffering serve only as amusement for my butcher. . . . — "Ah! I shall let thee see more of them, harlot," said *Roland*; "thou art not at the end of thy pains, and I wish thee to know even to the most barbarous refinements of misfortune." He leaves me.

Six obscure nooks, situated under a grotto round this vast well, and which were locked up like dungeons, served us as a retreat by night. As it arrived shortly after my being at this unlucky chain, they came to untie me as well as my companions, and they locked us in after having given us the portion of water, beans and bread of which *Roland* had spoken to me.

I was hardly alone when I quite freely gave way to the horror of my situation. Is it possible, said I to myself, there are men hard hearted enough to stifle in themselves the sentiment of gratitude?. . . This virtue to which I should give myself up with so many charms, if ever an honest soul put me in the way of feeling it, can it therefore be disregarded by certain beings, and must those who stifle it with so much inhumanity be anything else than monsters?

I was lost in these reflections, when all of a sudden I hear the door of my dungeon opening: it is *Roland*. The rascal comes to finish outraging me on making me serve for his detestable freaks: you easily suppose, Madam, they were to be as ferocious as his proceedings, and that the pleasures of love, in such a man, necessarily bore the hues of his hateful character. But why weary your patience by relating these fresh horrors to you? Have I not already defiled your imagination too much by infamous recitals? Ought I to risk fresh ones? — "Yes, *Therese*," said *Mr. de Corville*, "yes, we request of you these particulars; you take the harm out of them with a becomingness which damps all their horror, there only remains of them what is instructive to whatever person that wishes to know man; one does not imagine how useful these paintings are for the development of his soul; perhaps we are still most ignorant in this science, owing to the stupid discretion of those who wished to write on these questions. Enslaved by silly fears, they speak to us only of those puerilities, known to every booby, and dare not, while laying a bold hand upon the human heart, expose to our eyes its mighty errors." — "Well! Sir, I am going to obey you," resumed *Therese* moved, "and behaving as I have already done, I shall try and offer my sketches under the least shocking shades."

*Roland*, whom I must first describe for you, was a short, stout man, aged thirty-five, of inconceivable vigor, hairy like a bear, of gloomy mien, fierce look, very dark, manly features, a long nose, bearded to the eyes, black, thick eyebrows, and that part which distinguishes the men from our sex, of such length and of such huge a size, that not only nothing like it was ever offered to my sight, but it was also wholly certain that Nature had never made anything so prodigious: both my hands hardly went round it, and it was as long as from my elbow to my wrist. To these physics, *Roland* added all the vices which can be the outcome of a fiery temper, a deal of imagination, and a fortune always too considerable as not to have cast him into great irregularities. *Roland* got through his fortune;

his father, who had begun it, had left him exceedingly rich, by means of which this young man had already spent very much: satiated with ordinary pleasures, he had no longer recourse except to horrors; these alone succeeded in restoring to him desires consumed by too many enjoyments; the women who used to wait upon him were all employed in his secret debaucheries; and in order to satisfy some less dishonest pleasures in which this libertine could nevertheless procure the savour of the crime which delighted him better than all else, *Roland* had his own sister as mistress, and it was with her he finished extinguishing the passions he came to kindle with us.

He was almost naked when he entered; his face, greatly inflamed, bore at once proofs of gluttony, to which he had just given himself up, and of the abominable lust which was eating him away. He gazes on me an instant with eyes that cause me to shudder: "Remove these robes," he says to me, in tearing away himself those I had taken back to cover me during the night . . . "yes, remove all that and follow me; I made thee feel a little while ago what thou wouldst risk in giving way to sloth; but if thou gettest it into thy head to betray us, as the crime would be much greater, the punishment would necessarily be proportioned to it; come therefore and see what it would be like." I was in a state hard to be described, but *Roland*, not allowing my soul time to break out, directly seizes me by the arm and pulls me along; he led me with his right hand: with his left, he held a small lantern which dimly lighted us. After several windings, we find ourselves at the door of a cave; he opens it, and making me go in first, he bade me descend while he is shutting this first enclosure; I obey. At a hundred steps, we meet a second one, which is opened and shut in the same way; but after the latter, there was no other stairs, it was a small road hewn in the rock, full of windings, and the declivity of which extremely straight. *Roland* spoke not a word, this silence frightened me still more; he lighted us on with his lantern; we travelled thus nearly a quarter of an hour. The state I was in caused me to feel still more keenly the frightful dampness of those subterraneous passages. We had finally gone down so far, that it is no exaggeration to say the spot at which we arrived must be more than eight hundred feet in the bowels of the earth. On the right and left sides of the path we traversed, were several niches where I saw chests containing these malefactors' riches. In fine a last bronze gate presents itself; *Roland* opens it, and I was on the point of reeling over, in perceiving the dismal place to which this dishonest man was leading me; seeing me bend, he roughly pushes me, and so I find myself, without wishing for it, in the middle of this frightful sepulchre. Fancy, Madam, a round vault, of twenty-five feet in diameter, the walls of which, being furnished with black hangings, were only decorated by the most dismal objects; skeletons of every size, bones formed cross-wise, heads of dead persons, bundles of rods and whips scimitars, daggers, pistols; such were the horrors one saw upon the walls, which a three-wicked lamp, suspended from one of the corners of the vault, lighted. From the arch went a long rope which fell at eight or ten feet from the ground in the middle of this dungeon, and which, as you are shortly to see, was simply there in order to serve for dreadful expeditions; there was on the right a coffin which the spectre of Death, armed with a menacing scythe, was somewhat opening; alongside was a kneeling desk; one saw a crucifix above, placed between two black wax candles; on the left, the wax effigy of a naked woman, so natural that I was for a long while deceived by it: it was fastened to a cross, it was placed to it breastwise, so that all its hind parts were clearly seen, but horribly molested; the blood seemed to ooze from several sores, and flow along its thighs; it had the finest hair in the world, its lovely head was turned towards us, and appeared to implore forgiveness: all the writhings of suffering were distinguished, stamped upon its handsome face, and even to the tears which bathed it. At the sight of this terrible image, I had like to lose my strength a second time. The end of the vault was taken up by a vast black sofa, from which all the atrocities of this dismal place unfolded themselves to view.

— "There is where you shall die, *Therese*," *Roland* says to me, "if ever you conceive the unlucky idea of leaving my house; yes, I shall come here in person to take away your life, I shall here make you feel the agonies by all that will be possible for me to invent the hardest." In uttering this menace, *Roland* got inflamed; his nervousness, his disorder made him like a tiger ready to devour its prey: it was then he displayed the dreadful member with which he was supplied; he made me feel it, inquired of me if I had seen a similar one. — "Such as it is, wench," he said to me in a fury, "it must indeed be however introuced into the narrowest place in thy body, were I to split thee in two; my sister, being much younger than you, bears it in that same place; I never enjoy women otherwise: it must therefore split thee in two also." And not to leave me in doubt about the place he meant, he introduced into it three fingers armed with very long nails, in saying to me: — "Yes, it is there, *Therese*, it is there, I shall plunge by and by this member which frightens thee; it shall enter in all its length, it will tear thee, it will bleed thee; and I shall be intoxicated." He frothed on pronouncing these words, interlarded by oaths and heinous blasphemes. The hand with which he was patting the temple he apparently wished to attack, wandered then over all the adjacent parts, he scratched them; he did as much with my breath, he so bruised it that I suffered from it horrible pains during fifteen days. He next placed me on the edge of the sofa, rubbed with the spirits of wine that moss with which Nature adorned the altar where our species is regenerated; he set fire to it and burnt it. His fingers took hold of the fleshy excrescence which crowns this very altar, he rudely rumpled it; he next introduced his fingers into the inside, and his nails molested the membrane that decks it. No longer contented, he told me that, since he held me in his den, it was quite as well I should not leave it again, that this would spare him the trouble of bringing me down to it anew. I rushed to his knees, I ventured to remind him again of he services I had done him. . . . I perceived I was irritating him the more in recalling the rights that I supposed for his pity; he bade me hold my tongue, while knocking me down upon the floor with a blow of his knee with all his strength in the pit of my stomach. — "Come!" he says to me, on hauling me up by the hair, "come! get ready; I am certainly going to immolate thee. . . ." — "Oh! Sir!" — "No, no, thou must perish; I wish no longer to hear myself reproached with thy trifling favors; I like to owe nothing to anybody, it is the part of others to depend wholly on me. . . . Thou art about to die, I tell thee; get into this coffin, that I see whether it will hold thee." He carries me into it, he locks me in it, then goes out of the vault and pretends he is leaving me there. I never thought I was so near death; alas! it was about to offer itself to me under a still truer aspect. *Roland* comes back; he takes me out of the coffin.

— "Thou wilt be admirably well therein," he says to me; "one would say it was made for thee; but to allow thee to finish quietly in it, would be too fine a death; I am going to make thee feel one of a different kind and which fails not to have also its comforts. "Come! implore thy God, wench, beg him to hasten and avenge thee, if he really has the power of doing so. . . ." I throw myself upon the kneeling stool, and whilst I am opening my heart in a loud voice to the Eternal, *Roland* redoubles his vexations and tortures still more cruelly, upon the posterior parts I expose to him; he scourges these parts with all his might with a hammer studded by steel spikes, every blow of which caused my blood to spirt up to the roof. — "Well!" continued he while blaspheming, "thy God does not relieve thee; he thus allows unhappy virtue to suffer, he gives it over into the hands of wickedness; ah! what a God, *Therese*, what a God that God is! Come," he says to me next, "come, wench, thy prayer must be over." And, at the same time, he sets me on my stomach, at the edge of the sofa which formed the end of this cabinet. "Thou must die, *Therese*, I have told thee so!" He grips my arms, he ties them upon my groins, he then passes a black silk cord round my neck, both ends of which, being still held by him, can, on being tightened at will, squeeze my respiration and despatch me to the other world, in the longer or shorter delay it may please him.

— "This torture is sweeter than thou thinkest, *Therese*," *Roland* says to me; "thou wilt only feel death through inexpressible sensations of pleasure; the squeezing this cord will effect upon the mass of thy nerves is going to set the organs of voluptuousness on fire; the consequence is certain. If all the persons condemned to this torture knew in what intoxication it causes death, being less frightened by this punishment for their crimes, they would commit them oftener and with far more assurance; this delightful operation,

*Therese,* pressing likewise the place where I am going to set myself," he adds on presenting himself to a criminal route, so deserving of such a villain, "is also about to double my pleasures." But he vainly tries to open it; he might prepare ever so much the ways, being too hugely fitted to succeed, his enterprises were always repelled. His fury then knows no bounds; his nails, hands, feet help to avenge him for the resistances Nature opposes to him. He presents himself anew; the fiery sword slips to the banks of the neighboring canal, and with the vigour of the shake presents it nearly halfways. I scream; *Roland,* being furious at the mistake, gets himself out with rage, and this time knocks so vigorously at the other door, that the moistened dart is driven into it while tearing me. *Roland* takes advantage of the success of his first shake; his efforts become more violent; he gains ground. Accordingly as he advances, the unlucky cord he threw round my neck tightens, I scream awfully; savage *Roland,* whom this amuses, obliges me to redouble my yells; being too sure of their insufficiency, too much a master to stop them when he liked, he is inflamed at their shrill sounds. However, the intoxication is ready to come over him, the pressures of the cord are modulated in proportion to the degrees of his pleasure; my voice gradually dies out; the squeezings become then so violent, that my senses fail without however losing sensibility. Roughly shaken by the enormous member with which *Roland* tears my bowels, notwithstanding the frightful state I am in, I feel myself inundated with jets of his lust; I have still in my ears the cries he utters while pouring them out. An instant's dullness ensued; I know not what became of me, but my eyes are soon open again to the light, I am free, unbound, and my choice seems to return. — "Well! *Therese,*" my butcher says to me, "I bet if thou wilt be truthful, thou hast felt but pleasure?" — "What a deal of horror, Sir, what an amount of disgust, agonies and despair! — Thou art deceiving me; I know the effects thou hast just experienced; but whatever they may have been, it does not matter! thou oughtest, I fancy, to know me well enough to be perfectly aware that thy voluptuousness preoccupies me infinitely less than my own, in what I undertake with thee; and this voluptuousness I seek has been so quick, that I am going to help myself again to it for a few moments."

"It is on thee now, *Therese*," this notorious libertine says to me, "it is on thee alone thy days are going to depend." He then throws around my neck that rope which was hanging from the ceiling; as soon as it is firmly fastened to it, he ties to the stool upon which I was standing and which had raised me up to it, a string of which he holds the end, and goes and places himself in an arm-chair opposite to me; I have in my hands a sharp bill which I am to use in cutting the rope at the moment when, by means of the string he is holding, he will cause the stool to tumble under my feet. — "Thou seest, *Therese*," he says to me then, "if thou missest thy aim, I shall not miss mine; I am not therefore wrong in telling thee thy days depend on thyself." He excites himself; it is at the moment of his intoxication he is to pull away the stool, the removal of which leaves me hanged from the ceiling; he does his utmost to counterfeit this moment; he would be in his glory, were I to lack dexterity. But he might try ever so much, I foresee it; the violence of his ecstasy betrays him, I behold him making the fatal movement, the stool slips away, I cut the rope, and fall upon the ground; completely freed, there, at more than twelve feet from him, would you believe it, Madam, I feel my whole person inundated with the proofs of his delirium and madness.

Any other but myself, profiting by the weapon in hands, would have undoubtedly rushed upon this monster; but of what use would this act of courage have been to me? Without the keys of these subterraneous places, being ignorant of the windings, I should be dead before I could get out of them; besides, *Roland* was armed. I therefore got up again, leaving the weapon slightest suspicion of me; he had none; he had relished upon the ground that he might not even conceive the in its whole extent, and pleased with my mildness, my resignation far more perhaps than with my dexterity, he beckoned to me to go out, and we went up stairs again.

Next day I examined my companions better. These four girls were from twenty-five to thirty years old; although stupified by misery and deformed by the excess of labor, they still retained some relics of beauty; they had fine waists, and the youngest, called

*Suzanne,* together with lovely eyes, and still very pretty hair; *Roland* taken her at Lyons, he had had her first flowers, and after having carried her away from her family, under solemn promises of marrying her, he had led her off to this frightful castle; she was there these three years, and was besides, more especially than her companions, the object of this monster's ferocities: by dint of lash with the bull's pizzle, her buttocks had become callous and hard like a cow's hide dried in the sun; she had a cancer on her right breast, and an abscess in her womb, which used to cause her unheard of sufferings. All this was the work of perfidious *Roland* ; every one of these horrors was the fruit of his lubricities.

It was she who informed me that *Roland* was on the eve of setting out for Venice, if the large sums he lately had got passed in Spain returned him the bills of exchange he was awaiting for Italy, because he did not like to carry his gold beyond the mountains. He never sent any there: it was a different country from the one he intended to inhabit, that he was wont to get his forged moneys passed; by this means, being rich in the place he wished to settle down, only in bills of another kingdom, his roguery could never be found out. But all might fail in an instant, and the retreat he was thinking over wholly depended on this last transaction, in which the principal amount of his treasures was at stake. If *Cadiz* accepted his piasters, zechins, forged louis, and send him accordingly bills of Venice, *Roland* was happy for the remainder of his life; if the fraud was discovered, one day alone sufficed to overthrow the frail edifice of his fortune.

— "Alas!" said I on learning these particulars, Providence will be upright for once, it will not countenance the success of such a monster, and we shall be avenged. . . ." Great God! After the experience I had acquired, was it meet for me to reason thus!

About twelve o'clock, we were allowed two hours' rest, of which we profited to generally go singly to breathe and dine in our rooms; at two o'clock we were tied up again and made work until night, without its being ever permitted to us to enter the castle. If we were naked, it was not only because of the heat, but much rather to be in a better way of receiving the stripes of the bull's pizzle which our savage master came to lay on us occasionally. In winter, we were supplied with a pair of trousers and a waistcoat so tight to the skin, that our bodies were nevertheless exposed to the blows of a villain whose sole pleasure was to thrash us.

Eight days passed without my seeing *Roland.* On the ninth, he appeared at our work, and while *Suzanne* and I were turning the wheel with too much faint-heartedness, he dealt us out thirty lashes each of the bull's pizzle, from the middle of the loins to the calves of the legs.

At midnight of the same day, the nasty man came for me in my dungeon, and falling into a passion at the sight of his cruelties, he again introduced his awful club into the gloomy cavern which I was turning towards him, by the posture he was keeping me in while viewing the traces of his madness. When his passions were assuaged, I wanted to take advantage of the moment's calm in order to entreat him to mitigate my lot. Alas! I was not aware that if in such souls the moment of delirium renders the propensity they have for cruelty activer, nor does calmness either on that account recall them therefrom to the easy virtues of the good man; it is a fire more or less kindled by the fuel by which it is kept up, but which burns nevertheless though under the ashes.

— "And by what right," *Roland* answers me, "dost thou pretend I should ease thy chains? Is it on account of the caprices I am willing to pass with thee? But I am going to thy feet to crave thy favors, for the granting of which thou mayst request amends? I ask nothing from thee, I take, and I do not see why, because I use a right over thee, it would result therefrom that I must abstain from exacting a second one. There is no love in my case: love is a chivalrous sentiment thoroughly despised by me, and my heart has never felt its approaches; I make use of a woman from necessity, as one makes use of a round hollow vase in a different need; but I never bestow either esteem or tenderness upon that individual, whom my money and authority submit to my desires; indebted only to myself for what I rob, and never requiring of him but submission, I can not be bound accordingly to show him any gratitude. I ask those who would wish to force me to it, whether a robber who snatches away a man's purse in a wood, because he finds himself stronger than he, owes any thankfulness to that man for the wrong he has just caused him? It is the same with the outrage committed on a woman: it may be right for him to commit a second one, but never a sufficient reason for him to make amends." — "Oh! Sir," I said to him, "to what height you carry wickedness!" — "To the highest point," *Roland* answers me; "there is not a single peevishness in the world to which I have not given way, not a crime I have not perpetrated, and not one my principles do not excuse or legitimate; I have incessantly felt in evil a sort of attraction which always turned to the profit of my voluptuousness. Crime kindles my lust; the more frightful it is, the more it excites me; I enjoy, in committing it, the same kind of pleasure as ordinary people but taste in lubricity; and I have found myself on a hundred occasions, thinking of crime, giving myself up to it, or having just committed it, absolutely in the same state as one beside a lovely naked woman; it stirred up my senses in the same way, and I perpetrated it in order to be inflamed, as one approaches a fine object with the intention of lewdness." — "Oh! Sir, what you say is awful, but I have seen examples of it." — "There are a thousand of them," *Therese*.

"You must not imagine that it is a woman's beauty which best stirs up the spirit of a libertine: it is much rather the species of crime the laws have attributed to its possession. The proof whereof is, the more criminal this possession is, so much the more inflamed one is; the man who enjoys a woman he steals from her husband, a girl he takes away from her parents, is undoubtedly far more delighted than the husband who merely enjoys his wife; and the more worthy of respect the bonds which are severed appear, so much the more voluptuousness increases. If she is his mother, his sister, his daughter, fresh attractions for the pleasures felt; has one tasted all this? one should like the obstacles were still increased in order to give greater pains and charms in surmounting them. Now, if crime seasons an enjoyment, separate from this enjoyment, it can be therefore one itself; consequently, there will be then a certain enjoyment in crime alone. Because it is impossible, for that which lends savour, not to be itself well supplied with it. Thus, I suppose, the rape of a girl in her own behalf will afford a very lively pleasure, but the rape in behalf of another will give all the pleasure by which this girl's enjoyment was improved by the rape; the rape of a watch, a purse will likewise afford it, and if I have accustomed my senses to be affected with any voluptuousness at a girl's rape, considered as rape, this same pleasure, this same voluptuousness will be found in the rape of the watch, in that of the purse, etc. And this is what explains the caprice of so many honest people, who were wont to steal without being in need of doing so. Nothing plainer, henceforth, whether one tastes the greatest pleasures in all that will be criminal, or whether one renders, by everything imaginable, simple enjoyments as criminal as it will be possible to make them; in acting thus, one does not more than impart to this enjoyment the dose of savour which it lacked and which became requisite for the perfection of happiness. These systems lead far, I know, perhaps I shall even prove so to thee before long, *Therese*; but what matter, provided one enjoys? Was there, for instance, my dear child, anything simpler and more natural than to see me enjoy thee? But thou art opposed to it, thou requestest of me that this may not be; it would seem from the obligations I am under to thee, that I should grant thee what thou requirest. Yet I surrender to nothing, I break all the ties which ensnare fools, I subject thee to my desires, and out of the simplest, the most monotonous enjoyment, I form a truly delightful one. Yield therefore, *Therese*, yield; and if thou returnest to the world under the character of the strongest, misuse likewise thy rights, and thou shalt discern the liveliest and most acute of every pleasure."

*Roland* walked out on uttering these words, and left me absorbed in reflections which, as you easily imagine, were not to his advantage.

I was in this house six months, occasionally serving this rascal's notorious debaucheries, when I saw him entering my prison one evening with *Suzanne*. — "Come, *Therese*," he says to me; "it is a long time, it seems to me, since I made thee descend into that vault, which frightened thee so much. Follow me there both of you, but do ont expect to come up again in the same way, I must by all means leave one; we shall see to whose lot it will fall." I stand up, I cast bewildered looks at my companion, I saw the tears rolling in her eyes, . . . we march.

As soon as we were shut up in the underground place, *Roland* gloated at both of us with wild eyes. He delighted in repeating her doom, and in thoroughly convincing each of us tht one of us two would most certainly stay behind. — "Come," he says on seating himself, and making us stand straight up before him, "work each in her turn at the disenchantment of this spell-bound one, and woe to her who will restore it its energy!" — "It is wrong," said *Suzanne*; "she who will excite you best ought to be the one to obtain her forgiveness." — "Not at all," said *Roland*; "from the moment it will be proved that she inflames me best, it becomes certain that it is her death which will afford me most pleasure. Besides, in granting pardon to the one who is about to inflame me the sooner, you would each go at it with such ardor, that you would perhaps cast my senses into the ecstasy before the consummation of the sacrifice, and this is precisely what is not wanted." — "It is to will evil for evil, Sir," said I to *Roland*, "the completion of your ecstasy ought to be the only thing you should desire, and if you attain it without crime, why will you commit it?" — "Because I shall only thus attain to it deliciously, and because I come down to this vault but to commit one. I know perfectly well I should succeed in it without that, but I do wish this in order to succeed in it." And during this dialogue, having selected me to begin, I excite him with one hand before, with the other behind, while he is leisurely feeling all the parts of my body, which are exposed to him owing to my nakedness. — "That lovely skin, *Therese*," he says to me while fingering my buttocks, "is still very far from being in the state of hardness, mortification that *Suzanne*'s is in; one might burn that dear girl's, as she would not feel it; but thou, *Therese*, but thou . . . it is still as roses intermingled with lilies: we shall return to it, we shall return to it."

You do not imagine, Madam, how much this threat tranquillized me: *Roland* undoubtedly did not suspect, while uttering it, the calm he was infusing into me: for, was it not obvious that since he intended to subject me to fresh cruelties, he had not yet a mind to immolate me? I have already told you, Madam, everything strikes in misfortune, and, from that moment, I took courage again. Other additional good luck! I did nothing, and that huge mass, softly under itself, resisted all my shocks. *Suzanne*, in the same posture, was handled in the same places; but, as her skin was hardened quite another way, *Roland* fingered a good deal less; *Suzanne* was however the younger. — "I am persuaded," said our persecutor, "that the most frightful lashes would not succeed now in drawing a drop of blood from that backside." He made both of us stoop, and presenting to himself, by our inclination, the four routes of pleasure, his tongue frisked about in the two narrowest ones; the nasty man spat into the others. He took us again before him, made us kneel between his thighs, so that our two breasts were on a level with what we were exciting in him. — "Oh! as to the breast," said *Roland*, "thou must yield it to *Suzanne*; thou never hadst such beautiful nipples; look, see how full it is!" He squeezed, while speaking thus, this unfortunate girl's breast even to the bruising of it between his fingers. At this time, it was no longer I who was exciting him, *Suzanne* had replaced me; the dart was scarcely in her hands, when rushing from the quiver, it was already vigorously menacing everything around it. — "*Suzanne*," says *Roland*, "that is a dreadful success. . . . It is thy judgment, *Suzanne*; I fear so," continued this savage man, in pinching, in scratching her paps. As to mine he sucked and gnawed them only. He finally placed *Suzanne* on her knees upon the edge of the sofa, he makes her bow her head, and enjoys her in this posture according to the frightful manner natural to him. Being roused by fresh sufferings, *Suzanne* struggles, and *Roland*, who wants only to skirmish, content with a few incursions, comes to take refuge in me in the very temple where he sacrificed with my companion, whom he ceases not to annoy, molest during the while. — "There is a wench that is fiercely exciting me," he says to me, "I know not what I should like to do to her." — "Oh! Sir," said I, "have pity on her; it is impossible for her pains to be keener." — "Oh! yes!" said the rascal. . . . "One could. . . . Ah! if I had here that famous Emperor *Kie*, one of the great villains whom

China has witnessed upon the throne[2], we should indeed do quite a different thing. Between his wife and him, both of them, immolating daily victims, we are told used to prolong their lives twenty-four hours, in the cruelest agonies of death, and in such a state of suffering that they were ever ready to give up the ghost without being able to succeed in it, by the inhuman cares of those monsters who, causing them to fluctuate from reliefs to tortures, restored them this moment to life only to offer them death the next. . . . I am too mild, *Therese*, I am quite a stranger to all that, I am but a mere school-boy." *Roland* withdraws before finishing the sacrifice, and does me almost as much harm by this sudden retreat, as he had done me in introducing himself. He throws himself into *Suzanne*'s arms and adding sarcasm to outrage: — "Lovely creature," he says to her, "how I recollect with delight the first moment of our union! never did woman afford me livelier pleasures; never did I love any as thee! . . . Let us embrace, *Suzanne*, we are about to part from each other, perhaps for a long while." — "Monster," said my companion to him on pushing him back with horror, "be off; add not to the tortures thou inflictest upon me the despair of hearing thy horrible words; tiger, glut thy rage, but respect at least my misfortunes." *Roland* seized her, stretched her upon the sofa with her legs wide open, and the workshop of generation wholly in his reach. — "Temple of my former pleasures," cried this infamous fellow, "ye who procured me such pleasing ones when I gathered your first roses, I must indeed bid ye farewell. . . ." The wretch! he drove his fingers into it, and poking therewith, during several minutes, in the inside, while *Suzanne* screamed, he took them out only besmeared with blood. Satiated by these horrors, and clearly seeing it was no longer possible for him to contain himself: — "Come, *Therese*," he says to me, "come, dear girl, let us unravel all this by a short scene of the game of rope-cutting[3]" (such was the name of this fatal fun, of which I gave you a description, the first time I spoke to you about *Roland*'s vault). I get upon the tripod, the nasty man attaches the rope to my neck, he sets himself before me; *Suzanne*, although in a frightful state, excites him with her hands; at a moment's end, he pulls the stool upon which I am standing; but, armed with the bill, the rope is directly cut, and I fall upon the ground without any harm. — "All-right," said *Roland*; "thy turn, *Suzanne* : it is all over, and I pardon thee if thou gettest out of it with as much skill."

*Suzanne* is put into my place. Oh! Madam, allow me to conceal from you the particulars of this awful scene. . . . The unfortunate girl did not return from it. — "Let us go out, *Therese*," *Roland* says to me; "thou shalt not come back again to these places except it be thy turn." — "When you will, Sir, when you will" I replied; "I prefer death to the awful life you cause me to lead. Are there unhappy women as we are to whom life may be still dear?. . ." And *Roland* locked me up in my dungeon. My companions inquired of me next day what had become of *Suzanne*; I informed them of it; they were not astonished at; they were all awaiting the same lot, and they all, after my example, seeing therein the end of their evils, eagerly desired it.

Two years passed thus, *Roland* in his usual debaucheries, I in the horrible perspective of a cruel death, when tidings were at last spread through the castle that our master's desires were not only satisfied, that he not only received the immense quantity of bills he had requested for Venice, but that he was also asked again for another six million of forged moneys, the funds of which were to be transmitted to him according to his good pleasure, for Italy; he set out with an income of over two millions, without the hopes he could conceive: such was the fresh example Providence was preparing for me. Such was the fresh manner in which it wanted to convince me that prosperity was only for Crime, and misfortune for Virtue.

Such was the state of things, when *Roland* came for me to take me a third time down to the vault. I quaked on recollecting the threats he had made me the last time we went there. — "Cheer up," he says to me, "thou hast nothing to fear, it is about a thing which concerns only myself . . . a strange voluptuousness I wish to enjoy and which will cause thee to run no risks." I follow him. As soon as all the doors are shut: — "*Therese*," *Roland* says to me, thou are the only one in the house upon whom I dare rely for what is in hand; I wanted a very honest woman. . . . I have seen but thee, I confess, I even prefer thee to my sister. . . ." Filled with surprise, I begged him to explain himself. — "Hear me," he says to me; "my fortune is made, but whatever favors I may have received from Destiny, it may forsake me at any moment; I may be watched, I may be seized upon during the conveyance I am going to make of my riches, and, if this mishap befalls me, that which awaits me, *Therese*, is the rope; it is the same pleasure as I delight in causing the women to taste, that will serve me for punishment. I am convinced, as much as it is possible to be, that this death is infinitely milder than it is cruel; but, as the women whom I have made feel its first pangs never wished to be truthful with me, it is upon my own person I want to find out its sensation. I wish to know, from my own experience, whether it be not quite certain that this squeezing determines, in the one who feels it, the erector-nerve at the ejaculation; being once persuaded that this death is but a pastime, I shall face it far more undauntedly, for it is not the ceasing of my existence that frightens me: my principles are formed thereon, and being thoroughly persuaded that matter can never become but matter, I no more fear Hell than I expect Paradise; but I dread the torments of a cruel death; I should not like to suffer while dying: let us therefore make an effort. Thou wilt do to me everything I have done to thee; I am going to strip naked; I shall go upon the stool, thou wilt fasten the rope; I shall excite myself a moment: then, as soon as thou seest things settling down in a sort of steadiness, thou wilt pull away the stool, and I shall remain hanged; thou wilt leave me there until thou beholdest either the erection of my seed or symptoms of sufferings; in the second case, thou wilt loose me at once; in the first case, thou wilt let Nature act and wilt loose me only afterwards. Thou seest, *Therese*, I am going to place my life in thy hands; thy freedom, fortune, such will be the price of thy good conduct." — "Ah! Sir," I replied, "there is extravagance in this proposal." — "No, *Therese*, I require it," he answered on undressing; "but behave well; see what a proof I am giving thee of my confidence and esteem!" What would have been the good of my wavering? Was he not master of me? Besides, it appeared to me that the evil I was about to do would be immediately repaired by the extreme care I would take to conserve his life; I was going to be mistress of that life, but whatever may have been his intentions towards me, it would certainly be only to restore it to him.

We make ourselves ready; *Roland* over-heats himself by a few of his usual caresses; he gets upon the stool, I hang him up; he wants me to rail at him all the while, to reproach him with all the horrors of his life, I do so; his dart soon menaces Heaven, he himself beckons to me to pull away the stool, I obey. Would you believe it, Madam? there is nothing so true as what *Roland* had fancied: only symptoms of pleasure were depicted on his face, and almost at the same instant rapid jets of seed were shot to the ceiling. When all was spent, without my having aided him in any way whatsoever, fly to set him free; he swoons away, but by dint of attentions I soon recalled him to his senses. — "Oh! *Therese*," he says to me on opening his eyes, "one has no idea of those sensations; they surpass all that one can relate: let people do as they will with me now, I defy the sword of Themis. Thou art going to find me again very deficient in acknowledgment, *Therese*," *Roland* says to me on tying my hands behind my back, "but how wilt thou have it, my dear? people do not correct themselves at my age. . . . Dear creature, thou hast just restored me to life, and I never conspired so strongly against thine; thou hast complained of *Suzanne*'s fate: well! I am about to re-unite thee with her; I am going to thrust thee alive into the vault where she expired." I shall not describe my state to you, Madam, you understand it; I might cry, lament ever so much, I was not listened to. *Roland* opens the unlucky vault, he lowers a lamp into it that I may the better distinguish the host of dead bodies with which it is filled; he next slips a rope under my arms bound, as I have stated, behind my back, and by means of this rope, he lets me down twenty feet from the bottom of this vault and about thirty feet from where he was standing: I suffered awfully in this position, it seemed my arms were being torn asunder. With what fright must I not be seized, and what perspective presented itself to me! Heaps of dead bodies in the midst of which I was about to end my days and the loathsome smell of which was already stifling me! *Roland* stays the rope to a staff fixed across the hole; then, armed with a knife, I hear him exciting himself. — "Come, *Therese*," he says to me, "recommend thy soul to God; the moment of my delirium will be that on which I shall cast thee into this burial place, on which I shall hurl

227

thee into the everlasting abyss which is awaiting thee; ah! . . . ah! . . . *Therese*, ah! . . ." And I felt my head covered with proofs of his ecstasy, without his having luckily cut the rope. He draws me up again. — "Well, " he says to me, "hast thou been afraid?" — "Ah, Sir!" — "Thou shalt die thus, *Therese*, be convinced of it, and I was very glad to accustom thee to it." We went upstairs again. . . . Should I complain, should I praise myself? What a reward for that which I had just done again for him! But could not the monster have done more for it? Could he not make me lose my life? Oh what a man!

*Roland* was at last ready to depart. He came on the eve to see me at midnight; I throw myself at his feet, I most earnestly entreat him to set me free, and to give me whatever trifle of money he liked to bring me to *Grenoble*. — "To *Grenoble*? Certainly not, *Therese*, thou wouldst inform upon us there." — "Well! Sir," said I to him, on bathing his knees with my tears, "I swear to you never to go there, and in order to convince you of it, be pleased to bring me with you to Venice; perhaps I shall not find there hearts as hard as in my country, and once you are willing to bring me to that town, I swear that by all that is most holy, never to trouble you there."
— "I shall not give thee a single assistance, a single half-penny," this notorious rascal harshly replied; all that relates to pity, to commiseration, to acknowledgement, is far from my heart, that were I three times as rich as I am, I should not be seen bestowing a crown piece upon a poor man; the sight of misfortune excites me, it amuses me, and when I can not a myself do evil, I rejoice with delight at the one which the hand of Destiny causes. I have thereupon principles from which I shall not deviate, *Therese*. Poverty is within the order of Nature: in creating men of unequal forces, she has convinced us of the desire she had that this inequality should be maintained in the changes which our civilization would effect in her laws; to relieve the needy man is to destroy the established order; it is to be opposed to that of Nature, it is to overthrow the equilibrium which is the basis of her most sublime arrangements; it is to work at indolence and slothfulness, it is to teach the poor an equality dangerous for Society; it is to encourage man to rob the rich man, when it may please the latter to refuse his assistance, and that by the habit in

which these assistances will have placed the por man of obtaining them without labour." — "Oh! Sir, these are hard principles! Would you speak thus, if you had not been always rich?" — "That may be, *Therese*; every one has his own way of seeing, such is mine, and I shall not change it. People complain of the beggars in France: if people wished, there would be soon none of them; seven or eight thousand of them would be no sooner hanged, than this infamous brood would disappear. The political Body ought to have thereupon the same laws as the physical Body. Would a man devoured by vermin allow them to live upon him through pity? Do we not root up in our gardens the parasitic plant which injures the useful vegetable? Why then try to act differently in this case?" — "But religion," I cried, "Sir, benevolence, humanity. . . ." — "Are the stumbling-blocks of everything that pretends to happiness," said *Roland* ; "if I have consolidated mine, it is merely on the ruins of all those infamous prejudices of man; it is in mocking divine and human laws; in always sacrificing the weak man when I found him in my way; in cheating the public credulity, in ruining the poor man and robbing the rich man, that I have arrived at the steep temple of the divinity I was adoring; why didst thou not imitate me? The narrow route to this temple was offered to thy eyes as to mine; have the chimerical virtues which thou hast preferred to them consoled thee for thy sacrifices? There is no longer time, unfortunate one, there is no longer time; weep over thy faults, suffer and try to find, if thou canst, in the bosom of the phantoms thou reverest, what the worship thou hast rendered to them has made thee lose." Cruel *Roland* rushes upon me at these words, and I am again obliged to serve the filthy voluptuousnesses of a monster whom I so justly detested; I thought he would strangle me this time. When his passion was allayed, he took out the bull's pizzle and gave me more than a hundred lashes of it on the body, assuring me that I was very happy because he had no time to administer me more of them.

Next day, before setting out, this wicked fellow afforded us a fresh scene of cruelty and barbarity, of which the annals of Andronicus, Nero, Tiberius, Venceslas furnish no example. Everybody at the Castle thought that *Roland*'s sister would leave with him, he had got here therefore dressed; at the moment of mounting horse, he led her to us: "There is thy post, worthless creature" he said to her, while commanding her to strip naked; "I wish my comrades to remember me, on leaving them as a pledge the woman by whom they fancy I am most smitten; but as only a certain number is wanted here, as I am going to make a dangerous journey during which my weapons may perhaps be useful to me, I must try my pistols on one of these jades." On saying this, he loads one of them, presents it to the breast of every one of us, and returning at last to his sister: — "Away," he says to her, "wench," on blowing out her brains, "go and tell the Devil that *Roland,* the richest of imps on the earth, is he who most insolently defies both the hand of heaven and his!" This unfortunate girl, who did not expire immediately, struggled for a long while under her chains: a horrible spectacle which this infamous scoundrel looks upon in cold blood, and from which he at length tears himself away only on going away from us forever.

Everything changed on the day after *Roland's* departure. His successor, a mild and perfectly reasonable man, had us instantly released. — "That is no work for a weak and delicate sex," he kindly said to us; "it is the business of animals to work that machine; the trade we exercise is criminal enough, without still offending the Supreme Being by free atrocities." He established us in the castle, and put me, without exacting anything from me, in possession of the charges which *Roland's* sister used to fulfill; the other women were engaged in proportioning coins, an occupation undoubtedly far less tiresome and for which they were nevertheless requited, as well as I was, by good rooms and excellent food.

At the end of two months, *Dalville, Roland's* successor, informed us of the safe arrival of his colleague, at Venice; he was enjoying there all the rest, happiness he could have hoped for. The destiny of him who was replacing him was very far from being the same. Unfortunate Dalville was honest in his profession: it was more than was needed in order to be speedily undone.

One day as all was still at the Castle, as under this kind master's laws, the work, although criminal, was being carried on merrily, the doors are broken in, the fences scaled, and the house, before our men had time to think of their defence, is filled with more than sixty Marechaussean cavaliers. It was necessary to surrender there was no means of doing otherwise. We were chained like beasts; we were tied upon horses and conveyed away to *Grenoble.* O Heavens! said I to myself on entering it, the scaffold is about to do for me in this town where I was so foolish as to think that good luck was to begin for me. . . . O forebodings of man, how deceitful ye are!

The forgers' case was soon tried; all were sentenced to be hanged. When the brand I bore was seen, they almost saved themselves the trouble of questioning me, and I was just going to be treated as the others, when I endeavoured to obtain at length some pity from the famous Magistrate, the honor of this tribunal, an upright judge, a loved citizen, an enlightened philosopher, whose celebrated name wisdom and benevolence will engrave for ever, in golden characters, in the temple of Themis. He listened to me; convinced of my good faith and the truth of my misfortunes, he condescended to pay more attention to my trial than his colleagues. . . . O great man, I owe you my homage; the gratitude of an unfortunate girl will not be burdensome to thee, and the tribute she offers thee in making thy heart known, will be ever the sweetest enjoyment of her own.

M. S\*\*\* himself became my attorney; my declarations were heard and his manly eloquence enlightened their minds. The general depositions of the forgers, who were on the point of being executed, came to support the zeal of him who so kindly interested himself in me: I was found misled, innocent, entirely acquitted of the impeachment, with full liberty of becoming whatever I liked. My protector added to these services, that of making a collection for me, which yielded me more than fifty louis; my forebodings seemed at last realized, and I fancied I was at the end of my woes, when it pleased Providence to convince me that I was as yet very far from it.

At the time of getting out of prison, I had taken lodging in an inn facing the river Isere, on the side of the Suburbs, where I was assured I would be honestly. My intention was, according to M. S's*** advice, to stay there for some time in order to try and get a place in the town, or return to Lyons, should I not succeed, with letters of recommendation which M. S*** had the goodness to offer me. In this inn, I used to eat at what they call the *table d'hote,* when I perceived on the second day that I was closely watched by a stout, well dressed Lady, who got herself styled *Baroness* : by forcing of examining her in my turn, I thought I recognized her; we proceeded as two persons who had known each other, but could not remember where.

At length, the *Baroness* drawing me aside: — "*Therese,*" she says to me, "am I mistaken? are you not she whom I saved ten years ago from Jail, and do you not recollect *La Dubois* ?" Being but little flattered with this discovery, I however answer her politely, but I had to deal with the craftiest and most cunning woman there was in France: there was no means of getting out of it. *La Dubois* loaded me with politeness; she told me that she was concerned about my destiny with the whole town, but that if she had known this had interested me, there was no kind of steps she would not have taken with the Magistrates, many among whom were, she pretended, her friends. Feeble as usual, I allowed myself to be led into this woman's room, and related to her my misfortunes. — "My dear friend," she says to me on embracing me again, "if I have desired to see thee more intimately, it is to inform thee that my fortune is made, and that all I have is at thy service; look," she says to me on opening boxes full of gold and diamonds, "those are the fruits of my profession; had I extolled virtue like thee, I would be today locked in or hanged." — "Oh! Madam," said I to her, "if you owe all that but to crimes, Providence, which always finishes by being righteous, will not let you enjoy it long." — "Error!" *la Dubois* says to me, "do not imagine that Providence always befriends Virtue; let not a short instant's prosperity blinden thee to this degree. It is all one to the maintenance of the laws of Providence whether Paul indulges in evil, while *Peter* is doing good; Nature requires an equal sum of both, and the practicing of crime rather than virtue is the most indifferent thing in the world to her. Listen, *Therese*, pay a little attention to me," continued this corrupter on seating herself and making me place myself beside her; "thou art intelligent, my child, and I should like to finally convince thee.

It is not the choice man makes of Virtue, which causes him to find happiness, dear girl; for virtue is as vice, only one of the ways of conducting one's self in the world; there is no question therefore of following the one rather than the other; it simply treats of walking within the general route; he who deviates from it is always wrong. In a wholly virtuous world. I would recommend thee virtue, because the rewards being attached to it, happiness would infallibly depend thereon: in a totally corrupted world, I shall never recommend thee but vice. He who does not follow the route of others, inevitably perishes; everybody he meets with runs against him, and as he is the weakest, he must necessarily be crushed. "The laws vainly try to establish order and bring men back to virtue; being too biased for the undertaking of it, too unfit to succeed therein, they will remove an instant from the trodden way, but they will never cause it to be forsaken. When the general interest of men will incline them to corruption, he who will not be corrupted with them, will therefore struggle against the general interest; now, what happiness can he expect who continually thwarts the interest of others? Wilt thou tell me that it is vice which is opposed to men's interest? I should grant it to thee in a world composed of an equal share of good and bad people, because then the interest of the one evidently clashes with that of the other; but that is no longer the case in a wholy corrupted society: my vices then, while wronging only the wicked man, determine in him other vices which indemnify him, and we both find ourselves happy. The vibration becomes general; it is a host of shocks and mutual damages by which everyone, on retrieving immediately what he has just lost, is incessantly in a happy state. Vice is dangerous only to Virtue which, being weak and fearful, never attempts any undertaking; but when she shall no longer exist on the earth, when her fastidious reign is over, then vice, no longer wronging except the wicked man, shall make known other vices, but will alter no more virtues. Why shouldst thou not have failed a thousand times in thy life, *Therese*, by constantly taking contrary-wise the route which everybody was following? Hadst thou abandoned thyself to the torrent, thou wouldst have found the heaven as I have. Will he who wants to go up a river run over as much ground in one and the same day as he who comes down it? Thou speakest to me always of Providence: ah! who proves for thee that this Providence loves order, and consequently virtue? Does it not incessantly set thee examples of its injustices and irregularities? Is it in sending men war, the pest and famine, is it by having formed a Universe vicious in all its parts, that it manifests to thy eyes its extreme love for the good? Why wilt thou have it that vicious individuals displease it, since it acts itself only through vices, since all is vice and corruption in its works, since all is crime and disorder in its wills? But from whom, moreover, have we those movements which hurry us on to evil? is it not its hand which bestows them upon us? is there a single one of our sensations but comes from it? a single one of our desires whcih is not its work? Is it therefore reasonable to say that it would allow us, or give us inclinations for a thing which would be obnoxious to, or of no use to it? If then vices are subservient to it, why should we resist them? by what right should we labour to destroy them? and whence is it we should smother their voice? A little more philosophy in the world would soon set everything right, and let Magistrates, Legislators see that the crimes they blame and punish with so much rigor, have sometimes a far greater degree of utility than those virtues they preach, without practicing them in person and without ever rewarding them."

— "But when I should be faint-hearted enough, Madam," I replied, "to embrace your frightful systems, how would you arrive at stifling the remorse they would cause every instant to rise in my heart?" — "Remorse is a chimera," *la Dubois* tells me; "it is, my dear

*Therese*, but the faint murmuring of the soul too cowardly to dare annihilate it." — "Annihilate it can it be done?" — "Nothing easier; people repent only of what they are not in the habit of doing; renew often that which causes you remorse, and you shall soon extinguish it; oppose to it the fire-brand of the passions, the powerful laws of interest, you shall have it shortly consumed. Remorse does not prove crime, it simply denotes an easily subdued soul; let an absurd order be just issued to hinder thee from instantly going out of this room, thou wilt not leave it without remorse, however certain it be that thou dost no evil, nevertheless, by going out of it. Therefore, it is not true that only crime gives remorse. By convincing one's self of the nothingness of crimes, of the necessity they are , with respect to the general plan of Nature, it would be therefore possible to overcome the remorse which would feel after having committed them, as easily as it would become thee to stifle the one which would spring from thy going out of this room after the illegal order thou shouldst have received to remain in it. It is necessary to commence by an accurate analysis of all that men call crime; by convincing one's self that it is merely the infraction of their laws and national morals, which they so characterize; that what is styled crime in France, ceases to be so at two hundred leagues on the other side; that there is no action really considered as universally criminal upon the earth; none which, being vicious or criminal here, is not praiseworthy and virtuous twelve miles off; that it is all a matter of opinion, of geography, and that it is therefore absurd to try and force ourselves to practice virtues which are but vices elsewhere, and to flee crimes which are excellent actions in another country. Now I ask thee whether I can, according to these reflections, have still remorse, for having through pleasure or interest committed, in France, a crime which is simply a virtue in China; whether I ought to make myself exceedingly unhappy, constrain myself wonderfully in order to practice, in France, acts which would cause me to be burnt at Siam? Now, if remorse is only on account of the prohibition, if it merely springs from the violation of the curb and nowise from the act committed, it is a very wise movement so as to be allowed to exist in one's self? Is it not silly not to stifle it at once?

Let us accustom ourselves to consider the action which has just caused remorse, as indifferent; let us judge it as such from the profound study of the morals and customs of all Nations on the Earth; in consequence of this work, let us renew this action, such as it is, as often as possible; or still better, let us perform more violent ones than those we are combining, the better to accustom ourselves to the former one, and in a short time, habit and reason will defeat remorse; they will soon do away with this gloomy movement, the sole fruit of ignorance and education. We shall henceforth see that, since there is no real evil in anything, it is stupid to repent, and cowardly not to attempt doing what may be useful or agreeable to us, whatever may be the obstacles that must be over-turned to arrive at it. I am forty-five years old, *Therese* ; I committed my first crime at fourteen. This one freed me from all the bonds that were constraining me: I have not ceased since from running the hazard in a career bestrewed with them; there is not a single one of them I have not committed myself, or caused to be committed . . . and I have never known remorse. Be that as it may, I am drawing near the end; two or three more lucky times, and I shall pass from the state of mediocrity, in which I was to finish my days, to an income of more than fifty thousand livres. I repeat it to thee, my dear, never during this way safely ran over, did remorse make me feel its stings; were a frightful reverse to hurl me instantly from the pinnacle into the abyss, I should not feel it either; I should complain of men or my own awkwardness, but I should be ever at peace with my conscience." — "I grant it," I replied, "Madam, but let us reason a while according to your very principles; by what right do you pretend to require that my conscience should be as firm as yours, since it has not been accustomed from its infancy to overcome the same prejudices? With what right do you require that my mind, which is not organized like yours, should be able to adopt the same systems? You grant there is a total of good and bad in Nature, and consequently there must be a certain quantity of beings to do the good, and another to give themselves up to the bad; the side which I take is therefore in Nature, and wherefore would you have it accordingly that I should wander from the rules she lays down for me? You find, you say good luck in the career you are skipping over: good! Madam, whence is it I should not find it likewise in the one I am following? Do not fancy, moreover, that the vigilance of the laws leaves him who infringes them a long while at rest; you have just seen a striking example of it: out of the fifteen knaves among whom I dwelt, one escapes, fourteen perish ignominiously. . . ."

— "And that is then what thou callest a misfortune?" *la Dubois* replied. "But what does this ignominy matter to him who has no longer any principles? When one has outstripped everything, when honor is no more than a prejudice to our eyes, reputation an indifferent thing, religion a chimera, death a total annihilation; therefore, is it not the same thing, then, to die on the scaffold or in one's bed? There are two species of rascals in the world, *Therese* ; the one whom a powerful fortune, a wonderful renown shelter from this tragical end, and the one who shall not escape it if he is taken. The latter, being born without wealth, should have but one desire if he is intelligent: to become rich at no matter what rate; if he succeeds, he has what he wanted, he ought to be satisfied; if he is stretched on the rack, what shall he regret, since he has nothing to lose? The laws are therefore null with respect to all villains, from the moment they do not reach him who is powerful, and since it is impossible for the unfortunate man to be in dread of them, because their sword is his only resource." — "Ah! do you believe," replied I, "that heavenly Justice is not awaiting in another world him whom crime has not frightened in this?" — "I believe, retorted this dangerous woman, that if there were a God, there would be much less evil on the earth; I believe that, if this evil exists on it, either these disorders are ordained by this God, and then he is a barbarous being; or he is unable to prevent them: from this moment, he is a weak God, and in every case, an abominable being, a being whose thunder I ought to defy and whose laws I ought to despise. Ah! *Therese*, is not atheism better than either of these extremes? Such is my system, dear girl, it is in me since my infancy, and certainly I shall not renounce it during my lifetime." — "You cause me to quake, Madam," said I on rising; "permit me for being unable to listen further both to your sophisms and blasphemies." — "A moment,

*Therese,*" said *la Dubois* on holding me back, "if I can not get the better of thy reason, let me at least captivate thy heart. I want thee, do not refuse me thy help; there are a thousand louis, they are thine as soon as the deed is done." Heeding here only my eagerness to do good, I at once inquired of *la Dubois* what it was about, in order to prevent, if I could, the crime she was preparing to commit. — "Here it is," she says to me; "hast thou remarked that young Merchant from Lyons, who eats here those four or five days?" — "Who? *Dubreuil?*"— "Precisely." — "Well?" — "He is in love with thee, he has trusted me with the secret; thy modest and gentle look pleases him exceedingly, he likes thy candor, and thy virtue delights him. This romantic lover has eight hundred thousand francs in gold or notes in a little box near his bed; allow me to make this man believe that thou consentest to give ear to him: let it be so or not, what is it to thee? I shall persuade him to propose a walk to thee outside town; I shall prevail upon him to make thee his advances during a this walk; thou wilt amuse him, thou wilt keep him out as long as possible; I shall rob him in the meanwhile, but I shall not run away; his goods will be already at Turin, while I shall be still in *Grenoble.* We shall use all possible skill to dissuade him from suspecting us, we shall appear to be helping him in his researches; yet my departure shall be announced, it will not cause surprise; thou wilt follow me, and the thousand louis shall be counted down to thee on reaching the Piedmontese territory."

— "I accept, Madam," said I to *la Dubois,* fully bent on acquainting *Dubreuil* of the theft they wanted to commit on him; "but reflect," I added the better to deceive this wretch, "that if *Dubreuil* is in love with me, I can, on warning him, or in yielding to him, get much more from him than you are offering me to betray him?" — "Bravo!" *la Dubois* says to me, "that is what I call a good pupil; I begin to think that Heaven has given thee more craft than me for crime. Well!" she continued while writing, "there is my twenty-thousand crown note: dare refuse me now." — "I shall take good care not to do it, Madam," said I on laying hold of the note, "but attribute at least only to my unhappy state, both my feebleness and the wrong I am in by giving way to your seductions." — "I wished thy wit to have the merit of it," *la Dubois* says to me; "thou choosest rather that I should accuse thy misfortune for it, it will be as thou wilt have it; do my business in the meanwhile, and thou shalt be contented." Everything was arranged; on the same evening I began to put *Dubreuil* more at his ease, and I really saw he had a liking for me.

Nothing could be more perplexing than my situation: I was no doubt very far from consenting to the proposed crime, should there have been question of ten times more gold; but to inform on this woman was another grief for me; I disliked very much to bring a creature into danger, to whom I was indebted for my liberty ten years before. I should have been willing to find the means of preventing the crime without getting it punished, and with anybody else but a consummate rogue as *la Dubois,* I would have succeeded in it. This is then what I resolved on doing, ignoring that this horrible woman's secret manoeuvres would not only de-range the whole plot of my honest schemes, but would also punish me for having conceived them.

On the day appointed for the intended walk, *la Dubois* invites both of us to dine in her room. We accept, and the meal being finished, *Dubreuil* and I go down stairs to hurry the car which they were getting ready for us, I was a while alone with *Dubreuil* before setting out. — "Sir," said I to him very quickly, "listen to me attentively; no noise, and carefully observe especially what I am going to prescribe; have you a trusty friend in this inn?" — "Yes, I have a young partner on whom I may rely as on myself." — "Good! Sir, go at once and bid him not to leave your room a minute all the while we shall be out walking." — "But I have the key of that room; what means this over precaution?" — "It is more essential than you think, Sir: make use of it, I do beseech you, or I shall not go out with you; the woman with whom we have dined is a rogue: she is arranging the walk we are going to take together, simply to rob you more easily during that time; make haste, Sir, she is watching us, she is dangerous; hand your key quickly to your friend; let him go and set himself in your room and not stir out of it until we are back. I shall explain the rest to you as soon as we are in the carriage." *Dubreuil* understands me, he shakes my hand to thank me, flies to give orders concerning the advice he receives, and returns. We start; I unfold the whole adventure to him along the way, I relate my own to him, and inform him of the unhappy circumstances of my life, which brought me into acquaintance with such a woman. This honest and sensible young man expresses his warmest gratitude to me for the service I am so kindly doing him; he interests himself in my misfortunes, and proposes to soften them down by the offer of his hand. — "I am too happy to be able to repair the wrongs which fortune does you, Miss," he says to me; "I am my own master, I depend on nobody; I am passing over to Geneva for an extensive letting out of the sums which your kind advice are preserving for me, you shall follow me thither; on reaching there I shall become your husband, and you shall appear in Lyons only under this title. Or if you prefer it, Miss, if you have any mistrust, it shall be but in my own country that I will give you my name."

Such an offer flattered me too much that I should dare to refuse it; but it did not suit me either to accept it without making *Dubreuil* see that all might cause him to repent for it; he was pleased with me for my delicacy, and only pressed me the more eagerly. . . . Unhappy creature that I was! should good luck be only offered to me in order to penetrate me more keenly with the grief of being never able to lay hold of it! should no virtue therefore be able to spring up in my heart without preparing torments for me!

Our conversation had already brought us two leagues from the town, and we were just going to alight in order to enjoy the cool in a wood on the bank of the Isere, where we intended to walk, when all of a sudden *Dubreuil* told me he was ill. . . . He alights, frightful vomitings come upon him unawares; I get him at once put back into the carriage, and we speedily drive back to town. *Dubreuil* is so ill, that he must be carried into his room; his state surprises his partner whom we find in it, and who, according to his orders, had not gone out of it; a physician arrives, good Heavens! *Dubreuil* is poisoned! I scarcely learn this unlucky news, than I run to *la Dubois*'s apartment; the wretch! she was gone I go to my room, my press is broken open, the trifle of money and the little clothing I have are taken away; *la Dubois*, I am told, is running these three hours in the Turin direction. It was not doubtful but that she was the author of this host of crimes; she had come to *Dubreuil's* room; being nettled at finding people in it, she had avenged herself upon me, and she had poisoned *Dubreuil*, at dinner, in order that on returning, had she succeeded on robbing him, this unfortunate young man, more occupied with his life than with pursuing her who stole his fortune, might allow her to fly safely away, and in order that the accident of his death occurring, so to say, in my arms, I might be more likely suspected than she; nothing informed us of her combinations; but was it possible they should be otherwise?

I fled back to *Dubreuil's* room: I am not allowed to come near him again; I complain of these refusals, I am told the reason of them. The unfortunate man is dying, and busies himself no longer except about God. Yet, he exculpated me; I am innocent, he assures; he expressly forbids my being prosecuted; he departs. He has barely closed his eyes, when his partner hastens to come and give this news, on earnestly entreating me to be quiet. Alas! was it in my power not to weep bitterly the loss of a man who had so generously offered himself to take me out of misfortune! was it in my power not to deplore a theft which threw me back into misery, from which I was merely issuing! Thou frightful creature! I screamed; if it is to this thy principles lead, must we honest folks should punish them! But I was reasoning as an injured party, and *la Dubois*, who saw only her happiness, her interest in what she had undertaken, undoubtedly concluded quite otherwise.

I confided the whole thing to *Dubreuil's* partner, who was named *Valbois*, and what had been combined against him whom he lost, and what had happened to myself. He pitied me, regretted *Dubreuil* most sincerely and blamed the over tenderness which had hindered me from lodging a complaint as soon as I had been informed of *la Dubois's* schemes. We conjectured that this monster, who wanted only four hours to get into a land of safety, would be there sooner than we should have given notice of having her pursued; that it would cost *a deal of* expense; that the master of the inn, seriously compromised in the plaint we should lodge, and in clamorously defending himself, would perhaps end by undoing me myself, me . . . who appeared to breathe at *Grenoble* only as a gibbet-runaway. These reasons convinced me and even frightened me so much, that I resolved to quit this town without taking leave of my protector M. S***. *Dubreuil's* friend approved of this course; he did not conceal from me that if the whole of this adventure was set on foot again, the depositions he would be obliged to make, would compromise me, whatever his precautions might be, both on account of my intimacy with *la Dubois*, and owing to my last walk with his friend; that he advised me therefore for this reason to set out at once without seeing anybody, thoroughly certain that for his part he would never act against me whom he believed innocent, and whom he could accuse but of feebleness, in all that had just occurred.

While thinking over *Valbois'* counsels, I found them the better because it appeared as certain I looked guilty, as it was sure I was not so; because the only thing that spoke in my behalf, the recommendation given to *Dubreuil* at the moment of the walk, being, I was told, badly explained by him on the point of death, would not become so triumphant a proof that I should rely upon it; owing to which I speedily made up my mind. I informed *Valbois* about it. — "I should like," he says to me, "my friend had entrusted me with a few bequests favorable to you, I should discharge them with the greatest pleasure; I should even wish he had told me that he owed you the counsel of watching his room; but he did nothing of all this; I am therefore forced to confine myself to the bare execution of his orders. The misfortunes you have experienced for him, would incline me to do something on my own account, if I could, Miss; but I am beginning business, I am young, my fortune is limited, I am obliged to instantly remit *Dubreuil's* accounts to his family; permit therefore to confine myself to the sole trifling service which I entreat you to accept: here are five louis, and there is an honest trading woman of Chalon-sur-Saone, my native place; she returns there after having stopped twenty-four hours in Lyons, where business calls her; I give you into her hands. *Madam Bertrand,*" contin-ued *Valbois*, on bringing me to this woman, "this is the young person of whom I have spoken to you; I recommend her to you, she desires a situation. I beg you with the same earnestness as if there was ques-tion of my own sister, to be on the look-out as much as possible to find for her something in this town to suit her person, birth and education; let it cost her nothing for it until then, I shall settle with you for all at first sight. Farewell, Miss," continued *Valbois* on asking me leave to kiss me; "*Madam Bertrand* is starting tomorrow at day-break: follow her, and may somewhat more good luck accompany you in a town where I shall perhaps have the satisfaction of seeing you soon again."

The uprightness of this young man, who at the bottom owed me nothing, caused me to shed tears. Kind proceedings are very sweet, when one experiences for a long while hateful ones. I accepted his gifts, on swearing to him that I was just going to work only to put myself in a state of being able to give them back to him one day. Alas! thought I on retiring, if the exercise of a fresh virtue has just cast me into misfortune, at least for the first time in my life does the hope of consolation offer itself in this awful chasm of woes, into which virtue hurls me again.

It was early the need of breathing caused me to go down to the quay of the Isere, on purpose to walk about there for a few minutes, and, as it mostly always happens in a like case, my reflections carried me very far. Finding myself in an isolated spot, I sat down there to think more leisurely. However, night came on without my thinking of going, when all of a sudden I felt myself seized on by three men. One puts his hand upon my mouth, and the other two throw me headlong into a car, get into it with me, and we cleave the air during three long hours, without any of these brigands condescending either to say a word to me, or answer any of my questions. The coach arrives near a house, gates are opened to let it in, and are immedi-ately shut. My guides carry me, make me traverse several very dark apartments in this way, and at last leave me in one, near which there is a room where I perceive light. — "Stay there," said one of my ravishers to me, on withdrawing with his comrades, "thou art soon going to see acquaintances." And they disappeared, carefully shutting all the doors. Almost at the same time, that of the room where I saw the light opens, and I behold coming out of it, with candle in hand . . . oh! Madam, guess who it could be . . . *la Dubois*! . . . *la Dubois* in person, this awful monster corroded no doubt by the most ardent desires of vengeance. — "Come, charming maid," she says to me haughtily, "come and receive the reward of the virtues to which you devoted yourself at my expense. . . ." And shaking my hand wrathfully: "Ah! wicked creature, I shall teach thee how to betray me!" — "No, no, Madam," said I to her hastily, "no, I have not betrayed you: inquire, I have not made the slightest complaint that could cause you uneasiness, I have not uttered the least word that could compromise you." — "But didst thou not oppose the crime I was meditating? didst thou not prevent it, unworthy creature? Thou must be punished for it. . . ." And as we were entering, she had no time to say any more about it. The apartment into which I was made pass was as sumptuous as (it was) magnificently lighted up; there was, at the end of it, on an ottoman, a man of about forty years old, in a loose taffeta morning gown, I shall shortly describe him to you. — "*Monseigneur*;" said *la Dubois* on introducing me to him, "here is the little girl you wanted, the one in whom all *Grenoble* is interested . . . in a word, the celebrated *Therese*, sentenced to be hanged with false coiners, and since freed because of her innocence and virtue. Acknowledge my cleverness to be of service to you, *Monseigneur*; you expressed to me, a few days ago, the extreme desire you had of sacrificing her to your passions; and today I deliver her to you; perhaps you may prefer her to that pretty boarder of the Benedictines' Convent, at Lyons, whom you likewise desired, and who is just going to arrive: the latter has her physical and moral virtue, this one has only that of sentiments; but it forms a part of her existence, and you will find nowhere a more candid and upright creature. They are both yours, *Monseigneur*: you will either despatch both of them this evening, or one today, the other tomorrow. As for me, I leave you: your goodness to me obliges me to make known to you my adventure at *Grenoble*. A man dead, *Monseigneur*, a man dead! I make my escape." — "Ah! no, no, darling woman," cried the master of the place, "no, do stay, and fear nothing while I am protecting thee: thou art the soul of my pleasures; thou alone hast the knack of exciting and satisfying them; and the more thou redoublest thy crimes, so much the more is my head inflamed for thee. . . . But this *Therese* is pretty. . . ." And addressing himself to me: — "How old are you, my child?" — "Twenty-six, *Monseigneur*," I replied, "and many sorrows." — "Yes, sorrows, misfortunes; I am aware of all that, it is what amuses me, it is what I wanted; we are just going to put it into order, we are just going to end all your reverses; I warrant you that in twenty-four hours you shall be no longer unhappy. . . ." And with frightful roars of laughter: — "Is it no true, Dubois, that I have a sure means to end a little girl's misfortunes?" — "Of course," said this hateful creature; "and had not *Therese* been a friend of mine, I should not have brought her to you; but it is right I should reward her for what she has done for me. You would never imagine, *Monseigneur*, how useful this darling creature was to me in my last enterprise at *Grenoble*, you have kindly undertaken my gratitude, and I do entreat you to fully discharge it for me."

The obscurity of these discourses, those which *la Dubois* had made me on entering, the kind of man I had to deal with, again that little girl who was promised, all filled my imagination at once with a confusion which it would be hard to describe for you. A cold sweat oozes from my pores, and I am near falling into a swoon: such is the moment when this man's proceedings finally finish by enlightening me. He calls me, he begins by two or three kisses where our mouths are compelled to unite; he attracts my tongue, he sucks it, and his at the bottom of my throat seems to pump out of it even my very breath. He makes me lean my head upon his breast, and lifting up my hair, he attentively observes the nape of my neck. — "Oh! it is delightful," he cries on vigorously pressing this part; "I have never seen anything fastened so well; it will be excellent to be dislodged." This last discourse confirmed all my doubts; I saw clearly I was again with one of those cruel-passioned libertines, whose dearest voluptuousness consist in the enjoyment of the suffering or the death of the unhappy victims procured for them by plenty of money, and that I was running the risk of losing my life with him.

In this instant somebody knocks at the door; laDubois goes out, and forthwith brings in the young *Lyonnese* of whom she had just spoken.

Let us now endeavor to sketch for you the two new personages with whom you are about to see me. The *Monseigneur*, whose name or state I have never known, was, as I have told you, a thin, lean but vigorously constituted man of forty; constantly swollen muscles, rising upon his arms coated over with black shaggy hair, foreshadowed health and strength in him: his countenance was full of fire, small, black, mischievous eyes, fine teeth, and wit throughout all his features; his well shaped waist was about the middle size, and the goad of love, which I had only too many opportunities of seeing and feeling, was over eight inches in circumference by a foot long. This lean, sinewy, ever foaming tool, upon which were to be seen big veins making it still more formidable, stood up during the five or six hours that the performance lasted, without lowering a minute. I had never before lit on so hairy a man: he resembled those Fawns which Mythology depicts for us. His bony, hard hands were set off with fingers endowed with the force of a vice; as to his character, it appeared to me rough, hasty, cruel, his wit converted into a kind of sarcasm, niggardliness suited to increase the ills which one clearly saw were necessarily to be expected from such a man.

*Eulalie* was the name of the young *Lyonnese*. It sufficed to see her in order to judge of her birth and virtue: she was the daughter of one of the best families in the town where *la Dubois'* villainies had carried her away, under the pretext of uniting her with a lover whom she adored; she enjoyed, besides a bewitching candor and simplicity, one of the most delightful physiognomies that it is possible to imagine. *Eulalie*, being scarcely sixteen years old, had a real maiden's countenance; her innocence and chastity vied in embellishing her features: she had but little color and was the more engaging on this account; the sparkling of her lovely black eyes imparted to her pretty mien all the liveliness of which this paleness seemed at first to deprive it; her rather large mouth was supplied with the finest teeth, her already formed breast looked still whiter than her complexion: she was extraordinary handsome, and nothing was at the cost of her good ease; her shape was round and full, all her flesh compact, soft and plump. *La Dubois* pretended that it was impossible to see a finer backside: being but a poor judge in this matter, you will allow me not to decide. A light moss shaded the fore part; superb fair hair, while floating over these charms, made them still more pleasing; and, in order to complete her masterpiece, Nature, who seemed to form her at pleasure, had gifted her with the mildest and most amiable character. Tender and delicate flower, were you then to embellish the earth for an instant, but to be forthwith decayed!

"Oh! Madam," she says to *la Dubois* on recognizing me! . . . "Good Heavens! where have you led me?" — "You are just going to see my child, the master of the house says to her in pulling her roughly to him, and already beginning his kissings, while one of my hands is by his order exciting him. *Eulalie* wanted to defend herself; but *la Dubois*, while squeezing her unto this libertine, removes from her all possibility of getting away. The performance was long; the fresher the flower, the more this foul wasp loved to pump it. The examining of the neck succeeded his repeated sucking; and I felt that on touching it, the member I was exciting received still greater energy. — "Come," says *Monseigneur*, "here are two victims that are going to fill me with joy: thou shalt be paid well, Dubois, for I am thoroughly supplied. Let us go into my boudoir; follow me, darling woman, follow us," he continues while leading us away; "thou shalt leave tonight, but I want thee for the evening." *La Dubois* submits, and we go into this lewd fellow's cabinet, where we are made strip naked.

Oh! Madam, I shall not undertake to represent to you the infamies of which I was at the same time both witness and victim. This monster's pleasures were those of a savage. His sole voluptuousness consisted in cutting off heads. My unlucky companion. . . . Oh! no, Madam. . . . Oh! no, do not ask me to finish. . . . I was on the point of sharing the same destiny; incited by *la Dubois*, this monster was making up his mind to render my torture still more horrible, when a necessity for both of them to recover their strength invites them to sit down at a table. . . . What revelling! But am I to complain of it, since it spared me my life? Overcome by wine and food, they both fell blind-drunk with the leavings of their supper. I hardly see them in this state, than I spring upon a petticoat and mantle which *la Dubogis* had just taken off in order to be still more immodest in her protector's eyes; I take a candle, I rush towards the stairs: this house being supplied with valets, nothing is opposed to my escape; I meet with one, I tell him with a look of dread to fly to his master who is dying, and I reach the gate without encountering further resistance. I did not know the ways, I was not allowed to see them; I take the first I meet. It is the one to *Grenoble*; everything assists us, when fortune is pleased to smile a moment on us; they were still in bed at the inn, I get into it secretly and fly in haste to *Valbois'* room. I knock, *Valbois* wakes up and barely recognizes me in the state I am; he asks me what happens me, I relate to him the horrors of which I have just been at once both the victim and witness. "You can have *la Dubois* arrested," said I to him, "she is not far from here, perhaps it may be possible for me to show the way. . . . The wretch! besides all her crimes, she has taken again from me both my clothes and the five louis you gave me." — "O *Therese*," *Valbois* says to me, "you are certainly the most unfortunate girl in the world, but you see however, upright creature, in the midst of the evils which overwhelm you, a heavenly hand defending you; let it be another motive for your being always virtuous, good deeds are never without reward. We shall not persecute *la Dubois*, my reasons for letting her alone are the same as those I explained to you yesterday; let us simply repair the ills she has done you; first of all, here is the money she took from you." An hour after, a seamstress brought me two whole dresses and linen. . . . — "But you must start, *Therese*," *Valbois* says to me; "you must set out this very day, *la Bertrand* is relying thereon, I have persuaded her to wait a few hours for you, go and meet her. . . ." — "O virtuous young man! " I cried in falling into my benefactor's arms, "may Heaven restore you one day all the favors you do me!" — "Go, *Therese*," *Valbois* answered me while embracing me, "the happiness you wish me. . . . I already enjoy it, since your own is my work. . . . Farewell."

This is how I left *Grenoble*, Madam, and if I did not find in that town the felicity I had fancied, at least I encountered in none, as in it, so many upright people united to pity or alleviate my woes.

My conductress and I were in a small covered chariot drawn by one horse which we drove from the bottom of this car; where *Madam Bertrand*'s goods were together with a little girl of fifteen months old, whom she was still suckling, and whom to my bad luck I was not long before making as much friendship with as she who had given her life could do.

This *Bertrand* was moreover a pretty nasty, suspicious, prattling, gossiping, troublesome, shallow brained woman. We used to bring down all her goods every evening into the inn, and sleep in the same room. Things got on all-right up to Lyons; but during the three days which this woman required for her transactions, I had in that town an encounter I was far from expecting.

I was walking in the afternoon along the Rhone-wharf with one of the daughters of the inn, whom I had begged to accompany me, when all of a sudden I perceived the Reverend *Father Antonin* of *Sainte-Marie-des-Bois*, now Superior of the house of his Order situated in this town. This Monk accosts me, and after having severely upbraided me in a very low tone for my flight, and having brought me to understand that I was running great risks of being taken again, should he send word about me to the Convent in Burgundy, he said to me moreover, on softening down, that he would speak of nothing if I wished on the very instant to come and see him in his new abode with the girl who was accompanying me, and who appeared to him a good prize; then making aloud the same proposition to this creature: "We shall pay both of you well," said the monster; we are ten in our house, "and I promise you at least a louis from each, if your compliance is unlimited." I blushed exceedingly at these proposals; one moment, I try to make the Monk believe he is mistaken; not succeeding in it, I employ signs in order to keep him within bounds, but nothing cozens this insolent fellow, his importunities become only more violent. At length, upon our repeated refusals to follow him, he confined himself to asking our address immediately; in order to get rid of him, I gave him a wrong one: he wrote it down in his pocket-book, and leaves us while assuring us he shall soon see us again. While returning to the inn, I explained, as well as I could, the history of this unlucky acquaintance to the girl who was accompanying me; but whether what I told her did not suffice for her, or whether she had been vexed perhaps with an act of virtue from me, which deprived her of an adventure by which she would have gained so much, she tattled; I had only too much ground to perceive it from *la Bertrand*'s discourses, at the time of the unlucky catastrophe I am going to relate to you directly. However, the Monk did not put in an appearance, and we set out.

It being late when we left Lyons, we could sleep this first day's journey only at Villefranche, and it was there, Madam, that the frightful misfortune, which causes me to appear before you today as a criminal, befell me, without my being more so in this fatal circumstance of my life, than in any of those you have seen me so unjustly overwhelmed by mere chance, without anything having led me into the abyss, except the goodness of my own heart and the villainy of men.

Having arrived at Villefranche about six o'clock in the evening, we were in a hurry to take supper and go to bed, in order to begin a longer march next day. We were not reposing two hours, when we were roused up by a dreadful smoke; being persuaded that the fire is not far off, we rise in haste. Good Heavens! the progress of the conflagration was only too frightful already. We, half naked, open our door, and hear about us but the loud crash of falling walls, the cracking of the timber works while breaking, and the awful roars of those falling into the flames. Surrounded by those devouring flames, we no longer know where to flee; in order to escape their violence, we rush into their focus, and we find ourselves soon mixed up with the crowd of unhappy beings who are seeking, as we are, their safety in flight. I then remember that my conductress, more taken up with herself than her child, did not think of securing it from death; without advising her of it, I fly to our room through the flames which compass and burn me in several places; I snatch up the poor little creature; I rush to carry it to its mother, leaning upon a half burnt plank: my foot misses, my first move is to put my hands before me; this impulsion of Nature forces me to let go the precious burden I am holding. . . . It slips from me, and the ill-fated child falls into the fire under its mother's eyes. On this instant I am seized myself. . . . I am dragged; too affected to distinguish anything, I know not whether it is relief or peril that is surrounding me; but I am, for my misfortune, only too soon enlightened, when thrown into a mail coach, I find myself there beside *la Dubois* who, placing a pistol on my brow, menaces me with blowing out my brains if I utter a word. . . . — "Ah! wretch," she says to me, "I have thee now, and this time thou shalt not get away from me again." — "Oh! Madam, here you are!" — I cried. — "All that has just taken place is my doing," this monster answered me; "it is by conflagration I saved thy life, it is through conflagration thou art just going to lose it; I would have pursued thee even to Hell, had it been necessary, in order to have thee again. *Monseigneur* became furious when he learned of thy escape; I have two hundred louis for every girl I procure for him, and he not only wished not to pay me for *Eulalie,* but he threatened me with all his wrath if I did not bring thee back. I found thee out, I was within two hours of having thee at Lyons; I arrived at Villefranche yesterday an hour after thee; I set fire to the inn by means of satellites I have always at my wages, I wished to burn thee or recover thee; I have thee, I am reconducting thee to a house which thy flight threw into trouble and uneasiness, I am bringing thee back to it, *Therese,* to be there treated in a cruel manner. *Monseigneur* has sworn that he would not have tortures sufficiently frightful for thee, and we do not alight from off the car until we are at his house. Well! *Therese,* what dost thou think now of Virtue? — Oh! Madam, that she is very often the prey of crime; that she is happy when she triumphs; but that she ought to be the sole object of God's rewards in Heaven, if man's forfeits succeed in crushing her upon the earth. — Thou shalt not be long, *Therese,* without knowing whether there is a God who punishes or who rewards men's actions. . . . Ah! if, in the eternal nothingness into which thou art about to return presently, it was permitted thee to think, how thou wouldst regret the fruitless sacrifices which thy obstinacy has forced thee to make to phantoms which have never repaid thee but with misfortunes! . . . *Therese*, there is still time, wilt thou be my accomplice? I do save thee, I cannot bear to see thee always failing in the dangerous paths of Virtue. What! thou art not yet punished enough for thy wisdom and erroneous principles? What misfortunes wilt thou then have in order to correct thee? What examples are needed for thee in order to convince thee that the side thou espousest is the worst of all, and, as I told thee a hundred times, only mishaps are to be expected when, going contrary to the great mass of people, you wish to be alone virtuous in a wholly corrupted Society? Thou reliest upon a revengeful God: undeceive thyself, *Therese*, undeceive thyself, the God thou contrivest for thyself is merely a chimera, the existence of which is never met with except in fools' heads; it is a phantom, invented by men's villainies, having in aim to simply deceive them, or to set them in arms against one another. The most weighty service that could have been done them, would have been to slay on the spot the first imposter who thought of speaking to them of God. What a deal of blood one sole murder would have spared throughout the Universe! Come, come, *Therese*, the ever busy, ever active Nature has no need of any master at all to direct it. And if this master truly existed, would he deserve of us, after all the defects with which he filled his works, anything else but contempt and outrages? Ah! if thy God does exist, how I hate him! *Therese*, how I loathe him! Yes, if this existence was true, I grant, the mere pleasure of perpetually exasperating him who would be invested with it, would become the most precious amends for the necessity, I should be then in, of giving any credit to him. . . . Once more, *Therese*, wilt thou become my accomplice? A superb blow presents itself, we shall execute it boldly; I do spare thy life if thou dost attempt it. The Seignior, to whose place we are going, and with whom thou art acquainted, encloses himself up in the country seat where he carries on his games; thou knowest the class they are of requires it; only one valet lives with him there, when he goes there on pleasure: the man who is runing before this postchaise, thou and I, dear girl, here we are three against two; when this libertine will be in the heat of his voluptuousnesses, I shall snatch the sword with which he takes away his victim's lives, thou wilt hold it, we shall kill him, and my trusty fellow will in the meanwhile lay his valet low. He has money hidden in this house, *Therese*, upwards of eight hundred thousand francs, I am sure; the blow is worth the trouble. . . . Choose, wise creature, choose: death, or my service; if thou betrayest me, if thou informest him of my scheme, I shall charge thyself alone with the crime, and doubt not of my carrying it through the trust he always placed in me. . . . Think well before thou answerest me; this man is a villain: therefore in assassinating him we do no more than help the rigor of which he has merited. There is not a day, *Therese*, but this rascal assassinates a girl; is the punishing of Crime, therefore, the outraging of Virtue? And will the reasonable proposal I am making thee alarm again thy austere principles?" — "Do not doubt it, Madam," I replied, "it is not in view of correcting crime that you propose me this action, it is in the sole motive of committing one yourself: there can be then but a very great evil in the doing of what you say, and no showing of legitimacy. Nay more: had you even for design to merely avenge Humanity, for this man's horrors, you would be still wrong to go about it, this concern is none of your business: laws are enacted in order to punish the guilty, let them take their course; it is not to our feeble hands the Supreme Being has entrusted the power of their sword[4]; we should not make use of it without marring them. " — Good! thou shalt die, unworthy creature!" retorted *la Dubois* in a fury, "thou shalt die, hope no more to escape thy destiny."

— "What's that to me?" I quietly replied; "I shall be freed from all my ills, death has nothing to frighten me, it is life's last sleep, it is the unfortunate one's rest. . . ." And at these words that ferocious beast rushed upon me, I thought she was going to strangle me; she gave me several blows in the chest, but let go however as soon as I shouted, for fear the postilion might hear me.

Yet we are advancing very quickly; the man who was running ahead used to prepare our horses, and we stopped at no station. At the very moment of the relays, *la Dubois* used to take up her fire-arm, and set it against my heart. . . . What to attempt?. . . Indeed my weakness and situation disheartened one to the degree of pre-ferring death to the pains of defending myself from it.

We were near entering into Dauphiny, when six horsemen, gal-loping at full speed after our car, overtook it and, sabre in hand, compelled our postilion to pull up. At thirty paces from off the road there was a thatched house where these troopers, whom we soon recognized as being of the Marechaussee, ordered our postilion to bring the car: when it is there, they make us alight, and we all go into the countryman's house. *La Dubois*, with an unimaginable effrontery in a woman loaded with crimes, and being arrested, asks these troopers haughtily whether she was known to them, and what right were they thus using with a woman of her rank? — "We have not the honor of knowing you, Madam," said the Exempt; "but we are certain you have in your car an unlucky girl who set fire yester-day to the principal inn of Villefranche." Then staring at me: "Here is her description, Madam, we are not mistaken; kindly hand her over to us, and inform us how so respectable a person as you appear to be, could take charge of such a woman?" — "There is nothing extraordinary in this event," replied *la Dubois* still more insolent, "and I pretend neither to conceal it from you, nor to take this girl's part, if it be certain she is guilty of the frightful crime of which you speak. I was, as she, lodging yesterday at the inn at Villefranche, I left it in the midst of that confusion, and as I was getting into the car, this girl rushed to me imploring my compassion, telling me that she had just lost everything in that conflagration, and that she begged me to take her with me as far as Lyons, where she hoped to find a place. Yielding to my reason much less than to my heart, I complied with her requests; once in my chaise, she offered me her services; I again consented to everything imprudently, and I was bringing her into Dauphiny where my wealth and family are. It is certainly a lesson, I clearly see now all the inconveniences of pity; I shall profit by it. Here she is, Gentlemen, here she is; God forbid I should be interested in such a monster! I give her over to the rigor of the laws, and beg you to carefully conceal the misfortune I have had to believe her an instant."

I endeavoured to defend myself, I endeavoured to inform on the real culprit; my words were looked on as slanderous recriminations, which *la Dubois* simply denied with a contemptible grin. O fatal effects of misery and prevention, of riches and insolence! Was it possible that a woman who had herself styled the *Baroness de Fulconis,* who made a display of luxury, who bestowed upon herself lands, a family; could it be that such a woman could be guilty of a crime in which she appeared not to have the slightest interest? On the contrary, was not everything against me? I was without protection, I was poor: it was quite certain I was in the wrong.

The Exempt read *la Bertrand*'s complaints for me. It was she who had accused me; I had set fire to the inn to rob her more at my ease: she had been robbed to the last *sou;* I had thrown her child into the fire, in order that the despair into which this event was going to cast her, while blinding her about the rest, might not permit her to see my manœuvres; I was moreover, *la Bertrand* had added, a fast girl escaped from the gibbet at *Grenoble,* and of whom she had foolishly taken charge through complacence for a young man from her place, my sweetheart no doubt. I had publicly and in broad daylight accosted Monks at Lyons; in fine, there was nothing of which this nasty creature had not taken advantage in order to ruin me, nothing which calumny sharpened by despair had not invented to degrade me. At this woman's entreaties, there was a juridical examination made on the very place. The fire had broken out in a hayloft where several persons had sworn I had entered on the evening of this unlucky day, and that was true. Looking for a water-closet badly pointed out by the servant-maid to whom I applied, I had gone into this garret, not finding the place I was seeking, and I remained there long enough to cause what I was being accused of to be suspected, or at least to furnish probabilities; and we know they are proofs in this age. I might then defend myself ever so much, the Exempt replied to me only in preparing manacles for me: — "But, Sir," said I again before letting myself be bound, "if I had robbed my fellow traveller at Villefranche, the money must be about me: let me be searched." This frank defence but excited mirth; they assured me that I was not alone, that they were sure I had accomplices to whom I handed the stolen money, while making away. Then scurvy Dubois, who was aware of the brand I had had the misfortune to receive formerly at *Rodin*'s, feigned for an instant to have pity." — "Sir," said she to the Exempt, "there are so many errors committed daily about all those matters, that you will excuse me for the idea that occurs to me: if this girl is guilty of the deed she is accused of, it certainly is not her first forfeit; people do not arrive in one day at crimes of this nature: I beg you, Sir, to inspect this girl. . . . If you happen to find on her unfortunate body . . . but if nothing accuses her, allow me to defend and protect her." The Exempt consented to the verification . . . it was going to be performed. . . . — "A moment, Sir," said I on opposing it, "this search is needless; Madam knows well that I bear that frightful mark; she also knows well what misfortune is the cause of it: this shift on her part is an increase of horrors which shall be unmasked, as well as the rest, in the very temple of Themis. Lead me to it, Gentlemen, here are my hands, load them with chains; Crime alone blushes to bear them, unhappy Virtue groans under them, but it is not frightened at them." — "Indeed, I should not have thought," said *la Dubois*, "that my idea would have such success; but as this creature requires me for my goodness in her behalf by artful inculpations, I offer to go back with her, if necessary." — "This step is wholly useless, my *Baroness*," said the Exempt; "this girl is the sole object of our researches: her avowals, the brand with which she is marked, all condemns her; we want but her, and we apologize most humbly for having disturbed you so long." I was at once chained, thrown behind one of these troopers, and *la Dubois* departed while achieving her insults by the gift of a few crown-pieces, left with my guards through pity in order to relieve my situation in the sad abode I was just going to inhabit in awaiting my trial.

O Virtue! I cried, when I beheld myself in this frightful humiliation, couldst thou receive a more sensible outrage! What is possible that Crime should dare affront and prevail over thee with so much insolence and impunity!

We were soon at Lyons; on arriving I was thrown into the criminals' dungeon, and there I was entered into the jailer's book as an incendiary, a fast girl, an infanticide and a thief.

There had been seven persons burnt in the inn; I thought I would have been burnt myself; I wanted to save a child; I was going to perish, but she who was the cause of that horror was escaping from the vigilance of laws, the justice of Heaven: she was triumphing, she was returning to fresh crimes, whilst I, innocent and unhappy, had before me but dishonor, disgrace and death.

Being for a long while accustomed to calumny, injustice and misfortune; formed from earliest childhood to give way to sentiment of virtue, only on the assurance of finding thorns therein, my grief was more silly than heart breaking, and I wept less than I should have fancied. Yet, as it is natural to the suffering creature to seek all possible means of getting out of the abyss into which its misfortune has cast it, *Father Antonin* came into my mind; however slight assistance I expected from him, I did not refuse my self the desire of seeing him: I asked for him, he came. He was not told who wanted him; he pretended he did not recognize me: then I told the keeper that it was indeed possible that he did not remember me, having guided my conscience only when I was very young, but that I sought on this footing a private conversation with him. This was agreed upon by both sides. As soon as I was alone with this Monk, I rushed to his knees, I sprinkled them with my tears, conjuring him to save me from the cruel position I was in; I proved my innocence to him; I did not hide from him how the evil proposals he had made me a few days before had turned against me the person to whom I had been recommended, and who was now my accuser. The Monk heard me very attentively. — "*Therese,*" he says to me then, "do not fall into a passion as usual, as soon as one infringes on thy cursed prejudices; thou seest where they have led thee, and thou mayst easily persuade thyself now that it is a hundred times better to be a base woman, than wise and in misfortune; thy case is as bad as it can be, dear girl, it is needless to conceal it from thee: this Dubois thou speakest to me about, having the greatest interest in thy ruin, will certainly work at it underhand; *la Bertrand* will prosecute; all appearances are against thee, and only appearances are needed nowadays to incur the sentence of death. Thou art therefore a lost girl, that is clear. Only one expedient can save thee; I am on good terms with the Intendant, he can influence the judges of this town very much; I am going to tell him thou art my niece, and claim thee under this title: he will bring the whole process to nought; I shall request thee to be sent away to my family; I shall get thee carried off, but it will be to shut thee up in our convent out of which thou shalt never go during life . . . and there, I do not conceal it from thee, *Therese,* the servile slave of my oddities, thou shalt appease them all without reflection; thou shalt likewise give thyself up to those of my confriers: in fine, thou shalt be mine as the most submissive of victims. . . . Thou understandest me: the business is rude; thou knowest what the passions of libertines of our class are: make up thy mind then, and delay not thy answer. — "Away, father," I replied with horror, "you are a monster to endeavour to take advantage of my situation so cruelly, in order to place me between death and infamy; I can die, if necessary, but it shall be at least without remorse." — "What you will!" this cruel man says to me on retiring; "I could never force people to be happy. Virtue has succeeded so well up to the present with you, *Therese,* that you are right to cense her altars . . . Adieu: above all do not think of requiring me again." He was walking out; a stronger emotion than myself dragged me back to his knees. — "Tiger," I cried in tears, "open thy stony heart to my woeful misfortunes, and do not impose upon me, in order to end them, conditions more frightful for me than death. . . ." The violence of my emotions had caused the veils, which were covering my bosom to disappear; it was bare, my dishevelled hair floated over it, it was bedewed with tears: I excite desires in this lewd man . . . desires which he wishes to satisfy at once; he dares let me see what degree my state is inflaming them; he dares conceive pleasures in the midst of the chains which are encompassing me, beneath the sword ready to smite me. . . . I was upon my knees. . . . He knocks me over, he throws himself headlong with me upon the shabby straw which serves me for a bed; I try to cry, he madly plunges a handkerchief into my mouth; he ties my arms: being master of me, the infamous rascal scrutinizes me everywhere . . . all becomes the prey of his eyes, his handlings, and his base fondlings; at last he gluts his desires.

— "Listen," he says to me while untying me and setting himself to rights again, "you do not wish me to be of service to you, I am glad of it! I leave you; I shall do you neither good nor harm, but should you go about mentioning a single word of what has just taken place, while loading you with the most enormous enemies, I shall instantly remove from you every means of being able to defend yourself; reflect well before you speak. I am supposed to be the depository of your confession . . . you understand me: we are allowed to reveal everything when there is question of a culprit; therefore, comprehend thoroughly the sense of what I am going to tell the keeper, or I shall at once ruin thee completely." He knocks, the jailer appears: — "Sir," this traitor says to him, "that merry girl is mistaken, she meant to speak of a *Father Antonin* who is at Bordeau; I don't know her at all, I have never even seen her: she begged me to hear her confession, I have done so; I wish you both good day, and shall be always ready to make my appearance whenever my ministry will be deemed serviceable."

*Antonin* walks out in uttering these words, and leaves me as perplexed with his roguery, as shocked at his insolence and libertinism.

Whatever might become of it, my state was too horrible not to make use of every means; I bethought me of *Mr. de Saint-Florent*. It was impossible for me to believe that this man could slight me with respect to the behaviour I had observed towards him; I had done him a service signal enough, he had treated me pretty cruelly, to imagine he would not refuse to redress his wrongs in my regard in so essential a circumstance, and to acknowledge, as far as it was in his power, at least what I had done so uprightly for him; the heat of passions might have blinded him on the two occasions I had known him; his horrors were somewhat excusable, but in this case no sentiment ought, according to my mind, to hinder him from assisting me. . . . Would he begin afresh his last proposals to me? Would he set the frightful services he had explained to me at the rate of the help I was going to crave from him? Well! I would accept, and once free, I would easily find means to shake off the yoke of the abominable style of living in which he might have the meanness to engage me. Big with these reflections, I write to him, I describe my misfortunes to him, I humbly beg him to come and see me; but I had not sufficiently considered this man's soul, when I had thought beneficence capable of entering into it; I had not sufficiently remembered his horrible maxims, or, my ill-fated feebleness ever obliging me to judge others after my own heart, I had improperly supposed that this man should behave towards me as I should have certainly done towards him.

He arrives; and as I asked to see him alone, he was left at large in my room. It had been easy for me to see by the marks of respect lavished upon him, what his preponderance in Lyons was like. — "What! it is you?" he says to me casting disdainful looks at me, "I was mistaken about the letter, I fancied it from a more honest woman than you are, and whom I should have obliged with all my heart; but what will you have me do for an idiot like you? Why, you are guilty of a hundred crimes, the one more frightful than the other, and when means of earning your bread honestly are proposed to you, you refuse them obstinately? Folly was never carried farther." — "Oh! Sir," I cried, "I am not guilty." — "What must be done to be so? this hard-hearted man hastily retorted. "The first time in my life I see you is in the midst of a band of robbers who want to assassinate me; now it is in the prisons of this town, charged with three or four fresh crimes, and bearing, I am told, upon your shoulders the assured mark of former ones. If you call that honesty, teach me therefore what is necessary not to be so?" — "Good Heavens! Sir," I replied, "can you reproach me with the time of life when I knew you, and would it not be much rather my turn to make you blush at it? I was against my will, you know, Sir, among the bandits who arrested you; they wished to take your life away, I saved you, by favouring your flight, by both of us escaping; what did you do, cruel man, in order to return thanks for this service? Can you possibly remember it without horror? You wanted to assassinate me, you stunned me by frightful blows, and then taking advantage of the state you had put me in, you snatched from me what I held most dear; through an excess of unexampled cruelty, you robbed me of the little money I had, as if you wished that humiliation and misery should come to achieve your victim! You succeeded thoroughly, barbarous man; your success is complete indeed; it is you who plunged me into misfortune; it is you who set the abyss yawning into which I have not ceased from falling since that unlucky moment.

"I nevertheless forget all, Sir, yes, all is effaced from my memory, I even beg your pardon for venturing to reproach you with it; but could you dissemble that some amends, some acknowledgement are due from you to me? Ah! deign not to close up your heart, when the path of death is spreading over my sad days; this is not what I fear, it is ignominy; spare me the horror of dying as a culprit; all I crave from you is confined to this sole favor, do not refuse it to me, Sir, do not refuse it to me, both Heaven and my heart will reward you for it one day."

I was in tears, I was upon my knees before this savage man, and far from reading in his countenance the effect of the emotions with which I hoped to shake his soul, I distinguished therein only a change of muscles startled by that kind of lust, which springs from cruelty. *Saint-Florent* was seated before me; his black, cunning eyes scrutinized me dreadfully, and I noticed him handling his person, which proved that the state I put him in, was very far from pity; he nevertheless wore a false face, and rising: — "Look," he says to me, "your whole case is now in the hands of *Mr. de Cardoville;* I need not tell you the post he fulfills: suffice for you to know that your destiny depends wholly on him. He is an intimate friend of mine ever since earliest boyhood, I am just going to speak with him; if he agrees to any measures, you will be sent for about nightfall, that he may see you either at my place or his own; in the secrecy of a like inquiry, it will be much easier for him to turn everything to your favor, which he could not do here. If this grace is obtained, clear yourself when you see him, make good your innocence to him so as to persuade him; that is all I can do for you. Good-bye, *Therese*, be ready at all events, and especially do not put me to useless steps." *Saint-Florent* walked out.

Nothing equalled my perplexity; this man's conversations, the character I knew he was of, and his present behaviour were of so little conformity, that I feared some more snares. But be pleased to judge of me, Madam: did it become me to waver in the cruel position I was in? and should I not eagerly lay hold of everything that looked like assistance? I resolved therefore to follow those that would come for me: should it be to make a prostitute of me? I would defend myself as best I could; would I be led to death? be it so! it will not be ignominious at least, and I shall be rid of all my woes. It is striking nine o'clock, the jailer appears; I tremble. — "Follow me," this *Cerberus* says to me; "it is on the part of *Messrs. Saint-Florent* and *de Cardoville*: mind and profit, as you ought, by the favor which Heaven is offering you; we have many here who should like such grace, but who will never obtain it."

Decked out as best I can, I follow the keeper who delivers me into the hands of two exceedingly queer looking fellows whose wild aspect increases my fears; they do not speak a word to me: the hackney-coach advances, and we alight at a spacious mansion which I soon recognize as *Saint-Florent's*. The stillness everything appears to be in, serves only to increase my dread. In the meanwhile my conductors take me by the arm and we go upstairs to the fourth floor, into small apartments which appeared to me as tasty as mysterious. Accordingly as we were penetrating all the doors were shut upon us, and so on till we came to a back drawing-room where I saw no windows: there were here, *Saint-Florent* and the man who I was told was *Mr. de Cardoville,* on whom my case depended; this big, fat personage with a gloomy and savage countenance, might be about fifty years of age; although he was in home dress, it was easy to see he was a lawyer. A great air of severity was shadowed throughout his whole person; it deceived me. Cruel injustice of Providence, it is therefore possible for Crime to frighten Virtue! The two men who had brought me, and whom I distinguished better by means of the glimmering of the twenty wax candles with which this room was lighted, were not more than from twenty-five to thirty years old. The one who appeared to me the elder, whom they called *La Rose,* was a handsome brown man, shaped like a Hercules; the younger man's features were more effeminate, his hair was of the prettiest chestnut-color, and he had large black eyes; he was at least five feet ten inches tall, extraordinarily handsome, and of the finest skin in the world; his name was *Julien.* As to *Saint-Florent,* you are acquainted with him: as much roughness in his features as in his character, and withal some comeliness. — "Is every place closed?" said *Saint-Florent* to *Julien.* — "Yes, Sir," replied the young man; "your men are revelling by your orders, and the doorkeeper, who is alone on guard, will take care to let nobody enter." These few words enlightened me, I quaked, but what could I have done with four men before me? — "Sit down there, friends," said *Cardoville* while kissing these two young men, "we shall make use of you when we want you." — "*Therese,*" said *Saint-Florent* then on pointing me out to *Cardoville,* "there is your judge, there is the man on whom you depend; we have talked over your case; but it seems to me that your crimes are of such a nature that reconciliation is very hard." — "She has forty-two witnesses against her," said *Cardoville* seated on *Julien*'s knees, kissing him on the mouth, and allowing his fingers most immodest fondlings upon this young man's person; "we have condemned nobody to death this long time, whose crimes were proven clearer!" — "I, proven crimes?" — "Proven or not," said *Cardoville* standing up and coming impudently to tell me under my nose, "thou shalt be burnt, wench, if through an entire resignation, through a blind obedience, thou dost not instantly consent to whatever we are just going to require of thee." — "More horrors!" I cried; "what! it will be therefore only by yielding to infamies, that innocence may triumph over snares which the wicked set for it!" — "That is within the order," retorted *Saint-Florent*; "the weakest one must yield to the desires of the strongest one, or be the victim of his villainy: it is your case, *Therese*; obey then." And at the same time this libertine quickly tucked up my petticoats. I drew back, I pushed them off with horror; but having fallen through my motion, into *Cardoville*'s arms, the latter grasping my hands, exposed me henceforth without defence to his colleague's outrages. . . . The strings of my petticoats were cut, my bodice, neckerchief, chemise were torn, and I was at once under the eyes of those monsters as naked as when I was coming into the world. — "Resistance?" said both of them when coming to strip me . . . resistance?. . . this wench fancies she is able to resist us?. . . And not a single garment was pulled off, but was followed by a few blows.

When I was in the state they wanted, both of them seated in arched arm-chairs, and, sticking unto each other, were squeezing, between their empty space, the unfortunate fellow who was placed there, they examined me leisurely: while one was viewing the fore-side, the other was viewing the backside, then they changed and changed again. I was ogled, handled, kissed in this way upwards of half an hour, without neglecting any wanton episode in this examination, and I thought I noticed in what concerned the preliminaries, that the both had nearly the same fantasies.

"Well!" *Saint-Florent* says to his friend, had I not told thee she had a fine arse? — "Yes, by Jove! her backside is sublime," said the lawyer who was then kissing it; "I have seen very few groins moulded like those; how hard it is, how fresh it is! . . . how can that be reconciled with so dissolute a life? — But it is because she has never given herself up; I have told thee, nothing is so amusing as this girl's adventures! No one has ever had her except on violating her" (and he then drove his fingers together into the peristyle of the temple of Love), "but people have had her . . . unfortunately, for it is by far too wide for me: being accustomed to first flowers, I could never suit myself with it." Then, turning me again, he performed the same ceremony with my backside, in which he found the same inconvenience. — "Well!" said *Cardoville*, "thou knowest the secret." — "I shall also make use of it," replied *Saint-Florent* ; "and thou who hast no need of this same resource, thou who art contented with a fac-titious activity which, however painful it be for a woman, improves nevertheless the enjoyment quite as well, thou shalt have it only after me, I hope." — "That's right," said *Cardoville*, "I shall occupy myself, while observing thee, with these preludes so dear to my lust; I shall do the girl with *Julien* and *La Rose*, while thou art *masculinating Therese*; and the one is well worth the other, I think. — A thousand times better, no doubt, I am so disgusted with women! . . . Dost thou imagine that it woud be possible for me to enjoy those harlots, without the episodes which goad us both so well?" At these words, those lewd fellows having let me see that their state required realer pleasures, they rose, and had me put standing upon a large arm-chair, my elbows propped on the back of this seat, my knees upon the arms, and all the hind part wholly inclined to them. I was scarcely placed when they took off their breeches, tucked up their shirts, and were thus, their stockings excepted, quite naked from their waist down; they showed themselves to me in this state, passed and repassed several times before me, feigning to make me look at their arses, assuring me that they were quite different things from what I could show them. Both of them were indeed formed like women in that place: especially *Cardoville* offered the whiteness and shape, the elegance and plumpness of it. They polluted each other for an instant before me, but without emission. *Cardoville* had nothing but what was very ordinary; as for *Saint-Florent*'s it was a monster; I shuddered when I thought that such was the dart which had immolated me. Oh! good Heavens! why had a man of this proportion need of first flowers? Could it be anything else but ferocity that might guide such fantasies? But what fresh tools were, alas! on the point of being presented to me! *Julien* and *La Rose*, whom all this was undoubtedly inflaming, likewise rid of their breeches, advance pike in hand. . . . Oh! Madam, never did any such thing as yet defile my sight, and whatever my former descriptions be, this surpassed all I had been able to depict, as the stately eagle excels the dove. Our two lewd heroes soon grasped these menacing darts; they hug them, they pollute them, they bring them to their mouths, and the conflict becomes more serious in a little while. *Saint-Florent* bends over the arm-chair I am in, in such a way that my scattered buttocks are positively on a level with his mouth; he kisses them, his tongue is introduced into each of the temples. *Cardoville* enjoys him, offering himself to the pleasures of *La Rose*, whose frightful member is directly swallowed up in the nook presented to him, and *Julien*, placed under *Saint-Florent*, excites him with his mouth while gripping his haunches and modulating them to the shocks of *Cardoville* who, treating his friend brutally, does not leave him till the incense has moistened the sanctuary. Nothing equalled *Cardoville*'s transports when the crisis seized upon his senses: giving over with flabbiness to him who is serving him as spouse, but forcibly pressing the fellow he makes his wife of this notorious libertine, with rattlings in his throat like those of a dying man, then uttered terrible blasphemies. As to *Saint-Florent*, he contained himself, and the picture got displaced without his having as yet placed any of his.

— "Indeed," said *Cardoville* to his friend, "thou affordest me still as much pleasure as when thou wast only fifteen years old. . . . It is true," he went on while turning round and kissing *La Rose*, "that this fine boy knows very well how to excite me. . . . Hast thou not found me very wide today, dear angel?. . . Wouldst thou believe it, *Saint-Florent* ? it is the thirty-sixth time that I am so for the day . . . it was quite necessary that it should come out. Thy turn, dear friend," continued this abominable man, placing himself in *Julien*'s mouth, his nose stuck into my backside, and his own offered to *Saint-Florent*, "thy turn for the thirty-seventh time." *Saint-Florent* enjoys *Cardoville*. *La Rose* enjoys *Saint-Florent*, and the latter, at the end of a short career, burns with his friend the same incense as he had received from him. If *Saint-Florent*'s ecstasy was more concentrated, it was not less quickening, noisy, criminal on that account than *Cardoville*'s; the latter uttered everything that came in his head in yelling, the former forebore his transports without their being less active for it; he choose his words, but they were only still nastier and filthier owing to it: in fine, estrangement and rage appeared to be the characters of the delirium of the one; wickedness, ferocity were depicted in the other. — "Come, *Therese*, re-inflame us," said *Cardoville*; "thou seest those flambeaus are extinguished, they must be kindled anew." Whilst *Julien* was going to enjoy *Cardoville*, and *La Rose Saint-Florent*, the two libertines, bent over me, were to place their mossy darts alternatively in my mouth; while I was pumping one of them, I had to shake and pollute the other with my hands, then with a spirituous liquor, which had been given me, I was to moisten both the member itself and all the adjoining places; but I was not only to stop at sucking them, it was necessary that my tongue should twine round heads, and that my teeth should nibble them at the same time my lips were squeezing them. In the meantime our two patients were briskly shaken; *Julien* and *La Rose* changed, in order to multiply the sensations produced by the frequency of the coming-ins and going-outs. When two or three homages had at length flowed into those unhallowed temples, I perceived some thickness; *Cardoville*, although the oldest, was the first to announce it; a slap with all the force of his hand upon one of my paps was its reward. *Saint-Florent* followed closely; one of my ears almost lugged out was the price of my pains. They recovered themselves, and I was warned a little while after to get ready to be treated as I merited. Being fully apprized of those libertines' frightful conversation, I clearly saw that vexations were about to fall upon me. To implore them in the state both of them had just got into, would have served only to inflame them the more: they placed me therefore, naked as I was, in the middle of a ring they formed by seating themselves all four round me. I was obliged to pass before each of them in his turn, and to receive from him the penitence he pleased to impose upon me; the young men were not more indulgent than the old ones, but *Cardoville* above all distinguished himself by excessive teasings which *Saint-Florent*, all cruel as he was, came near only with pain.

A little rest succeeded those inhuman orgies I was allowed to breathe a few moments; I was ground, but what surprised me, they healed my sores in less time than it had taken them to make them; there did not remain the slightest trace of them. Lubricities were resumed.

There were moments when all those bodies seemed to form but one, and when *Saint-Florent*, the lover and mistress, received with profusion what the impotent *Cardoville* lent only sparingly; the moment after, acting no longer, but adapting himself to all ways, both his mouth and arse served as altars for frightful homages. *Cardoville* can not resist so many lewd pictures. Seeing his friend already with full erection, he comes to offer himself to his lust: *Saint-Florent* enjoys him; I wet the arrows, I present them to the places where they are to be driven, and my bare buttocks serve as perspective the lubricity of the one, as plastron the cruelty of the other: at length, our two libertines, having grown wiser through the pains which they have to repair, go hence without any loss, and in a state apt to frighten me more than ever. — "Come, *La Rose*," said *Saint-Florent*, "take that strumpet, and narrow her for me." I did not understand this expression: a cruel experiment soon disclosed to me its meaning. *La Rose* seizes me, he places my loins on a round stool which is not a foot in diameter; there, without other support, my legs fall to one side, my head and arms to the other; my four limbs are tied to the ground as far apart as possible; the tormentor who is going to narrow the ways is armed with a long needle at the end of which there was a waxen thread, and without troubling himself either about the blood he is going to spill, or the suffering he is going to cause me, the monster, in presence of the two friends whom this spectacle is amusing, closes up, by means of sewing, the entrance to the temple of Love; he turns me over as soon as he has finished, my belly rests upon the stool; my limbs hang, they are likewise tied and the indecent altar of Sodom is barricaded in the same manner. I do not speak to you of my pains, Madam, but you must imagine them; I was near fainting. — "That is how I want them," said *Saint-Florent*, when I had been replaced on my loins, and when he saw the fortress he wished to invade wholly within his reach. "Being accustomed to gather only first flowers, how could I without this ceremony receive any pleasures from this creature?" *Saint-Florent* was in the most violent erection, they curried it in order to maintain it; he advances pike in hand; under his eyes, in order to excite him still more, *Julien* enjoys *Cardoville*; *Saint-Florent* attacks me: inflamed by the resistance he meets, he pushes with an incredible strength, the threads are broken, the torments of hell do not equal mine; the more smarting my pains are, so much the more agreeable seem the pleasures of my persecutor. All gives way at last to his efforts, I am torn, the sparkling dart has touched the bottom; but *Saint-Florent*, who wishes to spare his forces, has done no more than reach it; I am turned over, same obstacles; the cruel fellow observes them while defiling himself, and his savage hands molest the outskirts in order to be in a better way of attacking the place. He comes to it, the natural smallness of the local makes the attacks much livelier, my formidable vanquisher has soon broken through every barrier; I am gory, but what does it matter to the triumpher? Two lusty blows of the groins place him in the sanctuary, and the rascal consummated therein a frightful sacrifice the pains of which I would not have born an instant longer.

— "My turn!" says *Cardoville*, getting me untied, "I shall not sew her, the darling girl, but I am going to put her upon a pallet-bed which will restore her the heat, all the elasticity her constitution or her virtue refuses us." *La Rose* forthwith takes out of a large press a very thorny, diagonal, wooden cross. It is thereupon that this notorious wanton wishes me to be laid, but by what episode is he going to improve his cruel enjoyments? Previous to attaching me, *Cardoville* himself takes a silvered ball, of the size of an egg, penetrate into my backside; he drives it into it by force of pomatum; it disappeared. It is hardly in my body, when I feel it swell and become burning; without my complaints being listened to, I am tied fast to this sharp rack. *Cardoville* penetrates while sticking to me; he presses my back, loins and buttocks against the spikes which are bearing them up. *Julien* places himself likewise in him. Being alone obliged to support the weight of these two bodies, and having no other prop but those cursed knots which are dislocating me, you easily imagine my soreness; the more I repel those who were crushing me, the more they throw me back upon the unevennesses which are lacerating me. During this time, the dreadful ball, having got up to my bowels, is scorching them, is burning and tearing them; I shriek: no terms in the world can describe what I feel. Yet my tormentor enjoys; his mouth, squeezed upon mine, seems to respire my pains in order to increase his pleasures by them: one does not imagine his intoxication; but, after his friend's example, feeling his forces on the point of being lost, he wishes to have everything tasted before they abandon him. I am turned again, the ball which I am made give back is going to produce at the vagina the same conflagration as it lit in the places it is leaving; it descends, it burns even to the bottom of the matrix: I am attached nevertheless upon my belly to the unlucky cross, and far more delicate spots are about being molested on the knots which receive them. *Cardoville* penetrates by the forbidden path; he is boring it while one is enjoying him likewise. Delirium at last comes over my persecutor, his fearful cries announce the completion of his crime; I am inundated, they untie me.

— "Come, friends," said *Cardoville* to the two young men, "seize upon this wench, and enjoy her according to your fancy; she is yours, we give her up to you." The two libertines lay hold of me. While one is enjoying the foreside, the other sinks into the backside; they change and rechange again; I am torn more by their huge size than I was by the breaking of the artful barricades of *Saint-Florent*; both he and *Cardoville* are amused at these young men while occupied with me. *Saint-Florent Sodomizes La Rose*, who is treating me in the same manner, and *Cardoville* does the same with *Julien*, who is exciting himself on me in a decenter place. I am the center of these abominable orgies, I am the given point, and spring; *La Rose* and *Julien* have already rendered their worship to my altars, four times each, whilst *Cardoville* and *Saint-Florent*, less vigorous or more enervated, are contented with sacrifice to those of my lovers. It is the last, it was time: I was near fainting.

— "My comrade has done you a deal of harm, *Therese*," *Julien* says to me, "and I am going to repair all." Being supplied with a flask of essence, he rubbed me over with it at several times. The traces of my tormentors' atrocities are effaced, but nothing assuages my pains; I never felt any so keen. — "With our skill in making the marks of our cruelties disappear, those who would like to complain of us would have a hard game at play, would they not, *Therese*?" *Cardoville* says to me. "What proofs for their accusations would they offer?" — "Oh!" says *Saint-Florent*, "charming *Therese* is not in the case of complaints; at the eve of being herself immolated, we should expect prayers from her, and not accusations." — "Let her attempt neither," replied *Cardoville*; "she would charge us without being heard; the consideration, the preponderance we have in this town, would not suffer anybody to pay attention to complaints which would still become all the same to us, and of which we would be the master on every occasion. Her torture would be only the crueler and the longer on that account. *Therese* ought to know that we have amused ourselves with her person, for the natural and simple reason which persuades force to ill-use feebleness: she ought to know that she can not escape her sentence: that it must be undergone; that she shall undergo it; that it would be to (no purpose to divulge her going out of prison tonight; she would not be believed; the jailer, wholly of our party, would belie her at once. It is therefore necessary that this lovely and gentle girl, so imbued with the grandeur of Providence, offer it in piece all she has just suffered and all that is still awaiting her; they will be so many expiations for the frightful crimes which are delivering her up to the laws. "Take up your garments again, *Therese*, it is not yet day; the two men who brought you are going to lead you back to your prison." I wanted to say a word, I wanted to cast myself at the knees of these ogres, either to soften them down, or to crave death at their hands. But I am dragged away and thrown into a hackney-coach where my two conductors lock themselves in with me; we were scarcely in it, when infamous desires inflame them anew. — "Hold her for me," says *Julien* to *La Rose*, "I must sodomize her; I never saw any backside I was more voluptuously squeezed in; I shall do thee the same service." The scheme is executed, I may defend myself ever so much, *Julien* triumphs, and it is not without fearful pains, that I undergo this fresh attack: the excessive size of the agressor, the tearing of these places, the fires with which that cursed ball devoured my bowels, all contributes to make me feel torments, renewed by *La Rose* as soon as his comrade has finished. Before arriving, I was therefore a victim once more of these base valets' criminal libertinism. We entered at last. The jailer received us; he was alone, it was still night, nobody saw me going in. — "Go to bed,

" he says to me, "*Therese*," while putting me back in my room; "and should you be ever willing to tell whomsoever that you went out of prison tonight, remember I should give you the lie, and this useless accusation would not get you out of the difficulty. . . ." And I should regret to quit this world! said I to myself as soon as I was alone. I should fear to abandon a Universe composed of such monsters! Ah! may the hand of God tear me from it on the very instant in whatever manner it may seem fit to it, I shall not complain of it; the only consolation that can remain with the unhappy one born among so many ferocious beasts, is the hope of leaving them soon.

Next day I heard nothing spoken of, and, resolved to give myself up to Providence, I got on without wishing to take any food. The day after, *Cardoville* came to question me; I could not forbear shuddering on seeing with what coolness this rascal came to exercise justice, he, the wickedest of men, he who, against all the rights of this justice with which he invested himself, came to cheat so cruelly my innocence and misfortune. It was useless for me to plead my cause, this dishonest man's craft invented crimes for me out of all my justifications. When all the charges of my process were clearly established according to this iniquitous judge, he had the sauciness to ask me whether I knew in Lyons a rich private man named *Mr. de Saint-Florent*; I replied that I knew him. — "Good," said *Cardoville*, "I want no more about it: this *Mr. de Saint-Florent*, whom you admit you know, is well acquainted with you too; he has deposed that he has seen you among a band of thieves wherein you were the first to rob him of his money and pocket-book. Your comrades to spare him his life, you advised it to be taken away from him; he succeeded notwithstanding to fly. This same *Mr. de Saint-Florent* adds that, a few years afterwards, having recognized you in Lyons, he had allowed you to come and pay your respects to him at his house upon your entreaties, upon your promise of good conduct at present, and that there, while he was preaching to you, while he was persuading you to continue in the safe way, you had carried insolence and crime even to choose those moments of his beneficence for the robbing him of his watch and a hundred louis which he had laid on his mantle-piece. . . ." And *Cardoville*, taking advantage of the indignation and anger such atrocious calumnies put me in, ordered the Register to write down that I owned these accusations by my silence and the impressions on my face.

I throw myself upon the ground, I make the vault resound with cries, I strike my head against the pavement on purpose to find thereby a more speedy death, and meeting no utterance for my rage: "You rascal," I cried, "I leave it to the good God who will avenge me for thy crimes; he will disintricate innocence, he will make thee repent the shameful abuse thou makest of thy authority!" *Cardoville* rings; he bids the jailer to get me in, seeing that, troubled by my despair and remorse, I am not in a state to follow out the interrogation; but, that furthermore, it is complete, since I have owned all my crimes. And the rascal goes out in peace! . . . And the thunder-bolt does not strike him down!

The case went at a great rate, carried on by hatred, vengeance and lust. I was speedily condemned and conveyed to Paris for the confirming of my sentence. It is during this unlucky journey, and treated, although innocent, as the greatest of felons, that the bitterest and most painful reflections came to rend my heart asunder! Under what ill-fated star must I have been born, said I to myself, that it should be impossible for me to conceive a single upright sentiment which does not plunge me forthwith into an ocean of misfortunes! And how is it that this enlightened Providence, while justice I delight in adoring, while punishing me for my virtues, offers me at the same time, in the highest position, those who overwhelmed me with their crimes!

An usurer wishes to persuade me, in my childhood, to commit a theft; I refuse him: he enriches himself. I fall into a band of robbers, I escape from them with a man whose life I save: for my recompense he violates me. I arrive at a debauched Seigneur's who gets me devoured by his dogs, for not having been willing to poison his aunt. I go thence to an incestuous and sanguinary Surgeon's, whom I endeavour to spare a horrible deed; the butcher brands me as a culprit; his forfeits are undoubtedly consummated: he makes his fortune, and I am obliged to beg my bread. I wish to implore the Supreme Being fervently from whom I receive nevertheless so many evils: the august tribunal where I hope to purify myself in one of our most holy mysteries, becomes the bloody theatre of my ignominy; the monster who misuses and stains me rises to the greatest honors in his Order, and I fall into the frightful abyss of misery. I try to save a woman from her husband's fury: the hard-hearted fellow wants to make me die by loosing my blood drop by drop. I wish to relieve a poor man: he robs me. I give assistance to a man in a swoon: he hangs me for his delight; the favors of chance surround him, and I am near dying upon the scaffold for having worked against my will with him. A base woman wants to corrupt me for a fresh forfeit: I lose for a second time the little wealth I have, in order to save her victim's treasures. A sensible man wishes to make me amends for all my woes by the offer of his hand in wedlock: he expires in my arms, before being able to do so. I expose myself in a conflagration to snatch from the flames a child that does not belong to me: the child's mother accuses me and brings a crim-inal case against me. I fall into the hands of my most deadly enemy, who wants to bring me against my will to the house of a man whose passion is to lop off heads: if I escape this rascal's sword, it is to fall again under that of Themis. I implore the protection of a man whose fortune and life I saved; I am so bold as to expect acknowl-edgement from him, he lures me into his house, he subjects me to horrors, he gets the unrighteous judge, on whom my case depends, to be found there, both of them ill-use me, both of them injure me, both of them hasten my downfall: fortune loads them with favors, and I run on to death.

That is what men have made me experience, that is what their dangerous intercourse has taught me; is it strange that my soul imbittered by misfortune, revolted at outrages and injustices, no longer aspires but to sever its ties?

A thousand apologies, Madam, said this unfortunate girl while ending here her adventures; a thousand pardons for having sullied your mind with so many obscenities, in fine, for having imposed so long upon your patience. Perhaps I have offended Heaven by filthy recitals, I have opened my wounds anew, I have disturbed your rest.

Farewell, Madam, farewell; the sun is rising, my guards are calling me, let me run to my fate, I no longer dread it, it will shorten my torments. This last instant of man is terrible only to the fortunate being whose days have sped without clouds; but the unhappy creature who has breathed but adder's venom, whose trembling steps have pressed but briars, who has beheld day's flambeau only as the lost traveller beholds in quaking flashes of lightning; she whose cruel reverses have snatched away parents, friends, fortune, protection and help; she who has no longer in the world but tears to quench her thirst, and tribulations for food, that one, I say, beholds death advancing without fearing it, she even wishes for it as a safe haven wherein tranquility will spring up again, for her, in the bosom of a God too good to permit that innocence, abased on Earth, should not find in another world the compensation of so many woes.

Honest *Mr. de Corville* had not heard this story without being deeply affected; as for *Madam de Lorsange* in whom, as we have stated, the monstrous errors of her youth had not extinguished sensibility, she was near fainting at it.

— "Miss," she says to *Justine,* "it is hard to listen to you without taking the liveliest interest in you; but must I confess it? an inexplicable sentiment, far more tender than I am describing it to you, drags me invincibly towards you, and makes your woes my own. You have concealed your name from me, you have hidden your birth from me; I do conjure you to confess your secret; do not fancy that it is a vain curiosity which attracts me to speak to you thus. . . . Great God! would what I conjecture be?. . . O *Therese* ! if you were *Justine?*. . . if you were my sister?" — "*Justine!* Madam! what a name!" — "She would be today of your age. . . ." — "*Juliette!* is it thee I hear?" said the unhappy prisoner throwing herself into *Madam de Lorsange*'s arms . . . "thou, my sister! . . . ah! I shall die much less unhappy, since I have been able to embrace thee once more! . . ." And the two sisters, closely pressed in each others arms, heard each other no longer save by their sobbings, no longer expressed themselves except by their tears.

*Mr. de Corville* could not retain his; seeing that it becomes impossible for him not to take the greatest interest in this affair, he goes into another room, he writes to the Lord Chancellor, he depicts in fiery strokes the horror of poor *Justine*'s destiny, whom we shall continue to call *Therese*. He goes bail for her innocence, he demands that, until the clearing up of the case, the pretended culprit may have no other prison than his castle, and engages himself to represent her at the first order from the sovereign Chief-Justice; he makes himself known to *Therese*'s two conductors, entrusts them with his letters, warrants them for the prisoner; he is obeyed, *Therese* is handed over to his charge; a carriage advances. — "Draw nigh, too unfortunate a creature," said *Mr. de Corville* then to the engaging sister of *Madam de Lorsange*, "draw nigh, everything is going to change in your behalf; it will not be said that your virtues shall always remain without reward, and that the good soul you have received from Nature shall never encounter but chains: follow us, it is no longer but on me that you depend. . . ." And *Mr. de Corville* briefly explains what he has just done.

— "Respectable and beloved man," said *Madam de Lorsange* throwing herself at her lover's knees, "this is the finest act you have done in your life; it is his duty who really knows man's heart and is skilled in the law, to avenge oppressed innocence. There she is, sir, there is your prisoner: go, *Therese*, go, run, fly at once and cast thyself at the feet of this upright protector who will not desert thee as the others. Oh! sir, if the ties of love were dear to me with you, how are they going to become more so to me, straitened by the tenderest esteem! . . ." And these two women embraced by turn the knees of so generous a friend, and watered them with their tears.

They reached the castle in a few hours; there, *Mr. de Corville* and *Madam de Lorsange* were busy in emulation of each other to make *Therese* pass from the excess of misfortune to the climax of ease. They fed her with delight on the most nourishing viands; they put her to sleep in the best beds, they wished her to command in their house, in fine, they used for her all the tenderness that it was possible to expect from two sensible souls. They got cures prepared for her during several days, she was bathed, fitted out, embellished; she was the idol of both lovers, it was a strife between the two to see which could cause her to forget her misfortunes the sooner. An excellent Surgeon undertook, with some close study, to efface that foul brand, the direful fruit of *Rodin*'s villainy. Everything corresponded to the cares of *Therese*'s benefactors: the traces of misfortune were already removed from the brow of this lovely girl; the *Graces* already reinstated their empire thereon. To the livid hues of her alabaster cheeks succeeded the rosy tints of her age, faded by so many vexations. The smile, for so many years banished from her lips, at length appeared on them again under the protection of the Pleasures. The best of good news had just arrived from Court; *Mr. de Corville* had set the whole of France on foot, he had stirred up the zeal of M. S***, who had joined in with him in order to depict *Therese*'s misfortunes, and restore her a tranquility so richly due to her. In fine, there arrived letters from the King, purging *Therese* from all the trials unfairly carried on against her, renewing on her the title of honest citizen, imposing silence for ever upon all the tribunals in the kingdom wherein people had sought to defame her, and granting her a pension of one thousand crown-pieces out of the gold seized in the false coiners' mint in Dauphiny. They would fain arrest *Cardoville* and *Saint-Florent*; but, according to the fatality of the star attached to all of *Therese*'s persecutors, *Cardoville*, one of them, had just been, before his crimes were found out, nominated for the Intendance of . . ., the other, manager for the general Colonial trade; each was already at his post, the orders met only with powerful families that soon procured means to allay the storm, and quiet in the bosom of fortune, these monsters' forfeits were forgotten in a little while[5].

As to *Therese*, as soon as she learned of so many agreeable things for her, she was very near dying of joy; she shed for them, during several consecutive days, exceedingly sweet tears, in the midst of her protectors, when all at once her mood changed, without its being possible to guess its cause. She grew melancholy, uneasy, pensive; she sometimes wept in the midst of her friends, being herself unable to explain the reason of her pains. "I was not born for so many felicities," she was wont to say to *Madam de Lorsange* ; ". . . Oh! my dear sister, it is impossible for them to be long." They might assure her ever so much that all her trials were at an end, she was no longer to have any uneasiness: nothing succeeded in soothing her; one would have said that this sad creature, solely doomed to woe, and feeling the hand of misfortune ever hanging over her head, already foresaw the last strokes with which she was about to be destroyed.

*Mr. de Corville* was still living in the country; it was about the close of summer, they were intending to take a walk which the coming on of a dreadful storm appeared to break off; the excessive heat had forced all to be left open. The lightning flashes, the hail falls, the winds blow, the thunder breaks through the clouds, it shakes them horribly; it seemed that Nature, weary of her works, was ready to blend up all the elements in order to force them into fresh forms. *Madam de Lorsange*, frighted, entreats her sister to shut every place, as speedily as possible. *Mr. de Corville* was coming in at this moment; *Therese*, eager to tranquillize her sister, flies to the windows which are already breaking; she tries to struggle a minute against the wind which drives her back; all at once a burst of thunder lays her low in the middle of the drawing room.

*Madam de Lorsange* screams dreadfully and faints; *Mr. de Corville* calls for help, cares are divided, *Madam de Lorsange* is restored to life, but unhappy *Therese* is stricken in such a way that even hope may no longer exist for her; the thunder-bolt had passed through her right breast: after having consumed her chest, face, it had gone out through the middle of her belly. This wretched creature was a fright to behold; *Mr. de Corville* orders her to be taken away. . . . — "No," says *Madam de Lorsange* rising most cooly; "no, leave her under my eyes, Sir; I want to contemplate her in order to strengthen myself in the resolutions I have just taken. Hear me, *Corville*, and above all oppose not the course I adopt, the designs which nothing in the world could make me now forsake.

The strange woes this ill-fated girl has gone through, although she has always reverenced her duties, contain something too extraordinary, as not to cause me to think of myself; do not fancy I am dazzled by those false glimpses of happiness which we have seen the villains, who have disgraced *Therese*, enjoy in the course of her adventures. Those vicissitudes from Heaven are enigmas which it becomes us not to unveil, but which must never mislead us. *O my friend! the prosperity of crime is merely the test to which Providence puts Virtue; it is as the thunder, the deceitful fires of which embellish the atmosphere for an instant, only to hurl into the abyss of death the unfortunate one they have dazzled.* Behold an example thereof under your eyes! the incredible calamities, the frightful and uninterrupted misfortunes of this bewitching girl are a warning the Eternal gives me to listen to the voice of my remorse and to throw myself at last into his arms. What a punishment am I to dread from him, I, whose libertinism, irreligion, and the forsaking of every principle have marked every instant of my life? What must I expect, since she is treated thus, she, who during her lifetime had not to reproach herself with a single real error? Let us separate, *Corville*, it is time; no link binds us, forget me, and deem meet of my going by an eternal repentance to abjure, at the feet of the Supreme Being, the infamies with which I have sullied myself. This frightful blow was necessary for my conversion in this life, it was so, too, for the happiness I dare hope in the next. Farewell, Sir; the last mark of your friendship I expect is to make no inquiries, to know what has become of me. O *Corville*! I await you in a better world, your virtues must bring you to it; may the mortifications where I am going, in order to expiate my crimes, to spend the unhappy years that remain to me, permit me to see you there again one day!"

*Madam de Lorsange* leaves the house at once: she takes a trifle of money with her, rushes into a carriage, gives *Mr. de Corville* the rest of her wealth while intimating to him pious donations, and flies to Paris, where she enters among the Carmelites, for whom, at the end of a very few years, she becomes an example and an edification, as much by her lofty piety, as by the wisdom of her mind and the regularity of her morals.

*Mr. de Covrille* worthy of obtaining the highest offices in the country, attained to them, and was honored thereby only to cause at once the happiness of the People, the glory of his Master, whom he diligently served, *though minister,* and the fortune of his friends.

O ye, that shed tears over the misfortunes of Virtue; ye, who pitied unhappy *Justine* ; while pardoning the sketches, perhaps rather hard, which we were forced to draw, may ye at least reap from this story the same fruit as *Madam de Lorsange* ! May ye be convinced with her, that true happiness is only in the bosom of Virtue, and that if in the intentions it becomes us not to sound, God permits her to be persecuted upon Earth, it is to recompense for it by the most flattering rewards!

**THE END**

# ENDNOTES

### PREFACE

(1) Translated from the French edition: *Paris, Liseux,* 1884.

(2) First Series, 1880. — *La Curiosite litteraire et bibliographique. Paris, Liseux,* 1880–1883, 4 vols.


### PART FIRST

(1) Sort of troopers that patroled the Country, now replaced by the *gendarmerie.* (*Note of the Translator.*)

(2) A troop formerly entrusted with the police duty during the night. **(Note of the Translator.)**

(3) O Future Ages! ye shall no longer behold this over-measure of horrors and infamy.

(4) A forest near Paris, which was for a long while infested with robbers. Allusion is often made to this particularity, when they say: **It is a forest of Bondy,** signifying thereby that the place mentioned is the strong-hold of thieves. **(Note of the Translator.)**

(5) Character of **Astree,** a famous Novel, by Urfe, a celebrated French Novelist who lived from 1568 to 1625. The name of this character has become, in French literature, a synonyme of a constant, rueful, discreet and bashful lover. **(Note of the Translator.)**

(6) Did the *Marquis de Bievre* ever make one which was worth that of the Nazarean to his disciple: "Thou art *Peter* (rock) and on this rock I shall build my church"? Let people come and tell us punning is of our time!

(7) See a small work entitled: **Les Jesuites en belle humeur.**

(8) See **Histoire de Bretagne,** by Dom Lobineau.


### PART SECOND

(1) Let not this be taken for a fable: this unhappy person has existed in Lyons itself. What is here said of his doings is correct; he cost fifteen or twenty thousand little unfortunate girls their honor; his operation performed, they were shipped on

the Rhone, and the towns of which there is question have been for thirty years peopled with objects of debauchery, only by the victims of this wretch. In this episode, the name only is romantic.

(2) The Chinese Emperor **Kie** had a wife as cruel and debauched as himself; the shedding of blood cost them nothing, and, for their pleasure alone, they daily shed floods of it; they had, inside their palace, a secret closet where the victims were immolated under their eyes, while they were enjoying. **Theo,** one of the Prince's successors, had, as he, a very cruel wife; they had invented a brazen column they used to redden, and upon which unfortunate people were bound under their eyes: "The Princess," says the historian from whom we borrow these extracts, "used to be amused immensely at the writhings and screeches of these sad victims; she was not pleased unless her husband frequently afforded her this spectacle." **Hist. des Conj., page 43, tome VII.**

(3) This game, which has been described further back, was greatly in vogue among the Celts from whom we descend (See **Histoire des Celts by** monsieur); nearly all these errors of debaucheries, these strange passions of libertinism, some of which are described in this book, and which today ridiculously rouse the attention of the laws, were formerly either pastimes of our forefathers who were better men than we are, or legal customs, or religious ceremonies: nowadays we make crimes of them. In how many pious ceremonies of the Pagans used flogging be employed! Several nations were wont to use these same tortures, or passions, for the installing of their warriors; this was called **Huscanaver** (See the **Ceremonies religieuses de tous les peuples de la terre**). Those drolleries, the only drawback of which may be at most a harlot's death, are at present deadly crimes! more power to the progress of civilization! How they co-operate with man's happiness, how we are far more fortunate than our forefathers!

(4) The power of life and death. **(Note of the Translator).**

(5) As to the Monks of *Sainte-Marie-des-Bois*, the suppression of Religious Orders will make known the atrocious crimes of that horrible brood.

# SUGGESTED READING

BADOU, GERARD. *Rene Pelagie, Marquise de Sade.* Paris: Payot, 2004.

BARTHES, ROLAND. *Sade, Fourier, Loyola.* Paris: Seuil, 1980.

BLANCHOT, MAURICE. *Lautreamont et Sade.* Paris: Minuit, 1963.

CARTER, ANGELA. *The Sadeian Woman and the Ideology of Pornography.* New York: Pantheon, 1978.

CROSLAND, MARGARET. *Sade's Wife.* London: Peter Owen, 1996.

HAYMAN, RONALD. *Marquis de Sade: The Genius of Passion.* London: I. B. Tauris, 2003.

HOOD, STUART. *Introducing Marquis de Sade.* London: Icon Books, 1999.

KLOSSOWSKI, PIERRE. *Conclusion in Sade.* Paris: Le Club francais du livre, 1966.

———. *Sade, My Neighbor.* Evanston, IL: Northwestern University Press, 1990.

LE BRUN, ANNIE. *Sade: A Sudden Abyss.* San Francisco: City Lights, 1991.

LELY, GILBERT. *The Marquis de Sade.* London: Elek, 1961.

NEIMAN, SUSAN. *Evil in Modern Thought.* Princeton: Princeton University Press, 2004.

PAUVERT, JEAN-JACQUES. *Sade.* Paris: Le Club francais du livre, 1966.

PAZ, OCTAVIO. *An Erotic Beyond: Sade.* Trans. Eliot Weinberger. New York: Harcourt, 1998.

REAGE, PAULINE. *Story of O.* Trans. Sabine D'Estree. New York: Random House, 1975.

SADE, MARQUIS DE. *Letters from Prison.* Trans. Richard Seaver. New York: Arcade, 1999.

SAWHNEY, DEEPAK NARANG. *Must We Burn Sade?* New York: Humanities Press, 1999.

SCHAEFFER, NEIL. *The Marquis de Sade: A Life.* Cambridge, MA: Harvard University Press, 2001.

THOMAS, CHANTAL. *Sade.* Paris: Seuil, 1994.

— — —. *Sade: La dissertation et l'orgie.* Paris: Rivages, 2002.